DRAGON MAGE

TEACUP
DRAGON
PUBLISHING

To all the dragons who dare to love.

BOOKS BY TAMERI ETHERTON

Song of the Swords*

The Prince of Dragons

The Stones of Resurrection

The Temple of Sacrifice

The Ruins of Betrayal

The Veils of Deception

The Keeper of Stars

The Fatal Fae*

Fatal Illusion

Fatal Assassin

Fatal Legacy

Fatal Forever

Court of Stars*

Sunset in Shadow

Chronicles of Eidyn*

Dragon Mage

Daring Ever Afters*

Enchant

*Books that are part of the Aetherverse: The fantastical realms of Tameri Etherton. Characters and storylines intersect within the books with magical consequences.

CHRONICLES OF EIDYN

DRAGON MAGE

USA TODAY BESTSELLING AUTHOR

TAMERI ETHERTON

CHAPTER
ONE

Trees blurred into a wall of silver as she ran through the forest. Her legs burned and each breath was fire through her lungs. She couldn't stop. Just a little farther and she'd reach the cliffs where even the most agile tracker dogs couldn't follow. The beasts' snarls were closer now, maybe fifty feet away. The cliff twice that distance.

Amaleigh pushed harder, fighting through exhaustion to find the last bit of strength she'd need. What an idiot to choose today, of all days, to steal from the palace.

She hadn't intended to, had sworn that she never would, but that dagger had called to her, and she, fool that she was, answered.

It would've been much simpler to steal a heavy purse from one of the nobles strutting along the boulevard like a gilfern displaying his magnificent feathers.

Rot it all, but she knew why she'd stolen that specific dagger with its gold hilt and sparkling jewels. Not for bragging rights. Not for any sort of glory. Not for personal wealth. She'd stolen it to barter her freedom.

If she could unshackle herself from Antonio's suffocating

grip... Even the thought of being free from him gave her a boost of energy and she sped faster toward an uncertain destiny. Perhaps then Gwilym—she stopped herself from imagining a future she knew could never happen. She and Gwilym might be best friends, but that didn't negate the fact that he was a prince and she an orphaned thief. Friends was all they could ever be, no matter how much she wished for more.

A pinch twisted her gut and she swallowed a lump of shame. What would Gwilym think of her now? He'd trusted her. Surely, he would understand this was too important. He had to realize that without the dagger her life was forfeit. Somehow, he would find a way to forgive her.

She was grasping at hope, more so now than ever before in her miserable life. Despite their differences, or perhaps because of them, they'd accepted each other, flaws and all. But she'd never tested their friendship by stealing from his father. Until today.

"Blood and poxes!" Pain ricocheted across her scalp where a branch tore a clump of hair from its roots. She kept moving, head lowered. Almost there. Can't stop. She couldn't let thoughts of Gwilym sway her resolve. Especially when those thoughts made her heart warm and face flush.

Damn fool of a woman! They might be just friends, but that didn't prevent her from appreciating the muscular lines of his body or the way the light would catch in his eyes, making them shine like rare sapphires.

Oh, bless, she was losing her mind. Or she had a death wish. This was not the time to daydream about the prince's eyes. The dogs' baying was close. Too close. The hounds were almost upon her, the trackers not far behind.

Mooning over the prince had distracted her and now there wasn't time to adjust her speed and climb down the bluff. She'd have to jump and pray she missed the crags. Gods willing, she'd land in the treetops. It was a wish borne of desperation, and all she had left at the moment.

With a last surge, Amaleigh leapt from the cliff. Fly or die, she thought, and thrust her arms out. Given the choice, she'd rather not die this day.

Wind rushed past, smoothing her crimson hair off her face. She closed her eyes and basked in the sun's warmth, allowing a rare moment of serenity. Far below, the hounds prowled the empty cliff, their noses snuffling the ground. A lone beast sniffed the air and whined. The trackers' calls reached her ears and a cheeky grin lifted her lips. She'd outwitted them yet again.

For one perfect moment, she gazed across the land to the palace sitting in the center of Eidyn like a multifaceted jewel in a rather ornate crown. She clearly saw the gardens and lawns of the palace, the turrets where she and Gwilym had played when they were younger. Radiating out from the palace were the districts of Eidyn, all carefully monitored by the king's guards. The university sat solemnly to the east as if a sullen child not allowed to join the adults at the dinner table. To the west was the elite district, and to the south, the harbor where Amaleigh dreamed of one day sailing to new adventures.

The hounds bayed and brought her back to the reality she now faced. There would be no sailing away just yet. First, she had to lose the trackers. A giggle bubbled from her belly as she watched their irate faces grow smaller the higher she rose.

Her breath caught.

She should be plummeting to the trees, not lifting into the air. A strange little thrill of excitement ran through her terror.

She reached for the satchel slung across her torso and found…nothing. She twisted her body to better see, and her blood turned to ice, chilling her insides. Gone were her scrawny arms, replaced with sturdy legs covered in glittering scales. Not quite blue, not altogether green…more like the color of an abalone shell she'd found on the beach when she was little. The memory pinched her heart. That was before, when everything was good and food a given.

Amaleigh gasped at the long talons protruding from her feet. Or were they hands? Paws? She flinched and a wing swung forward, blocking the sun. A thin membrane stretched between bones and a vicious-looking claw stuck up from the top. What the pox was happening?

Scales. Wings. Talons.

Flippin' barnacleballs, she was a dragon. A dragon! Great, just bloody great. How the hell did dragons fly?

She flapped her wings and propelled herself backward, toward the trees. The more she fought to fly up, the quicker she went down. Try as she might, she couldn't right herself, and her panicked flailing only sped the descent.

The trackers' cries faded as she fell. It was impossible to know whether they saw her, but how could they not? A clear, sunny summer day would do fuck all to hide a dragon. Unless the sun was in their eyes. She clung to that mad thought like the hope-starved cretin she was.

Stealing the dagger already came with a death sentence. If she was found to be a dragon, the punishment was worse, so much worse.

As the ground rushed to meet her, she finally accepted her fate. The gods had deserted her. Again.

Gwilym. She threw the thought to the wind. *Please forgive me.*

CHAPTER

TWO

Men shouted in the hall outside the sitting room where Prince Gwilym sprawled with his legs over the arm of a rather comfortable sofa. He sat up, the book he was reading slid to the floor with a thud.

Gwilym, please forgive me.

Amaleigh. He pressed the pads of his fingertips to his temple, sure he'd imagined his friend speaking in his mind. They'd grown close over the years, but never had he heard her when she wasn't in the same room.

Guards rushed past the open door and Gwilym rose to follow them. They barged into the king's private study, more of a conference room with one large oval table in the center and a dozen chairs set at equal intervals around it. At the head of the table, his face a thunderstorm, his rigid body leaning over the gleaming mahogany tabletop, was Gwilym's father. Rage brewed in King Heshen's features. Strong arms rested on knuckles that ground into the wood surface.

Gwilym slowed his steps. He'd not seen his father in a state such as this since the Purge.

"Son, come in." Heshen beckoned his son forward and Gwilym obediently went to his side.

"There's been an incident." His father breathed out, his nostrils flaring with his anger. "Someone snuck into the palace and stole one of my daggers."

Gwilym hid his confusion. His father had dozens of weapons, daggers, swords, bows with arrows tipped with iron. Why a single dagger would cause such ire was beyond him. He looked to the guards and other high-ranking nobles in the room. Their ashen faces and solemn expressions corroborated his father's claims.

"Who would do such a thing? The palace is well guarded."

His father straightened and faced him with a look that could flay a pig. "I was hoping you could tell me."

"Me? I had nothing to do with—" he lifted his hands in a supplication, "whatever this is."

The king's stern glare made Gwilym's insides pinch and shrivel, but he kept his expression blank. He honestly had no idea what his father was hinting at, but he knew that look— understood it was not to be questioned.

"You have a, ah, female friend you entertain at the palace, do you not?" His father kept his tone casual, but there was meaning behind the words. Meaning Gwilym didn't comprehend.

"A female friend?" He rubbed his temples. There wasn't a woman in his life. Never had been. There had only ever been Amaleigh.

The truth hit him in the solar plexus hard enough he nearly wheezed as if actually punched.

"Erma comes by sometimes." Gwilym said the name he'd insisted Amaleigh use at the palace more than a decade and half earlier. It was to keep her safe, to hide her identity, and now...he wasn't sure why he used it when he knew the king most likely had her real name written on a death warrant somewhere in this very room.

"And where does Erma live?"

Gwilym shrugged and spoke the truth. "I don't know." Impulsively, he added, "She's a student at the university." The last part was pure fabrication. Protecting her was built into the very fabric of his being.

His father motioned to a guard who ran out of the room with two others following.

"Your friend stole a valuable object from me this afternoon. When I find this Erma, trust that she will not live to see the sunrise. No one steals from me."

Gwilym's frow creased with disbelief. "I can't believe she'd steal from the palace. Steal from you. Are you absolutely certain it's her?"

"We'll find out soon enough. My inquisitors are very good at their job."

Amaleigh had promised him a thousand times she'd never steal from him or the palace. If she did take the dagger, she must've had a good reason for it. One that put her life in danger. All he could think about was getting word to her that the king was looking for her, but anything he did from this moment forward would be watched and analyzed.

Besides, he honestly didn't know how to reach her. She always came to him, never the other way around. No matter how many times he'd begged, she insisted on keeping her life separate from his, for his own safety.

Gwilym sat heavily upon a chair, his expression one of resignation. He knew his father well enough to know not to question his motives. Not yet. As long as Amaleigh wasn't caught, there was still hope.

CHAPTER

THREE

A jab to Amaleigh's ribs brought her fully awake. Well, mostly awake. Another poke and she gritted her teeth. If they hit her again, she'd show the urchin she wasn't to be messed with.

Jab. Poke, poke.

In one swift movement, she grabbed the stick and rolled with it clutched to her chest, then used it to propel herself upright. She blinked into the bright sun, startled and confused. The alleys she once called home were always in shadow. A lone figure stood before her, much taller than the street rats who made a game of annoying her.

She jutted the staff at the stranger. "What do you want?"

The more she blinked, the better he came into focus. Tallish, but then, most everyone was taller than her. Not old, but older, perhaps in his mid-forties. Chestnut hair, grey eyes. Handsome. Damn fine handsome. A fleeting half-forgotten memory of his face pushed against her skull, and then was gone before she could snatch it fully. Not one of Antonio's men, nor a merchant she recognized. His clothing suggested money, but not wealth.

"Who are you?"

"So many questions." His gaze flicked behind her, and a shadow passed over his features. "We should go. They lost your scent, but if the wind changes, it won't be long before they suss out your location. Come on."

He turned before she had a chance to argue. For a brief moment, she followed his gaze and the morning crashed into her thoughts. She clutched at her bag, and cool relief flowed from her forehead to her toes. The dagger was there, snugged against the bottom of the satchel.

She looked at her hands, at the staff she held, and her skin. No wings. No talons. No glittering scales. She'd hallucinated. Had to be. The leap from the cliff had made her brain misfire. Or maybe it was the fall. She'd dreamt the dragon. Yes, that was it.

"We don't have all day." The mysterious man stood several paces from her, an eyebrow raised. "Unless you'd rather spend the night in the castle dungeons."

As a matter of fact, she would not. With as much speed as she could muster without appearing to rush, she caught up to him and handed him the staff. He hadn't tried to take it back when she'd jabbed him with it, which she found odd and disconcerting. Now, he took it with a curious glint in his eyes, as if he found her actions surprising.

"You have questions, but now is not the time for a chat." Again, his gaze flicked to the cliff and his pace increased. "This way."

He led them off the path and through tightly packed trees. Amaleigh was slight and he was not, yet somehow, he managed to squeeze through openings that caused her difficulty.

"Are you a mage?" The question came unbidden, and she bit her lip to keep from blurting anything else that might get her killed.

Again, the raised eyebrow, but this time he wore a smirk. "Are you?"

She was nobody. An orphan without a home, family, or purpose. "I'm a thief."

"Of course you are."

The tone of his words—the half-mocking way he said everything—made her want to smack him with his stupid staff that she'd foolishly given back to him. She could always stab him with the dagger.

"Wait." He put a finger to his lips and cocked his head. A crooked smile lifted his right cheek. "Oh, you've vexed them good this time. They're looking for a body, but they'll be sorely disappointed. Well done, girl."

The compliment sounded sincere, but she'd learned long ago to never trust kind words.

"Do I know you?" She peered closer, but still didn't recognize him. Even so, a slight buzzing at the back of her head said they might've been acquainted once.

"Later. This way." He stepped around a huge trunk, and she ran into his back when he stopped suddenly. "Rather clumsy for a thief."

Rude. Why was she even following him? She could outwit the trackers without his assistance. She was about to leave when his movement stopped her cold. Not just her body, but her breath, and worryingly, her heart. Just for two blips, but she felt it and held her chest. Impossible came to mind, but then, that word was on her lips often that day.

He whispered words that tickled her attention. Words from long past that burned through memories and emotions she'd buried ages ago. His right hand stretched forward to touch the old tree's trunk, and a shimmering door appeared in the bark.

Too stunned to scream or cry or run, Amaleigh almost pissed herself.

Magic of all kinds was forbidden. Illegal. Just being near

this man would bring certain death if the trackers saw her. Not since the Purge had anyone practiced magic.

Not since the Purge had there been dragons in Eidyn.

An uncomfortable prickling covered her skin, and her fingers twitched toward the dagger. Words circled in her mind, like lullabies learned as a baby. Her lips moved, but she didn't speak the dreadful syllables.

Visions accompanied the lyrical sentences. A warm hearth, a strand of crimson hair similar in shade to hers, the face of a young boy laughing at something. Love buttressed against the walls she'd built around her heart, surging forth with frightening force. In a blink, the images were gone, leaving her reeling from the powerful emotions they evoked.

Questions swirled in her mind. Who were they? Where were they? What did it mean?

"If you want answers, follow me." The stranger held out his hand toward the doorway in the tree trunk.

It might be a trap. Lure her into a magical cell where she'd rot the rest of her life. No thanks. When she didn't move, the man's eyes softened and his grin slipped.

"They won't stop until you're dead. It isn't some daft trinket you stole, not this time."

He moved aside and motioned her forward, through the tree.

Something in his eyes made her believe she could trust him, but also lurking in the grey depths was a frantic sort of desperation. She didn't know him. Couldn't trust him. She hadn't survived this long by blindly trusting strangers. Especially those who possessed magic. Her mind screamed to run, but her legs wouldn't budge. She gripped the bottom of the sturdy canvas bag and closed her eyes. He somehow knew about the dagger. Maybe he looked in her bag while she was knocked out. If so, then it was more than passing strange he didn't steal it.

"You have no idea what you've taken, do you?"

She blinked and stared at him, uncomprehending. Of course she bloody well knew what she stole. She'd risked everything to get the damned thing. She sure as flox wasn't going to let him or anyone else take it from her. Or lead her straight to the palace dungeons. Despite his kind-sounding words, there were only two people in this world she could count on, and he wasn't one of them.

A bark sounded to her right, startling her into action. Her legs pumped and chest heaved with the effort. The stranger called after her as she bolted through the trees. He might've even said her name. His face swirled through her thoughts as she ran up a fallen tree trunk and leapt to a branch. Familiar, yet not. She scrambled to pull herself up and climbed higher until she reached a branch that would allow her to jump to the next tree.

Just a few more leaps and she felt certain the dogs couldn't follow her scent. She landed on the ground with a jarring thud and darted between two huge boulders to a hidden cave. Her legs churned like wagon wheels as she ran, never stopping to look back. Too afraid of what she might see.

CHAPTER
FOUR

By the time Amaleigh emerged from the secret entrance tucked behind the old gate house, merchants were closing their shop windows in preparation for the celebrations. Gods, but she hated this day. For her, there was nothing to celebrate.

Her stomach gave a vicious pinch, reminding her that her last meal had been far too long ago. She pressed a fist against her abdomen and strode down the street with cautious optimism.

She'd outrun the trackers this time, but the stranger's words haunted her. As far as she could tell, there wasn't anything special about the dagger. It had been in an unlocked case with other weapons. She'd taken it for the jewels embedded in the hilt and planned to toss the blade once she removed the gems. Her hand snaked to the bottom of her bag, and she pushed against the weight of the dagger. It had a nice heft to it. Perhaps she could sell the blade to a blacksmith for scrap. That might afford her a proper meal. The gems would buy her freedom.

On the way home, she swung by her favorite bakery and

swiped a loaf of day-old bread from the shelf. It wasn't so much stealing as taking what the baker always left for her. Two doors down, she picked up a hunk of cheese. The merchants on this street were as close to family as she'd ever get. She'd grown up racing beneath their windows and been scolded by each one of them in turn. They were her uncles, aunts, and cousins. But they could never be her mami or papi, nor would they ever replace her brother.

Not that she had many memories of them—just the occasional image of smiling faces at the seashore. Always there, never anywhere else. Unless the vision she'd had earlier was of them. She'd never seen them in a warm home, or heard lullabies, now that she thought about it. The voice she'd heard was soft and feminine, perhaps her mother. Amaleigh tried to recapture the sense of belonging she'd felt, the feeling of being where she was loved, where she was safe, but it eluded her.

With a firm shake of her head, she dispelled the encroaching sadness that always came with recollections of her family. Instead of seeking the memories, she refortified the walls around her heart until a cool indifference flowed over her. She wouldn't allow herself to wallow in self-pity, not tonight. Instead, she'd force herself once again to forget that horrible night fifteen years earlier when she was three and her whole world burned.

Bruno the butcher waved her over and gave her a thick roll of hard sausage. "Best stay put, dear. The guard's been out thick as flies on honey." His gaze went to her bag. "Word is, someone robbed the king right beneath his sniveling nose."

"Not a problem. I hate this night, anyway. The whole thing sickens me." Celebrating mass murder wasn't her idea of a good time.

"Shhh, now. If they hear you sayin' that, you'll find yourself in the dungeons. Get along now." He turned back to his shop with a wave.

He was right. If she was overheard speaking against the king, they'd throw her down the darkest hole and forget she existed. Not even Gwilym could help her then. If she was caught with the dagger, she wouldn't make it as far as the hole. Once again, she wondered whether her friend would be angry with her. She placed a hand over her heart and felt the steady beats. An image of Gwilym grinning in that way he did when he was proud of her accomplishment came to her, and she exhaled the stress she'd been holding. It might've been wishful thinking, but imagining him like this was far better than the alternative. She didn't care whether she pissed off the king or Antonio, but Gwilym...well, that was another story.

Antonio. Fuck. She'd have to deal with her controlling boss at some point. Any other time, she would've gone to him right away, but it was too dangerous tonight. She'd take the dagger to him in the morning, when the guard wasn't so heavy. Maybe she'd get lucky, and Antonio would have a whopper of a hangover. It would certainly help with her negotiations.

He'd tell her how she owed him her life, how he'd taken her in after she was orphaned, how he was like a father to her. All stories she'd heard before, and all stories that made her sick to her stomach. No child deserved a man like Antonio in their life. He'd broken her more times than she cared to remember, but it was her own fierce will that had taken all his abuse and used it to survive the streets.

She might be a thief, but it wasn't for her own profit. If she had her way, she'd give everything she stole back to the people. The king taxed the working class and kept them in poverty while he dined on mutton and pheasant every night. He drank the finest wines while her friends made do with sour cider pressed from last season's rotten apples.

The only person worse than the king, in her opinion, was Antonio. King of the slums, he ran his gang of urchins with more military precision than the king his army. What she pilfered from the wealthy went into Antonio's coffers, but she made sure part of her score found its way back to the common folk. It wasn't as if she cheated Antonio, exactly, she just didn't tell him about everything she stole. It was a difficult life balanced between survival and utter ruin.

Antonio might've kept Amaleigh alive after the Purge stole her family, but there were many times she wished he'd let her die.

She checked the street and surrounding area before she snuck into her building and clambered up the stairs that led to the tiny attic room she called home. It wasn't much, but it kept her dry and out of the alleys. It had taken her a week to bugger up the courage to tell Antonio she had her own place. He liked to keep his gang close, where he could control their every move. She'd rather risk the king's dungeon than live in the alleys again. She was at an age where she couldn't hide her curves, and there were too many men who saw her as an easy target for their lustful desires. Why pay a whore when they could take her for free? Fuck that.

It meant constant moving, which was exhausting physically and mentally. A place of her own afforded her a tiny modicum of safety, but even that was far more than the sewers and alleys gave. Besides, all the time she'd spent sneaking through the palace showed her how the other half lived. Unlike most of the urchins who ruled the underbelly of the streets, Amaleigh dreamed of a better life away from the grime and piss and vomit.

Fireworks lit up the sky outside her tiny window, and with each bang, she flinched as if struck with a leather strap. Flickering rainbows chased the shadows out of her shabby room.

She sat with her back to the window and turned the dagger over in her hand. Rubies, sapphires, diamonds, opals, and emeralds covered the hilt. A serpentine blade ended with a vicious-looking hooked curve.

She ran a finger over the flat part of the blade and shivered. Whether ceremonial or used for fighting, this dagger knew death. Ancient power thrummed from the iron to her skin. A comforting calm washed over her like a loved one's embrace.

Another boom shook the rafters, and she swallowed a cry. The celebrations were a revolting reminder of the Purge that had taken a good portion of the city's inhabitants. King Heshen liked to remind his subjects it was done out of charity, that he had to purge Eidyn of the dragons and mages for their own safety. She might never know the truth of why he slaughtered those with magic, other than to rid the kingdom of people who had abilities he himself did not. Maybe he was afraid of magic. Or he was afraid of mages. But why, she'd never understand. For hundreds of centuries the palace always had mages at court as advisers. And a few lucky rulers even had dragon mages—men and women called Aerlghots who had a dragon soul and could shift into the magnificent beasts. They were once considered a high honor for a monarch, as their mere presence elevated that ruler's prestige.

Whatever changed, it had nearly destroyed Eidyn. For three days and nights, the city burned while Heshen and his army went house by house, murdering anyone—including children—who showed signs of having magic. And now, they celebrated the Purge with fireworks and feasts. Such a disgusting insult. Fifteen years of lies and corruption to cover up genocide.

Amaleigh wrapped the dagger inside her bag and tucked it under her straw mattress. It was late and too dark to work. In the morning, she'd remove the gems from the hilt. Flashes of red, green, and blue colored her room, followed by crackling.

Memories threatened to overtake her, of a night where flames burned bright against the night sky, and the cries of her brother were heard above the shouts of her parents. She recalled being warm, too warm, and more frightened than she'd ever been before or since. Fire blocked her vision, but not the awful wails of terror. Then an ominous silence followed, and it was there memories of her family ended.

She crawled beneath her thin blanket and pulled it over her head to block out the colorful fireworks reflected on her walls. If only blocking the sounds outside her window, and inside her mind, was equally as easy. With each whoop of celebration, she heard her parents' deaths.

CHAPTER
FIVE

Fire raged through the house and she cried out, but no one answered. She was alone, frightened, and young. So very young. In the haze of flames, a face appeared—not human. The little girl recoiled from the scaled snout that stretched toward her, but there was nowhere to run. She was trapped. She would die.

The dragon's mouth opened to reveal fangs taller than her.

"Amaleigh, step inside. I won't hurt you."

"No." She whimpered and cried out again, but only the roar of flames answered.

"Come now, child. There's no time."

Death awaited her, no matter the choice. Amaleigh stepped into the dragon's maw.

Bright sunlight momentarily blinded her when she sat upright, shaken from the nightmare. It had seemed so real. Her skin crackled as if singed by the blaze, and she rubbed her arms to rid herself of the unwelcome sensation. Bloody dreams. Every Purge, she had the same nightmare, but this time she actually took the final step beyond the dragon's jaws.

The harder she tried to recall details of the dream, the quicker they evaporated into smoke.

"Curse it all." She scrubbed her palms over her eyes and shook off the remnants of sleep. "I don't have time to waste on illusions."

She crammed a chunk of bread and some cheese into her mouth. A quick peek out the window told her the rest of the city was still asleep. The sooner she took the gems to Antonio, the better. If everything went to plan, she'd have a full belly by sunset.

An hour later, she threw her penknife across the room in a fit of rage. No matter what she tried, the stupid gems wouldn't come free of their settings. She studied the dagger with renewed interest. It looked old, probably from the second age. The ornate hilt and swoop of the blade were foreign to her, but that didn't mean much. She wasn't an antiquarian who studied such things, and the only person she knew who did would turn her over to the king the moment he saw the dagger.

Damn. If she couldn't remove the gems, maybe Antonio would take the whole thing as payment. It was worth a shot and really, she didn't have anything to lose by asking. Except her freedom.

Reluctantly, she shoved the dagger back into the canvas bag and left her tiny room. As she made her way across town, she kept to the shadows to avoid being seen. Antonio lived in one of the wealthier districts, but not the wealthiest, a fact that irked him to no end. He might be king of the urchins, but he would never be an equal to Eidyn's elite.

As she made her way through the posh avenues, she practiced what she would say to convince him she'd earned her freedom. Everything rested on Antonio. She prayed he was in a generous mood.

Fortunately for her, Antonio was nursing a major headache

after a night of debauchery. Celebration night was one of the most lucrative for his urchins—plenty of drunk citizens with heavy coin purses begging to be snatched. She'd once been one of the select few who Antonio sent into the wealthy districts of Eidyn. That was before she moved into her attic. Since then, Antonio kept her at a distance, as if she'd personally insulted him by leaving the alleys.

And that kept her weakened. He was slowly killing her, and he knew it. A deliberate move to starve her into coming back to the fold.

Flox that.

"Why you here so early?" Antonio's greasy black hair hung in clumps over his pockmarked face. He'd been handsome once, but that was before he discovered a love of eirislip—a nasty green alcohol that was said to be brewed using dragon intestines. Considering dragons were slaughtered during the Purge, Amaleigh tried not to think how long they'd been using the same disgusting entrails.

"I want to work out a trade." She gripped the bag and stepped close enough she could see his bloodshot eyes. "This, for my freedom. No more thieving for you, no more constantly being watched, no more allegiance to your urchins. An amicable separation."

His guttural laugh went to the dark place of her self-confidence like a battering ram.

"There's nothing in this kingdom that could pay off your debt. I took you in when—"

"When I was a child. Yes, we all know the story of your benevolence. With everything you've had me do, I think I've more than earned my freedom."

"Why you talk like an elite? You always think you so much better'n the rest of us. We both know you ain't got no more education than me."

That wasn't true—Amaleigh had the education of a prince, thanks to Gwilym. But Antonio couldn't know that. Her friendship with the prince was the only secret she'd managed to keep from her boss. And one she'd die protecting.

"I must've picked up elite slang from the wealthy streets when you trusted me." Amaleigh shrugged as if it mattered little to her how they spoke.

Antonio shifted in the huge chair he liked to use for meetings because he believed it made him intimidating, but Amaleigh saw past the façade. He was an old man slowly dying from his addictions, clinging to every last scrap of control he could. She would've killed him years ago if she thought she could get away with it, but he still had men loyal to him who would've hunted her far better than the king's trackers. And they wouldn't have stopped at throwing her into a dank cellar to die.

"You come here to insult me, girl? I trust thems who steal what I tells them to steal. You ain't earned shit." His pasty skin glowed translucent beneath the flicker of candlelight.

This wasn't going well. She went down to one knee and extended the tattered canvas. "Maybe this will change your mind." She couldn't bring herself to apologize or agree with him, even though that's what he wanted.

He eyed her a moment before beckoning one of his flunkies to take the bag from her. A rather revolting fellow whom Amaleigh had previous altercations with leered at her as he grabbed the satchel. A canker sore near his mouth oozed, and she suppressed the disgust that made her want to look away. If she could kill them all, she would, but she wasn't a murderer. A thief, yes, but never a killer.

Gerzer peeked inside the canvas bag before handing it to Antonio with a shrug. The king of urchins glared at Amaleigh, as if not trusting what he might find inside. After a tense few moments, he lifted the flap. His jaw clenched and eyes widened, then narrowed, all in the space of a heartbeat. By the flared nostrils and slight tremor of his hand, she sensed his apprehension, or fear, of the dagger. Antonio shoved the bag at Gerzer and flicked his hand toward Amaleigh.

Head cocked in question, Gerzer held out the satchel.

"You trying to get me killed?" Antonio's voice lowered in a stern rebuke. "Take that away and don't yous ever bring it near me again."

"It's just a dagger," Gerzer argued, then clapped his mouth shut.

"Just a dagger." Antonio stood and smacked his flunky across the side of his head. "You're too stupid to know any better."

Amaleigh stood quietly, happy that Gerzer had said the words she'd been thinking and that she'd had the wherewithal to keep silent.

"If you won't accept the dagger as payment, what can I do to buy my freedom?" Desperation clung to her words, and she struggled to keep from letting her disappointment show. Weakness would be punished.

Antonio settled onto his chair and wiped his palms down the front of his legs. He knew she wouldn't prostitute herself, but by the way he was licking his lips, she feared that would be the answer.

"Fifty thousand gold feathers. You bring me that much, and your service to me will end."

Gerzer's mouth gaped, as did Amaleigh's.

"You and I both know that dagger is worth four times as much." Antonio's voice softened. "Haven't I always looked out for you, Amaleigh? Took you in, gave you a home and a purpose. This is how you can repay my kindness. Besides, you should have no problem getting the money. I'll give you two moon-turns. That should be plenty of time." He sat back with a wicked grin. "If you don't get me the money by that time, you'll forfeit any claim to independence and will serve me in whatever capacity I see fit for the rest of your life."

The change in his tone to concerned father figure sent chills down her spine. If Gerzer noticed, he didn't show it, but Amaleigh heard the elite speak Antonio pretended to hate so much. Everything with him was an act, even his slum slang. She saw the truth of how he'd risen to king of the urchins, and it wasn't from his kindnesses.

Sickness churned in her belly, and she fought to keep from being ill right there. Two months. She had to sell the dagger quickly. How? Who? Her mind spun with a few answers and settled on the only option that made sense. Danteneux. If he couldn't sell the dagger, she'd join his crew and sail far from the stinking city.

"And don't yous think of leaving Eidyn. I have spies in every kingdom. I'll find you, and you won't like your punishment." He rubbed his hands together and nodded to Gerzer. "But I's will."

Gerzer's laugh wheezed from his congested lungs, and he spat a glob of something foul on the floor at her feet.

She swallowed hard and curled her nails into the soft skin of her palms.

"Fine. Fifty thousand gold feathers for my freedom. Consider it done." She pivoted and strode from the room without being dismissed. Several gasps followed her, but she didn't look back.

She could feel Antonio's stare upon her back and knew the punishment he was planning was far worse than she could ever imagine. Prostituting herself would've been preferable to what he'd demand of her. She couldn't let that happen. Whatever it took, she had to buy her freedom from Antonio.

SIX

Danteneux had never let Amaleigh down in the past. With any luck, her favorite unscrupulous captain would be in port and they could work out a deal. Knowing she'd be followed, and not really caring, she practically ran back to her attic and crammed her only gown, cloak, and gloves into the bag on top of the dagger.

Getting to the dock would take a little more care, and subterfuge. She spotted two of Antonio's urchins loitering across the street from her building and had to stop herself from waving at them. Instead, she slipped into the alley and took several more cramped walkways before turning onto busier streets, hoping to lose them in the crowd. By the time she circled back toward the harbor, she'd managed to lose both urchins several blocks over. It gave her a moment to relax, but not fully. Those two would be replaced by even more soon enough. She'd have to conduct her business quickly to keep Antonio from knowing her plans.

The dock was quiet as she approached. Nothing to be worried about, but it kept her on edge all the same. To her relief, the *Sundancer* sat moored in the harbor. At this time of the day, and after a raucous night, the captain wouldn't be on his ship—he was most likely in one of the whorehouses on the next street.

A burly man with coarse black hair and sunburnt skin sat on a rickety chair outside the front door of one, his gaze firmly set on her. Probably a spy. In her business, it paid to be paranoid.

Amaleigh scurried into a doorway where she would see Dante coming or going from either his ship or one of the whorehouses but kept her out of direct sight of the burly man. She positioned herself toward the front of the doorway, using shadows to hide her presence. It didn't take long before Dante ambled down the road, looking as if he'd been ridden hard and put away wet. He waved to the doorman, who raised a hand in return, a wide smile breaking across his features.

She slipped further into the doorway and waited until Dante was close enough he would hear her whisper. "Got a minute?"

Dante glanced up, a frown making deep creases in his forehead. "What the fuck are you doing here?"

"I've got a business proposition for you."

He tucked in his shirt and raked his hands through his hair in an attempt to tame the mess. After a quick glance to the doorman, he leaned against the wall near where she hid. "What's so damn important you had to interrupt my morning?"

"Seems to me your business was already concluded." She shifted the bag to her right hip. "Have you heard about anything being stolen from the palace?"

Dante shook his head. "Can't say that I have, but then, I've been busy."

"When do you sail again?"

He looked toward the horizon and then to his ship. "On the early tide, in about two hours' time."

Amaleigh stepped to the back of the doorway, where they'd

be sheltered from passersby and prying eyes. "I'd like you to sell this, far from Eidyn. Take your usual commission, of course."

He sidled beside her, his height crowding the small space. She opened the flap of her bag to show him the dagger, and he whistled through his teeth.

"You stole that? From the palace?" A callused hand rubbed his chin. "That's worth a king's ransom. Why the whole piece? It would be easier to shift without the steel."

"I tried. The gems won't budge."

Dante moved so that his back was to the street and held the dagger in his hands. He ran a thumb across the blade, whistling again. "It's a beauty. I might be tempted to keep it for myself."

"I need fifty thousand for it. I don't care who ends up with the thing." If Dante wanted it, fine. Coins were coins. It didn't matter where they came from, as long as they bought her freedom.

He tucked the dagger beneath his shirt and pulled her into a hug, surprising her.

"The hell you doing?" Her muffled protest was lost in his embrace.

"In case anyone's watching. Let them get an eyeful of something besides a trade." He lifted her face to his and kissed her hard.

His firm lips locked onto hers in what many a lady would consider a passionate kiss, but only brought about feelings of spite in her. How very dare he! Sputtered curses were silenced by his fierce hold, and despite her squirming, didn't deter him one bit. His hands stroked her grimy hair and his body moved rhythmically against hers. He was a handsome man, and in a different situation, she might've enjoyed the attention, but the fact he'd been with another woman not more than half an hour earlier made her already delicate stomach churn.

At last he pulled away and gazed at her adoringly. "Make it

look like you're upset I'm leaving. Sell the lie. Tears might be nice."

She snorted. "Sorry, I don't cry."

"Fake it."

"Fine." She screwed her face into the best heartbreak she could. Dante didn't laugh, but his snicker didn't give her confidence.

"Good enough." His lips brushed her forehead and for a moment, it felt like real affection. "You sure I can't convince you to be part of my crew?"

"And have you slobbering on me every day? No thanks." No way could she tell him Antonio would kill her if she tried to run. She trusted Dante with the dagger, but not her life.

"Tis a pity, lass." He turned with a last wave. When he stepped from the doorway to the street, he adjusted his breeches as if he'd had a last shag before sailing. Sell the lie. What a rogue.

She watched him go, her emotions skittering like dice thrown across the pavement. At the gangplank, he paused, half-turned, then shook his head and strode to the ship. Amaleigh waited until he was out of sight, then wiped dry eyes as if she were crying. It wouldn't convince anyone, she knew, but she felt a need to play along with Dante's charade. In a way, he did hold her life in his hands. That dagger was the beginning of a new life for her. She wouldn't allow herself to breathe just yet, but the prospect of living without the constant fear of Antonio's whims controlling her every waking moment was enticing.

Finally, she could dare to dream of the life she wanted. Could dare to believe she would become more than an urchin and a thief. Could dare to think that maybe, just maybe, she deserved to love and be loved in return.

Perhaps even by a prince.

CHAPTER
SEVEN

Morning sun filtered through the windows of the library in rays of light that momentarily blinded Gwilym as he entered the room. This was one of his and Amaleigh's favorite places to hide. Not that they actually had to hide—more like no one ever used this room and therefore they always had the space to themselves.

The walls rose two stories high with shelves stretching from one end to the other. Books, scrolls, parchments older than Eidyn itself, and other antiquaries were stuffed into any available crevice. He'd spent hours upon hours in this room with Amaleigh, at first helping her learn to read, and then later, sitting in comfortable quiet as they each leafed through a book. Amaleigh preferred a mix of historical texts and romances, but Gwilym often chose chivalric adventures. They'd tease each other endlessly about their choices, but in the end, he didn't care what book lay upon his lap, as long as she was by his side.

Today the library felt claustrophobic and empty at the same time. He missed his friend. Missed Amaleigh's laughter and the way she had of mocking him when he got too uppity. He turned away from the bright sunlight and stood before a plain, almost unremarkable cabinet that had always been in the library.

Inside the cabinet, forty-three weapons were displayed against a crimson velvet backdrop. They ranged from a saber to a rapier with words etched into the blade, several daggers of various sizes and shapes, to mysterious stars that looked lethal in their simplicity, and to other items he had only vague ideas how they could be used in combat. Two golden pegs sat empty in the center of the cabinet.

"Why do you suppose she stole that dagger?" His father's voice came from the shadows and Gwilym steadied himself to keep from jumping at the sudden sound.

"I don't know." He cocked his head and studied the empty space, trying to recall the dagger's details. He recalled a wavy blade that ended in a vicious curl, and a hilt worth a king's ransom. "It was the handsomest of the lot, perhaps she was drawn to the gems."

"Hmmm, yes, perhaps. But there are others with far more valuable diamonds that I suspect would be easier to remove." The king approached from Gwilym's left where an alcove with several overstuffed chairs made excellent hiding places that he and Amaleigh had made use of many times over the years. "Surely, profit was her motivation."

Gwilym faced his father. "I truly don't know. I trusted her. I thought we were friends." Sadness clung to his words.

"Yes, well, friends are the ones who betray us the harshest, I suppose." His father stared at the cabinet, his eyes glassy as if he were far away in memory.

"I'm surprised no one's ever stolen a weapon before now. I mean, it's not as if the cabinet is locked, and it's kept here in the library with no guards to keep watch." Those very facts had often made Gwilym curious about the cabinet, but there was always something more interesting to draw his attention and he never followed up on his musings. Until now.

The king nodded, his lips quirked. "We never needed a guard." He pointed to the cabinet. "Get me that ishikenshi, will you?" At Gwilym's frown, the king continued. "The one that looks like two crescent moons back-to-back, just there."

"Ah." That was a name he didn't recognize. So many of the weapons' names were lost to him since he'd only been trained with daggers and swords. The king's elite army would use the more lethal weapons like the ishikenshi, but never the prince.

Gwilym reached for the simple gold handle to open the cabinet. A sharp stinging snapped against his hand and he pulled it back, shaking his fingers to alleviate the pain. He sucked in the swear word on his lips and tried again. This time, the stinging turned to razor-like rips up the back of his hand to his forearm. He stared at his unmarked skin, and then at the cabinet. Dawning washed over him with deep dread.

"Magic. But how?" He turned to his father, who was watching him with curiosity clear in his eyes. "You knew it was spelled to keep anyone from opening the cabinet. But, you hate magic. You're quite public about it as well."

He didn't say the words that begged to be spoken. That it was magic that caused the king to go on a murderous rampage fifteen years prior. The Purge was meant to wipe out magic users and yet here was a cabinet cloaked in the very thing that brought about so much heartache and upheaval. It didn't make sense.

"It's true, I abhor magic and those who use it. But this particular cabinet, well, I suppose the irony amuses me." The king's gaze tracked each weapon, a small smile on his lips.

"What do you mean?"

His father opened the cabinet with nary a flinch and withdrew one of the ishikenshi. "Each of these weapons was given as a gift to those who served the crown. Some by me, others by my father, great-grandfather, or those who came before them. All given with gratitude for their loyalty." He turned to Gwilym, his gaze now filled with meanness that unnerved him. "All filthy mages. I won't be deceived like my predecessors."

Gwilym had never understood his father's hatred of mages. It was no secret he didn't agree with the king, but anytime he brought it up he was treated with the equivalent of a pat on the head as if he were a toddler and too young to understand. He'd been six when the Purge took place. Old enough to remember the chaos, the anxiety of those around him, and the screams of those who were butchered. It was three days and nights of sheer terror.

"Why keep them here and not in the weapons room?" Gwilym eyed the lethal dual scythe-like weapon his father gripped in his hand.

"Because I don't wish to see them." He handed the ishikenshi to Gwilym. "Put this away."

He took the strange blade and hesitated. "But I can't. It won't let me."

"You speak as if magic is alive. Don't be deceived, my son. Magic is vile, but not sentient." He jutted his chin toward the cabinet and Gwilym reached for the handle.

This time, there was no shock, no stinging pain. He opened the door without issue and returned the weapon to its place. His gaze went to the empty golden pegs.

"You're curious about the one your friend stole." It wasn't a question. The king crossed his arms, his eyes glassy as if he were lost to memory. "It belonged to the Lord High Mayor. I killed his family myself." This was said with pride and Gwilym swallowed his disgust. "His wife was your mother's protector." His father's face creased with revulsion. "An Aerlghot. Despicable traitors."

Gwilym had a vague recollection of the couple, but it was hazy as were so many of his memories from that time. Momentary gratitude washed through him that his mother hadn't lived to see the king's madness. She'd died before the Purge of a mystery illness that no one was willing to talk about, especially not to him. There were days Gwilym could recall his mother's face with clarity, but other times he struggled with what her hair color was. He remained silent, willing his father to say more.

The king rarely spoke about the Purge and said even less about his late wife. Gwilym hung on his every breath, greedy for even a scrap of information about his mother. But none came forth.

"I seem to remember two children..." the king moved his hand through the air as if to stroke someone's hair. "But no, there was only one."

"Father?" Gwilym touched his father's arm lightly so as not to startle him out of his reminiscing.

The king blinked and looked at his son as if confused where he was. "Yes, as I was saying, these weapons are a reminder that the throne is absolute. No one," at this he looked at Gwilym, "shall contest my decisions."

Threat understood. Although, Gwilym hadn't said or done anything to challenge his father. Unless his father considered the theft of the dagger Gwilym's personal responsibility.

"You did as you saw fit, as a king should." The words felt like sand in his mouth.

He knew the game, had played it his whole life. Appease the king at all costs. His gaze went to the empty place in the cabinet, and his chest tightened with worry. The entire conversation was a warning. His father wanted him to know he knew who had stolen the dagger, and yet, he seemed confused about it at the same time.

Gwilym waited until his father left the library before he searched the archives for information about the Purge. The palace staff kept meticulous records of everything that happened at the palace, and, morbidly, of every soul murdered in those three days. Whatever memory his father had been lost to, Gwilym was certain he'd find it in the records.

A chill of dread wrapped around his spine and a gentle voice whispered through his mind, *Be careful what you wish for.*

CHAPTER
EIGHT

After walking around the block four times and doubling back twice, Amaleigh settled into a booth inside the tavern across from Danteneux's ship. When she saw the crew preparing to set sail, her heart quickened and she sat on her hands to keep from biting her nails down to the quick. She'd not seen any urchins sneaking around the harbor, but she knew better than to think she'd escaped them completely. Antonio had eyes everywhere.

Once the ship was a speck on the horizon, she left the tavern by a back door and made her way to the public baths. Instead of going to the pools sectioned off for the poor, she wove between the rooms through the tunnels built into the walls for heating. When she found an empty pool reserved for exclusive use of the city's elite ladies, she squeezed from the cramped space and set her bag on a bench. She shook out her gown and let it drape to remove the wrinkles.

Next, she stripped off her dirty clothes and threw them into a smaller pool servants used to wash the ladies' feet before entering the larger, heated pool. The clothes needed a good scrubbing, as did she. It had been too long between baths, and she stank. Washing the clothes took longer than she'd have liked, but once they were clean, she laid them out in front of the small fireplace that kept the room warm. She took extra care bathing herself until her hair squeaked and skin tingled. The scent of the soaps and scrubs reserved for ladies of privilege made her swoon. Lavender, rosehip, even a touch of cinnamon perfumed the air.

For a long time, she floated in the warm water and let her mind wander. A dream—no, a vision played out in her mind, but it felt real as if it were truly happening. Fire raged, just as it had in her nightmare. Beyond the flicker of flames, a woman's voice spoke to Amaleigh, her voice tender, maternal.

"Borne of ash, you cannot be burned. Borne of air, you cannot fall. They cannot cage you, my child of fire, for you are more powerful than they could ever imagine. Remember this. Always."

Amaleigh tasted tears and searched the empty room for the woman, but she was alone. As always. She rolled until her face was submerged in water. The vision followed, and she saw herself standing in front of a chimney in a destroyed house. Ash fell from the rafters like snow. Behind her, the face of a dragon rose, its ruby scales glinting violet in shadow. Her eyes glowed with inner fire.

Amaleigh curled into herself and willed the vision to leave, but it wormed its way into her marrow. There hadn't been dragons in Eidyn since the Purge. They were detested by the king and slaughtered, along with anyone who showed signs of magic. But now she'd had two dreams about them. One, the nightmare that always came with the Purge celebrations of a dark-scaled dragon, and now this one. If it was a warning, she didn't understand the meaning. If it was a memory, she'd do well to erase them from her mind. Nothing good could come of remembering dragons.

Her head broke the surface, and she gulped in humid air. She coughed and sputtered against the moisture entering her lungs. She needed dry air—she needed fire. On hands and knees, she crawled out of the pool to the small hearth. The heat of the flames beckoned, and she stuck her face as close as she dared and inhaled. A soothing burn traveled down her throat to fill her lungs and she breathed deeper.

Pale, abalone-hued scales rippled across her skin, and she stared in horror at her hands. She thought she'd hallucinated the dragon when she leapt from the cliff. But there, in the firelight, she clearly saw scales where flesh should've been. It was impossible. Fuck impossible. To even entertain the idea of having scales was tantamount to suicide. She cast a wary eye to the corners and shadows, where secrets lingered. Whatever this affliction was, she didn't want it.

The fire popped, and she scuttled backward like a crab, as far from the flames as she could get without entering the water. Huddled alone and naked, a dam burst deep in the place where she shoved her emotions, and she wept.

Fifteen years' worth of unshed tears left her a sobbing mess. If questioned under torture, she couldn't have said why she cried. Nor did she care. In a bizarre way, it felt good, so good to let go. To be vulnerable to her emotions. A long overdue release came from letting the tears flow. If nothing else, she was tired of pretending to have it all together. Exhausted from constantly having to build walls and force people away. Especially the one she cared for most. Her heart pinched as she thought of Gwilym. His sweet smile and easy acceptance of her lifestyle had always seemed like a blessing. She'd loved him from the moment they met, but always kept her feelings hidden for fear of losing his friendship. He was a prince. One day, he would marry a princess. That's the way royalty worked, and though it was a bitter pill, she swallowed it readily. Gwilym's happiness always came first.

Fanciful imaginings popped into her head of what could become of their friendship once she was free. They would sit together at an open-air café to drink tea and gossip about the courtiers. What a lark. Surely, their clandestine meetings become a thing of the past. Or would he insist she sneak into the palace, afraid to be seen with her in public? The unspoken question nearly broke her heart. Not him. Not her Gwilym. He'd never, not once made her feel inferior even though she was the lowest of the low and he the heir to the throne.

Fresh tears wracked her, and she curled into herself, afraid to face the truth of the matter. He wasn't hers. Would never be hers, no matter how much she wished otherwise. Her face throbbed with each beat of her heart, and her breathing came in gasps that left her spent. Gwilym could never know about her dragon nightmares, or her hallucinations. For that's what they were. She hadn't become a dragon when she leapt from the cliff. Impossible. And the scales on her flesh? Just a lack of food and too warm water. She was human. She was nobody. She was just a thief. Nothing more.

Exhausted from running, from worrying, from just bloody trying to survive, she wiped the last of her tears and rested her head in the crook of her arm. Her thoughts lingered on Gwilym, as they always did when she thought of a somewhere she might be safe. The fool boy probably didn't even know he was the only one who made her feel protected. One day she'd make it up to him.

The sound of voices and shuffling outside the arched doorway woke Amaleigh with a start. Stupid woman! Falling asleep for the Gods knew how long could be a fatal error.

With no time to lose, she rushed to pack her now dry clothes in the carryall. She pulled the gown over her head and slipped behind the wall into the tunnel just as several chatty young women entered the room. Their giggles hid any sound Amaleigh might've made as she moved swiftly through the tight space.

At the door leading to the city, she paused and made sure she looked appropriate for the wealthier neighborhood. She draped her cloak over the bag to conceal its tattiness and stepped through the door with the confidence of a noblewoman. The darkened sky surprised her, but she made sure to keep the shock from her features. She'd lost an entire day in the baths.

No one noticed the attractive young lady dressed in a fine blue gown with cascading curls the color of garnets. And if they did, it wasn't to remark on her dirty clothes or smudged face like usual. Her clean skin and shining hair were a mark of class.

Amaleigh had used her borrowed time in the palace studying the noble girls—learning how to mimic their walk, talk, and the way they condescendingly sneered while simultaneously wearing a beguiling smile. Gwilym used to roar with laughter at her impressions. Hell, it was he who had procured the gown she now wore. He thought it riotously funny to nick a dress or bauble from the snooty girls and give them to Amaleigh. She never thought of them as gifts, per se, but a token of friendship for making his lonely life a little less awful.

She flicked a curl off her shoulder and demurely dropped her gaze from a handsome young man's appraisal. His belt lacked a heavy pouch. Pity for that, but she was on the hunt for a nice score that would tide her over until Danteneux returned. The thought of the scurrilous pirate made her blood chill. Idiot. She'd let him kiss her. Now he'd think he could do it anytime he liked. The next time she saw him, she'd make sure he knew there'd be no freebies, and she wasn't for sale.

A plump little partridge came into view, and she slid her

best simpering waif face into place. The man waddled near, and she wiped an imaginary tear from her eye.

"Hey ho, what's the matter, darlin'?" The man wheezed closer and bent down as if she were a child. All a ruse to get his beady eyes nearer to her breasts.

"I'm afraid I've gotten myself lost. My brother and I came in for the celebrations and now, I don't know where he's gone." She lowered her voice and whispered, "I've never been in the city before. It's ever so terrifying."

The man leaned in, almost touching her as if to better hear, and inhaled a surreptitious sniff of her hair. For his troubles, she cleanly cut the leather straps from his purse.

"Oh! There he is!" Amaleigh rushed off, slipping between a group of ladies.

She heard the man cry out, but his voice was soon lost to the din of the city as she hurried to the next block.

Two streets over, she slowed to catch her breath. As she rounded a corner, she ran into the solid chest of a man.

"Pardon me." The apology came out breathy, and she fluttered a hand in front of her face.

"No harm done."

At the sound of the man's voice, her nerves jangled. She cautiously glanced up into the damn handsome face of the stranger who'd made a doorway out of a tree trunk. A magical doorway. Her brain screamed *Danger!* And told her to run. But again, her legs wouldn't move.

"Well, well, if it isn't my little thief." His tone conveyed amusement, but his eyes were hard bits of granite. "Do you live around here?"

She took a step backward and it felt like trudging through mud. "Are you following me?" It was an absurd thing to ask, but his presence in the wealthy district unnerved her. Why would a mage be here? What could be important enough to risk being caught by the king's guard?

"Following? No. Hoping to find you? Yes."

His honest answer did nothing to settle her already frazzled mind. "Why?"

His gaze went to the cloak she gripped beneath her arm. "Do you still have it?"

"I don't know what you're talking about."

"You still don't know what you stole, do you? In the wrong hands, that dagger could wreak untold destruction."

A peculiar burning sensation ripped through her veins, and blood roared in her ears. She licked her dry lips. "I don't have it."

His eyes narrowed, and she felt his disappointment down to her core. It wasn't pleasant, or familiar, but at the same time, it was familial. Such a strange thing to think from a man she didn't know and had only spoken to twice in her life.

"Where is it? You must get it back." The amusement was gone from his tone.

A carriage approached, and the man sunk into the shadows of an alley. Amaleigh took advantage of the moment and darted in front of the carriage, startling the horses. The driver shouted at her, but she was already on the other side of the street, melding into the crowds. As she ran, she slipped the bag's strap over her head and draped the cloak around her shoulders. When she returned to her attic, she vowed to burrow herself beneath the only thin blanket she owned and not venture out until Danteneux returned. Between Antonio's spies and the mystery man, she couldn't chance encountering any more enemies.

CHAPTER

NINE

Shadows ghosted past the small window of her attic room, and she ducked into an alcove across the street where she couldn't be seen. For nearly an hour, she watched men move back and forth in her tiny room. Snippets of their conversation drifted down to her, unsettling her already frazzled nerves. They weren't Antonio's men, but the king's guard. The emptiness of her stomach and wild ups and downs of the day finally caught up with her. She choked against dry heaves and pressed her back against the cool building. How the pox had the king figured out she stole the dagger?

No one in the palace saw her, she was certain of it. If Gwilym suspected it was her, he definitely wouldn't say anything. Dante was gone, so who?

Antonio? Fucking hell, it had to be him that snitched on her. But, why? To what end?

She'd always suspected he worked with King Heshen, but she didn't want to believe it. Realistically, though, the king would have to know about Antonio. It wasn't like the urchins were a secret. Hell, half the city was indebted to Antonio in one way or another.

No. She refused to believe Antonio would betray her like this. Couldn't believe it. Despite everything, he'd taken her in when she was just a small child. He'd given her shelter, food, a purpose. True, that purpose was to steal and enrich his coffers, but he'd also looked out for her and made sure no one physically assaulted or abused her. That was a privilege reserved only for him. Besides, they had a code of honor among the dysfunctional family that they were. No ratting on each other. Ever.

Gerzer? Naw, the man didn't have the nerve to betray Antonio.

The stranger.

Dammit. It had to be him. She nodded and rubbed a finger along her lips. The handsome mage. Only four people knew Amaleigh had the dagger, and of them, only one she didn't know.

Barnacleballs, she'd really stepped in it this time.

The only thing she could do was wait for the king's men to clear out and hole up until Dante returned. She'd need food, but that would be easy enough. Bruno would make sure she didn't starve. The pouch full of coins nestled deep in her bag beneath her thieves' clothing was a far cry from the fifty thousand gold feathers Antonio wanted, but it was enough to keep her belly full for a little while.

If only she knew why the stranger would turn her in. Or how he knew she had the dagger in the first place. Who was he, and why this sudden interest in her? As far as she could recall, she'd never met him or even seen him in Eidyn. It was a rather disconcerting coincidence that the day she steals a dagger from the king, he appears and offers help.

Was he a friend? Or foe?

If he had turned her in to the king, that answered that question. But if he hadn't and his offers of help were sincere, well that was a whole other pickle. She hated coincidences.

She knew one thing for certain—she was glad Dante had the dagger and was far from Eidyn. The guards wouldn't find what they were looking for, which meant she wouldn't spend the rest of her days in the dungeons.

When finally the guard left through the front door, she cautiously made her way up the back of the building using drainpipes and window ledges as supports. It was tedious and annoying, but getting surprised by a lone guard left to watch for her was a shittier option.

She reached her floor and crawled through the window, her gaze sweeping from side to side, but the landing was empty. For several long moments she stood still, listening, but the only sounds she heard came from the streets below where revelers were ramping up their celebrations for the second night. Only one more to go after this night. Three nights, that's how long Heshen had taken to purge Eidyn of dragons and mages. And every year, three nights of celebrations to commemorate his atrocity. He was the one who should be in the dungeons, not her.

With a cautious sigh, she pushed open the door. Whatever she'd imagined she might find, the reality was far worse.

She stared at the wreckage of her room, willing her legs not to buckle and her stomach not to pinch and heave yet again. She didn't have many possessions, but what she did own was strewn across the floor with careless apathy. Straw from her mattress littered the window nook and her small desk lay in splinters. Their thorough search had destroyed everything. It looked as if they took great pleasure in making sure nothing of hers could be made useful ever again. She imagined several unladylike things she would do to the assholes who got off on ruining her life so violently.

Rage whipped through her veins, and she sank to her knees as fresh tears rolled over her cheeks. She swiped them away with a fist. What was wrong with her? She wasn't some sappy waif. In fact, until that day, she hadn't cried in years. Material possessions meant nothing—they were easily stolen or, in her case, broken. She knew better than to place any importance on stuff.

Her anguish went deeper than the loss of her belongings. The guard had been in *her* space. Her refuge from the world was violated. Not even Antonio or his goons had ever been to the attic. The attack felt personal. As if they were sending a message. Her nerves tightened and hands shook as she looked out the small window into the night. She wasn't safe here. Not now, not ever again. The guard knew where she lived and could come back at any time.

That, more than anything, unsettled her.

She kept away from the window in case it was being watched, which she had no doubt it was, and did her best to tidy the room. It was silly, she knew, but somehow, the act of straightening the mess gave her a sense of control. The few items that weren't completely destroyed, she tucked into her bag as if they were talismans of her survival.

With the threat of the guard returning, she knew she shouldn't sleep there that night, but the thought of returning to the sewers or alleys filled her with a dread so deep and abiding that she resolved to take the risk and stay in her attic. She would find other accommodations tomorrow. If the king thought she'd be easily caught, he was mistaken. She knew Eidyn better than most and had several places she could hide, but they were places best secured during the daylight because with nightfall came threats of another kind—Antonio's thieves and assassins. If she were caught sneaking through the streets after word got out that the guard had been to her room, there were too many of Antonio's men who would be only too happy to slit her throat for the reward she was sure the king would give them.

After rigging several alarms and traps just in case anyone thought to creep up on her, she fell asleep to the sound of more fireworks and revelers continuing Purge celebrations. If she never had to endure another night of celebrations, it would be too soon. She made a promise to herself that if she survived the night, she would find a way out of Eidyn. Whatever it took.

CHAPTER
TEN

When Amaleigh woke the next morning, tangled in the mattress fabric and with straw sticking out of her hair, the sun was already past her window. Only a handful of times before had she slept so late. Without a job to do, or anywhere to be, she had no reason to wake up early. It was indulgent to have a bit of a lay-in, but after all she'd been through, she deserved it.

Just then, the realization stunned her.

She was alive. She touched her face, her heart, her throat. Yes, alive. Warm flesh, heart beating rapidly, but strong. No one had come to kill her. Nor had she had the nightmare that always accompanied every night of the Purge celebrations. Not one to scoff at a gift, she said a silent prayer to the ancient gods of Nasus, thanking them for one more day of life.

Soothing relief washed over her as she rolled over to untangle herself from the fabric. Her hand smacked something hard. Immediately, the relief turned to dread. She dared not look for fear she'd find a guardsman sitting opposite, grinning at his captive.

Cool steel met her exploratory touch, and a buzzing

tormented her belly. Every prayer she'd ever learned was whispered to those ancient gods, despite the fact that she'd never believed in them. She hoped they saw past that one tiny detail. Leaning away from the floor as if there might be a viper waiting to strike, she brushed aside a clump of straw and sucked in a breath at the sight of a flared blade and jewel-encrusted handle. She snatched her hand away and blew on her fingertips as if burned by some imaginary flame.

How in the name of fishcakes did the dagger get in her room?

She scrambled to a sitting position and scanned the room, but it was empty. Her traps were still set. No one had entered. She stared at the beautiful weapon as if it could give her answers. Most importantly, she wished to know why Dante would return it to her. There was only one way to find out.

In a matter of minutes, she was dressed in her thieves' clothing and had shoved what little remained of her belongings into the bag. The dagger she wrapped in the gown and covered them both with her cloak. She pulled her hair into a sloppy braid and shoved it under a cap to help hide her identity. She passed for a boy often enough, she hoped she could one more time. Of course, that was before her body betrayed her and sprouted hips and breasts.

An initial scan of the area didn't show anyone lingering suspiciously, but she wasn't taking any chances. She went to the roof and hopped from her building to the one opposite, and another two for good measure before she crept down the stairs on silent feet. At the street, she dodged carts and horses, putting as many people as possible between her and would-be pursuers.

As with the day before, she took a circuitous route to her destination, circling back several times. When satisfied she wasn't followed, she slipped into the flow of pedestrians and headed for the harbor.

The docks were a hive of activity when she arrived. Several ships were docked in the large harbor, but not the *Sundancer*. She made her way to the harbormaster's office and asked a harried-looking man whether Danteneux's ship had sailed that morning.

He scratched his chin while looking over the shipping records. "He sailed out yesterday."

"But he came back in, right?" She peered at the logs. Only one entry for the *Sundancer* and it was the previous day.

"I've been here since early this morning. He hasn't come back on my shift." Something caught his attention outside, and he hustled her out the door just as a well-dressed woman entered.

Amaleigh ignored the woman's sneer and decided to ask a few of the men unloading boxes from a cart whether they'd seen Dante or his ship. They all gave the same answer as the harbormaster—not since yesterday. It was entirely possible he snuck into a cove somewhere up the coast, but why would he? If caught, he'd lose his sailing license and Dante needed the king's permission to dock in Eidyn.

She stood in the middle of the bustling dock without any clue what to do or where to turn. Nothing made sense. A dagger that mysteriously appeared. The king's guard searching her room. The stranger.

People jostled her and knocked her aside. She got swept up in the flow and walked toward the city with an increasing sense of dread. The dagger was her way out of Eidyn. Her freedom. Somehow, she had to convince Antonio to take the damn thing. Even if not as payment, then to just get rid of it. A nagging worry kept itching the back of her skull that, for some asinine reason, the stranger wanted her to get caught with the dagger.

She just couldn't understand why. If only she knew who he was, and who she was to him. She couldn't fathom how he benefitted if she were caught. If there even was a reward, perhaps that was it. But he'd known she had the dagger while the trackers were chasing her. No one was that good at tracking. Or were they? Especially if they had magic. It didn't make sense, and that frustrated the hell out of her.

The only answer that did make sense was Antonio. He'd set her up to fail so that he would own her. She didn't want to admit it, but it was the less insane possibility.

Gerzer answered the door to Antonio's lavish house, and she grimaced at the look of superiority he wore.

"What you want?"

"I don't answer to you. Take me to Antonio."

He sucked his teeth and made an obscene gesture that she ignored. "He won't be pleased if you ain't got his money. Yesterday, he had to discipline a young one for stealing from him."

Amaleigh's insides coiled. No one stole from Antonio and lived to tell about it. They might not die right away, but they would soon enough. The time between discipline and death was pure torture, though—Antonio saw to that.

The king of urchins sat on a balcony overlooking the busy street below. When Amaleigh and Gerzer approached, he put down the orange he was peeling and gave her his best fatherly smile.

That look meant trouble. Her muscles turned to jelly, but she kept upright and walked to within a few feet of him.

"You have my money?"

"Did you send the king's guard to search my room?" She watched his face intently, waiting for any telltale signs he would lie. His eyes narrowed slightly and the corner of his lip twitched, confirmation he had. The bloody floxy bastard. And to think, she'd convinced herself it couldn't be him, that he wouldn't betray her like that. What a fucking fool she'd been.

"Why would I do that?" His manipulation of answering her question would've been humorous if her life wasn't on the line.

"To get the dagger. Possibly even a reward for turning it in. Is that why you refused to take it yesterday? They didn't find it, by the way. It's gone. Now that you've got the king's guard sniffing around, I doubt you or I will see a single coin."

"Well then, if you can't pay," Antonio leaned forward to look out at something on the street, "I have another proposition for you." He waved a hand dismissively. "To earn your freedom."

Perspiration dotted her upper lip, and she scraped a hand over her hair. Fuck him. He'd squealed to the king to set her up. She hesitated, not wanting to know what she'd have to do for fifty thousand gold feathers, but also knowing curiosity would win out.

"Go on." She fluttered a hand with practiced nonchalance.

Antonio turned to her with a steely gaze. "Kill the prince."

She blinked rapidly, certain she misheard. "What?"

"Kill the prince. You have until the end of celebrations tomorrow night. If you fail, you belong to me." He rested his elbows on his knees and leered at her.

The salty, acrid smell of his sweat assaulted her nostrils, and she took a step back. "I'm not—I can't. I'm a thief, Antonio. I've never killed anyone. I couldn't."

"Well then, if that's your answer. Gerzer, take Amaleigh's things to my room."

Gerzer stepped forward, and she put out a hand to stop him.

"Wait." Her mind spun as quickly as her churning gut. This wasn't happening. Couldn't be. She needed time. Needed to think. Needed to plan. To escape. But there wasn't time. She was trapped. Antonio had played her perfectly. She was utterly and completely fucked. "I'll do it."

Gods help her, she needed a miracle. It wasn't just her life on the line now.

"If you fail, you understand the penalty?"

"I do." She swallowed the sickness that crept up her throat. "I won't fail you."

"I'll hunt you down myself if you try to run."

"I understand." The air grew thick, and her head pounded.

He waved her off, and she practically ran to the front door. When Gerzer slammed it behind her, she gulped in drags of air and fought to remain standing on wobbling legs. How the hell was she going to get out of this mess? And all because of the stupid dagger.

She stumbled down the busy street, not seeing the faces of those she passed. Her view was tinged in red, with only the dagger in her mind. She'd take it back to the palace. Get rid of the cursed thing. But what about the prince? What about Gwilym?

CHAPTER
ELEVEN

The cabinet stood silent in the darkened room. It looked the same as it always had, with the notable exception of the missing dagger. She crept close and opened the glass door. Why would they leave the cabinet unlocked with so many valuables inside? It didn't make sense.

With a stab of disappointment that hurt her heart, she unfurled the gown to reveal the gorgeous weapon. To own such a work of art would be a blessing. But her life wasn't blessed.

Almost reverently, she returned the dagger to its place and sighed.

"I've never heard of a thief returning their stolen goods."

Amaleigh froze, her hand on the door, heart in her throat.

"I could call the guard right now and have you arrested."

The glass door clicked shut, and she turned. "But you won't, will you, Gwilym?"

The prince sat in a chair, his face a mix of conflicting emotions. Affection warred with—what? What hid within his brilliant blue eyes? Disappointment? No. Concern. He was worried for her.

She glanced over her shoulder, half expecting armed guards

to come racing into the room. He might not call the guard, but the king surely would.

"My father was quite vexed to learn someone had infiltrated the palace and stolen one of his prized possessions." Gwilym smiled then, a genuine grin that erased his unease. "I knew it had to be you, and truth be told, I'm glad to know I was right."

"Are you angry with me? I broke my promise to never steal from you or the palace."

His chuckle warmed places that she didn't know existed. "Angry? Perhaps a little. But mostly I'm proud as hell. You're a remarkable woman, Amaleigh. And apparently, a brilliant thief."

A blush stained her cheeks. "I wouldn't have taken it if it wasn't important."

"I know." He rose from the chair with the grace of a cat and stood before her. He removed the hat she wore and slid her braid between his fingers. "I knew a woman once with hair like sparkling garnets. She was fierce and strong, like you."

His eyes sought something in hers, and she waited, afraid of what he might find. After an interminable moment, his hand slid down her arm to clasp her hand in his. Words plunked in her brain, but she couldn't speak. The woman he spoke of was a stranger to her, and she despised the jag of jealousy that came with his statement. The woman might've been a lover. Or perhaps just a friend like Amaleigh. Or even a princess he might one day marry. Traitorous tears bit her eyes, and she blinked them away with a sigh. He was never meant for her.

"Tell me what's so important you had to steal from my father?" Again, that penetrating look.

"I—" A lie sprang to her lips, but she swallowed it whole. He was her best friend and deserved the truth. "I thought I could buy my freedom from Antonio. But that didn't work out so well. He demanded fifty thousand gold feathers. Da—I mean, a friend was going to take it away to sell, but somehow the damned thing returned to me." She shrugged, as if it were a small thing. "So I returned it."

"Fifty thousand? Is that all? You would think the king of urchins would know what this dagger is worth." Gwilym chuckled again. "Far more than what he asked." A shadow crossed his features, and she stifled a shudder from the chill it gave her.

"If it's so valuable, why isn't the cabinet locked?"

Gwilym turned them to face the display case. His hand didn't leave hers, and she gave him a soft squeeze. A cheeky grin lifted his lips, but he didn't look at her. Instead, he stared straight ahead where several items glittered in the dim light, but none more so than the dagger.

"It is locked. With magic." He glanced down, and her veins cooled with the intensity in his eyes. "Only someone with powerful magic in their blood could open the cabinet."

"No." She shook her head and stepped back. "I don't have magic. Please don't make that claim, Gwilym. You've known me my whole life. Was there ever a time you suspected me of being a mage?" She thought of the stranger's question in the forest when she'd asked if he was a mage and he countered with the same to her.

Gwilym reached a hand to stroke her face, and she leaned into his touch. Since before she could remember, she'd been sneaking into the palace. At first, it was just to snatch a silver spoon or two, but one day she saw Gwilym with his tutor and she'd stayed hidden, listening. When, a few months after that, Gwilym caught her, he'd helped fashion a little nook where she could do the lessons without being seen. Later, he'd go over her writing and help her understand some of the more difficult concepts. Then he'd give her a few coins to take back to Antonio so he wouldn't be wise to what she was really doing. She never stole from the palace again until now.

It had been a friendship borne of loneliness and desperation but benefitted them both. He knew her better than most, but he didn't know all of her. The thought sat heavy in her mind. Neither did she. There were pockets of her life that were blank mysteries. Sometimes she would catch a snippet of her past, but those were fleeting and never made sense. A vision of the dragon she'd become when she leapt from the cliff burst to the front of her thoughts and then in the baths, the scales shimmering upon her skin.

No. No, no, no. Those were caused by stress. She wasn't, couldn't be, what he suggested.

Gwilym smiled fondly at her, warmth emanating through his touch. "I didn't know for certain, but there were times I suspected."

His fingertips trailed along her forehead to her chin. Her mind screamed at him to kiss her, but he she held herself steady. How ludicrous to be thinking of his lips on hers at a time like this. But then he lowered his face until they were nose to nose and she inhaled his dark, spicy scent. Her nerves tightened and snapped. Desire spiraled through her, stealing her breath.

"You caught onto convoluted theories too easily and surpassed me in many areas."

His lips were close to her own. It would be so easy to turn ever so slightly and brush her against his.

"You never told me that. You always said I was decent, but had to try harder." Her words were breathy, full of lust.

"If I told you how smart you were, you might not've come back." He cocked his head and raised a brow. "Whenever you showed up, my life became a little bit brighter." His lovely lips pulled away, his eyes hard and bitter. Cold whooshed between them, leaving her reeling in the sudden draft. "But not this time. Father intends to make a public spectacle of whoever stole the dagger."

The abrupt change in his behavior unbalanced her, but she didn't have the sense it was from anything she'd done. She had to hope it didn't.

Gwilym's gaze went to the case. "That dagger belonged to the Lord High Mayor. Father used it to murder him and his family."

Amaleigh's vision darkened, and she swooned, suddenly lightheaded. Her desire was replaced by fear, raw and primal. The image of flames licking a collapsing ceiling played out, and she saw King Heshen stride through the wall of fire. The dagger winked and caught the light as he moved.

"But I returned it. He can't be angry now."

"You don't know him, Amaleigh." Deep, troubling sadness covered Gwilym's features. He was three years older than her. Old enough to remember the Purge.

She chewed the inside of her cheek, debating her choices. They all led back to one thing—her death. Despite Antonio's claim, she had to escape Eidyn. Somehow, someway. But to do so meant leaving her best friend. She clasped his hand in hers and squeezed too tightly, not wanting to let go. Never wanting to lose him. But of course she would. There was no way she could carry out Antonio's wishes, and that meant she wouldn't survive the night.

"Gwilym, there's something you should know. I, erm, I heard Antonio talking and he said by tomorrow night you'd be dead." Her voice trembled as she spoke, as did her legs. "You're not safe."

Despite being told there was a death warrant for him, Gwilym remained calm. "I had a feeling it would come to this." His jaw worked from side to side, and he held their gripped hands to his heart.

She could feel the rapid beating beneath her palm and fear rode over her senses.

"I've been vocal about my distaste for the Purge celebrations—so much so, some of the courtiers have been tossing around words like traitor and illegitimate."

Sounds came from the hallway, and Gwilym's face lost all color.

"Go, Amaleigh. I'll distract them, but you must leave." He held her tightly for one moment before giving a gentle shove.

By the time he turned to the hallway, she was halfway to the door hidden behind a heavy painting. She wedged herself inside and pulled the painting in place without a sound.

"You there!" Gwilym shouted a few moments later. "Where is my father? I must speak with him at once."

The sound of footsteps retreating echoed the beating of her heart. She didn't waste time celebrating. Instead, she turned and ran down the cramped passage and through the maze of crawl spaces only someone as slight as she could get through. It had been years since she and Gwilym first found the tunnels and explored them from one side of Eidyn to the other. If only she could remember where each one led. It would have to be trial and error. She raced on, sadness and rage fueling her. Leaving Gwilym was the hardest thing she'd ever done, but they both knew it was for the best.

At the end of the cramped space she came to a door, and peered through a tiny gap to see it led to a tunnel roughly hewn into the stone. She crept inside and shuddered at the chilling blackness. At least in the crawl spaces there had been ambient light from the palace, but here there was nothing.

She fumbled in her bag for flint and kindling. It took several more tries with shaking hands to light the bloody thing. The scant amount of light it provided was enough to allow her cautious movement. As for how long she was in the tunnel, she couldn't say. It might've been an hour or a day. She kept moving, placing one foot in front of the other. When her kindling ran out, she used strips of cloth from her tunic.

At last, she came to a door bolted from the inside. A secret passageway to the palace, but with no idea where it led. She thought she knew every nook and crevice in Eidyn, but she'd never seen this tunnel. She jerked on the latch and grimaced at the loud screech the hinges made when she opened the door.

Stars blanketed the night sky and a vista of sandy bluffs went from the tunnel to the ocean. She stared at the scenery, not quite believing what she saw.

She knew this place.

Charred remains of buildings littered the beach, and she tread carefully over the bluffs. The closer she came to the first pile of ash, the quicker her heart beat. Breathing slowed, shadows lengthened, and her world narrowed to just the ruins in front of her.

She stepped over the burned timbers and into what was once a home. Memories seized her, and she sank to her knees. A mother. A father. Her brother. Safety and laughter and love. Her gaze went to the remaining bricks, where the fireplace once stood. Something pale shimmered beneath the soot, and she crawled over to better see.

Terror like she'd never known seized her as she reached out with trembling hands. Her heart knew what she'd find, but her mind refused to accept the inevitable. This alone could get her killed but the secrets it held might provide answers to questions she'd long withheld in the depths of her memories. Warmth infused her entire body when her fingertips touched the glittering, dangerous thing. She was home.

CHAPTER

TWELVE

Tears slipped from Amaleigh's eyes as she brushed ash off a rounded, pebbled surface. She traced an oval with her fingertips and slid them into the soot and dirt. When she lifted her hands, a stone about the size of her head rested between her fingers. Not a stone. An egg.

The skin on her hands and forearms glistened with scales the color of abalone. The same color as the egg. She almost dropped the thing from fright, but instinct made her clutch it to her chest.

"Amaleigh."

She stilled, her breathing shallowed. She knew that voice.

The stranger.

"Amaleigh, it's time to go."

The dragon.

Slowly, she turned to see the handsome man standing a few feet away.

"Don't you dare hurt us!" She gripped the egg as if her life depended on it.

"Amaleigh, I'm not going to hurt either of you, but we have to go now." He held out his hand, and she shook her head.

"You told the king about the dagger." In her heart, she knew it was a lie, knew Antonio had told King Heshen, but she wasn't thinking rationally.

"I would never do that. Heshen doesn't understand the power of the dagger. Only a mage of pure blood can harness its capabilities."

She stroked the egg like she would a baby. "I don't understand."

"Where's the dagger now?" He took a step closer, and she cowered into the ruined fireplace.

"It's cursed. Dante was supposed to sell it, but it came back, so I returned it to the palace."

His eye twitched and a look of consternation crossed his features. "It's with Heshen?"

"No."

They both turned to see Gwilym walking toward them. He cocked his head at the stranger.

"Cornelius? I thought you were slain in the Purge." Gwilym's lips thinned and eyes narrowed.

"Are you sad I wasn't?"

Gwilym reached out a hand, and the man called Cornelius took it. They embraced like old friends.

This was a dream. Had to be. Nothing made sense.

Cornelius. Amaleigh searched her memory for that name. It was there, but she couldn't reach it. Locked inside the vault of her mind with the rest of her memories of her life before Antonio.

"I was devastated to hear about you and the Lord High Mayor." Gwilym's glance slid to Amaleigh. "I didn't fully figure it out until you returned the dagger."

"Figure what out?" She rose, still clutching the egg to her chest.

"Is that—" Gwilym stepped forward, but Cornelius put a hand up to stop him.

"The less you know about this, the better. Your father already wants you dead."

"My father ordered the killing?" He blew out a breath. "It's worse than I thought. I hope they send someone skilled. I'd hate to suffer."

"They sent me," Amaleigh admitted. Her heart broke a little to hear her own words. "It was payment for my freedom, but I couldn't do it."

"You gave up freedom for me?" His words were barely a whisper. "Why?"

There was that look again. The one that searched her soul and made her feel exposed, yet unafraid.

"You're my only friend. My best friend. I could never hurt you." There was more, but she held those words sealed in her heart. He didn't need to know that she loved him. Had possibly always loved him. He was a prince and she...was something she didn't even understand.

Gwilym's face softened, and he reached inside his cloak. Cornelius moved to shield her from the prince, but Gwilym ignored the man and withdrew the dagger to hand to her.

"This belongs to you. It's your legacy to protect." His gaze returned to the egg. "For all of our sakes."

Amaleigh took the dagger and held it alongside the egg. Light-headed, exhausted, and starving, her mind played tricks on her. Her legacy? Snippets of her life before the Purge slid into place.

A man holding a young boy on his lap, reading from a book. A woman singing soft lullabies to Amaleigh as her lids grew heavy. Those things happened, here, in these crumbling ruins of a once loving home.

"He was my father, wasn't he? The Lord High Mayor?" She didn't have a face to go with the memories, just hazy images.

"He was. And your mother was the best dragon rider Eidyn ever knew." Cornelius scanned the ruins. "This was your home."

Not just a dragon rider—Amaleigh's mother was one of the rare warriors who was half dragon, half mortal. Like her. And she had crimson hair, the same as Amaleigh. Gwilym had known her parents. He had information that could help fill in the gaps of her memories. If only they'd known. All those years of friendship, and they'd never discussed her family. Why would they? Amaleigh was an orphan with no knowledge of who her parents were.

She eyed the stranger. "You knew my parents?"

"Enough to call them friends." Melancholy fell across his features. "It was a difficult time for all of us." His gaze flicked toward the city. "Still is."

In the distance, fireworks lit up the night sky.

"I have to go. And you should be off as well." Gwilym looked to Cornelius. "I am glad you're alive. You'll protect her?"

"With my life. Your father won't be able to follow us or find us, of that be assured."

Gwilym stroked her cheek and she leaned into his touch. "I'll miss you. I hope when next we meet, it will be in happier times."

She turned her head to kiss his palm. "You're the best friend I ever had. Don't die."

"I'll do my best. Now, off with you. This isn't a night to linger." Gwilym grinned and turned to leave. He stopped after two steps and returned to her.

Her heart leapt and knees buckled. He was coming with them. Hope beyond hope bloomed in her chest that he would stay with her.

His hands gripped her face and those gorgeous blue eyes of his bore into hers. Then, ever so slowly, he lowered his face to hers, and her whole body trembled with anticipation. She wasn't dreaming. This was truly happening.

Gwilym's lips brushed hers, tentative and unsure. She softened her mouth as invitation for him to deepen the kiss and he accepted. Tingles of desire raced through her veins, warming her all over and igniting her nerves like flares that rivaled the fireworks that lit up the sky over Eidyn.

His tongue stroked hers, now strong and sure. She melted against him, safe in his embrace. This was home. He was home. He'd always been her port in the storm and now, she strove to be his. His arms encircled her as she gripped the dragon egg and dagger. This was how it was meant to be—her, Gwilym, the egg, deep down, she knew this was important, how it was meant to be.

Tiny sparks of magic flashed from the dagger, but they didn't hurt. Nothing hurt. She was floating on a cloud of happiness that she wished would never land. They could talk to the king, explain her situation. Reality struck her with the chilling truth. The king would see her dead, and who knew what would happen to Gwilym. She had to leave, even though she desperately wanted to stay. Risking everything with Gwilym was better than living without him.

"It's time, Amaleigh." Cornelius touched her arm, interrupting the lovely moment.

Gwilym's hold tightened and his lips suckled hers as if taking one last taste to remember her by. "Be well, my sweet friend." His gaze was shrouded with something intangible. Not pain, but close.

"You too." She didn't want to let go, but Cornelius tugged her sleeve, and she reluctantly took a step away from Gwilym. A piece of her heart cracked seeing him turn to leave.

He gave a last wave before disappearing over a bluff.

Cornelius directed her to a wavering patch of air. "There's nothing left for you here."

Before she stepped into the unknown, she said a silent farewell to the life she'd lived before and after the Purge. Daughter. Sister. Orphan. Thief. Friend. Finally, she was free.

But that freedom came at too dear a cost. Cornelius was wrong. There would always be something left for her in Eidyn. Gwilym. She turned to see the beach one last time. To burn it into her memory.

Fireworks lit the sky in the distance, but here it was deserted save for the ruins of her home. A bittersweet night of discovery. As she said goodbye to her past, she touched her lips where Gwilym's taste lingered. It was more than just a kiss between friends. It was her first true kiss—not one stolen by a scurrilous pirate, but one that she reciprocated and desired. Gwilym was now, and always had been, her first love. She could admit the truth to herself without fear of reprisal, even if she didn't know what that mean for the future.

Her gaze scanned the bluff, hoping to find Gwilym beckoning her to stay. But the beach was empty. She sent a silent prayer to him that if he ever needed her, he only had but to ask and she'd be there. This couldn't be the end of their story. Not after that kiss.

"I know it's painful, but trust me, you need to forget everything about Eidyn. You can't ever return." Cornelius reached for her but didn't touch her sleeve. "When I said I knew your parents, that was only part of the story. It was I who saved you from the Purge the night Heshen murdered your family. I left you with a family I trusted to take care of you. Never in my wildest dreams did I think they would give you to Antonio. But I've come back to make amends. My returning for you is at great risk to myself."

She took in this new information, her mind spinning. "The dragon, that was you?"

His eyes narrowed. "A dragon? No. I'm just a man, Amaleigh. I could never hope to be what you are." He took her hand in his. "We can discuss everything later. Time is getting away from us and you're a wanted woman. We need to leave. Now. For good. If you ever return, either Heshen or Antonio will see to it that you'll wish you never had. If you truly want to live —free, beholden to none, you must come with me."

The Gods knew, she did want to live. And yet, she'd be leaving Gwilym.

"But you walked the streets unharmed." She was grasping at straws, desperate for an alternative. Anything that might allow her to stay.

"You saw the real me, but everyone else saw a reflection of a man of their choosing. It's a trick I can teach you, but not here." His gaze razed the beach before looking up at the fireworks. "Never here."

His eyes shimmered as if he fought back tears and Amaleigh averted her gaze. He'd told Gwilym he would protect her. She had to believe he spoke true. One thing he wasn't lying about was the death warrant on her head. She had to leave Eidyn. The words were a sword blade through her heart.

"Then let's go where you can teach me everything I need to know." She wiped tears from her cheeks and lifted her chin. If she truly wanted to be free of Antonio and the king, she had to leave. She just wished it wouldn't hurt so much. She turned away from the bluffs, no longer looking for Gwilym, but staring into the shimmering oval that would change her life.

Eidyn was her past.

Magic was her future.

CHAPTER
THIRTEEN

*A*maleigh.

Gwilym's voice whispered in her mind and Amaleigh shuddered against the intrusion. Over the years she'd often dreamt of him, usually about that kiss he gave her just before she left, but he'd never, not once, contacted her.

It was a fluke. She was using too much magic and had overextended herself to the point she was hallucinating. Or wishful thinking. Either way, it was dangerous. Too dangerous to hope Gwilym had broken through her wards and contacted her now. She shook her head as if to dispel his presence, whether real or not, and returned to her casting.

Focus. Breathe. Calm. Amaleigh repeated the mantra twice more out of desperation it would work. Visualize the dragon. She knew it was in there. Had actually shifted once, long ago.

Seven years, to be exact. Seven long years of wishing for something she feared was forever lost to her. And it wasn't just her dragon. But thoughts of Gwilym only ended in heartbreak and she'd promised herself she would close off her heart. Promised herself she'd forget the one man who haunted her dreams. Promised herself she was fine not knowing if he survived the night she left Eidyn.

Lies. All lies.

For seven years she tried in vain to pretend Gwilym didn't exist.

In every new place, she would look for him in the shadows. Search the reflections of shop windows hoping to get a glimpse of him, even though she knew it was futile. If Gwilym had survived that night, the king wished him dead, and the next assassin would've been far more skilled than her. She reminded herself for the millionth time that Eidyn was her past.

Imagining she heard him now would only end in further heartbreak.

She had the life she'd always dreamed of—beholden to no one, able to move about freely without fear or worry. But it wasn't truly the life she'd wanted. That life included Gwilym, and try though she had, she couldn't forget him.

The sea roared with the oncoming storm, sending a spray of salt water across her face, bringing her thoughts squarely to the present. She hovered twenty feet above the sea, sitting cross-legged, hands resting on knees. Not even the encroaching foul weather could deter her from training. This was too important. She was determined to master her casting before the festival and surprise Cornelius. To see the look on his face would be its own reward.

A snort broke her concentration, and she winced against the biting wind. Her careful balance wobbled, tilting her toward the white surf. With practiced calm, she righted herself, her back rigid to prevent any further teetering. Surely Cornelius wouldn't mind that she'd kept a secret from him. He claimed to hate surprises, but he'd be proud of her accomplishment.

If she got it right. Flippin' barnacleballs, she had to or else—
She stopped the thought from taking shape. It would work this

time. It simply must. She'd been such a disappointment to him already, and after he'd risked his life for her, the least she could do was show him his efforts weren't in vain.

She took a cleansing breath and relaxed her features. A fresh spray of water dampened her skin and brought a wistful smile to her face. She knew she'd succeed. Could feel it. While breathing in and out in measured counts, she drew on the sea's energy to fuel her casting. Her focus narrowed, and she envisioned her dragon in all her majesty. She delved deeper and enticed the dragon from where she dwelled inside Amaleigh's spirit. *Come forth*, she coaxed, *be free*.

Ghostly wings unfurled behind her, glistening pale blueish-green in the scant afternoon light. Strong scaled legs stretched forth, and her dragon's head tilted upward to sniff the air. She was even more magnificent than Amaleigh could imagine. The dragon loomed around her like a protective bubble. *Finally*.

Her breath slowed, and she closed her eyes. What she saw came through the dragon's vision, not hers. The world became sharper, clearer. She blinked and looked down through the churning water to see tiny creatures skittering across the sandy bottom. Along the horizon, birds soared several leagues away. Her smile grew into a bliss-filled grin.

"Fly," she whispered, and the dragon took flight while her human form continued to hover above the waves. Her heartbeat tripled with excited triumph.

She'd done it! A pinch of guilt swayed her confidence. Cornelius didn't know she'd been practicing casting, or that she'd first learned about it from an entry in one of his books. He might be angry that she'd read his books without asking. Everything came easy to him, but she struggled with even the most basic magical commands. Just once, she wanted him to be proud of her.

The luminous dragon flew low, skimming the tops of the

waves with her talons. The sense of freedom invigorated every fiber of Amaleigh's being. She was an Aerlghot—half human, half dragon. She should've been able to shift into a dragon with ease, but ever since she left Eidyn, her inner dragon had stubbornly remained out of reach. Although patient with her, she knew her mentor was equally frustrated.

The one and only time she'd unleashed her dragon had been out of desperation. Those few moments when she escaped the king's trackers by flinging herself off a cliff had been a terrifying and electric experience. Casting, although thrilling, wasn't the same as being her true dragon, and a sense of longing filled her heart.

The ghostly shape of the dragon waned and Amaleigh brushed aside the melancholy to concentrate. Her dragon lifted into the air and flew over the meadows. She banked and coasted over the little cottage she and Cornelius shared. It wasn't much, but it was a roof over their heads and a hearth to keep them warm until they moved again. Theirs was a life in constant motion, only staying on one world long enough to search for others like her, or rescuing orphaned dragons like the twins.

Two little scaled heads peeked from beneath a pile of straw, and Amaleigh chuckled at the dragonlings. They were such mischief, but also pure joy. They pranced around the barnyard, lifting their snouts toward her with happy yips. She'd found them high atop a cliff in a shallow cave. Their mother's body lay beside the nest, her scales drawn taut over her ribs. Of the five eggs she recovered that day, only the twins had hatched. The other three eventually cracked and oozed their contents into the fire where they were kept.

Amaleigh still mourned the lost dragons and refused to speak of it to Cornelius. He couldn't understand the fear she had that the same would happen to the egg she'd found in the ruined fireplace of her family home. For now, it remained buried in the ashes of the fire, as solid and unblemished as ever. Even though it hadn't hatched, it didn't crack like the others. Cornelius warned her that the dragon inside—if one existed—was most likely dead. A part of her knew he might be right, but even so, she refused to give up hope that, one day, her egg would hatch.

She circled the cottage twice before she spotted Cornelius walking toward the barn to check on the dragonlings. He scolded them for making a mess and herded them inside the barn for the night. She held her breath, waiting for him to glance up and see her, but when his gaze traveled to the sky, he made no sign of recognition. A giddy thrill traveled through her human veins. If the great Cornelius couldn't see her, then she doubted anyone could.

Her phantom dragon returned to her, and she arched into the connection, feeling at once whole. The power she drew from the sea kept her aloft, but had it not been for that, she would've collapsed. Casting would take time to perfect, but she'd get there. At least now she could go to the festival with a light heart. She'd tell him about her secret afterward.

Her vision darkened and searing pain ripped through her mind, followed by an image straight from a nightmare. A face pinched in agony, his skin raw as if he'd been recently beaten. Through the swollen cuts and oozing blood, she recognized Gwilym. Her heart ached at the sight even while she rejoiced that he might be alive. Adrenaline rushed through her veins, spiking her excitement. Her magic swirled with heightened intensity. And caution. If this was a hallucination, it was too real to discount.

Amaleigh. His voice croaked in her mind, and she winced. *I need you. Please come. I—they—my father—I need your help. Please.* She heard a scream, not Gwilym's but that of another man's, and she put her hands over her ears. It did no good. The cry came from inside her skull and couldn't be silenced.

The connection with Gwilym severed, and she hovered above the waves, shaking violently. Sickness teased up her throat. The surf rose to touch her robes, and it was then she remembered she was drawing power from the sea. She unclenched her fists in the hopes it might calm the seas and her heart. This was no illusion or enchantment, of that she was more certain than she'd ever been in her life.

Gwilym was alive. Relief swept over her, and guilt—raw and dirty, seeped through her veins. She'd been the one sent to kill him that final night in Eidyn. Yet she couldn't do it. Instead of killing the only man she'd ever loved, she ran away. And never stopped.

The realization that somehow, he'd survived his father's assassins struck her just below her heart where a painful wedge of heat stayed trapped. All those lies she told herself that he didn't matter were laid bare. All those years of pretending indifference flooded her with emotions too powerful to control.

There was no time to waste pondering questions she couldn't answer. He called out to her. He needed her.

The discomfort beneath her breastbone waned and a different kind of warmth infused her body at the memory of his lips seeking hers, of the love she'd felt in their kiss. Of the hope she'd had for one brief, shining moment that they could defy his father and be together. But then reality had crashed over them both and he'd left her with Cornelius.

From the depths of her being, a dangerous truth threatened, one that she'd spent seven long years denying—she'd loved Gwilym then and still did. Damn that man. He wasn't the first man to kiss her, but he was the only man she'd ever longed to be kissed by again.

She was treading on dangerous waters. Literally and figuratively. The surf tumbled beneath her, mimicking her roiling emotions. Any other time, she would've stopped to consider the hows and whys, but she had to hurry. Cornelius needed to know what happened.

The mage was waiting at the top of the bluff when she scrambled over the last few rocks. Of course, he'd already know. He did everything in his power to keep their presence hidden from anyone in Eidyn who might be searching for them.

"What happened? I sensed a spike in your power and an... intrusion through my protective spells."

"It was Gwilym. He was hurt and—"

Cornelius grabbed her arms a little too roughly and looked her full in the face. His magic flared around him in powerful streaks. "Did you say anything? Did you return the connection?"

"Of course not." She removed her arms from his grip and rubbed where his fingers had dug into her skin. "It was too sudden. I didn't have a chance. Gwilym said he needed help, and maybe his father, too. That's all. Then I heard a scream and the connection ended."

Cornelius paced a circle and tapped his lips with trembling fingers, then blew out a long breath.

She'd never seen him this agitated, and his lack of control unnerved her. More than twice her age, he held himself with a grace and serenity she usually admired. Unflappable was how she'd describe him, but not now.

"This could be a trap. If Heshen found out what you are, he'd tear apart his world to find you."

"We're not on Nasus. We're light-years from Eidyn, isn't that what you said?" They'd been safe for seven years. The first several of which Amaleigh had woken every night with the same nightmare—of King Heshen striding into her home and slaying her mother, father, and brother with an ornate dagger. The same dagger she'd stolen from him. It had taken her a long time to feel safe enough that the nightmares ended.

"Aye, we're far from that whoreson's reach. Which makes me wonder—why now? Why after all this time is Gwilym reaching out? And how the hell did he break through our wards?" Cornelius glared at the sea as if it was the cause of his ire, but she knew it was Heshen who he was angry at. Cornelius had suffered from the Purge, too. Even though he wouldn't discuss it, she saw the sadness that edged the corners of his eyes each time he spoke of those horrible nights so long ago.

Amaleigh pressed her clenched fists against her hips, exhaustion tugging at her fading energy. Purge or not, Gwilym needed her. "In the vision, he looked as though he'd been beaten. If he was desperate enough, maybe he flung the thought into the void, hoping it would reach me."

As much as she wanted to rush to the cottage and pack, she had to be smart about this. It wasn't just her life she'd endanger if King Heshen drew her into a trap. Her gaze went to the yard where the dragonlings play-fought. They were fat and happy and finally growing to trust her. They needed her and she, them. Yes, she desperately wished to see Gwilym again, and to help him in any way possible, but Gwilym was Heshen's son, and the king had a death warrant with her name on it. She couldn't separate one from the other, no matter what her heart wished.

Cornelius brushed a lock of crimson hair from her forehead and held her face between his hands. "I would go to the ends of the universe for you. You know I would. But I can't go back to Eidyn. Not now. Not after everything we've done here."

He was right. They'd made good progress with the twins and had plans to explore more of Cilachaem. She'd heard rumors of elves living to the north in Elvenwood, and of one kingdom called Faerie where two amicable queens reigned.

This was a place where magic wasn't feared. Thus far, this world had proved friendly to dragons. It was somewhere she wouldn't mind settling down and raising the twins. Perhaps if she were stable, her mage abilities would improve. Both her parents had been powerful mages and she had magic, but hers was...elusive. Frustratingly so.

"Let's not decide anything just yet. We've the festival to attend." He kissed her temple and wrapped an arm around her shoulders. "I know you've been looking forward to it."

It wasn't so much the festival she'd been looking forward to but mingling with the villagers. The loneliness of moving every six months weighed on her, and she longed to be near others, even if she only existed on the fringe of their community. With Cornelius as her sole companion, sometimes for months on end, having the company of others was a treat. It fueled her desire to find a permanent home. To belong.

A battle roared in her heart—on one side she was desperate to rush back to Eidyn and help Gwilym, but the other side cautioned calm. To not make snap decisions based on emotions. Cornelius couldn't understand what it meant to her to hear Gwilym's voice again after so many years. He'd left Eidyn with no regrets, unlike her.

"I need to rest first." She shuffled to the cottage, surprised at how difficult it was to walk. Casting and Gwilym's vision must've depleted her energy stores, which was odd, but her exhaustion made it difficult to think. After a brief nap, then she could decide her next move.

Cornelius was right about one thing—she needed to know how Gwilym had broken through the wards. Maybe then she would understand why her power had surged when he did.

Maybe then she could suss out if it really was a trap.

CHAPTER

FOURTEEN

Despite the dark clouds, the festival was in full swing by the time Amaleigh and Cornelius arrived. A band played a lively jig while dancers twirled on a makeshift stage. The villagers clapped to the music or raised a mug in toast to those brave souls kicking up their heels in merriment. As Amaleigh and Cornelius strode past, the ladies curtseyed, and the men bowed low.

When they'd found this little hamlet, they'd been relieved to find the villagers welcoming of mages. Then when they brought the twins to the cottage, they weren't attacked by an angry mob, but treated with curiosity and kindness. If Cilachaem had ever known the existence of dragons, it was a time long past and forgotten. The villagers revered Amaleigh and Cornelius with near-godlike devotion.

It was a mantle she wore with discomfort. Healing those in need was one thing, but she understood the peril of what could happen if the villagers turned on them. One bad plague, or failing crops, and she'd find herself skewered on the pointy end of a pitchfork. Thus far, they'd been lucky, but Amaleigh never took such things for granted. She'd lived through the hell one power-hungry man could inflict and never wished to do so ever again.

It was her fear of King Heshen that had won the argument to stay and attend the festival. Until she knew for certain Gwilym's plea wasn't a trap, she couldn't risk returning to Eidyn. Every inch of her hoped it wasn't, but seven years was a long time and as Cornelius explained several times already, people change.

She strolled through the village square, content in her good fortune to find a place as welcoming as this. Even if she were a disappointment to Cornelius with her spells, her healing abilities exceeded all expectations. There wasn't a fever she couldn't lower or a bone she couldn't set. Just a touch of her magic was enough to mend most any ailment. For that, Cornelius had showered her with praise.

Damn it, she'd meant to surprise him with her casting, but it had gotten lost in the excitement of Gwilym's vision. But she *had* casted. None of her past failures could take that away from her. Her thoughts flickered back to the rush of magic she'd felt when Gwilym's face appeared in her mind. It was more than she'd ever experienced, and a greedy part of her wanted more. The sensible part of her wanted answers. Gwilym's presence seemed to affect her magical abilities. Perhaps blocking her memories of him somehow diminished her power. Far-fetched or not, she couldn't deny something had happened when his vision broke through her wards. She rubbed her temples as if to soothe her thoughts. Her brain hurt from demanding answers that refused to come forward.

She hadn't blocked memories so much as willed herself to forget. It was impossible to forget her best friend and first love. But remembering him was dangerous not just to her heart, but to their lives. Cornelius made it clear after their first year of running that they could never, ever return to Eidyn. Despite her hope that one day they might, his constant reminder that she had a death warrant on her head eventually dismissed all her hopeful wishing. But now, Gwilym had reached out to her. She couldn't ignore him, or the pull of magic that he'd somehow unlocked.

The clop of horses' hooves sounded behind her, and Amaleigh turned in time to see a young boy rush to herd several goats across the road. A baby goat, too little for the horse and rider to see, stumbled behind the group, and right into the horse's path.

"Stop!" she cried out and darted forward to snatch the goat just as hooves thundered to the ground, inches from her face.

The kid bleated and squirmed in her grip, but she clutched it to her chest. Its little heart beat even quicker than hers, and she trembled with the effort.

"What's the matter with ye? Daft woman, running out in front of me horse like that. Could've gotten yerself killed, ye could've." The rider glowered down at Amaleigh from astride his chestnut. He pointed a gloved hand at the kid and shook his head. "Savin' a fool goat's not worth the trouble."

Amaleigh stood tall and lifted her chin. "Every life is worth the trouble, even creatures deemed disposable by people like yourself."

The boy approached, eyes wide. "Thank you, miss." He bowed at the waist, and she handed him the little goat with a wan smile.

"Keep an eye on this one. I have a feeling it'll bring you good fortune." Fool goat, indeed. That little critter was damn lucky she was a fool herself.

The rider left a string of expletives in his wake as he rode toward the village green. She inhaled through her nose and smoothed her hair with shaky fingers.

"Ye look like ye could use a drink." The village elder handed her a mug of something dark and spicy, and she raised it in a silent toast before taking a sip.

It warmed her mouth and throat, slinking to her belly with a satisfying burn. The taste of chocolate and chilies lingered on her tongue.

"This is delicious. What is it?" She tipped the mug to her lips for a longer sip.

"'Tis called grhom, my lady. It be a recipe from the elves." He moved in close and placed a finger alongside his nose. "Me mam worked in the palace as a young lassie. Stole the recipe, she did. Them elves don't like ta share, but we got it now, don't we?" He gave her a saucy wink and grinned.

"Your secret is safe with me." She downed the rest of the grhom and licked her lips. "Any chance I could get the recipe?"

"I'll do ye one better. I'll send me boy around tomorrow with the ingredients. You've been so kind ta all of us here, it's the least I can do." His gaze followed where the rider had disappeared in the crowd. "That man might take ye for reckless, but I thank ye for helping thems that are in need."

She gripped his hands with gratitude. Perhaps they would accept her into their lives as one of them and she would find peace, at last.

At a table displaying amulets and trinkets, she stopped to chat with the woman who made them. As they spoke, Amaleigh's attention was drawn to one pendant in particular. Tiny sculpted branches wrapped around a glass vial. Inside, miniature trees made up a forest. She could almost see the gravel paths and overgrown shrubs contained within. But that was impossible. The vial was no larger than her thumb.

"I'll take this one." Amaleigh paid the woman and held the pendant against her palm. A soft thrumming came through the glass—comforting and disturbing at the same time. Warped and muted, but what she sensed had to be magic. She wrapped her fingers around it and said a silent prayer of grace. Whatever divine providence brought the lovely pendant to her, she was thankful.

Revelers laughed at the antics of two villagers performing in the square. Amaleigh flinched slightly, but that was all. There was a time when the sound of merrymakers would bring about terrors and night frights, a remnant from the Purge celebrations.

Amaleigh reminded herself that she was safe, that she could enjoy the laughter and raised voices of those around her, which was a testament to how far she'd come from those nights in Eidyn when she'd hid beneath her blankets, trembling. Here, no fireworks lit up the night, dredging up memories of the fire that burned through her house the night her parents died. Just a simple village fete celebrating life.

Her thoughts drifted to Gwilym and the vision. To return to Eidyn would put her life in danger, certainly. But if he were in dire need, which was the only reason she could fathom he'd reach out to her, then surely it was worth the risk to help.

"You're thinking of going to him, aren't you?" Cornelius squinted at the glass vial as he approached and frowned. "What have you there?"

Amaleigh tucked the trinket into a pocket and faced him with a forced smile. "Just a pretty bauble. As for your other question, I'm...conflicted. I was eighteen when we left Eidyn. Not a young girl, not quite a woman, yet far too street smart for my own good. I didn't know if Gwilym would survive the night, much less seven years. I keep asking myself what's happened that he felt I was the only one who could help?"

Cornelius turned her to face him and met her anxious gaze with his own. "I've asked myself the same question. Why you?"

Indeed. Why her?

She was a known thief, a fugitive, a potential dragon shifter, and a mage. Any one of which was enough for King Heshen to have her executed.

Gwilym had been her only friend growing up. The only person she trusted. No one, not even Cornelius knew how she truly felt about Gwilym. She'd kept that secret deep in her heart, not even trusting herself to tell the prince how much she loved him. Yes, he was her first, and only, love, but he was also heir to the man she hated.

That was a long time ago. Gwilym might've been her friend once, but in the long years since she'd seen him, anything could've happened. His mind could've been poisoned with Heshen's radical beliefs, or he might've grown tired of rebelling against his father. Whatever the case, she told herself she didn't know Gwilym anymore and had to think of herself and the dragons. Yet deep down, nestled alongside where she hid her feelings for the prince, lay the truth of it—she'd never forgiven herself for abandoning him.

It was an impossible choice—forsake Gwilym once again, or desert the dragonlings and everything she'd built over the last few months. Because Amaleigh knew if she returned to Eidyn, her hopes of a quiet life on Cilachaem would die.

She and Cornelius had traveled to worlds where magic was dying, and others where magic was already dead. She'd seen lands ravaged by war and technological terrors that gave her nightmares. But never, in all her traveling, did she encounter a horror as soul crushing as Heshen's Purge. To willingly return to the place that hated her kind, to put herself at risk on a whim, was nothing short of suicide.

CHAPTER
FIFTEEN

A wild wind spun against Amaleigh as she stood on the cliff's edge. The storm had finally broken, and she wrapped her shawl tighter. Lightning flashed across the darkened sea, and she sucked in its energy.

Her mind roiled like the shifting clouds. Her relationship with Gwilym was complicated, at best. She'd been three when his father murdered her family, Gwilym six. Both too young to understand the king's reasons for the Purge. Hell, she still didn't know. One thing was totally clear—it was the Purge that stole her childhood. She grew up not knowing who her parents were, or their fate in the massacre. Cornelius had shared some stories with her about her parents, but she couldn't remember their faces or what they looked like. For most of her life, she thought she was an orphan, nothing more.

Antonio had led her to believe she'd been abandoned at his doorstep. Under his tutelage, she became a thief who had honed her anger and fear until she'd hardened her heart against everyone. Everyone except Gwilym.

Ironic then, that it took stealing the dagger to learn who her parents were, and of his father's role in their death. She was glad of her innocence. If she'd known Gwilym was the son of the man who murdered her family, she would've hated him as well. Instead, she grew up knowing him not as a prince, but as a boy equally as lonely and frightened as her.

Amaleigh trembled against her memories. They served no purpose to her life now. Except, that was a lie. They were the reason Gwilym had reached out. He knew she would risk facing his father to save him. They had a bond stronger than friendship. One that he'd solidified with a kiss just before saying his last goodbye. If not for the king, they might've had a future together.

Not just the king—Antonio had ruined her life as well.

Fucking Antonio. What a vile man he was to send her to the palace to kill Gwilym—the prince's death for her freedom. She was a thief, not a murderer, but Antonio didn't care. He was as cruel and sadistic as the king.

She would never understand why Cornelius had left her with Antonio. He claimed it was to hide her identity—the best way to keep her safe was to place her with the one man the king ignored. According to her mentor, after he saw to her safety, he helped as many mages as he could and then escaped Eidyn before Heshen found him and added to the death toll.

As much as she'd wanted to hate Cornelius for leaving her, she couldn't. He'd been young and scared himself. A man who knew nothing of raising a child. It had taken her far too long to forgive him, but she eventually understood he'd made the best out of a terrible situation by leaving her with the king of the urchins.

If Heshen knew she existed, he'd have murdered her, too. Every mageborn child was killed in the Purge, whether they showed magical promise or not. The urchins were invisible to the king. Although she hated that Cornelius left her to Antonio's whims, she couldn't fault his logic. Heshen never knew about her. Hopefully still didn't. Unless Gwilym had turned against her and used their past to set a trap.

She shook her head and loosened several tendrils to the wind. No. She wouldn't believe Gwilym had changed. She knew now, just as he'd known when she was sent to assassinate him, that their friendship surpassed politics and court intrigues.

Tears rolled down her cheeks, and she wiped them away with the edge of her shawl. Even with freedom on the line, she hadn't been able to kill Gwilym. Instead of being angry with her, he'd given her the dagger and told Cornelius to keep her safe. Then he'd walked away to face his father and his fate.

She touched the pads of her fingers to her lips. Gwilym hadn't given her a simple kiss between friends. At least, it hadn't felt that way to her. There was emotion behind the press of his lips to her. Emotion she readily recognized and returned. It would've been much easier if he'd simply left without stirring up feelings that were better left in the dank darkness of her cold heart. But he hadn't, and she'd always wondered why. Wondered—and dared to hope—that he returned her love. But that was a fool's wish, and she'd buried her feelings long ago.

Despite telling herself it was for the best, a lump of guilt settled in her belly with stubborn permanence. Hell, it had been there since they'd escaped. She should've stayed and made sure Antonio didn't find someone else to go through with the assassination, but she'd run like a coward. Too concerned with her own life to worry about Gwilym's.

That wasn't entirely true. At the time, even though Cornelius demanded she never return to Eidyn, she'd always secretly hoped they would. She never imagined Cornelius would keep them hopping from one world to another, constantly looking over their shoulder, never to see their home-world again.

But now she had a chance to help Gwilym, to repay him for all his kindnesses. If she could save him, then perhaps the sour lump in her gut would finally go away. Perhaps then she could settle her mind and heart.

And maybe, just maybe, she could discover why his vision had empowered her magic. Even now, stirrings of power swirled in her veins. The magic she'd tried to grasp, but always eluded her, Gwilym might have the answers why. If he died, he'd take those answers with him.

A pair of strong arms wrapped around her, and she tensed.

"Did the storm wake you?" Cornelius's soft breath warmed her cheek.

"Not entirely." She turned to face him, taking a half step back as she did. He kept his arm loose around her shoulders, his grip light yet firm. She looked into his grizzled face, not seeing the scars or the grey in his beard. She saw only concern, and fear.

"What were you doing when the vision came?"

"I was meditating above the sea." She moved to his side and her gaze drifted to the surf. "I'd just completed a successful casting and was grateful for the sea's strength in helping me. Then I was thinking about the festival."

"Hmm. So, you were drawing power from the elements?"

"I've done that hundreds of times. You taught me to use the energy around me so that I don't deplete all my resources."

"I did, that's true. And I'm delighted you paid attention." The snark in his tone didn't lighten the mood. "You successfully casted, did I hear that right?" A light blazed in his eyes, giving them an eerie greenish glow. Pride beamed across his features.

"I did. I even flew over you and the twins, but you didn't

notice." She glanced toward the barn. "I'm pretty sure they knew, though."

Now he did smile, but it was tempered. "Your mother always told me you were something special. Called you her child of fire. You're a lot like her, you know."

Amaleigh's heart skipped a beat, and her cheeks warmed. "I hope I've made her proud."

Cornelius mussed her hair with a chuckle. "She'd be more than proud." His grin faded and his gaze went to the horizon. "She was the late queen's fiercest protector. One of the finest Aerlghots I've ever known." He lifted her chin with his forefinger. "One day you'll be as strong as she was. You'll find your dragon."

"It's here. I know it is."

"In time, you'll unleash her." His eyes narrowed and jaw tightened. "I think it best to forget you saw Gwilym's vision. We're safe here."

"I wish I could." She raised a hand to caress his cheek and sighed. "If it was me reaching out, and you knew you had a chance, even a slim one, to help, would you ignore me?"

He shook his head and kissed the inside of her palm. "I'd move worlds to save you." He touched a scar at his temple. "Almost died trying twenty-two years ago when you were but a wee thing and I found you in your parents' ruined home."

He meant the night of the Purge, when Heshen murdered her family. Tears flowed unbidden over her cheeks. "I don't remember much of that night, just being too scared to move. I still have nightmares that he'll come for me." She remembered something else—a deep-green dragon that had come later, after the killing, to take her away. But that was impossible, because Cornelius was the one to rescue her and he wasn't an Aerlghot.

Cornelius flicked his fingers in the way he did when troubled. "I doubt he knows you exist. In the fighting and smoke, he must've believed he'd killed your entire family." A sardonic grin quirked his lips. "Besides, you hid in the fireplace." His gaze met hers, and she saw flames dancing in his eyes. "Where a blazing fire roared."

Her gasp popped between them. "In the fire?" She looked at her unblemished arms. "You never told me that part of the tale before. Am I fireproof?"

"It would appear so. Although, until you master your spells and casting, I don't recommend experimenting with fire to be certain." He tucked a strand of hair behind her ear. "I think you were protecting the egg."

The dragon egg she'd found buried beneath a layer of cold ash in the ruined fireplace of her family home. The very same egg that was now buried in the hearth of their little cottage, warm and snug, Gods willing, not empty as Cornelius believed. She refused to let him dash her hope it would ever hatch. It was a source of contention between them, one that she tried hard not to provoke. To him, the egg represented the Purge, but to her, it was an extension of her family. Whether it hatched or not, it had belonged to her parents, and was the only physical reminder she had of them besides the dagger that once belonged to her father.

She and Cornelius rarely spoke of their lives before leaving Eidyn. During his exile, he'd drifted from world to world until he felt compelled to return the same day she stole the dagger. She never told him the depth of her friendship with Gwilym, only that they'd been friends as children. Of her time with Antonio, she said nothing. She didn't want him to have any guilt for leaving her with the king of urchins.

A crack of thunder startled her, and his grip tightened around her shoulder. A flash of lightning followed. She sensed Cornelius pulling on the storm's energy and fought the urge to do it as well. He'd taught her everything she knew about being a mage and although there was still more to learn, she hoped it would be enough to face whatever challenges came her way in Eidyn.

"You're going, aren't you?"

"I have to. I feel it here." She tapped her breastbone above her heart. "I know it could be a trap—hell, most likely is. But if Gwilym needs me—"

"I thought that might be your answer. I need to stay here to look after the twins. That doesn't mean I won't be watching over you, though. If the situation becomes dire, I'll be there."

She faced him and held his hands between her own. "Thank you. Knowing you're with me helps."

He bent low and pressed his lips to hers. There was a desperation she'd not felt before, as if her leaving changed their dynamic, somehow. It didn't. It couldn't. She waited for a surge of passion or hell, even a tickle, but nothing came. She didn't return the kiss, and yet she didn't pull away from him either. It had been the same with Danteneux all those years ago—more of an obligation than a desire. Only one man had ever made her dream of more sweet kisses.

If she'd let him, Cornelius would've been her lover as well as her protector. He'd never forced himself on her, nor made any awkward declarations of love, but she knew his heart. She loved him, too, in her own way.

Just not in the way she suspected Cornelius would've liked. She'd only ever allowed herself to love one person the way Cornelius desired, and she kept those feelings locked up tight for fear that if they were known, they could be used against her. It came with growing up in the alleys and never knowing who to trust. Even after all this time, it was hard to let go of the lessons Antonio had beaten into her. She couldn't afford to show emotion. Emotion got you killed—or worse.

One hand cradled her head while the other snaked across her hip. His fingers splayed across her lower back and his power thrummed against her skin. He kept his affection in check, but there was no denying the depths of his attraction to her. If she knew how, she would've returned that passion. The gods knew she'd tried. But her heart wasn't meant to be shared with another. She'd spent too long shutting it away and building walls around it.

She pulled away, ending the kiss, and he captured several strands of hair to tuck behind her ear. The pain in Cornelius's eyes went straight to the lump of guilt in her gut.

"I had hoped by now you would trust me enough to love me." His hair twisted wildly in the wind.

He was still as damn handsome as the first time she saw him. Grey eyes that brooked no nonsense, but were kind. Chestnut locks that fell in his eyes when he was working. Although he was twice her age, their kind lived to be several hundred years old, so the age difference wasn't much of an issue. In a perfect world, she would've loved him. On paper, they were the perfect companions for each other.

"I do love you. Just—not how you want me to." She tilted her head and sighed. They'd been through this before, and it still made her uneasy. Although she appreciated everything he'd done for her, and for his constant protection, watching him wait for her heart to open was like inflicting a thousand paper cuts each day. He deserved someone capable of returning his love. "I've tried. Believe me, I have, but I don't know how to love that way." She lied.

"It's not something you learn. It's something you feel, naturally. It can't be forced." His eyes stayed rooted to hers, and his nostrils flared. "Love doesn't make you weak, Amaleigh. It doesn't make you vulnerable or a victim. It strengthens you, wholly. It gives you purpose and something to fight for. One day, I hope you can let down your guard and love in return."

"I'm sorry." She refused to look deeper into his eyes for fear of reading his soul. Or him reading hers.

"Hey." He lifted her chin until she was forced to look at him. "Don't be sorry. Maybe when you get back from Eidyn, things will be different." His lips grazed her forehead and then he pressed her head against his shoulder in a protective embrace.

Nothing would be different when she returned—if she returned. He was a fool to hope. A nagging in the back of her mind asked why he thought things might be different, but she brushed the answer aside. Cornelius wasn't jealous of Gwilym. It was silly of her to even entertain the idea. He was dead set that Gwilym was using her, baiting her to return so that Heshen could finish what she started with the Purge and kill her. Cornelius was worried about her. That had to be the reason for his sudden show of emotion.

Ignoring the audacious thoughts unfurling in her mind, she unfolded from his arms and walked beside him to the cottage. She had to pack and to plan. She needed to think. Her heart beat fierce beneath her ribs, and she fought the urge to fly off that instant. If Heshen was setting a trap for her, she needed the element of surprise.

Cornelius followed her into the small room she called her own. It wasn't much more than a bed, a bureau, and a dressing table, but it was hers. This was one of the few times Cornelius had ever been in her space and it felt strange to have him there. He folded a cloak and put it into an old ratty bag. The same one she'd used when she was thieving for Antonio.

"Not that one. I might be recognized from it. Here." She tugged an exquisitely made, hand-embroidered tapestry bag from beneath her bed. Cornelius had given it to her a year previously on her birthday, and she'd joked she had nowhere to use such an expensive, lovely gift. Ironic that it would be perfect for her journey now.

Once they had her clothing sorted, Amaleigh went to her dressing table and opened the bottom drawer. Strands of her magic swirled—wards she'd placed on the drawer recognized her touch. She withdrew a silver coffin and placed it atop the table. Inside, an ornate dagger lay safely ensconced on a bed of rich velvet. Her breath caught, and she stroked the curved blade. Whispers tangled in her mind. Words sung to her by her father brought tears to her eyes.

Gems glittered on the handle and she ran the pads of her fingers over them. The dagger had belonged to her father—it was a gift from the king, and what Heshen had used to murder her family. When she'd stolen it from the cabinet in Heshen's palace, she hadn't known the significance of the dagger. She'd only wanted it for the gems to buy her freedom from Antonio. In retrospect, perhaps the dagger had called to her that day. It and the egg were the only reminders she had of her family. They were her most valued possessions.

"That will get you recognized and executed. Are you sure you want to bring it?" Cornelius stood at her side, his gaze firmly upon the weapon.

He was right, of course, which irritated her. Still, she sensed the dagger needed to be with her in Eidyn, but she couldn't be caught carrying it around. With a wave of her hand, the dagger disappeared. She sent it to a place out of time or physical space, where it would remain until she needed it.

"I suppose that's that, then." Cornelius stood with his hands at his side, looking helpless and a little lost.

"I'll be safe. I promise." She wished she could guarantee she'd return.

She looked away from his concern and made a circle in the

air with her right hand. The air shimmered and a pale-blue portal elongated enough to allow her passage.

"Amaleigh."

She turned slightly and winced at the tears shimmering in his eyes.

"Take this." He held out a slim gold chain and locket. "I was going to give it to you for your birthday."

She opened the locket and a small cry escaped her lips. Two tiny portraits stared back at her. She couldn't remember what they looked like, nor had she ever seen paintings of them, but she knew the faces gazing from the locket were her parents. Helena and Selmar, the queen's protector and King Heshen's Lord High Mayor, respectively. Her parents had been close friends of the king. Which made their deaths all the more despicable. A shudder wracked her spine.

"Thank you." She ran a thumb over the portraits. "I'm fortunate they were your friends. The night we escaped from Eidyn, Gwilym was surprised to see you, and said he thought you'd died with the other mages. I often wonder how many others survived the Purge."

"I know of a few, but I can't be certain how many. For those days and nights during the Purge, I did my best to help our kind escape. I wish I could've done more."

"You did what you could. For that, I'm sure those you helped are grateful."

She clasped the pendant around her neck and tucked it beneath her gown before hugging Cornelius tight enough he let out a small oof. Power thrummed through the charm. Hers, Cornelius's, her mother's, her father's—she sensed all their magic in the ornately carved gold. The chances of anyone at the palace recognizing the tiny portraits inside were slim, but to be safe, she'd have to hide the pendant beneath her clothing.

Knowing her parents would be with her on this dangerous undertaking gave her much-needed strength.

She'd delayed long enough. Somewhere on the other side of the portal, Gwilym waited. She took a step toward the shimmering air and focused on where she needed to go—the last place King Heshen would think to look for her. His palace.

Unless it was a trap and Gwilym the lure. Then she was walking straight into her death.

CHAPTER

SIXTEEN

The air settled, and Amaleigh stood still for several long moments, listening. Drawing from memory, she'd selected a room just off Gwilym's sleeping chamber. It was where he used to take lessons as a boy, and also where he'd built a little enclave where she could hide and participate in the lessons without being caught.

A thief and a prince. What an unlikely pair they were. But the friendship had satisfied them both and given each someone to confide in—a safe harbor in their respective storms. Although, to be fair, Amaleigh didn't know what being a prince was like, nor could Gwilym claim to understand her torment of surviving Antonio's brutal regime. It didn't matter. They were friends. Innocent allies in a world that wanted to use them both.

The room had changed little since she'd last been there. In the corner was the screen that had hidden her from Gwilym's tutors, now draped with waistcoats and cravats. A wave of nostalgia overcame her, and she put out a hand to steady herself. Images of them racing through the long corridors of the palace, being chased by a nanny or guardsmen and laughing so hard their sides hurt, burst through her thoughts.

They'd run the entire length of the palace, but never got caught. Probably because Amaleigh knew of every hidey-hole and crevice where they could hide. Sometimes it was more difficult for Gwilym because he wasn't as skinny as her, but they always managed. That seemed to be the mantra of their lives back then—somehow, they always succeeded, even when the odds were against them.

"One last adventure, eh, my friend?" She spoke softly to the empty room, a lump of emotion caught in her throat.

Not one given to moments of fancy, she pushed her shoulders back and lifted her chin before striding toward the door. There was no time for nonsense or melancholy. She had work to do.

Before her hand touched the gilded knob, she hesitated. Did she look the same? Would she be recognized? Within the space of a heartbeat, a visage slid over her features, altering them to make her unrecognizable. A gifted mage might be able to see through her mask, but unless Heshen had lost his mind a second time, she had little worry of encountering one in the palace.

A quick peek in a mirror confirmed that her crimson hair was now a lustrous chocolate and her light eyes were equally dark. She doubted even Cornelius would recognize her. With grim determination, she turned the door handle and peeked into the next room. The stillness and quiet gave her confidence to proceed.

A huge four-poster bed dominated the space, and Amaleigh looked quickly away from the masculine bedding. She'd never bothered with Gwilym's love life, unless it was to tease him about his lack thereof, which was terribly childish of her. Things most likely had changed for the prince since her absence. Her gaze crept back to the bed, and she jerked her head to the left to keep from peeking at the primly folded duvet and thick hanging curtains that would block out light, sound, and curious onlookers.

What the flox was wrong with her? It was a bed. She'd seen lots of them. What did she care that it was Gwilym's?

"What are you doing here?"

A feminine voice came from behind Amaleigh, and her stomach twisted.

She spun around to face a lovely young woman with hair the color of straw and a creamy complexion. Pretty, but not overly so. The woman stood with four others, their faces drawn in question, but not alarm. Two were pale, and the other two dark skinned, with eyes so deep brown Amaleigh couldn't see irises. They wore similar clothing to the princess, but their bearing set them apart. Regal, yes, but they had a lethalness to them that made Amaleigh wary.

"I, erm, I'm looking for the prince." Amaleigh couldn't stop staring at the woman's face. If she wasn't mistaken, the stranger wore a magic-enhanced mask over her features.

"He's not here at the moment. May I ask what business you have with him?" Her tone was pleasant—curious, even.

Amaleigh's thoughts reeled. Her tone implied she meant he was out of the palace for a few hours. But, if Gwilym were missing, surely the young woman would be upset. Instead, she stood with her ladies looking as if they were discussing nothing more important than the weather. Amaleigh had a sudden desire to learn everything she could about the woman. Especially what her relationship to Gwilym might be.

"I'm afraid I can't share my reasons for seeing the prince. I'm happy to wait until he returns, if you'd like to show me to an appropriate room." The sooner she got out of Gwilym's bedchamber, the better.

"Certainly. He should return within the hour. I'm Princess Cassia from Aenglebreck. And who might I have the honor of speaking to?" The lilt of her voice and graceful way she moved sent warnings through Amaleigh's mind.

Aenglebreck was across the seas from Eidyn, a human kingdom. She'd studied all the kingdoms with Gwilym when they were younger, but the lessons were too long ago for Amaleigh to know if Cassia were telling the truth. There was no reason why she would lie about her origins. Yet something nagged at the back of her mind that the princess wasn't being completely honest.

Amaleigh curtseyed to the princess and bowed her head. "It's an honor, Your Highness. I'm Erma. Erma Kielder." She chose a name Gwilym would immediately recognize. Erma was his nickname for her—his way of protecting her identity should anyone question her presence in the palace. When alone, he always used her given name, but around others, she became Erma. She'd loved the game and now hoped it protected her still.

"Erma. What a lovely name for a lovely girl. Come, I'll show you to a sitting room where we can wait for the prince. Tell me, Erma, where are you from? I don't recognize your clothing and that bag is simply divine." Princess Cassia chatted the entire way from Gwilym's rooms to a cozy sitting room in another part of the palace.

As they walked through the maze of halls, Amaleigh adjusted her plan. She hadn't counted on a princess being in the palace. And certainly not one comfortable enough with Gwilym to enter his private chambers unannounced. Nor had she thought she might be discovered so soon after arriving, which made her cautious of the princess.

"Erma, sit beside me. I wish to know all there is about you. It's been ages since anyone's come to the palace, and I'm simply starved for gossip." Cassia patted a worn cushion, an expectant look on her face.

Amaleigh did as asked and sat next to the princess. The four ladies took chairs opposite, near enough to join in the conversation, but at a discreet distance if the princess wished to say something in confidence.

Silence settled in the room and it took Amaleigh a moment to realize Cassia was waiting for her to speak. Her mind whirled like the wild winds on the cliff. She had no gossip.

"I...erm, I'm afraid to disappoint you, but I don't keep up on current events. Surely you hear everything, living here." Amaleigh waved her arm to indicate the palace and stopped when her gaze landed on a mural covering an entire wall.

She nearly rose from the couch, but stopped herself. Her fingers itched to grasp her locket, but she held them firmly in her lap. There, blazoned from one side of the room to the other, was a painting of a woman with crimson curls riding a dragon with sea-green scales. Beside her, another woman rode a cobalt dragon. Their hair danced on the wind and smiles widened their faces, as if they laughed at a private joke.

Amaleigh didn't know the woman on the blue dragon, but the other one she recognized—it matched the miniature portrait in the locket Cornelius gave her. Her mother.

All those years traipsing through the palace with Gwilym, and they'd never set foot in these rooms. All that time, her mother's image had been here, in life-size painted glory. Forgetting protocol, Amaleigh stood and approached the mural. She stretched her fingers to touch the shimmering scales of her mother's dragon.

A thread of magic sparked from the wall to her fingertip, and she jumped at the shock. She knew this magic, had felt it as a child. Warm, maternal, wise. It was her mother's power that flowed into her now, though she had no idea how. She glanced around the room and saw tiny threads of magic, some ragged and fraying. Centuries and centuries of wards, probably.

She placed her palm flat on the wall and closed her eyes. *Mother, I'm here. Your Amaleigh.* A slight pulsing came from the portrait, and Amaleigh sighed with happy contentment. She wasn't alone in the palace. Whatever traps or intrigues she found herself in, she knew her mother's spirit would give her strength. She just hoped it would be enough if she were caught by the king or his guard.

CHAPTER

SEVENTEEN

A figure moved beside her, and Cassia placed her hands on the mural in the same way Amaleigh did. She caught a whiff of Cassia's sweet, yet exotic scent. It wasn't one she recognized. Floral, soft like gardenia, but with a tang. Everything about the princess was a study in opposites. Her capriciousness was undermined by a strength Amaleigh sensed in the girl. She'd need to watch her words and deeds around the princess.

"Does it upset you? I can pull the tapestries closed if it does," Cassia asked, and Amaleigh shook her head.

"I'm just surprised, is all. I had heard rumors the king despised dragons." Amaleigh dragged her gaze back to Cassia and saw the pinch of pain at the corners of her lips, the spark of anger in her eyes. A moment later, it was gone.

"You heard true." Cassia took several steps backward and gazed up at the painting. "These were the queen's rooms. Neither the prince nor the king ever comes in here, and I find the painting...comforting. It's the freedom in their expressions, I think."

"They're lovely. Do you know who they are?" She knew her mother and could guess the identity of the other woman.

Cassia's laughter was like the tinkling of bells. "You certainly aren't from here if you don't recognize Queen Maire. She's the king's late wife. Died in childbirth with their second son. Gwilym would've been young, about five, I believe."

Of course, long after the fact, Amaleigh had heard the rumors of Queen Maire's death—those who lived on the streets thrived on gossip from the palace—but in all the time she'd spent with Gwilym, they'd never talked about their dead parents. The queen had died exactly one year before Amaleigh's family was murdered. It was an anniversary neither she nor Gwilym had wished to remember. For her, she lived with the terrors of Purge celebrations, and looking back, she now understood he was mourning his mother's passing those lonely nights of fireworks and revelry. No wonder he'd hated them as much as her.

Cassia returned to the sofa, and Amaleigh followed. They sat for a moment, admiring the painting.

"And the other woman? Is that the queen's sister?" A raging desire to learn everything about her mother surged through her, and if Cassia could provide anything at all, she had to know.

"In truth, I'm not entirely sure who she is. The queen only had a brother, I believe. They look to be rather close, though." Cassia sighed and cupped her cheeks in her palms, her elbows resting on her knees. "So carefree. I should like to know that kind of unbridled bliss one day."

"If the queen of Eidyn can have joy, then certainly so can a princess of Aenglebreck."

"From your lips to the gods' ears." Cassia turned toward Amaleigh with a bright, if slightly forced smile. "That's a lovely locket. May I see the portraits inside?"

A fissure of panic seized Amaleigh's brain. She didn't speak or move, but simply stared at the princess for several heartbeats. A multitude of thoughts rushed her brain. She thought she'd tucked it safely away. She couldn't risk wearing it in the palace. It was foolish of her to think she could. If Cassia saw it, she'd be found out. Especially since they were just discussing the woman featured on the mural and in Amaleigh's locket. She was doomed.

"Have I said something to upset you?" The princess sat upright, her features scrunched with concern.

"No, I'm sorry, Your Highness. It's just, I haven't eaten today and I'm afraid my stomach is none too pleased with me at the moment." Amaleigh made a face as if she were trying hard not to be sick or pass wind. She had no idea what she looked like, but by the alarm that crossed Cassia's features, she assumed it worked.

"Do you need to lie down? Merigold, grab a blanket. Isla, get some pillows for our friend."

"Please don't fuss on my account. It's just a bit of gas, I hope. Perhaps I should come back later when the prince is available?"

As if remembering Amaleigh was there to see Gwilym and not actually her, Cassia's expression fell and her lips trembled.

"Do you have to go? Since you're a friend of the prince, I could have one of the servants make up a suite for you and once you've recovered, we could dine together." She grabbed Amaleigh's hands. "Please."

The desperation in the girl's voice and the way her hand shook gave Amaleigh pause. She'd planned to stay at an inn, but if the princess were willing to vouch for her, then a comfortable bed was much preferable to a straw mattress.

"You are too kind, Your Highness. I would enjoy spending time with you."

If nothing else, she might discover why the girl was willing to befriend a complete stranger—and a commoner at that. If Cassia were truly who she said she was, and just lonely in the huge palace, perhaps she could be an ally. But if she was lying, about anything, then Amaleigh had to be even more careful with her words and actions.

"Let's see about that room, shall we?" The princess beamed at Amaleigh, but she saw the tightness around her eyes, the slight panic residing in their depths.

Amaleigh's presence might not be as welcome as Cassia wanted her to believe. They passed a mirror, and Amaleigh caught the princess's reflection. It showed a young woman who appeared to be touched by frost. Her shimmering white hair hung near to her buttocks, and her dark, almost midnight skin gave her an ethereal bearing. White lashes fringed ice-blue eyes and silvery brows made feathered arches. Even her four ladies' features were altered in the mirror. The angular cut of their jaws were more rounded, and their high cheekbones not as pronounced.

Elves. Amaleigh sucked in a gasp and covered it with a cough. Why would an elf be in the palace? They were the hereditary caretakers of dragons. All the dragons Heshen slaughtered had come from Aerithilyn, the elven kingdom. After the Purge, King Heshen became the elves' sworn enemy. She remembered Gwilym telling her his father sought war with the elves, but they hid their kingdom behind a wall of mist and Heshen never found them.

Cassia glanced at her in alarm, but she waved the princess off. "Caught a bit of dust in my throat."

"It's those damn tapestries. They hold in filth for centuries. Come, we'll get you a glass of water."

"You're very kind. Really, you don't have to go out of your way for me."

"Don't be silly." Cassia shrugged her off and turned down a narrow hallway.

From her days roaming the palace with Gwilym, Amaleigh knew they were headed for the kitchens. "Is the king in residence?" She tried to keep her tone casual, despite the tremor that thinking of the murderer brought about.

"He's hunting. Or something. Won't be here for at least a fortnight is what I believe the prince said." Cassia looked to one of her ladies, who nodded.

Amaleigh tried to recall how often the king hunted, but she'd made avoiding him an art and scarcely knew when he was in residence or not. Her sole focus back then had been Gwilym and his happiness.

Ten steps later, she smelled the aromas coming from the cavernous space and swooned. She hadn't lied when she said she'd not eaten that day. In the rush to pack, she'd forgotten about food. How far she'd come from the days of living in the alleys and thieving. The predominant thought in those times was of when and where her next meal would come. Now, she had the luxury of forgetting to eat without worry. How very far she'd come indeed.

A growl loud enough to wake a giant came from her midsection. "Excuse my rather rude tummy." She placed a hand over her stomach with a slight giggle.

"We'll sort out food first, then get your rooms settled." Without saying a word to her ladies, Cassia turned Amaleigh to the right and they went to the left, into the kitchens. "We'll dine in my private rooms to be certain we're not disturbed."

She'd hoped to have a minute away from the cheery princess to think—to alter her plan, and most of all, to remove her locket before anyone else noticed it. When Cassia stopped to give a servant orders for preparing Amaleigh's rooms, she casually slipped off the pendant and tucked it inside a pocket in her bag. She could send it where she'd hidden the dagger, but that used magic and she couldn't risk doing so with Cassia so near.

When the princess turned back to Amaleigh, her eyes narrowed, but she said nothing.

Amaleigh felt the weight of Cassia's disapproval, as if the girl had known what was in the locket all along and now knew Amaleigh tried to hide something from her. But unless she was clairvoyant, she couldn't know.

Fucking elves. They had powers ordinary mages could never understand. Theirs was a magic as old as the worlds they inhabited. Which made it all the more intriguing why Cassia was pretending to be human. She'd have to be clever to uncover what an elf princess was doing in Eidyn. That is, if she really was a princess. Cassia could be an assassin. The more they walked, the more unsettling the thoughts swirling in Amaleigh's mind became.

They turned a corner, and Cassia let out a noise that sounded like someone had stepped on a large rat. Or a small dog. Not quite a yelp, but more than a squeak.

"Your Highness!" Cassia immediately lowered almost to the ground, with her arms extended in a formal curtsey.

Amaleigh startled at not only the sound she made, but her effusion of protocol. The very air surrounding them altered with an unseen tension.

Then her brain processed Cassia's words. She glanced up to see Gwilym standing not more than three feet from her. Excitement whipped through her blood, but she clamped it down. It wouldn't do to burst into tears at seeing her only childhood friend. Time froze, as if nothing had changed. He looked exactly as she remembered him—dark curls framed a ruggedly handsome face, but the mischief she recalled in his deep-blue eyes was no longer there. Neither was any sort of recognition. Of course not; she had made sure she didn't look like herself. Still, a bitter pang throbbed in her heart. A pain she didn't quite understand.

The whole point of a disguise was not to be recognized, and yet, she'd hoped he'd see through the mask and know it was her. She'd hoped their years of friendship meant as much to him as they did her. But he smiled genially without a hint that he knew it was his friend.

Also missing was any sign of being tortured. Not a scratch marred his perfect complexion. Unlike in the vision she saw while casting. Which could only mean the prince hadn't sent it. That would mean she had imagined it. It could've been a trick of her magic, playing out her worst fears. Perhaps her guilt had built to such a degree that she saw things that weren't real.

Seeing Gwilym unhurt should've been a relief, but instead it ratcheted her anxiety. The nagging in her mind screeched that something was off. It went beyond Cassia's pretense and Gwilym not recognizing her. Whatever the hell was going on here, she was determined more than ever to find out.

She dropped into a curtsey that would've made King Heshen pleased and rose at the same time as Cassia.

"Cassia, darling, who is your friend?" Gwilym regarded them both with curiosity, and for a moment, the princess faltered.

The carefree, chatty girl was gone, replaced with a meek little thing.

"Your Highness," Amaleigh cut in before Cassia could speak. "I am delighted to find you in good health. When last we spoke, you were under a bit of duress. It's been a while, but you helped me at a time when I needed it most, and I have come to return the favor. How may I be of service to you, my lord?" She swept the floor in a second curtsey and hoped Gwilym understood her veiled meaning.

"Forgive my memory, kind lady. Although I don't recall the specifics, I cannot turn away someone who has offered to repay a debt. I would be honored if you would grace our home with your presence."

Despite his words, the way he peered at her, as if trying to see beyond the mask, robbed her of any sense of security.

"She's called Erma, Your Highness," Cassia offered.

"Erma Kielder." Amaleigh hoped using the name of his most favored dog as a surname would garner some sort of reaction. None came. Even if Gwilym didn't recognize her, surely he knew the name of his pet. Unless...unless he'd been tortured to forget his past. Was it possible? Or, more likely, he purposefully pretended not to know her and her worst fears were true—it had been a trap to lure her out of hiding. Her heart hammered in her chest loud enough to drown out Cassia's twittering.

"Well met this day, Erma Kielder." A sardonic grin twisted his lips, sending panicked jabs through her gut. He took her hand in his and raised it to his lips. His eyes never left hers, and she repressed a squirm.

Even though he followed protocol, something about his intensity sent a warning through her mind. Not only did he not behave like the friend she remembered, his scent and touch weren't the same. The firm grip he had on her fingertips wasn't princely, but controlling. As if he meant it as a silent threat.

It was possible Gwilym had changed in the years she was gone, but to this extent? They knew each other, really and truly. Had lain beneath the stars and shared their deepest secrets and fears with each other. She refused to believe the boy she grew up with had become this stranger.

Whatever game he was playing, Amaleigh knew one thing for sure—the man standing before her, who looked so much like her childhood friend, either had changed a great deal since she last saw him, or he was not her Gwilym.

EIGHTEEN

Water dripped somewhere. In the corner, perhaps, or near the door. Close, but not on them, thank the gods. Gwilym shifted his weight to better sit against the cold stone and reached his bound hands toward his father.

The king lay on the floor, face down. His whimpers echoed in the empty space, making a morose counterpart to the constant dripping. By his estimation, they'd been in the cell six days. The king's men should be looking for them, but until Gwilym knew where they were, he couldn't expect a rescue any time soon.

He grabbed his father's sleeve and pulled him closer to combine their body heat. It was their only chance of surviving the frigid cold. Heshen grunted and flopped to his back, landing half on Gwilym's lap.

"Father, sit up." Blood filled his vision, and he wiped his forehead with the hem of his sleeve.

Heshen shifted and scooched until his back was against the stones. Gwilym was in bad shape, but the king had taken the brunt of their beatings. For every punch Gwilym got, his father received five. Which made him believe this was personal.

They'd been kidnapped while out hunting—at a time when the king's guard was distracted, leaving the monarch vulnerable. Gwilym had nearly skipped the hunt that morning, but his father had insisted. After seven hard years of earning his father's trust, Gwilym had learned long ago not to agitate the king or he'd find himself locked out of meetings and, on occasion, locked in his rooms. As the king grew older and Gwilym more trusted, his father also became more complacent.

Once the most feared ruler in the surrounding kingdoms, Heshen had softened with maturity. Still a tyrant, still the most selfish man Gwilym had ever known, his father was at least willing to listen to reason. It had been seven years of hard-fought change, but they were getting there.

Baby steps, as they said.

Little of that mattered now. Reason wouldn't get them out of the dank cell, nor would softened resolve ease the ire of their abductors. His father had already promised more gold than they had in the treasury. Women, wine, country homes—he'd promised whatever the miscreants wanted, and they'd laughed. The vile men with cold eyes and brutal fists had laughed at the king.

That, more than anything, had broken the man. No one laughed at King Heshen.

It was the king's own damn fault. Any other time, Gwilym might've had sympathy for the abusers. After all, his father hadn't made their lives easier. Hadn't made any of their lives easier, including his.

Gwilym rubbed his hands along his father's arms and chest, trying to get his blood circulating. The king's teeth chattered like rickety old wagon wheels over cobblestones. If he didn't get them warm soon, they would die. It was summer outside, but these cellars were made for storage and never knew warmth.

He crawled on hands and knees around the perimeter of the room, just like he'd done dozens of times already. Stone walls, cold slab floors, no fireplace nor windows. It was a cellar in someone's house. But where? And whose house? He continued around the small space, his hands sweeping wide across the slabs, hoping to find what he knew wouldn't be there. Something, anything they could eat or burn. Six days without adequate food or water, and only the damp chill to keep them company.

Whoever the abductors were, they knew how to torture a man: deprive him of sight and scent and sensation.

He returned to his place beside his father and continued to rub his arms and legs. A low moan came from the king. Gwilym swallowed a lump of guilt. If he'd been a better son, this wouldn't have happened. That night, all those years ago, when he'd let Amaleigh escape with the dagger—Gwilym stopped himself with a harsh reprimand. It wasn't Amaleigh's fault. Of everyone, she was the most innocent.

Gwilym's guilt started long before Amaleigh stole the dagger from his father's magically locked cabinet. He'd been trying to undermine his father's rule for several years, and that alone almost got him killed. Amaleigh stealing the dagger only enhanced his father's fury.

The fact that Gwilym let her escape with the powerful blade nearly caused the king apoplexy. It had taken surviving two assassination attempts for Heshen to finally see that Gwilym might be made of sterner stuff and have something to offer.

Assassinations the king himself had ordered.

Gwilym grimaced and leaned his head against the stone. Whatever had happened in the past was done. There was no sense in letting it darken his remaining days, however few or many they may be.

"I forgive you, Father."

"For what?" The words were more a wheeze than spoken.

Gwilym started at the sound of the cracked voice. He hadn't expected his father to hear him, much less respond.

"For trying to have me killed." He gripped Heshen's hand in his own. "You always told me to have my own thoughts—that a king must rely on his own counsel before taking advice from others."

"I did, didn't I?" A phlegmy laugh came from his father's chest. "Thank you." Heshen patted their clasped hands. "For your forgiveness, and your continued love. There are days I'm not sure I deserve such kindness, especially from a son I once wanted dead. I was wrong about so many things. Listened to ill-conceived advice. Knowing that I have your forgiveness, I shall go to my grave lighter of heart."

For all his father's faults, he believed his father meant it.

"May that be many years from now." Gwilym raised their hands and kissed his father's fingertips. "Sleep and conserve your energy."

The king sighed a long, mournful whistle. "The Purge was a mistake. You've told me as much many times, and with each telling, I knew it was true, but hubris has a way of twisting our thinking. I should've listened to you. Above all else, only you have spoken the truth, harsh as it was to hear." Another sigh, followed by the soft snuffles of someone who hid their tears. "He told me the prophecy, my son. He said dragons will tear the crown asunder. I'm so sorry. I thought I had no choice."

"What prophecy?" A wiggle of memory teased his mind. Something from long ago—something his mother had told him, but it wouldn't form into a coherent thought. "Who told you?"

His father's body relaxed as if speaking had exhausted him, and Gwilym turned slightly to cover more of the king's body with his own. They would survive this. Had to. Gwilym had worked too hard over the years to bring peace to his troubled kingdom. It had taken diplomacy and determination, but he was winning over the merchants and elite of Eidyn. And now, his father finally saw reason. Once they were free of their kidnappers, he and the king would work together to rebuild Eidyn.

Whatever this prophecy his father mentioned was, he couldn't let it derail his progress. A sharp stab against his chest warned that it might've played role in their abduction. He rubbed his breastbone, his mind circling around the problem. It was possible the prophecy went further back in their history. Even as far back as before the Purge. If his father had believed dragons would destroy the kingdom, that would be motivation to rid Eidyn of them. But to slaughter all the mages, too—it didn't make sense. Gwilym shook his head. Perhaps it wouldn't make sense *now* for the aging king, but in his youth, Heshen was hot-headed and consumed by power.

He remembered the rage his father displayed when Gwilym's mother died in childbirth. Heshen blamed the mages, screaming they'd killed the queen. Even the queen's brother couldn't escape the king's wrath. That had been a dark time for Gwilym. Until, one day, a skinny little girl with hair like garnets snuck into his study rooms and they became the most unlikely of friends.

He closed his eyes and thought of the one person who had never wavered in her friendship. The one person he trusted most. His body warmed with the memory of his lips upon hers. What had possessed him to kiss her? Not that he hadn't wanted to for ages, but on the night he said goodbye to her for possibly ever, he'd been compelled to, as if he might forever lose his chance.

Amaleigh, if you can hear me, we don't have much time.

His other attempts to reach her had all gone unanswered, but he wouldn't give up. She was out there, somewhere. By the grace of their gods, he hoped she could help. It was a wild risk, asking her to return to Eidyn after everything she'd been through. He couldn't say for sure why he thought she could help, only that he believed in her, and every time he closed his eyes, it was her face he saw.

In all the years they'd known each other, she was the only person who accepted him as he was—as just Gwilym. She'd never called him Your Highness or bowed to him. Nor had she ever treated him with false deference. Most of all, she'd never betrayed him. He'd confided in her his most daring secrets and hidden fears, and she'd listened without judgement. Even when Antonio had ordered her to kill him, she risked her own safety to defy the bastard.

Gwilym shuddered not from the cold, but from the memory of Antonio's fury that she'd escaped. He'd set her up to fail so that he would own her. When Gwilym heard of Antonio's plans for Amaleigh, he'd been sickened and also relieved that he helped her escape the madman's clutches. He'd never understood why Amaleigh continued to work for Antonio. But then, he'd never been starving or freezing—until now.

"I'm sorry, Amaleigh. I should've been a better friend." It was his day for penance. If he survived, he vowed to do better. No longer would he tolerate his father's whims. The people of Eidyn had been punished enough. He'd work to mend the relationship with Aerithilyn and restore the dragon mages to their place of respect and reverence. Eidyn had been prosperous once, before his father destroyed everything with the Purge.

A chain rattled, and Gwilym tensed. It was time for their

daily beatings. His father roused himself and muttered several curses beneath his breath. He was frail and failing daily. One more beating might be the end of the king.

"Take me and leave him for the day." Gwilym was on his feet and shuffling toward the door before it even opened.

"Aye, playing the hero, are we? Well then, let's get on wit it." A ghostly hand extended from the darkness and grabbed Gwilym by the ear.

He fell forward and a knee came up to meet his gut. The air whooshed from his lungs, which earned him mocking laughter from his abuser.

"Not so princely now, are ye? Git moving or there'll be hells to pay."

"Feed my father, please." Gwilym choked on his own blood and stumbled down the hallway.

"Never you mind 'bout him."

They climbed two flights of stairs before turning down a cramped corridor. A door opened to their right, and Gwilym was shoved inside. Thus far, the beatings had all happened near the cell where they were being kept. The change intrigued Gwilym, and he blinked to make out details of the room. Anything that might help him place exactly where they were.

Two chairs sat in the middle of the otherwise empty space. Tacky wallpaper—the kind those with new money bought to appear fashionable—peeled from the walls. This might've been an important house once, but it was falling to ruin. Either the owner had lost their money, their prestige, or their life, and now someone else squatted in the building.

The man shoved Gwilym onto a chair. A rope slid over his chest from someone behind him—someone he'd not noticed in the shadows. The man who'd taken him from the cellar kicked his feet and someone else tied them to the chair legs. He peered at his abductor, but he wore a dark mask over his face. If they meant to kill them, it seemed odd they would hide their identities. Unless, they weren't going to kill them. Or, Gwilym might recognize them.

He listened harder to their speech patterns as they discussed the extent and execution of Gwilym's beating. Street speech. If he was still in Eidyn, he knew exactly where he was.

Before the first punch hit, Gwilym closed his eyes and went to the place in his mind where their brutality couldn't reach him. He felt the blows and accepted the pain, but he didn't cry out. Only occasionally did he grunt or pull against his restraints. He refused to give them the satisfaction of seeing him whimper like a child.

Amaleigh. He sent the thought into the ether and tried again to reach her. Being aboveground, he had the wild idea she would better receive his message. *Please hurry. I think we're a—*

A chain slammed into Gwilym's cheek and a flash of light lit through his skull before everything went black.

NINETEEN

The prince laughed at something the princess said and raised her fingertips to his lips. They shared a private look that Amaleigh wasn't supposed to see, but she couldn't turn away. The whole dinner was an elaborate pantomime that she found horrifying and yet mesmerizing. The actors—Prince Gwilym and Princess Cassia. The sole member of the audience—Amaleigh.

Bizarre didn't even come close to describing the events at the palace. After their introduction, Prince Gwilym demanded she join them for dinner, without ever asking what debt she needed to repay, and Cassia hadn't questioned her further as to why she was in Gwilym's rooms. It was as if neither really wanted to know her purpose for being in the palace, and yet, they both required her presence. For what, she wasn't sure. A distraction from each other? Most likely, some macabre game royals enjoyed playing.

Cassia's ladies dined with them, as did two of Gwilym's friends, but they spoke only to each other and ignored what was happening between the prince and the princess. Only when Gwilym shouted down the table at them did they look in the prince's direction. Their steadfast avoidance of Gwilym's pathetic behavior only served to intrigue Amaleigh more. In fact, the whole charade would've been laughable if it weren't so tragic.

Gwilym went out of his way to show Amaleigh how much he adored Cassia, and the princess, well, she did her best to return that adoration. The tiny flinches, and the strained expression as if she wore a corset pinched too tight, gave her away. Amaleigh doubted Gwilym even noticed. Her best friend had definitely changed, and not for the better. If anything, he was more like his father and less the compassionate man she'd known, which was quite un-Gwilym-like.

The moment they were alone, Amaleigh would ask Cassia what the flox was really going on. She raised a glass of water to her lips and tipped the rim toward the couple in a silent toast. At the very least, they deserved a round of applause for their performance.

A stinging pain lashed across her cheek, and she cried out. The crystal goblet crashed to the table, splintering into several shards of kaleidoscopic prisms. In one, Amaleigh clearly saw Gwilym—not the prince sitting opposite her, but another Gwilym, seated in a dimly lit room, bound to a chair. Shadows prowled around him, tigers stalking their prey. A blow to his abdomen caused her to wheeze as if struck herself.

"Erma! What's wrong?" Cassia rushed to her side and put a hand to Amaleigh's forehead. "Is this the affliction you had earlier? Come, we must get you to your room."

Amaleigh didn't fight the princess. Whatever was happening, she preferred it not be in front of an audience. She couldn't tell if the vision was a premonition of what was to come. Or if it was happening concurrently.

"Can you stand?" Gwilym was at her side, his hand outstretched. He appeared the very definition of chivalrous.

With all her heart, she wanted to believe this was her Gwilym, but the instinct to recoil from his touch was too great to ignore. If he wasn't the real Gwilym and the man in the dark room was, then who was pretending to be the prince? And why?

The wretched realization washed over her that if she wanted answers, she'd have to play his game. At least, for the time being.

"Thank you." Amaleigh put her hand on his sleeve and steadied herself.

Cassia took her other arm and together, they led her to the suite of rooms that had been prepared for her stay. Once there, Gwilym stalked the room while Cassia settled Amaleigh into a chair and ordered tea and cakes to be brought.

"Dear child, what got into you?" Cassia's softened tone and fretting was the opposite of how she spoke to the prince. She fussed with Amaleigh's long, wavy hair, gathering it into a bun, then letting it hang loose.

Her need to be useful was palpable, and Amaleigh had a moment of pity for the woman.

"I'll send for the physic." Gwilym turned to face them, his brows set.

"I'm fine, really. I don't need a doctor. I'm sorry to have disturbed your meal." Amaleigh stood as if to prove her point and hoped her face hadn't paled. The mask she wore mimicked her natural skin, which meant if she blushed, it showed on her mask. "I sometimes get fierce pains when I eat rich foods or drink too much wine."

"But you had water," Cassia offered.

"And it's a good thing, too. I can't imagine how much worse I'd be if I'd had all that food and wine as well."

"You poor dear. We'll make up a list for Cook tomorrow of suitable foods you can eat." The princess was behaving more like a doting mother than a young woman who'd only met Amaleigh a few hours earlier.

Definitely odd.

"Darling, we should let our guest rest. I'll walk you to your room."

"You go on. I want to make sure Amaleigh is right as rain before I retire."

Gwilym glared at Cassia for several moments before he strode to the door. His fingers flicked at his side as he hurried out.

As soon as the door clicked shut, a collective breath was let out by the princess and her ladies.

Now that they were alone, Amaleigh had several questions for Cassia, but hesitated. If she came on too strong, the princess might shut down. She'd have to start slow to earn her trust.

"Merigold, see about running a bath for Erma."

Cassia's lady gave her a sharp look, but hid it quickly. She strode to a door hidden in the corner, and Amaleigh watched her with keen interest. The way she held her shoulders taut, yet let her arms dangle to appear loose, struck a familiar chord. It wasn't the way a lady would walk, certainly.

"Lady Merigold doesn't have to run my bath. I'm perfectly capable of taking care of myself."

"Pish posh. *Lady* Meri doesn't mind at all, do you, love?" The amusement in Cassia's voice as she called after Merigold added another layer of mystery to the woman.

The dark-skinned beauty returned with a deep scowl on her features. "Not at all, Your Highness." Her gaze went to Amaleigh. "Would the lady like me to help her undress?" Her tone softened, surprising Amaleigh.

"I can manage, thanks."

Cassia tilted her chin toward Amaleigh, and the four women approached in unison. They were a flurry of hands, untying stays and unbuckling the little belt Amaleigh wore around her waist. A moment later, both her gown and her chemise were drawn over her head, leaving her standing naked and quite perplexed about what to do about it.

"Come now." Cassia took her hand and guided her to the bathing room. A massive tub nestled against the far wall with a cascade of steaming water filling it from an unseen source. All those times she'd dreamed of bathing in one of the palace's luxurious tubs when she was younger, she'd never have guessed it would eventually happen—nor that an elven princess would assist.

She stepped into the tub and settled low enough for the bubbles to cover her nakedness. One of the ladies, Isla perhaps, wet a sponge and began dragging it over her skin. Cassia herself poured a pitcher of water over Amaleigh's head and laughed when she sputtered. A little warning would've been nice, but the ladies weren't interested in what Amaleigh wanted. They took their charge of bathing her seriously.

A pair of soapy hands massaged her shoulders while Cassia rubbed sweet-scented shampoo into her hair. Despite desperately wanting to take full advantage of the warmth, she stayed alert. Machinations were afoot in the palace, and Cassia's determined friendship set off several warning bells. A life of thieving had taught her being a little paranoid and distrustful wasn't a bad thing.

She stretched her legs and arched, delighting in the heat on her muscles. Cool air swept across her nipples, and she lowered back to the warmth.

"No need to hide your body from us," Cassia whispered close to her ear. "You're lovely, Erma."

A soft prodding at her temple should've irritated her, but Amaleigh silently chuckled at the princess's attempt to read her thoughts. Elves were known for their telepathic abilities—their skill unequaled in infiltrating a mind so completely the person wouldn't know whether the thoughts were his own, or the elf's. Amaleigh had learned long ago how to close off her thoughts, either entirely or just enough to let the seeker get only the information Amaleigh wished to share. She might not have the skill of elves, but she could defend her mind from them.

She imagined a made-up life for Erma and allowed Cassia to access only those thoughts. To close herself off completely would've caused suspicion and unwanted questions. Although, the mere fact Cassia felt the need to pry told Amaleigh the princess didn't quite believe her story. The more she got to know the princess, the more she admired her.

While Cassia rooted through Amaleigh's made-up memories, she sent a thread of her magic to the girl's mind. As expected, she was met with a hard barrier, but that didn't daunt Amaleigh. Every wall had a crack somewhere; she only had to find Cassia's.

It came through a memory of Gwilym, as Amaleigh had hoped. Anything that caused discontent was a weakened area easily exploited.

The water swished, and Amaleigh opened one eye to see Merigold enter the bath. Her naked body gleamed in the candlelight. Lean and lithe, she had the build of a soldier. Perhaps she was one of the famed Fianna Bel'en—a select few warriors bound to their charge, usually a prince or princess of high standing. If so, that meant Cassia wasn't just any princess, but likely heir to the elven throne.

Merigold took Amaleigh's right leg in her hands and worked the muscles until a sigh escaped Amaleigh's lips. The bath was a ruse, meant to relax Amaleigh enough Cassia could extract the information she wanted. Amaleigh would go along with it—after all, she was naked and vulnerable, surrounded by possible elven warriors and their princess. Let them think they were in control. Let them believe she was a simple, trusting lass. But Amaleigh knew bloody damn well a blade might quickly appear, and just as swiftly slice a vein. If Cassia wanted her dead, an apparent suicide wouldn't put suspicion on her.

Except, Amaleigh didn't sense the princess wanted her dead. By her own admission, she was lonely. From what she witnessed at dinner, Cassia didn't return the prince's affections. Most likely, Cassia wanted to know whether she could trust the stranger who appeared out of nowhere in Gwilym's rooms. Possibly to know whether she had an ally or a foe. Amaleigh wondered the same about the princess.

Warm water was poured over Amaleigh's head while Merigold worked on her left leg. When her fingers inched closer to her sex, Amaleigh floated in genuine happy contentment. Merigold lightly fluttered her fingers against Amaleigh's bud in an obvious attempt to arouse her. Amaleigh allowed it, curious what her body would do. The answer was a big fat nothing. As with Cornelius, her body didn't respond to sexual stimuli. Not only was her heart a craven wasteland, but it appeared her passion was as well.

Whatever their reasons for manipulating her, and despite her attention being on alert, she quite enjoyed the bath. Every inch of her tingled from where their hands had stroked and kneaded. Cassia's power withdrew from Amaleigh's mind, and she let out a sigh of her own.

"Let's get you dried and in some clean bedclothes." Cassia's brusque tone meant the pseudo seduction was concluded. She must've gotten the information she wanted.

Amaleigh stood with a disappointed sulk. She could play Cassia's game, too.

"You really are lovely, Erma." The princess held up a towel, and Amaleigh stepped into it.

"Are you this hands-on with everyone you've just met?" She

kept her tone light, joking, but was also curious about the attention Cassia paid her. How she'd love to know what the princess had extracted from her mind.

"Only those who intrigue me." A sly smile lifted her lips, and she giggled. "Actually, my father would be mortified to see me holding a towel for a commoner. You are a commoner, am I correct?"

"I am, Your Highness." Amaleigh wasn't offended by her blunt question. It was a fair assumption to make. She hadn't introduced herself properly, and her reason for seeing the prince was dubious at best. Even so, it wasn't as if she'd just come off the street and stumbled into Gwilym's rooms by accident.

Which, in a way, she had when she was a wee lass of five and had discovered a secret entrance to the palace through one of the tunnels she loved to explore. It was the day she'd first seen Gwilym with his tutor and she'd hidden behind a chair, listening. That had been one of the best days of her life. It took Gwilym two months to finally speak to her, and when he did, it wasn't to chastise or tattle on her, but to take her hand and explore the palace together. That was long ago and now, she stood shivering in one of the many palace rooms, wondering how the hell she could get away from the prying princess and her ladies.

They dressed her in a sage-green sleeping gown and rubbed a towel through her hair until it was nearly dried. She sat on a chair in front of the fire, a cup of tea in her hand and a piece of cake sitting on the table beside her. Cassia sat opposite, eating her cake with bird-like bites.

"I like you, Erma. There's something about you that I find compelling and yet, you frighten me, too." Her gaze went swiftly to her ladies, then back to Amaleigh, as if admitting that had broken an unspoken rule.

"I'm honored by your compliment, but really, there's nothing to fear, Your Highness."

"Oh, please. Call me Cassia. I really dislike formality and all the scraping and bowing that goes on at court." She licked her thumb and rested her chin on her palm. "Why do you frighten me, do you suppose?"

Amaleigh swallowed hard as a dozen answers sprang to mind. She could tell Cassia it was because she'd guessed who she truly was, or that she suspected who her ladies were, or even that she knew the spectacle at dinner was fake. But she said none of those things.

"I really couldn't say. I don't consider myself all that imposing and, as you pointed out, I am just a commoner. In reality, it's you who intimidate me."

Cassia laughed hard. A full-bellied laugh that made her ladies pause in their tugging.

"Me? Truly? If so, then only because I'm a princess." Cassia leaned forward and whispered conspiratorially, "Don't let a silly tiara or musty old traditions scare you. The gods know I haven't." She leaned back and pinched a rather large chunk of cake between two fingers. "Truth be told, I envy you. Come and go as you please. No protocol. No one watching your every move. No pretending." She plopped the hunk into her mouth and chewed. "I'd love to know what it's like to live your life."

Now it was Amaleigh's turn to laugh. Which life would the princess choose? A starving thief who had to be on constant watch or end up dead? Or an exiled mage who ran from world to world to keep from being found out and perhaps killed?

The ladies resumed their braiding, and Amaleigh winced against the force they used. Whatever issue they had with her, they were taking it out on her scalp.

"Trust me, Your Highness, my life isn't worth giving up a palace for." She sipped her tea, a dangerous idea forming in her mind. "Although, if you'd like to experience what life is like outside these walls, I could arrange a foray into the city."

Cassia glanced nervously at her ladies. "For all of us?"

"For you. If you truly want to be discreet, you'd have to lose the chaperones."

A rather firm tug jerked her head backward, and Amaleigh swore under her breath. A tendril of magic raced through her blood, but she quenched it before she did any harm.

"I'll think on your offer." Cassia stood and beckoned her ladies. "I believe Merigold would be happy to stay with you tonight, if you feel the need for company."

Amaleigh rose as well and faced the stunning woman. If she'd felt even a spark of passion, she might've accepted. But it appeared her heart was empty of affection. She placed a hand over her chest and chose her words carefully. "I am honored by your generous offer. At this time, I must decline, but please do not think it is in any way because I am not attracted to your lovely lady. I fear my night will be restless at best and I'd hate to keep you awake."

Merigold smiled and it was as though the night sky suddenly lit with stars. "I rarely sleep more than a few hours. Should you find yourself in want of a companion, you have but to ask." She inclined her head and placed her hand over her heart.

Amaleigh curtseyed low, her head bowed. A lady-in-waiting, especially if she were a Fianna Bel'en, would never incline their head to a commoner. She wondered again what, exactly, Cassia had found while rummaging through her mind. And what, if anything, had she told her ladies?

She escorted them to the door, only half sorry to see them leave. Their company, although strange, also kept her from having to worry about Gwilym. She smoothed a hand over her throat and swallowed the lump of anxiety stuck there. The elf princess might pretend to be a sweet lass from Aenglebreck, but the casual way she led Amaleigh into a vulnerable position where she would be easily coerced, spoke to a woman who was much more skilled at espionage than she'd ever admit. Amaleigh definitely needed to be cautious. With both the princess *and* the prince.

She checked her reflection and made a face at the multitude of braids hanging down her back. Not one to fuss with elaborate hairstyles, she rarely did more than brush her curls in the morning. She twisted a braid around her finger and felt the subtle thrum of magic in the weave. Clever. With only a few twists and plaits of her hair, the ladies had made Amaleigh a spy without her even being aware. Even at that moment, she was certain Cassia could see and hear everything Amaleigh was doing.

With a resigned sigh, she blew out the candles that were lit all around the room and crawled beneath the heavy blanket on her bed. Thoughts of Cornelius and Merigold swirled in her mind, and she chided herself for being a loveless witch.

The gods knew she craved love. Had even dared hoped for it once, but that was nearly a decade ago and everything had changed since then. Including her, and Gwilym. She didn't want to be unfeeling or uncaring. To experience the intensity of unbridled passion would be a welcomed thrill. Cornelius was wrong—letting her guard down would leave her vulnerable.

Over the past seven years, she'd come to realize that to love another was to open herself to weakness and that was something she could never do. Not when there were men like King Heshen and Antonio in the world, who sought to exploit weakness for their own gain.

It was better to remain cold and impartial than to love. If only she could convince herself that was true. If she were as cold-hearted as she'd like others to believe, then why had she left everything to help Gwilym? For her own selfish reasons. For answers about her past and to ascertain how he'd been able to cut through their wards. It left her feeling defenseless and exposed that he'd so easily burst into her mind.

Another possibility shoved past her easy explanations. The terrible truth that perhaps she'd allowed him access. That maybe she'd wanted him to break through her walls. The answers she sought weren't just about her past, but to even entertain the idea of asking them made her tremble not out of fear, but from what might transpire given the chance.

She rolled over and burrowed deeper into the warm blankets. From what she witnessed this evening, Gwilym didn't need her help. Perhaps it was a trap, but not from King Heshen. This might be some twisted game—but to what end? Why call out for her if he wasn't in peril?

The more she spun questions in her mind, the clearer it became that whatever was happening at the palace didn't concern her. On the morrow, she'd return home, where she knew what was real. Let Gwilym and Cassia play their games. She'd have none of it.

The image of Gwilym in the shard of glass seared her skull. The lashing had felt too real to be hallucinated. Both tricks easy enough to conjure from a skilled mage. Or an elf.

A little tickle in her mind told her that if she left now, she'd never get her answers. Barnacleballs and pox it all. She rolled to her side with a huff. Fine. She'd give the scheming royals one more day, but she wouldn't wait around the palace for answers. She knew where to find them, and it was somewhere neither Cassia nor Gwilym would ever think to look.

CHAPTER
TWENTY

A shadowy figure ghosted through her room while Amaleigh pretended to sleep. She tracked their movements, from the little table where she and Cassia had left their cups and plates, to the en suite bathing room. Whoever it was spent several minutes in there, lifting items and setting them gently back down.

Amaleigh heard it all, and wondered whether Cassia did as well through the magic laced in her braids. By the heaviness of the intruder's steps, she guessed it was a man who prowled through her belongings. They hadn't lit a candle, but the moon shining through the gauzy window coverings let in plenty of light by which to see.

She shifted in her bed, making sleepy noises in the hopes whoever it was might be frightened off. Fighting an unknown assailant in the darkened room in only her nightdress didn't sound the least bit enticing. But if their intentions weren't honorable, fight she would.

They left the bathing room and came to stand at the side of the bed. Their shallow breathing sounded muffled, as if they wore a cloth over their face. Why would someone hide themselves in an unlit room? Perhaps they worried she might wake and light a candle, exposing them. If so, they must've assumed she was a light sleeper. Curiosity tugged at her. There were only a few people in the palace she'd recognize. Unless her mysterious visitor wasn't staying at the palace. Curiouser indeed.

A hand reached forward, and Amaleigh stiffened. Her heart thumpity-thumped in her chest, loud enough for the intruder to hear. Soft fingers stroked one of her braids, skimming it from her head to the tip. Such an intimate thing to do. Every nerve in her body wished to lash out, to scream until her throat bled, but she kept silent in part to gather more information about her possible attacker. Also out of curiosity to see whether they would indeed try to assault her. During her days of living with the urchins, many had tried. None succeeded.

She shifted again, turning her face upright, and stretched slightly to forcibly remove her braid from their fingertips. A slight grunt was all she heard. To sell the ruse, she blinked as if just waking and looked toward the intruder, but the space was empty.

The door clicked softly as they left, and Amaleigh put a hand over her racing heart. What the hell was that about? If they'd wanted to rape her, why search through her room first? Yet she didn't sense assault was the intended goal. Nor did she feel they were looking for something. After all, if they were, why spend so much time in the bathing room? It was all rather bizarre and left more questions than answers.

She slipped from the bed and found her bag in the armoire where she'd left it. The locket containing her parents' portraits was where she'd hidden it earlier, and her belongings appeared untouched. Robbery wasn't the purpose of her midnight visitor. Assault might've been, but she'd interrupted their plans. Possibly. But again, she didn't think so.

For a long time, she sat on the floor with her things clutched to her bosom. The moon traveled from one side of the windows to the other and still she had no answers. When her back ached from the awkward position, she dressed in an embroidered silk tunic and sleek black trousers. She might not be a thief anymore, but she'd long ago learned the value of dressing for all possibilities and for that, a gown wouldn't do. She'd been prepared to leave the palace, but she couldn't leave until she discovered what was going on. A changed Gwilym, a secret princess, and someone snooping in her rooms—she'd told herself the palace intrigues didn't concern her, but she was wrong.

She smoothed her hands over her braids and whispered a counter spell to the eavesdropping magic Cassia's ladies placed in the plaits. She didn't need silent company where she was going. Next, she used a tiny thread of magic to create a pocket in her traveling bag where she could hide the locket. She should send it where she'd hidden the dagger, but the thought of being separated from it tore at her heart. On impulse, she slipped the little trinket she'd bought at the festival around her neck. Calm passed over her, and she left her rooms with renewed optimism. She'd get answers, and knew just where to go first.

The palace had changed little in the years since she'd roamed the secret spaces and wide-open halls with Gwilym. Even the paintings were the same, with imposing figures looking down on her as she sped across the thick carpets. Splashes of gold were everywhere—a decadent display of King Heshen's wealth. Wealth that her own parents had helped build. Their reward had been death at the hands of the man they served.

Amaleigh shut out the voices in her head that would incite her to treason. *Find the king. Kill him. Avenge your mother and father.*

Killing Heshen would bring a momentary sense of satisfaction, but then what? She wasn't certain this new Gwilym be any better of a king than Heshen. There were no guarantees Heshen's death would change anything. Bloody royals. What did she care who was on the throne of Eidyn? She'd left the city for a damn good reason. Her place wasn't here anymore. The dragonlings needed her, and she had a good life on Cilachaem.

A jag of pain ripped across her chest, and she heaved in a strangled breath. Avenging her mother and father wouldn't bring them back, but maybe, just maybe, she could bring the Gwilym she knew back from wherever he was hiding in the cruel prince. Then, she could leave Eidyn knowing they had a caring ruler on the throne.

What mattered most was that the people of Eidyn lived in peace and prosperity. They should have celebrations of life instead of the Purge celebrations that commemorated death. No matter where her travels took her, Eidyn was her home. A part of her would always remain there. She paused in front of a tall door. Her affection for a city she thought she hated surprised her. She placed a hand on the darkly stained wood to support herself. The revelation rocked her to the core.

For seven years, she'd told herself she was better off being far from Eidyn. A tendril of truth unraveled in her mind. She'd missed the city. Even missed Antonio and the urchins—a dysfunctional family at best, but better than nothing. As sad as it was, she'd had a home here. And she'd had Gwilym.

Her breathing quickened, and she rolled her lips between her teeth. She hadn't imagined the vision. Gwilym *had* called out to her. She just had to sort out why and if he had, then who was pretending to be the prince? The puzzle pieces swirled in her mind, elusive to her grasp. She'd figure it out, but needed help.

The library door swung open with a comforting whoosh, and she stepped inside the familiar space. She and Gwilym had spent hour upon hour there, huddled behind stacks of books. It was their refuge—him from the demands of being a prince, and her from the hostile city outside the palace.

A soft glow emanated from a cabinet to her right. She tried valiantly to ignore it, but the pull was too great. The magic surrounding the display cabinet called to her like a parent their child. She reached a finger to touch the threads and hesitated. The last time she'd been in this room, it was to return the dagger she'd stolen. The magic hadn't harmed her then, but would it now?

Back then, she didn't know she was descended from two mages, nor had she discovered her own power. Since letting her magic free, would the barrier around the cabinet look on her as a friend or a foe? It wasn't worth the risk.

She lowered her hand to her side and gazed at the weapons on display. Each of them had belonged to high-ranking officials in King Heshen's court. Each of them had been used to slaughter their owners—by King Heshen's hand. He'd systematically murdered every mage who had trusted him. Her hands shook with silent fury. Her jaw clenched and nostrils flared. Hatred flowed through her veins.

Centered in the display of jewel-encrusted daggers, knives, axes, and swords, one spot was conspicuously empty. The dagger she stole—her father's dagger—should be there. All she had to do was reach out and it would appear. For now, it would stay hidden.

She turned from the cabinet and let her eyes adjust to the dimness of the library while her breathing slowed and her heart rate mellowed. Anger wouldn't bring her parents back. Impotent rage wouldn't punish the king.

Heavy curtains blocked the moonlight, but mages had a way of seeing even in the darkest of places. A scent drifted to her, the same citrusy floral as the shampoo Cassia had used, but the smell didn't come from Amaleigh's hair. A slow inhale brought other odors—mustiness from the library, dirt brought in on someone's shoe, and the unmistakable acidic smell of wine. She was not alone.

Two options presented themselves: leave at once, or stay and see who her companion was. She chose the latter. Whoever hid in the darkness, they didn't know she knew they were there, and had lost the element of surprise. If they were curious about the information she sought, they would be mightily disappointed.

Stacks of books rose from the carpeted floor, piled high up to a vaulted ceiling. She knew exactly where the book she sought was, but with the newfound complication of a silent witness, it would be best if she at least pretended to search for it. The first shelf held books for reading pleasure. These she skimmed, and chose a few that looked interesting. Depending on her length of stay, they might provide comfort during the long nights.

Five shelves down, she found the book she sought and pulled it from its place just at arm's reach. Heavier than she remembered, the once-smooth leather cover was now stained and cracked. It had been one of the few books she and Gwilym studied again and again. Within the pages were maps and catalogs and listings of every kingdom of the whole of Nasus, the world Eidyn belonged to.

She took the tome to a chair and used a match kept in a silver jar next to a group of thick candles to give her light. It would've been a simple thing to light the wicks with her magic, but that might draw attention. Whoever was in the library was trying very hard not to breathe hard, much less make any sound, but she sensed their presence. Now that she knew someone lurked, she kept an awareness of them in her mind.

The pages made a nice fluttering sound when she opened

the book. She spread her hands wide and smoothed the edges. It had been ages since she held a book in her hands. The sensation was really quite like nothing else. After a moment of inhaling the book's essence, she searched for the section on Aenglebreck first. Her aim was to refresh her memory about the elven kingdom, but not until she'd left a trail of misdirection. If her silent companion was a mage, it would be easy enough to follow where she'd read in the book. It wouldn't even take a spell, just a single thought and every page Amaleigh touched would be highlighted for their perusal.

A devilish grin accompanied a soft snort. It would serve them right if she touched every fucking page in the book. She wouldn't be quite that cruel, but she did read several unnecessary chapters and made sure she left her imprint on enough other pages that her companion would have a hard time deciphering exactly what she was looking for. If she thought she wouldn't be disturbed in her room, she would've taken the book with her, but the library provided quiet and relative privacy, her silent companion notwithstanding.

By the time she finished, the sun peeked from beneath the heavy drapes. She set the book aside and stretched, yawning loudly in the process to give her companion a chance to rouse themselves in case they'd dozed off. She slid the book into its place and gathered the few smaller novels on her way out. As she passed a darkened corner, the scent of shampoo drifted to her, and she resisted the urge to look into the shadows.

They were still there, watching her. It really should've unnerved her more than it did. Her calm acceptance that someone might stalk her was more alarming than the actual fact that she was being watched. Whoever it was, she didn't perceive them as a threat.

The thought puzzled in her mind as she left the room. Several sleepy servants scuttled out of her way, and she smiled to each one in turn. Being a morning person, she never understood people's reluctance to greet the day with the sun's rise.

At the first hallway, she turned sharply and pressed herself against the wall. With any luck, the mystery person would leave the library, and she could put a face to her silent companion. It might be the same person who visited her room in the middle of the night—the scent of her shampoo wasn't a coincidence. She lifted a braid to her nose and sniffed. Citrus and a powdery floral. Not something she would've chosen for herself, but nice in a fresh kind of way.

The library door opened and a booted foot stuck out. A moment later, Gwilym exited, looking up and down the hallway, eyes narrowed.

Amaleigh turned and fled to her rooms before he saw her. Questions crammed into her skull with dizzying speed. Why the pox would Gwilym be sneaking into her room? Whether or not he had recognized her, why not just wake her? And what's up with the shampoo? Did he douse himself with it?

She tossed the books on the bed and flopped onto her back. The answers would have to wait. She had more pressing matters to consider. Namely, Princess Cassia. Or rather, Cassia's real home—the kingdom of Aerithilyn. The elven kingdom had once been Eidyn's greatest ally. Relations grew frosty with the old king—Heshen's father, and completely severed after the Purge.

She closed her eyes and placed her hands over her heart. *What have you gotten me into, Gwilym?*

In the silence of her room, she heard the irregular, rattling heartbeat of someone close to death.

Amaleigh. You've come.

I'm here, Gwilym. At the palace. Where are you?

Cold. Dark.

His wheeze choked her mind. She sat up and stared at the

cold fireplace. Sounds from the palace came to her, but inside her skull went still.

Gwilym?

For a long while, she perched on her bed, ready, but he didn't answer.

CHAPTER
TWENTY-ONE

The street leading to the docks was crowded, more so than it should've been so early in the day. Amaleigh scanned the faces of those she passed, noting downcast eyes and grimly set lips. In all her years as a thief, she'd never seen the people of Eidyn this despondent. She cocked her head to better hear, but all that came to her were mumblings and grunts.

The buildings themselves looked the same, if a little shabbier. In her absence, the city hadn't changed; the people had. Where before there existed a pulse of excitement—of pride, even—now she sensed an undercurrent of apprehension. She kept her body alert, her mind attuned to those around her.

She rounded the corner and glanced toward the harbor, hopeful. If Danteneux was in port, he might have information not only regarding the change in Eidyn, but about Gwilym and the king. The scurrilous pirate had vital insight into the city, and probably all the surrounding kingdoms. His public display of being a legitimate businessman didn't fool her. She'd helped him with too many of his seedier dealings to think he'd changed much in seven years.

The *Sundancer* bobbed on the morning tide, and Amaleigh breathed a sigh of relief. Getting aboard wouldn't be a problem. Convincing Danteneux to help her, while not showing her true face, would be.

She ducked her head and scrambled up the gangplank to the deck without any interference from those coming and going. At the top, however, a shortish man with ginger hair and a full, bushy beard put out a hand to stop her.

"Eh there, lass. Where do ya think yer going, eh? No women allowed aboard the *'Dancer.*"

Amaleigh narrowed her eyes and settled her feet shoulder-width apart. Her fists balled on her hips as she glared at the man. "If that isn't the most asinine, sexist bullshit I've ever heard! No women? Why? Are you afraid we might be better sailors than you?" Her gaze dipped to his crotch, and she chuckled. "Or are you worried we might steal your bedmates each night?"

"You little harpy!" He raised his hand as if to strike, and she braced to defend herself.

"Eaman! What the clunge you doing, man? We don't hit people. Especially ladies. Remember what we talked about." Dante strode across the deck, stopping a foot in front of the man, who was literally frothing at the mouth.

Dots of white bubbled at the corners of his lips, and Amaleigh's stomach churned at the sight. So much rage for such a small man.

"Ye told me to use me words, Cap'n." Eaman dropped his hand to his side. "She ain't no lady, though." He huffed off, muttering curses that Amaleigh clearly heard.

She tucked a few new-to-her words away for later. She thought she'd heard them all during her years as a thief, but Eaman's lexicon of swear words was impressive.

"You must forgive Eaman. He comes from a land that's, shall we say, not as liberated as Eidyn."

"Liberal. I think you mean liberal. Liberated would intimate the people have been freed from something."

A wide smile broke across his face, and he winked with a cocky tilt of his head. "I knew a lass once, used to talk me silly about the right words. She disappeared many years ago, though. You remind me of her."

"I hope that's a good thing?" Amaleigh held out her hand. "I'm called Erma."

"Erma, eh? I'm Danteneux." He held her hand for a moment too long and she feared he might kiss her fingers like a proper gentleman. Then she'd know Eidyn had well and truly lost its damn mind. "How can I be of service?"

Amaleigh removed her hand from his grip and glanced at the sailors milling about. "Is there somewhere private we can talk?"

Dante eyed her like a fighter sizing up his opponent. "I don't see any weapons on you, but that doesn't mean you don't have a dagger hidden in your bag."

Now it was Amaleigh's turn to smile. Fucking Dante. Of course he saw through her disguise. He was one of the rare creatures who listened when people spoke—usually to use their words against them later. In truth, she was relieved he knew who she really was. It would make negotiations much smoother.

"I have no weapons, I promise." She held up her hands and turned in a slow circle. Dante's appreciative whistle made her cheeks warm.

He led them to his quarters and locked the door behind him. "I never thought I'd see you again."

"And you haven't. If anyone discovered I'd returned..." She

left the words hanging. He knew the cost of her being in Eidyn more than anyone. How many times had he tried to get her to leave with him? To be part of his crew or to just get out of the city. More times than she could count.

He closed the space between them and her heart beat in her throat, making it hard to swallow the lump of—what? Fear? Anxiety? Lust? Damn the man. He wrapped her in a hug and although she didn't exactly rebuff his embrace, she didn't cling to him, either. She settled for a quick squeeze and pat on his back. He pulled away with that cocky grin of his that melted all the ladies' hearts. Fortunately, not hers.

"It's been awhile, Ama—Erma." His fingertips rose to his lips, and his tongue lashed out to lick their tips. "The last I saw of you was when you kissed me in exchange for selling your dagger."

She pushed his chest hard until he backed up a few steps. Despite his audaciousness, she suppressed a chuckle. "You stole that kiss and you know it. I'd never willingly kiss the likes of you." She wiped her mouth with the back of her hand to prove the point.

"Well, I am a pirate."

The growl in his voice sent a stupid giddiness whipping through her belly.

"You pretend to be cold-hearted, but I feel your heat. Can smell your...curiosity."

She cursed beneath her breath, but it lacked conviction. The scoundrel was the only person to have that effect on her. It wasn't that she fancied him, not in the least—unless she'd like to contract an array of sexually transmitted diseases—but he had a certain charm that even she found hard to resist. Her lips burned at the memory of the kiss he'd given her. Stolen from her. She didn't give permission for the kiss, nor had he asked.

Stop it. No thinking of Dante's lips, or that kiss, or his mighty fine ass.

He blinked, and the air in the cabin shifted. His shoulders relaxed, and he leaned against a table as if they discussed the day's menu. It was part of his allure, and ever so infuriating. The worst part was that it wasn't magic, which he didn't have to begin with. Oh no, the seductive sultriness was all Danteneux.

She took a long, slow breath to clear her thoughts. She released her mask, more of a sign of trust than anything else. He knew it was her beneath the disguise and, if only for a few minutes, she wanted to be Amaleigh again, wholly and completely with her friend.

The way his eyes widened and the slow nod of his head half made her want to put the mask back, but the damage was done. She'd come to him wearing a face that wasn't hers and yet he'd guessed it was her. That mask didn't come from thin air—he had to know she possessed magic.

"I'm risking everything by revealing myself. I hope my trust isn't misplaced. Do I have your word you won't tell anyone you've seen me?"

Dante spit into his palm and held it out for her to shake. She hid her grimace and clapped her hand to his.

"I swear to you on the pirate's code, I'll take your secrets to my grave."

"Thank you." She wrapped a thread of her magic around their hands to seal his word. If he broke it, he'd suffer mightily.

He wiped his hand on his vest with narrowed eyes. "It's probably too late for an apology, but I lost the dagger. I woke up the next morning and it was gone. Tore my ship and crew apart looking for it, but it vanished." He dragged his fingers through his dark hair and exhaled slowly. Cracks edged his eyes when he squinted. He looked tired. Still handsome, but the years had worn on him. "By the time I returned to Eidyn, you were also long gone. Antonio said you were told to kill the prince, and when you failed, he sent men after you. I even dispatched some of my most trusted men into the city looking for you, but you'd vanished."

"You risked pissing off Antonio for me? I didn't know you cared, Dante." She really didn't. They'd always had a grudging friendship, but didn't think he was capable of true affection. Like herself.

"You know I care. What happened to you, Ama—Erma? Where did you go? And why come back now?"

Amaleigh took a long drag of breath and settled her shoulders. "I had no plans to return. The night Antonio sent me to kill the prince, I couldn't do it. I might be a lot of things, but I'm not a murderer. I had to run." She couldn't tell him about Cornelius or being a full mage. Not yet.

"Where have you been this whole time? I sent out feelers at each port I stopped in, but no one had seen a crimson-haired waif. I had no idea you'd matured into such a beauty." He stroked a long braid. "I like the new look."

"Thanks. I think. It doesn't matter where I was or why. I'm only back because I think the prince is in trouble."

"Why would you want to help him, of all people?" He snorted and tugged her braid.

She winced and removed her hair from his grip.

Dante didn't know her history with Gwilym or that Heshen had butchered her family. He knew as much as she'd allowed him to know. Which was how she'd kept all her acquaintances —at arm's length. All of them except Gwilym. If she'd known he was the son of the man who killed her family, everything would be different. But she hadn't known, and now she couldn't turn her back on him. But how could she explain her reasons to Dante without giving away too much?

He sat in a chair and leaned back with his arms crossed behind his head. Muscles bulged along his biceps, and she looked away.

"It's complicated."

He indicated a chair, and she took a seat. Exhaustion washed over her, and she rested her head in her palms. Dante took one of her hands and held it, his thumb stroking over her skin. It felt nice, familial in a way. She wanted to trust him, she really did, but lives were at stake and flox it all, she was so damned tired.

"You look like you could use a friend. I've never betrayed you before, and I won't now. What's going on, Erma?"

She leaned forward and gripped his hands from across the table. Maybe it was time to risk letting someone in, even if just a little. Antonio used to say a shared score benefits everyone. Not that it ever benefited her as much as him, but the sentiment might be the same for a shared worry. And Dante was right—he'd never betrayed her even when it might've been lucrative for him to do so. She nodded to herself and rolled imaginary dice. She'd find out soon enough whether her instinct was right.

"I don't know, truly. I had a vision, of the prince in torment, and he said he needed help. I'm just a girl, Dante. A thief. What can I do for a prince? I came back because I'd hoped maybe things had changed in Eidyn, but they haven't. The prince is at the palace—healthy and alive, from what I could see. Have you heard anything? Even the silliest thing might make a difference. Not just for the prince, but for all of Eidyn."

Dante rubbed the day's growth of stubble on his chin. Black hair hung across his forehead, down to his shoulders. He flicked a forefinger across his lips several times before shaking his head.

"I can't think of anything unusual. Antonio no longer runs the underground, so my spy network's not what it used to be."

"Antonio's still alive? He was a walking corpse when I left. How the flox is he still breathing? Who took over?"

"There was a coup after you left. Some of the upper lieutenants scrabbled among themselves and one came out victorious. A particularly nasty fellow called Gerzer."

"You're kidding me? He's an idiot."

"That's what he'd like you to think, but he's also wily and outwitted the others to overthrow Antonio. Took most of the urchins with him, and a goodly sum of Antonio's treasury. The old man was left to rot in his palatial manor."

Amaleigh processed what Dante said. Gerzer knew she had the dagger. Her leaving Eidyn without killing Gwilym might've allowed Gerzer to assume Antonio was weak. Or he'd been planning a coup already and the timing coincided. Either way, she had to be extra careful in the city. If Gerzer recognized her, he wouldn't hesitate to strike. To say they hated each other would be an understatement.

A thump behind her drew Dante's attention, and he scrambled to stand. "Cover up. We've got company."

Amaleigh drew the mask over her face and spun around to see a pair of grubby feet dart past a small round window. She and Dante raced up the stairs and reached the deck just as the urchin slipped over the side of the ship. She pivoted to follow, but Dante held her back.

"Follow that boy. I want to know where he goes and don't lose him," Dante directed one of the sailors. A moment later, he sprinted down the gangplank. To her, Dante whispered, "Patience, Erma. We don't know who sent that cub, but we can make an informed guess. You might be walking into a trap."

Barnacleballs, he was right. Amaleigh went to the side of the ship and tracked the urchin as he wove in and out of people.

There was no way the sailor could follow him. The urchins knew every escape route through sewers and back alleys. Within moments, he'd vanish. She flicked her wrist and sent a flare of magic toward the retreating back of the lad. Her power would allow her to follow him undetected. The presence of an urchin on Dante's ship could only mean one thing—either Antonio or Gerzer had sent him. The question was: were they spying on her, or Danteneux?

CHAPTER

TWENTY-TWO

Amaleigh waited several tense minutes until finally, the sailor reappeared alone. Dante slammed his fists on the railing and sputtered several curses. The sailor trotted up the gangplank, out of breath, and shook his head. Amaleigh knew he'd lose the urchin, but Dante had faith in his crewmember. She did her best to feign indifference. As soon as her business with Dante concluded, she'd follow the imp and uncover who was spying—and of whom.

"I'm sorry, Cap'n. He was too fast and too little. I lost him in the crowd." The sailor held his cap and bowed to Amaleigh. "M'lady."

Dante's snicker didn't go unnoticed, and the sailor looked from his boss back to her. When neither of them commented, he slunk away to do whatever chore he'd been doing before Dante commanded him to follow the boy. A cry from the bow of the ship drew their attention, and she looked up to see the nasty fellow who'd almost hit her stumble forward. Bright-red blood flowed from between his fingers and down his face.

"What the flox?" Dante strode to the man, and Amaleigh

followed. "Eaman, what in the name of the sea king happened?"

Eaman wobbled toward them, his face ashen. "Took me eye off the rope t' see what the commotion be about. Got snapped for me trouble. 'Tis nothing, Cap'n."

"Best take a look to be certain." Dante motioned for Eaman to follow him belowdecks.

Amaleigh hesitated a moment, then followed.

Prickles rose up Amaleigh's spine. It was an accident, nothing more. Yet the presence of the little spy on the ship followed by a strange mishap didn't sit well with her. She scanned the rest of the crew, noting how many men bustled around them. Ten in all. Had there been more? Less? Her senses went on full alert, and she balled her hands into fists to keep from blanketing the ship with a protective ward. Using the scant amount of power to follow the boy wouldn't be traceable, but a spell powerful enough to cast a ward would be felt by anyone with magical abilities.

The three of them crowded into the galley, and Eaman eyed her suspiciously. "What'n she here for?"

Amaleigh shushed him and instructed Dante to find a clean cloth. She'd seen the handiwork of too many ship captains and wagered her healing skills far surpassed Dante's. He handed her a reasonably clean strip of muslin, and she gently blotted the wound. Eaman shifted and groused, but she ignored him. The wound wasn't deep, but untreated could become infected.

"Do you have any cleaning spirits?" Before she finished her question, Dante handed her a bottle of clear liquid. She poured some onto the cleaner edge of the cloth and met Eaman's worried gaze. "This might sting."

"Jus' be done wit' it, woman."

He only flinched twice while she cleaned the wound. Before he could pull away, she ran a finger along the skin surrounding the cut. Her magic worked its way beneath the skin to begin knitting the wound together. A foreign sensation pulsed against her—not unfriendly, more like...inquisitive. She prodded deeper and sucked in a breath. A powerful ward suppressed Eaman's own magic.

Buried within the threads of his warding, she sensed his anguish and rage and feelings of impotence. She ran her fingers over the no longer bleeding skin and infused his wound with healing strength. As long as he didn't bump his head, he'd heal with barely a mark.

Eaman felt along his forehead. His scowl slowly faded to a look of wonder, then apprehension. "What did ye do t' me, woman?"

Amaleigh put a hand on Eaman's shoulder, and he flinched from her touch. She dropped her hands at her side and stepped away from him to appear less frightening.

"Who warded you, Eaman?"

He crossed his arms and jutted his chin at her in defiance.

"Was someone close to you a mage?" She wouldn't be deterred. Eaman had magic swirling in his blood. Magic that someone tried to hide.

Both men gasped, and Dante reached behind her to close the galley door.

"Are you trying to get us killed? You can't just ask someone that, *Erma.*"

"I'm sorry. It's important. Please, Eaman, I need to know."

He looked to his captain before answering. When Dante nodded, Eaman sunk into his chair and nodded grimly. "Me nan. She were powerful, all right. When t' king had the Purge, she was killed with the rest of 'em. Me mam took us far away so's we wouldn't be killed too. It weren't fair. Me nan was kind and gentle." Tears welled in his eyes and all signs of the brute who almost smacked her vanished. He wiped his eyes with the same cloth she'd used to clean his wound.

She put her hand on his forearm. "I'm sorry, truly I am."

They shared a look and in that brief moment, Amaleigh felt Eaman's heartache as if it were her own. Perhaps it was hers—they shared losing a loved one to the Purge. Except, Amaleigh didn't remember her parents. Clearly, Eaman's memories of his nan were still fresh. It might've been her power Amaleigh sensed in his wards. Her last act was to protect the grandson she loved. Tears shimmered in her eyes, and she let them fall. For Eaman, his nan, her family, and for all the others who still suffered because of King Heshen's Purge.

Eaman shuffled out of the galley, and Dante wiped her tears with his thumb. "What's going on, Erma? I can't ever recall a time I saw you cry."

"It's all so senseless. The Purge, I mean." She glanced around the small kitchen and shrugged. "How many others are there like Eaman? Warded to hide their magic, living in fear of being discovered. Now I know why he's so angry."

"Not once in all the years I knew you did I suspect you for a mage, but here you are concealing your true self and healing my crewman. What happened when you were gone?"

"That's a story for another time. I have more pressing concerns right now."

"Ah, yes. The bewildering prince and his mysterious request."

"I see your flair for the dramatic hasn't improved. How long will you be in port?"

"About two weeks."

They left the crowded galley to return topside. Amaleigh breathed in the salty air and stretched her head from side to side. How much had the little spy seen? Did he glimpse her face, her real face? What of her hair? Certainly, he saw ruby braids and not the dullish brown she now wore. It was entirely possible the urchin wasn't spying for either Antonio or Gerzer. She peered at the horizon toward Aenglebreck.

"What do you know about Princess Cassia?"

Dante's smile widened, stretching his tanned skin. His deep-brown eyes sparkled, and Amaleigh groaned. Such a slut. It was nice to know some people hadn't changed in her absence.

"Now that's a woman I might give up the sea for. Comes from Aenglebreck, been here six months or so. I wager she's got a bid to wed the prince, but there's been no rumors, so who can say? Those ladies of hers." He whistled between closed teeth. "I'd take them all to bed."

"Seriously, Dante, you'd bed anything with breasts and a pussy."

"You wound me! I do have standards, you know."

Her snort was answered with a glare from the scoundrel.

"Well, at least you have the good sense not to fall for my charms." His eyebrow raised in silent challenge, and she laughed at how ridiculous he could be.

"Is it any wonder why? I'm surprised your dick doesn't fall off from disease or overuse!" She turned to leave, and he put a hand on her forearm.

"Be careful. This Gerzer fellow's not right in the head. King Heshen refused to make the same concessions to him that he had with Antonio, and Gerzer's never forgiven him for it."

Amaleigh considered his words. "Do you think he's angry enough to kidnap the prince and king?"

"You mean like for ransom?"

"I mean like for revenge."

"Are they missing?"

Amaleigh shook her head. "I'm not sure."

Dante leaned in close, and the air around them vibrated with suppressed tension.

Anxiety—his. The scent of sweat and resin filled her nose, and she inhaled without thinking. Her eyes rested on his broad chest. The top two buttons of his shirt were open, revealing a patch of dark curls.

He took a braid between his fingertips. "You smell good." His action reminded her of Gwilym snooping in her room. An involuntary shudder wormed its way across her skin.

"Imprinting my scent for later?" She meant it to sound joking, but that's what Gwilym might've been doing.

"Just trying to remember why we never got together."

"Because you're a whore and I'm incapable of love."

He smoothed several braids from her face and smiled. "I don't believe that for a second. You're just scared of caring because of your past. I can respect that."

"Thank you, Dante." She reached up and kissed his cheek. "Please, if anyone comes looking for me, let me know? I don't know how you saw through my mask, but if others can, I'm in danger."

"When aren't you in some sort of trouble?" His laughter rumbled from his chest and tickled her ear. "Where are you staying? I'll get word if I hear of anything about you, or involving the prince and king."

They stood on the deck, with others milling about. She glanced nervously at the sailors. Any one of them could be a spy. Hell, Eaman knew she had magic, but she also knew he was warded. Hopefully, their respective secrets would keep her safe.

She bit her lip with indecision. "I'm at the palace, which complicates matters. They know me as Erma Kielder."

Again, he whistled. "The palace? I'd love to hear the story of how that came about."

"One of these days I'll tell you the whole sordid tale over a pint. You're buying, of course." She grinned and pinched his cheek.

He took her hand in his. "For what it's worth, I didn't recognize you by your looks. Still don't." His gaze drifted to her hair and down to her lips. "If you passed me on the street, I would've appreciated a pretty woman, nothing more. But that sass...that, I recognized. I suppose it was wishful thinking. Since that damn dagger disappeared, and then you were gone—" He paused to press her palm to his cheek. "I thought I'd somehow gotten you killed."

Her heartbeat flipped a moment, and her vision clouded. Not from his touch, which admittedly wasn't as terrible as she pretended, but from the honesty of his words. He wasn't being a braggart or smooth to get his way. She had the sense he spoke from his heart and that wasn't something she expected.

"I'm sorry I left you with questions. I didn't have time for goodbyes." She met his concerned gaze and held it. In the depth of his dark eyes, she saw how much her disappearance had affected him and was truly sorry. She'd been selfish to leave without a word.

"Consider it forgotten. Will you be here long?" He kissed her palm once more before releasing her hand.

"I'm not sure. I'll say a proper farewell this time, though."

His grin matched hers. "You better, but not before I get the whole story. Now, scram." He shooed her toward the gangplank with a pretend kick to her ass.

She'd love to sit with him at the Shoogly Dragon and hear all about his adventures and share her own. But not yet. Not until she found out who sent the urchin spy and what, if anything, that had to do with Gwilym. As she trotted down the gangplank, she felt Dante's gaze on her back. She'd taken a huge risk trusting him, and only time would tell whether she'd made the wrong call. Her instinct told her she hadn't, that Dante would keep his promise...but like everything else in Eidyn, Dante might be putting on a façade and not be exactly as he appeared.

CHAPTER

TWENTY-THREE

Amaleigh followed the urchin's trail until it disappeared behind a pile of rubbish in a narrow alley. She knew that hidey-hole. Had used it many times growing up. A nostalgic grin settled on her lips. At least this, too, hadn't changed. She wished she could say the same for the rest of Eidyn.

The shabbiness she first saw on the way to the harbor increased the farther away from the palace she ventured. Eidyn was laid out like a web, with the palace in the center and six districts stretching outward. The manors closest to the palace belonged to the wealthiest citizens. Even though the elite only lived within the boundaries of their district, they were happy to claim every square block of land surrounding the palace grounds as their places of worship, businesses, and university.

Unlike other palaces Amaleigh had seen on her travels, Eidyn's rulers didn't live behind a wall or upon a high hill. She tapped her cheek in thought. It would take a strong ruler to live in the open, or a feared king. Or... Her mind whipped through possibilities, with one coming to the forefront of her thoughts. The palace was protected by an invisible force. Perhaps even a magical ward. She let her imagination soar and a vision came to her of dragons flying over the palace: wings spread wide, their scales glittering in the setting sun.

Dragon magic. More powerful than humans, dragons could easily protect the palace. Yet another reason it made zero sense that Heshen would slaughter them.

A tingling washed along her skin, and goose bumps raised the hairs on her arms. Her dragon shifted, and she *felt* her. Could almost put out a hand and touch her. A barrier prevented her from reaching the dragon, but she knew she was there, desperate to be unleashed. Equally as frustrated as Amaleigh. Even if it killed her, she'd find a way to destroy the invisible wall separating them.

She checked her surroundings, confident she was alone, and ducked behind a stack of barrels. Eyes closed, she concentrated on her dragon and coaxed her out. In her mind, she saw the abalone-colored snout, could feel the warmth of her dragon's breath. So close. Just a little more and they'd connect. She extended her mind further into the invisible wall and sensed it flexing with her effort. The dragon snuffled and pushed toward her, but the barrier kept them apart.

Her heart thudded in her chest, but it wasn't alone. Two heartbeats. Excited anticipation shot through her veins and she stretched harder, ignoring the jolts of pain in her brain. She could scarcely breathe. This was the closest she'd ever come to reaching her physical dragon on purpose. This wasn't casting. Nor was it some ghostly image of her dragon. If she could just break through the barrier, she could shift into her dragon and they'd both be free.

Her ears rang and blood trickled from her nose with the effort. One last push. The invisible wall snapped taut, and she was flung backward into a hard wall. Her head cracked on the stones and stars lit from behind her eyelids. Tears rushed to fill her eyes and overflow across her cheeks.

The loss of her dragon presence was worse than any injury she suffered. Her mind was achingly empty. Nothing but a dark expanse of loneliness met her thoughts.

She leaned against the wall, grateful for the barrels that hid her from view. For several minutes she remained there, silently mourning the loss of the connection and simultaneously cursing whatever force kept her from becoming who she truly was—an Aerlghot dragon shifter.

Her anger drifted to Eaman, and icy tentacles reached into the soft places of her heart and mind. Only a powerful mage could block her from reaching her dragon. A horrible thought set its hooks into her mind, and she shuddered against it. She could be warded, the same as Eamon. That would account for why only the simplest magic came easy to her and everything else she had to work hard to achieve. It would explain everything. If only she knew who would ward her. Or why. Or even when. Her parents might've the night of the Purge, but they'd had no warning. No time to protect her or her brother.

She rubbed her temples and then wiped her face with the edge of her tunic. There was, however, someone else she could think of who might possibly benefit from her being warded. Antonio. If he knew who her parents were, and there was a good chance he did considering Cornelius had left her with him, then he'd want her magical abilities hidden. No sense having the king snooping around his business any more than necessary. And finding a witch to ward a kid would've been no problem for Antonio. His contacts were vast and varied. He was a man who bartered in secrets. She could only guess what it would cost to perform something that illegal, but Antonio always got what he wanted. One way or another.

Amaleigh set her sights toward the elite part of the city. If Gerzer took over Antonio's business, then maybe the dethroned king of the urchins would be more amenable to give her answers. The last time she went to Antonio's lavish home, she was ordered to kill Gwilym. Gerzer had been there, hulking like a lapdog over Antonio. She'd been wrong to dismiss Gerzer so easily then; she wouldn't make the same mistake again.

The overgrown yard and battered shutters were a far cry from the opulence the manor once held. Amaleigh sighed at the front gate. Still lovely but worn. Tired. Like her, perhaps. Although, she'd never thought of herself as particularly lovely. Mildly attractive, perhaps, but no great beauty. Definitely tired, though.

Constantly running from one world to another left her depleted. Cornelius had promised not so long ago that they were safe, they needn't run from King Heshen or Antonio anymore, but she'd been too afraid to stop. And now, she was about to walk into the same man's home who had threatened unspeakable pain the last time she saw him.

She wasn't the same scrawny thief who had left his home trembling, faced with the task of killing her only friend or submit to being Antonio's possession for the rest of her life.

Nor was she the parentless orphan she'd believed herself to be. She couldn't bring her mother and father back, but at least now she knew who they were, and the positions they'd once held at Heshen's court. Antonio couldn't hurt her with his callous words.

She set her shoulders and pushed open the gate. It creaked loud enough to cause a neighboring dog to bark. There was no turning back. If Antonio had heard, he knew someone was coming and would be prepared. Hell, he probably knew she was coming when she turned the corner. As far as spies went, he was the best. He'd deny being a spy, of course, but nothing happened in Eidyn without Antonio knowing.

Amaleigh knocked on the front door and tried to settle her thoughts. She willed calm to her buzzing belly and knotted her hands into fists, then unclenched them, only to repeat the clench and release several more times.

The door opened and a haggard-looking woman peered from the darkness into the day's sun. "What you want?"

"I'm here to see Antonio. My name is Erma Kielder. He won't remember me, but I was an associate of his long ago."

"You were what? Eh, never mind. Follow me." The door widened, and the woman scratched her ass as she turned toward the large foyer.

A chandelier hung overhead, its crystals missing or broken. Half-melted candles clung to their pots or hung precariously to the side. An acrid stench assaulted her nostrils, and she breathed as shallow as possible to avoid gagging. Feces, urine, and garbage lined the walls of Antonio's little palace.

The woman grabbed the banister and used it to haul her slight frame up the stairs one at a time. Amaleigh followed, desperate for the woman to hurry so they could be out of the filth. Whatever staff stayed loyal to Antonio, they weren't earning their keep.

They reached the top of the stairs and turned toward Antonio's audience chamber. She'd been in that room more times than she could remember, and never for anything good. Her stomach churned at the thought of entering it again. This manor should've been a place of refuge, where her found family resided, but instead it was a symbol of the abusive institution she'd been forced into. From the depths of darkness where she shoved her bitterness and hate, a sliver of acrimony slid along her thoughts.

Cornelius had been the one to leave her with Antonio. All the logic in the world didn't make it easier to forget that he could've taken her with him to whatever world he'd escaped to, but instead, he left a confused and frightened three-year-old with a psychopath. She dug her nails into her palm and reminded herself that Cornelius did the best he could in a terrible situation. Her anger shouldn't be with him, but Antonio.

A silent mantra played on repeat through her mind. She was a strong, capable woman. Antonio couldn't hurt her anymore. She was a mage. A dragon shifter. Powerful.

Despite her own words, the child she'd been when Antonio trained her to be a thief was still present. That fearful girl who dared defy the king of urchins lurked alongside the independent woman Amaleigh had become. They were one and the same.

Nothing could have prepared Amaleigh for the shock of Antonio's appearance. A cadaver had more life in it than did her ex-tormentor. Sunken, watery eyes watched her as she approached. No recognition shone from them, for which she was grateful. His chalky lips trembled, but no sound came out.

"This here lady says she be needing to speak at you." The woman flung a hand toward Amaleigh. Having done her part, she flopped onto a couch, as if the effort had been too much.

"Who you?" Antonio's hands shook violently as he tried to lift a cup to his lips.

Amaleigh watched with attempted impassivity. Dark liquid sloshed over the rim to puddle on the table. More out of irritation than any genuine desire to help, she placed her hands around his to steady the tremors. The chill of his flesh stunned her, but she didn't recoil.

He drank noisily, slopping most of the liquid onto his shirt.

A vicious grunt indicated he was finished, and he pushed his hands toward the table. "Can do it meself."

Amaleigh sat in the chair opposite, ignoring Antonio's angry harrumphs. He blinked toward her, but not at her. A watery film covered his eyes, giving them an eerie incandescence. As if light burned from inside his skull. He turned from her direction and glanced over the banister toward the street. She doubted he saw anything happening below them. If he wasn't completely blind, he was nearly there.

Amaleigh considered this new information. Without his sight, he wouldn't notice the filth surrounding him, but certainly he could smell it. She leaned forward and rested her arms on the table. "I'm looking for someone, and I heard you were the person to seek if I need to be discreet."

The woman on the couch, who reclined with a forearm tossed over her eyes, shifted slightly. No doubt to better hear.

"It'll cost you. Information's not cheap." Antonio rubbed his forefinger and thumb together. "Gold feathers."

Amaleigh's chest tightened at the words. Fifty thousand gold feathers was the price Antonio had set for her freedom. An impossible sum. She'd often wondered whether it had all been a setup. King Heshen desired his son to be killed, and Antonio chose her as the assassin. He'd hoped she'd fail so that he would own her for the rest of her life. Or perhaps he'd hoped she'd succeed and the king would be forever in his debt. An easy bargain for Antonio to make. An impossible choice for Amaleigh. Neither option was one she could live with. Fortunately, Cornelius gave her a third choice—escape.

"How much?" She wouldn't let him sense how much those two words had rocked her core. She repeated her mantra and stiffened her resolve.

"Depends on what you looking for." He leaned forward and wheezed with the effort.

The pungent smell of eirislip hit her like a punch. It was a miracle he still lived. That drink was pure poison, and he'd been sipping it for as long as she could remember. Made using the entrails of dragons, the fermentation process alone was enough to cause permanent damage.

A wail came from somewhere in the manor, and Amaleigh sat up straight, senses on full alert. "What was that?"

The woman bolted from the couch to stand behind Antonio. She rubbed his arms and cooed into his ear as if he were a baby. The look she gave Amaleigh said she'd best drop it.

Like hell she would.

Another cry echoed through the rooms, followed by several more, accompanied with gruesome thumps. Someone was being beaten. More memories flooded through her mind, threatening to drown her. She'd been beaten too many times to count in this very house. By the very man who sat before her. Sometimes for infractions worthy of a whipping, other times for no reason at all—simply for Antonio's enjoyment.

She half stood, ready to blow the house to ashes. Her magic swirled with ferocious intent, more so than she'd ever encountered before. Fuck the laws banning magic. If she was caught and punished, it would be worth it. The astonished look on Antonio's face stopped her.

His head swiveled in her direction, his focus somewhere near her shoulder. "You hear it, too. Don'tcha? I tole 'em. I did. I says something ain't right here, but theys tell me I'm crazy. I hear things." Antonio tapped his head and nodded. "Thems the crazy ones."

"It's just the house settlin', my love. Nothing to worry yerself about." The woman bent low and turned Antonio's face to hers. She opened her mouth and covered his with her lips.

Amaleigh turned away to keep from seeing more. Her stomach was already upset enough. She steadied herself against the table. Clearly, something was going on that someone didn't want Antonio to know about. Her mind kept spinning to Gwilym and his father, and each time, a pit sank deeper in her heart. It was most likely some random urchin being beaten.

But what if it wasn't?

After all, Cornelius had hidden her with Antonio because it was the last place anyone in the palace would look. Maybe things hadn't changed so much in that regard. The question was—who would use Antonio as a scapegoat if they wanted to kidnap and torture the king and his son? Only one man was foolish enough to try.

Amaleigh looked the woman full in the face. "Where's Gerzer?"

Fire flashed through her eyes, and her lips flattened.

Antonio's hands flailed and his jaw worked with agitation. Spittle formed at the corners of his lips. "That whoreson stole what's mine. He took her, and she was mine. Mine. I'll kill him with my bare hands if he shows his face."

"Ain't no one here by that name. I think it's past time you leave." The venom in the woman's expression and tone would've felled a lesser foe.

"Took whom?" She ignored the woman and asked Antonio directly.

"Amaleigh."

Antonio sighed her name, and her legs buckled. She steadied herself against the table to keep from falling.

"I waited all night for her to return. That whoreson stole her before I had a chance. She failed me. She was mine."

Despite the wobble in her legs and bile in her throat, Amaleigh feigned ignorance and asked the woman, "Who's Amaleigh?"

"Some bitch who stole from Antonio. Disappeared the night

she was supposin' to finish a job for him. Piece of shite, if you ask me."

Well, no one asked her, and Amaleigh didn't like her tone. An overwhelming desire to flame her ass, and Antonio's, rushed through her blood. She gripped the table to keep from losing control.

The sound of men arguing came from the hallway, and terror crossed the woman's face. "You ought not to be here. Theys won't be happy to find an associate of Antonio's in the house."

"I'll show myself out." She turned to go, but Antonio grabbed her by the wrist. She struggled against his grip, but it was strong despite his age and frail appearance. "Let go of me."

He brought her hand to his face and sniffed along her skin. She gagged against his touch and jerked her hand away. The bemused smile on lips lingered in her mind as she hurried from the room and down the stairs. Whatever the hell had that been, she pulled her focus away from him and slowed, being careful not to encounter anyone.

At the landing on the ground floor she paused. Her attention tugged toward the back of the house, and she took two steps in that direction, only to be stopped by the sound of more men coming from the dark hallway. They might be Antonio's goons, or Gerzer's; either way, they were trouble she didn't need.

As she twisted the doorknob, she whispered a spell that would allow her to enter unnoticed later. She'd wait until dark, then return to see who was being beaten—and who held the whip. An unusual tingling started in her hands and traveled up her arms. She rubbed herself, unsure whether it was her use of magic—tiny though it was—that caused the discomfort.

Nothing in Antonio's house *felt* spelled, nor did she detect any magic nearby, but magic could be warped for deception.

Which could mean, either someone in the house possessed power and was skilled at hiding it, or there *was* a spell on Antonio's manor but it was cloaked somehow. Either way, she had to be extra careful. If another mage were in residence, she was in deep shit.

CHAPTER
TWENTY-FOUR

Screams ripped through the walls to where Gwilym hunched in the corner. His father couldn't take much more, but the men came anyway. Even when Gwilym offered to take the beating in his father's place, they dragged the half-conscious king down the hall to where they'd set up a mini-torture chamber.

Each time they took him out, Gwilym memorized how many steps it took to get to the stairs, and how many steps up to the ground floor. He counted the doors on each side of the hallways and planned how he'd carry his father to safety. Then the beatings would commence and all energy needed to free them would evaporate until the next time he had a chance to rest and recover.

The daily beatings were carried out at irregular intervals—most likely to keep him and his father from regaining too much strength. Or, and this terrified him more than any other thought, whenever the abductors were bored, they'd come for Gwilym or his father just to have some fun. One thing Gwilym had learned during his captivity was his jailers loved inflicting pain.

Fucking sadists.

He recounted the steps in his mind, planning yet again how he'd get his father to freedom. He held onto the hope that if he could free his father, and they both recovered, then King Heshen would be the ruler Eidyn needed. He could reverse the damage done by the Purge and forge a way forward for Gwilym's reign. The easy answer would be to leave his father to rot in the cellar and escape on his own; then he could take the throne. But Gwilym never took the easy way out of anything. He wanted his father to atone for his heinous crimes and only then would Gwilym wear the crown and give the people of Eidyn peace. A fantasy, perhaps, but it kept his mind engaged and off the beatings.

Another cry was followed by a low moan and a loud thump. He could clearly visualize what tools they used to torture the king. Knew them intimately himself.

An argument sounded above him, and he cocked his head to better hear. Two, possibly three men squabbled. He couldn't make out complete sentences, but four words were repeated that caused him alarm: dispose of the bodies.

Chilling dread spiraled from the top of his head down his spine, tightening his chest and stifling his breaths. These men weren't interested in a ransom. This was far more serious than a random kidnapping.

Gwilym tugged at the rope binding his wrists. He was fairly certain the miscreant in charge of securing them had been a sailor. Only a seaman would use the intricate knots that held his hands together. He stared at the rope, willing it to burn.

A buzzing started in the back of his mind, and he sat straighter. Memories long buried wafted through his thoughts. He lay curled in his mother's arms, warm and safe in her embrace. The rumble of her chest tickled his ear as she sang lullabies. In those moments, he knew how very much he was loved.

Gwilym rocked as if he were still in his mother's arms and listened closely, delighting in the sound of her voice. The more she sang, he realized they weren't lullabies at all—they were spells. Spells his mother taught him when he was just a lad in short pants. Was it real? Or was he succumbing to madness? Did it matter?

More memories floated closer, of his father doting on them both. Etched in his memories was the concern his father felt when his queen would fly on her dragon with her warrior protector—Amaleigh's mother. He grasped at those memories, but they retreated to the darkness. He barely remembered his mother. She'd died when he was young, and his father had forbidden him from talking about her. Her soft voice echoed to him now, urging him to embrace all that he knew to be true.

Gods, but he missed her. Missed her laughter and her strength.

Let go, my son. The path before you is difficult, but will open if you have the courage to prevail.

Brilliant. A dead mother giving him advice. He was well and truly fucked.

Let go, she'd said. If only he knew how. Amaleigh would know. She was always brilliant at finding ways to ease his worries. Gwilym flopped against the wall, his bound hands useless in his lap.

The awful truth was, he had nothing left to lose. Might as well try. He breathed in and focused on those two words. *Let go.* Of fear, of expectation, of all the rules his father had hammered into his psyche.

He relaxed his hands and visualized a flame dancing along the threads of the rope that held him hostage. A moment later, a tendril of smoke rose from where he focused. Impossible.

Utterly and completely impossible. Gwilym had no magic. Hell, if he had, his father would've murdered him during the Purge.

A dangerous thought tickled the back of his mind, and he fought against it. If he had magic, it was hidden, locked behind layers of wards so strong he'd never once suspected he might be mageborn. His mind spun with this new information.

No. Impossible.

But...his mind whispered, his mother had been a mage, and her brother as well. Fine. He might have magic. But why now? Why the sudden ability to use magic? He was hallucinating. Had to be. There was no way he was magical. It was the lack of food, the cold, the near-deathness of his situation.

Trust, my son. Believe.

The smoke lengthened, and he blinked several times, just to be sure he was actually seeing what he thought he saw. Not only could he see the smoke, but his vision became clearer. Things unseen until that moment came into view. The outline of the door, bricks in the wall, detritus tossed in the corner: he saw it all. Including several boards covering a small window. Too small for him to crawl through, but if he could get the boards off, he could shout for help.

The buzzing grew into excitement, and he took several long breaths to keep from shouting his triumph to the rafters. Doubling his efforts and focus, he stared at the rope and commanded it to burn. A spark lit forth, singeing the hairs on his wrist. He muttered several curses between his laughter.

He'd done it. Somehow, someway, he'd conjured fire. Most remarkable. His excitement at discovering he had mage gifts was tempered by the fact that he couldn't tell anyone—not yet. Especially not his father. Later, he'd explore the how and the why. Then he would fully examine what this meant for him and his people. But first, he had to survive.

A small flame burned the threads, and he tugged at them to

release himself from the rope. A moment later, it lay in a heap at his side. Angry red marks circled his wrists where the rope had been tied too tightly. He rotated his hands in wide circles to bring circulation back to his fingers.

A key scraped in the door, and Gwilym grabbed the singed rope, carefully wrapping it around his wrists before the men returned. They opened the door and tossed the unbound king into the cellar without even looking in Gwilym's direction. They didn't need to tie up the king. He was barely conscious. They must've thought the king no longer a threat to leave his hands free.

His father huffed to the wall, where he collapsed. He kept an arm wrapped around his midsection, and Gwilym gently felt along his ribs, counting at least two that were broken. It would complicate matters, but he was determined to free them before the next beating.

He cradled his father in his arms until the old man snored softly. They'd made a makeshift bed with their jackets, and Gwilym lowered the king to the pile. He used his own jacket to cover him, knowing it wouldn't bring much comfort or warmth.

The slats hiding the window were hammered in place with thick nails that didn't budge when Gwilym tugged on them. Even his newfound magic didn't shift the rusted metal. He searched the rubbish in the corner for anything that could be used for leverage, but found nothing. Not even an old bone. He'd searched the room dozens of times, and with each sweep of the area, he'd hoped to find something, anything, but never had. He sat back with a heavy sigh and leaned his head against the stones, as he'd done hundreds of times. The brick shifted with his weight, and Gwilym turned with renewed hope.

Bits of old mortar crumbled beneath his finger when he swiped along the brick's edges. He used the rope to remove more mortar until the brick loosened just enough he could dig it out with his fingertips. After failing to remove the nails with magic, he resisted trying to use it now on the highly probable chance it was a fluke and he didn't actually possess magic. It wasn't like he had many options, the least he could do was at least give it a try. Ignoring his doubts, he focused on the brick and willed it to loosen. He grunted and strained, but the brick stayed stubbornly in place. Despair slunk through his thoughts. He wasn't mageborn. It had been an accident, nothing more.

After only a few minutes of digging around the brick, his fingers became bruised and bleeding from the effort. Unwilling to give up, Gwilym wrapped his fingers in the discarded rope and used it to scrape out bits of mortar. Sweat rolled across his brow to drip to the floor. His shoulders ached with the effort, but he kept scraping until finally the brick came free of its bindings.

He sat back with a stupid grin and hefted the brick in his hands. It would be a useful weapon the next time their abductors came to take one of them. He'd have one chance. If he missed, they'd overpower him and all his efforts would be for naught.

He shuffled to the door and put an ear to the wood. No sounds came to him. Footsteps scurried across the floorboards above his head. These usually came after one of their beatings. In his imaginings, he pictured the room as a kitchen, and after the men finished torturing their victims, the cook scrambled to feed them.

As if on cue, scents of beef cooking drifted to him. He might be imagining it or not; it didn't matter. Just the perceived smells made his stomach knot with emptiness. He couldn't remember the last time they'd been given food or water. Beatings and starvation—certainly not the way he'd imagined himself dying.

Gwilym held the brick to his chest with both hands. It had to work.

Amaleigh. He cast the thought into the void. He tried to imagine what she looked like now. In his mind, her hair was just as brilliant as it had been, shining in the sun's rays like garnets. He hoped she was happy. He'd often wondered whether she found somewhere safe to live where she could explore all it meant to be a mage. He imagined her using her gods-given gifts to help others. Despite her insistence she didn't like people, he saw a softer side to her that she tried desperately to hide. She'd make an excellent mage. Both her parents had been talented with magic. A bitterness crept up his throat. Being mages had cost her parents their lives.

His gaze went to his father, and the familiar twinge of guilt tightened around his heart. His father had murdered Amaleigh's parents out of spite. Not spite, not exactly.

Still, how could a woman love a man whose own father was a brutal killer?

Even seeing the king now, brought low from his incarceration, could she forgive him? Why would she? The possibility of her forgiveness was what drove him to save the king. If he could convince his father to atone, perhaps Amaleigh, and others like her who were hurt during the Purge, could heal.

Part of him hoped Amaleigh was far from Eidyn, where she was safe. He hoped she stayed there and never returned to the city. King Heshen's death warrant for her was still on the books. Even though everyone, including Antonio, thought she was dead, the king had refused to remove her name.

Gwilym settled beside his father and put a protective hand on his back while cradling the brick with his other hand. He closed his eyes and tried not to think of Amaleigh, but it was no use. If he wasn't replaying the route to escape, his thoughts centered on her. It had taken him far too long to realize that he loved her. Had loved her his whole life, ever since he first saw her sneaking into his study rooms. What a brazen, stupid thing for an urchin to do. But he hadn't thought of her as a thief. Only as a friend. She'd once promised she would never steal from the palace, but he knew that wasn't true. The first time they met, she'd stolen his heart.

Keeping it secret had been unbearable. There were countless times he'd wanted to confess to her, but he was afraid she'd laugh at him. Call him silly and too full of himself. She couldn't imagine a world where a prince and a thief could be together.

He had. He'd envisioned their future so many times he could recite it verbatim to anyone who asked. What had possessed him to kiss her that final night? Maybe it was realizing who she truly was that had broken his restraint. When he saw her crouched in front of the fireplace of her ruined childhood home, everything had fit into place for him. He'd realized then who she was—not the orphaned thief he knew, but the child of two of his father's most respected officers.

They'd never spoken about her family all those years they spent roaming the palace and studying with his tutors. Nor did they ever talk about his mother. It was an unspoken agreement that benefited them both. But that night, her last night in Eidyn, he'd realized with crushing clarity that he'd known her parents—had spent the first seven years of his life seeing them daily at the palace while Amaleigh and her brother were at the family home with their nanny. She and her brother never came to the palace, or if they did, he couldn't recall meeting them. He was the heir to the throne; he met scores of people daily and two children would've blended into the mix of faces. Thinking about it now, he was ashamed not to have spent more time getting to know Selmar and Helena's children.

The fact that he knew her parents better than her but had never connected that she was their daughter the entire time they were friends growing up, still haunted him. If he could, he'd go back and give her the time he'd spent with Helena and

Selmar so that she might have memories of them. Not just the smoldering remnants of their deaths.

Amaleigh, wherever you are, please forgive me.

The key scratched in the door, and Gwilym tensed. They were coming for him, this time. He crept to the darkened corner next to the door and crouched low, waiting. When his would-be abuser entered, Gwilym rose up and brought the brick down upon his skull.

A sickening crack was followed by a squelch that made bile creep up his throat. He wouldn't waste time mourning the man who'd brought them nothing but agony. The man fell to the floor in a lifeless heap.

CHAPTER
TWENTY-FIVE

Streetlamps were just being lit when Amaleigh exited the Shoogly Dragon. She'd spent the afternoon hiding out in the pub, hoping to overhear anything useful about Gwilym, the king, Antonio, or even Gerzer. Several drunken men had approached with insulting offers for a quick romp in the sack, but otherwise, it was as if the patrons did their best *not* to talk about the former king of the urchins.

She had the sense she'd walked into the middle of a turf war and the citizens were waiting to side with the victor. Twice, she thought she'd heard Gwilym's voice. Each time, she scanned the room, hope surging through her, but both times she was disappointed.

What her afternoon at the pub had given her was a chance to plan her next steps. Something wasn't right about Antonio's manor, but she wasn't sure that's where her next move should take her. Everything kept pointing to the palace. There would be many questions about her absence when she returned, and she didn't have the patience to deal with the game-playing prince and princess. Yet that's exactly what she needed to do—

play the game. First and foremost, she had to discern once and for all whether Gwilym were truly the friend she knew growing up, or if someone was impersonating him. And if they were, why?

She could return to Dante's to see whether he'd heard anything, but in truth the only reason she'd go back to his ship was to be with someone who knew who she was and she felt safe with. Not that she trusted him with her life, but at least she didn't have to pretend to be Erma Kielder with him. That was a lie. She *had* trusted him with her life by showing him her real self. Something she'd never done before. Indecision wracked her as she half-turned toward the harbor.

A huge white beast came into her view, and Amaleigh slowed her step. Not just her step, but time itself seemed to lengthen. The air softened. Seconds stretched to minutes, into hours. All around her, people moved in incremental movements, as if not quite frozen.

Her gaze went from the golden eyes of the wolf to the silver hair and piercing blue eyes of a woman. Beside her strode an elf, his long hair braided not unlike her own. The woman inclined her head and moved past. In a hiccup of a moment, she stood directly before Amaleigh, but she hadn't backtracked. She simply appeared without moving. A frown marred the strange woman's beauty.

"What world is this?"

"Excuse me?" Amaleigh squinted against the woman's radiance. A starburst glowed just beneath her skin.

"Is this Faerie? On the world Cilachaem?" The woman's gaze drifted to Amaleigh's chest.

"No, this is Nasus. You're in the city of Eidyn." It wasn't every day someone asked whether they were on a different world. In fact, she'd never known anyone to ask such an impudent question. Most people were content knowing their city and possibly their kingdom, but didn't expound further than their own lives.

"You have something from Faerie in your possession. It doesn't belong here." Her gaze was unsettling, yet not combative.

The elf at her side touched her sleeve. "Taryn, we do not have time to spare."

"You're right, it's just...I can feel his anguish."

"Who?" Amaleigh put a hand over her chest, where the pendant she'd bought at the festival rested. It was the only thing from Cilachaem she had on her. The charm might've come from Faerie, but she couldn't be sure. Still, the way the woman spoke with certainty unsettled her. She'd said the man felt anguish, but Amaleigh didn't see a man besides the elf.

"May I?" The one called Taryn held out her hand, and Amaleigh hesitated.

"Why are you interested in a trinket?"

"It's much more than that. I promise I won't harm him."

"Who?" Amaleigh wasn't sure she spoke aloud.

Something about the woman brought calm to Amaleigh's nerves. She had no reason to trust the stranger, yet she felt compelled to obey.

"I can feel magic surrounding the vial, but it's twisted. Do you know what it is?" Amaleigh removed the pendant from around her neck and reluctantly placed it on Taryn's palm.

Taryn's fingers curled around the pretty bauble. "There's a faerie trapped inside. Alive, but unconscious." Taryn met her startled stare with a look of grave concern. "I met a woman once. She was from Faerie and had a similar amulet. Did you get this here?"

"Definitely not. Magic is forbidden in Eidyn."

The woman's gaze went straight through Amaleigh. Even the elf stared hard at her. She shifted beneath their scrutiny.

"But you have ShantiMari." Taryn's eyes widened and lips trembled. "The pendant. Where did you get it?" The woman glanced over her shoulder, a worried expression on her face.

They were strangers, but Amaleigh sensed no danger from them, only hope and peace. She raised a hand as if to touch the woman, then dropped it to her side, embarrassed.

"From the village near where I was living. On Cilachaem, south of the faerie kingdoms." Amaleigh struggled to recall exactly what the villagers had told her about the world. Elves, trolls, ogres, brownies—all sorts of details crowded her mind. She hadn't explored enough of Cilachaem to give definite locations.

People continued to move in tiny steps as they stood talking about other worlds and trapped fae. The beast watched Amaleigh with a curious glint to her golden eyes. Not a wolf as such, she was much larger than any Amaleigh had seen.

"She's a grierbas. From Aelinae, our world." Taryn searched Amaleigh's eyes and scrunched her lips to the side.

The man at her side looked behind them and took Taryn's hand. "We must hurry."

A darkness slithered from the edges of her vision. Something vile and dangerous that made Amaleigh shiver.

"Who are you?" She cast another glance toward the threat. "What's chasing you?"

Taryn tucked the pendant into a pocket in her unusual trousers. Not quite leather, not of a cloth she recognized. "Nothing for you to worry about. It will leave with us." She reached out and touched Amaleigh's cheek with warm fingertips. "Our meeting was not coincidence. I hope to see you another time." She patted her hip. "I will return him to his home."

"Thank you." Amaleigh had the overwhelming desire to kneel, along with a sense that she'd been witness to something far greater than herself but couldn't say what.

As they turned to leave, time returned to normal speed and the darkness blinked out. Amaleigh heard the silver beauty say to her partner, "Rhoane, she has a dragon soul."

She gazed after them and met the moss-green eyes of her companion.

His whispered words came to her on a breeze. *"Dearth lach nothrin de las vendrigas, der darathi vorsi."* Then he touched his thumb to his forehead and lips before placing his fist at his heart.

Tears flooded her eyes, and she lived his pain in that single moment. His people had known great tragedy, and he bore the weight of their loss.

Amaleigh stared, bewildered, as they headed toward the Shoogly Dragon. The words were similar to the language of dragons she used to communicate with the dragonlings, but altered. A different inflection of a word here, or shaper snap to a word ending there. More formal, definitely. She didn't understand his words, but desperately wanted to—they were important, yet just out of reach. She gazed at him, at his beauty, and thought perhaps she could drown in his eyes. His was an intelligence centuries old.

When she blinked the tears away, the threesome was gone. A moment later, she sensed the use of power coming from the Shoogly Dragon. Not magic like the mages used, but power similar to Cassia's. She ran to the pub and caught the eye of the bartender. He shrugged and cocked his head toward the back room. When she got there, it was empty. Only a slight shimmering around a doorway remained.

Amaleigh put her hand to the wood. Even knowing it might

be destructive to herself, she had to know where they'd gone. Question upon question built in her mind. Desperate to learn who they were and how they knew about other worlds, she needed to know what their appearance meant for Eidyn. More importantly, she wondered if their being here was significant to her quest.

Warmth emanated from the wood, and Amaleigh sucked it in like a starving goat at its mother's teat. This was no power she knew. Strange. Ancient.

Amaleigh.

She heard Gwilym's voice and jerked her attention away from the mysterious threesome. She raced to the common room, but again, he wasn't to be seen. Either she was losing her mind, or he was somewhere close. Her worst fear was that it was the former. It didn't make sense that she kept hearing Gwilym's voice when he was at the palace, for all appearances, safe. Again, doubt crept through her thoughts that the prince wasn't her Gwilym.

Gwilym, where are you?

Silence answered. More riddles. More games. The madness was taking over too quickly. If it was madness. She shuddered to think it was Gwilym playing a sick and twisted game with her. In a macabre way, she hoped Gwilym and his father were being held captive at Antonio's. Then at least she'd know it wasn't madness or him purposefully trying to hurt her.

Outside, the first stars blinked in a dusky sky. It would be full dark soon and she could investigate Antonio's place. Stalls on the market square were closing up as she strolled past. It was a quick five-minute walk to Antonio's, but she didn't want to appear rushed or draw attention to herself.

At his street, she did increase her pace and arrived at his door slightly breathless. She touched the doorknob and it turned without complaint. A fresh wave of magic tickled up her arm. If another mage had set an alarm on the door, then she'd learn soon enough who was responsible for the source of magic she kept feeling.

No one came to the stairs, nor did any footsteps hurry along the hallways above or in front of her. An eerie silence had descended on the house.

She crept through the foyer, holding her nose closed to avoid the stench. A large sitting room opened to the left, and to the right was an unfurnished room. If memory served, it was where Antonio used to host elaborate dinner parties. Gone were the days of his importance. Now the grand fireplaces sat empty and cold.

A doorway led to the kitchens, and Amaleigh smelled the scent of cooking beef. Muffled voices came from the dark hallway, and she hurried past to the last door. It led to the cellars, where she knew of at least three escape routes to the sewers. Unless Antonio had blocked them.

She reached for the doorknob and flinched at the cold steel. Not magic, exactly, but some kind of spell had been placed on the metal. A necromancer, perhaps? She touched the knob lightly with her fingertip. Immediately, a slick oiliness covered her senses. As much as she wanted to withdraw her finger, she forced herself to stay connected to the metal until the full impact of the charm was made clear.

It wasn't an enchantment to keep anyone from entering the cellars, quite the opposite, in fact. Whoever had placed it on the door wasn't experienced in necromancy but knew enough to be dangerous. She lifted her finger and wiped it on the hem of her tunic. Not that the spell left anything tangible on her skin, but the mere act of experiencing the nasty charm made her want to bathe to rid herself of the filth.

It was a protection spell to keep whatever ghoulishness

might creep forth from the cellars from entering the house. Her stomach pinched violently when she imagined what kind of horrors took place down there to warrant the protective barrier. In all the times she'd been punished, it had been in Antonio's rooms upstairs. She knew some were taken to the cellars, and those she never saw again.

Blowing out her cheeks with a deep breath, she girded herself for the worst. Unsettled spirits were the least of her concern as she opened the door and crept down the stairs. She kept her step light and avoided the boards she remembered as being prone to creaks. Even though it had been seven years, the memories were ingrained in her psyche.

At the bottom of the stairs, several corridors ran off in different directions. The passages to the sewers were hidden behind crates and barrels in the storage cellars. If Gwilym and the king were down here, she doubted they'd be in one of those rooms. Still, it might be prudent to make sure she had a way out in case the stairs became inconvenient.

Two torches burned along the stone wall that led to the storage rooms. She passed them quickly, not wanting to linger too long in a brightly lit space. At the first cellar, she ducked inside. Bags of flour were stacked along a high shelf next to several baskets of withered beans. She scanned the walls and floor, recounting how the room had looked a decade earlier. More food on the shelves, definitely—not that any of it went to her, and she knew better than to steal any. Food was more valuable than gold feathers when it came to Antonio's control of the urchins.

If memory served, there should've been a hatch in the floor beside an unused and boarded-up fireplace. She brushed dirt away with her hands, but found only stone slabs. Frustrated, but not defeated, she hurried down a set of short steps to the next room. Not even a bag of rice was on the shelves. Two barrels sat in the corner, and she climbed over them to look for the boards she'd worked to loosen over the course of several months when she was barely eight. Even then she'd understood her life hung precariously on Antonio's whims and she always needed an escape plan.

The sound of keys jangling echoed down the passageway, and she held still until the sound died down. Her fingers shook as she ran them over the wooden slats, pressing each in turn. Two of the boards gave way, and she sat back on her heels. Relief washed over her. It was enough for a slim child to squeeze through at best. Another two more slats and she'd fit, no problem.

She jerked on the first board, grimacing at the wretched sound it made. She listened for approaching footsteps. A sick crack like someone smashed a coconut with a rock was followed by a heavy thump.

Amaleigh grabbed the board and jerked it from its place. She crouched behind the barrels and stilled her breath as much as possible. Blood rushed through her ears, and her lips went dry. After several minutes of agonizing silence, she hopped over the barrels and stood in the middle of the passageway, listening.

What the hell was she even doing there? Whoever was being beaten wasn't her concern. She didn't work for Antonio anymore, nor did she owe any of his urchins her loyalty. Then why stand in the middle of the fucking hallway, holding a wooden board like she was some warrior wench ready to brawl?

Because she'd been there. Because she knew the hell of living a life she didn't want and being beholden to a man who didn't deserve a second of her time.

Muffled grunts came from her left where the torches didn't reach, and she crept along the hallway to where another passageway intersected. She paused and closed her eyes. Her senses were already on high alert, but she pushed harder, sending waves outward like scanners. A thump came from her right, and she took a tentative step in that direction. A figure loomed at the end of the corridor, silhouetted in the doorway.

Amaleigh gripped the board and held it waist high. Ready for whatever came next.

CHAPTER

TWENTY-SIX

The king's body slumped in Gwilym's arms, and he shifted to hoist his father up for a better grip. There wasn't time to fashion any kind of carrier, so he had to make do with half-dragging himself and his father through the dark cellar.

He peered into the shadows and counted his steps to the stairs. The king groaned and slid farther down his side. Gwilym's heart sank with him. There was no way he could get himself and his father up the stairs unnoticed. For a single heartbeat, defeat burned his thoughts.

No, he wouldn't let his abductors win. He'd gotten them this far, and he would find an exit. What was it Amaleigh had always told him? Every cellar had its secrets. If they were in Eidyn like he believed, then those cellars would have at least one entrance to the sewers. According to Amaleigh's stories, that's where Antonio ruled supreme. An underground system of pathways unnoticed by those on the streets above.

He shuffled farther down the hallway and paused at the sound of wood creaking. More like something was torn off its hinges. Silence descended, and he continued to the first doorway he found.

Inside, crates were tossed haphazardly into piles. He set his father down on a rickety box and closed the door behind them. Finding no lock, he set several of the crates in front of the door. They wouldn't stop an intruder, but they might slow them down. The last crate he moved revealed a rough-hewn door cut into the stone wall. Its planks were half rotted with decay. When he touched the handle, the door soundlessly swung open.

Moving quickly now, he lifted his father and backed into the blackness of the open doorway. Several steps in, he set the king unceremoniously on the damp ground and returned to the storage room. He kicked at the edge of the soft wood until he made a small hole in the plank. All the crates he'd placed against the door he returned to their place in front of the secret door and stretched his arm through the hole he made to pull them close as he closed the door.

It wasn't a fail-safe, but it might buy them enough time to escape. He hoisted his father up to rest on his hip and shuffled through the pitch black with one hand stretched out in front. After counting seventy-seven steps, a dim light came from the end of the tunnel. Gwilym almost cheered with relief.

Emboldened by the soft glow, he hurried his steps, counting them until he reached the source of light and another, wider tunnel. A grate above their heads allowed in light from a street-lamp. People walked past, unaware of Gwilym's presence. He stilled and listened. He recognized their words, their cadence, their language. They were in Eidyn, as he'd hoped.

In fact, they were in the elite district, which meant they had been at Antonio's like he'd guessed. Was it Antonio or Gerzer who was responsible for their abduction and subsequent torture? It didn't matter. He'd find them both and gut them like fish. They deserved no less.

Rage infused his veins, and a curious calm washed over him. *Kill,* a voice whispered. *Kill them all. Kill all the urchins. Kill the masters.*

Gwilym shook his head. He'd heard those words before. Long ago, in the palace. Someone had said them to him. No, not to him. He redoubled his grip on his father and it came to him—someone had said those hateful words to the king.

Who would want the urchins dead? His father used to call them thieving little grubbers, but he hadn't expressed a desire to slaughter them. The was probably a long list of people who hated the urchins, and by association Antonio. But only one person that Gwilym could recall hated them so much he would suggest the king commit infanticide. The who eluded him, and he grunted in frustration. When they were safe, he'd find the answers he sought. He'd dig deep into his memories for a name and face of the person who had whispered vile things into the king's ear. It was there, somewhere, but elusive as if he had consciously blocked himself from remembering. Or someone had warded him. He wriggled his fingers where the fire had sparked from the tips. If someone had blocked his memories with magical warding, it wasn't the same person who had shielded him from his magic. Of that he was certain.

Gwilym surveyed his surroundings with a sinking sense of dread. Tunnels stretched in every direction. Surely one would take him to the palace, but he had no idea which one and loathed the idea of becoming lost in the underground maze. He glanced up again and was about to cry out for help when an echo stopped the words in his throat.

His heart cramped in his chest and a pit formed in his gut. They'd been found.

Slowly, as if to delay the inevitable, he turned toward the sound. A small boy, perhaps no more than five or six, stood ten feet from them—his dark eyes huge in his face, his little mouth open in an O. He looked just as frightened of Gwilym as he was of the boy.

"Please," Gwilym croaked, surprised at the sound of his own voice. "Please help us. My father needs a healer."

The boy shook his head, but he didn't scream or run. The rags he wore vibrated as if he shivered or was trembling.

"We won't hurt you. I promise. We need to get out of these sewers." What had Amaleigh said about the urchins? They were always hungry. "If you can help, I'll make sure you never miss a meal ever again."

His eyes lit up, and he took a tentative step toward Gwilym. "Ye won't tell thems bosses abouts me helpin', will ye?"

Gwilym shook his head. "No one will know you've helped us. I promise."

The boy turned and motioned for Gwilym to follow.

He lifted his father and whispered, "We're almost safe. Just a bit more."

The king groaned and rolled his head, his eyes closed. They walked a short distance through the tunnel before the boy slipped between two narrow arches. Gwilym carefully maneuvered his father through with the help of the boy before he squeezed between the bricks. His vision blurred with the effort, and he steadied himself against the damp wall.

"How much farther?"

The boy pointed to a long alley. "I sleep just there. Not far."

By the time they reached the pile of rags the boy called a bed, Gwilym's last reserves were spent. He lay his father on the dirty fabric and collapsed beside him.

"Please," he said to the boy, "keep us safe for one night."

Their lives were in his hands. If they survived the night, he'd make good on his promise and not only make sure the child was fed, but he'd also find a place for him in the palace. Once he rested and regained his strength. No sooner than his head touched the rags, he slipped into a deep sleep.

CHAPTER
TWENTY-SEVEN

A low chuckling came from the shadows, and Amaleigh tensed. The figure lumbered forward into the flickering light of a torch. Antonio's face emerged, his black hair slicked with something dark and thick. Crimson streaks ran from his scalp to his neck. One hand gripped his head while the other flailed for the wall.

Amaleigh tightened her hold on the board. She eased backward, toward the stairs.

"I knew ye heard 'em too." Antonio lunged at her, and she raised the board to strike. But he wobbled and fell against the wall.

"You don't look too good. Who did this to you?"

"Didn't see 'em, did I?" He twisted until his back rested against the stones and closed his eyes. "'Course, can't see much of nothing no more." He inhaled and a sickly smile covered his face. "Can smell, though. And I still gots me ears." His head turned in her direction. "I knew ye would come back if'n you weren't dead. Knew ye wouldn't betray me."

"Where's the king? What have you done with him and the prince?" She couldn't let Antonio know how much his words unnerved her. He wanted her to believe he knew who she really was, but she wouldn't give him the satisfaction he so obviously craved. He was a master at manipulating emotions, but not hers—not anymore.

"Gone." He waved a hand in the direction of the corridor he'd come from. She darted past him, but he grabbed her wrist and twisted until she stopped. His bony grip held her fast. "I made a deal with a demon. Put me out of me misery. Have mercy on one who cared for ye all those years."

His rank breath assaulted her nostrils, and she turned her head to avoid seeing his decayed, yellow teeth.

"I'm not who you think I am. But I know you don't deserve mercy. Whatever deal you made, you deserve to suffer the consequences."

His grip released, and she shook out her arm. When she was two steps from the end of the hallway, he said, "I stole a child once. A wee thing, not more'n three, maybe four. Stole her from the home of an elite who didn't know what they had livin' under their very roof."

Amaleigh slowed, her nerves tightened.

"She had power." Antonio sucked in his breath and smacked his lips several times. "Such glorious power. But magic gets ye killed in Eidyn, so I's warded her and hid her from thems that would steal her soul. In doing so, I saved hers." His head flopped toward her, his gauzy eyes penetrating to the depths of her heart. "That deserves some mercy, wouldn't ye think?"

He meant her. Dear gods, he still had the ability to pull her feet out from beneath her even when she no longer lived under his rule. Her head throbbed and thoughts muddied. All those years Cornelius had lied to her. He made her believe he'd left her with Antonio, but now her tormentor was telling a different tale. Someone was lying, and she feared it wasn't the man who lay dying before her.

"Why would you steal a child, then hide her magic? Why didn't you exploit her for your own gain?" Amaleigh asked the easy questions, shying away from the harder truths she wasn't ready to accept.

A warbled chuckle lifted Antonio's chest. "Oh, I did. I used her good. She was cleverer than most. Faster, too. Learned tricks in weeks that took others years to master. She was my best thief. Me favorite."

Rage ignited in her veins, and she fought to control her magic. It swirled unfettered, more powerful and beautiful than she'd ever realized she was capable of. Why here of all places would she come into her power? Why now? The unknowable questions banged against her skull with cruel insistence. She sneezed against the musty odors of the cellar and forced herself to contain her magic. There were answers she could get, but time was ticking.

"If she was your favorite, then why did you abuse her? Why were you so brutal? She was just a little girl."

"Because of this." He pointed to her, and she flinched. "Even warded, ye are more powerful and dangerous than most of them mages Heshen slaughtered. Had te protect ye. Even if'n it weren't what ye deserved."

She staggered against the wall and clutched her stomach. "You warded me?" she rubbed her temples, trying to make sense of it all. "You're still warding me? How?"

"Not me." He slumped to the ground, and a loud moan came from deep inside him.

"Who warded me? Tell me!"

"Don't matter none now." Blood drooled from his lips. "Mercy, Amaleigh. Please."

"I told you, I'm not a killer."

He reached a hand toward her. "It's not killing if I'm already dead inside. It's a release."

She looked at the board in her hand and shuddered. No way could she slay him. Even though she hated every inch of his being, she couldn't do it. It might be a ruse to lure her near. If she touched him, he could steal her magic and overpower her.

"I can't. I'm sorry."

"Ye can. Stop me heart. Just takes a thought."

Just a thought. She could send a thought to his heart, couldn't she? It wasn't like he wouldn't die on his own.

"Tell me who warded me and I'll do as you ask."

"'Twas…" The word came out slurred, and his hand dropped to the ground. His body slid sideways until he was a crumpled mass on the stone floor. A pool of blood haloed his head.

She gripped the board and held it out until it touched his shoulder. She sent a tiny thread of her power through the wood to his heart. The organ beat an irregular rhythm. As if it were trying to decide whether to keep going or give up.

Dammit. She'd never know who warded her now. It was a secret he'd take to the grave. A mad thought rushed through her skull that she could force the words from him. If she could stop his heart with a thought, she could certainly use the same tactic to trick his brain into giving her the information. Desperation flooded her senses. The brain was far more complicated than a beating organ. He'd toyed with her until the very end, promising one thing and then snatching it away.

Fuck him. Fuck him and his stupid tricks. Fuck him to every fucking ring of hell that ever existed.

She kept a death grip on the board, wary he might grab it and leap up, but he didn't move. He didn't need her mercy. Whatever demon he'd made a deal with apparently had no more use for him. She spoke an Eidynite blessing more out of personal protection from the unseen and turned away from the man who had made her childhood a living nightmare. Witnessing his passing didn't bring her joy or closure. His death left her with more questions than answers, but at least he'd confirmed that Gwilym and the king had been there.

Antonio had recognized her voice, something Dante had hinted at, which meant she needed to be more careful. She had no doubt Antonio would tell the others she'd returned if he had the chance. He would crow about it to Gerzer, using her as some fucking trophy. It was best he was gone. She watched him for several minutes before prodding him with the board a final time.

His body jostled with her force, but he didn't blink or moan or make any movement. She sent one last thread to his mind, hoping to sift through recent memories, but it was a dull, grey emptiness. Her magic traveled to his now-still heart, and she shuddered a sigh. Antonio was truly dead.

For one terrible moment, she paused to let her emotions sort themselves out. Sadness, anger, relief, and finally, acceptance flowed through her. His words had confused her, but she would deal with that later. Gwilym was her priority. Antonio's death was not.

She left her tormentor on the cold floor and hurried down the hallway, grabbing a torch from the wall for light and protection. At the end of the hall, she listened for movement, but none came. A door stood open to her left, and she crept forward, board in hand. She pushed the door farther open to reveal an empty room. Foul smells rose from the damp floor, and she scrunched her nose against the stench. She was about to turn away when something pale caught her attention.

At the bottom of several steps, she found the burned remnants of rope. When her fingers touched the singed strands, a vision of Gwilym hit her hard enough to knock her backward onto the steps. His agony tore through her psyche, and she clutched the rope to her chest. He'd been in this room.

She sniffed the air, retching at the foulness, but also

searching for scents of the real Gwilym. This was her proof that the prince in the palace was a pretender. Well, the proof she needed. Convincing anyone else would take more than a vision and some singed rope.

Antonio had said the king and Gwilym were gone. It might've been them who had bashed Antonio's head. She scanned the floor and saw a brick lying a few feet away. Crimson splotches covered one end. They'd been there the whole time she'd been upstairs with Antonio, and then while she wasted time at the Shoogly Dragon, waiting for night. Antonio's wound was fresh, which meant Gwilym and the king had escaped minutes before she found him. She'd been in the cellars, but didn't see them. They might've tried escaping up the stairs or found an exit through one of the other storage rooms in the cellar.

She closed her eyes and thought of Gwilym, the rope firmly in her grasp. The smell of soiled laundry came to her. And fresh bread. It meant nothing to her, but she would find him. He was in the city—now she knew for sure he was close.

Her gaze traveled down the dark corridor to a closed door. Through there was one of the entrances to the sewers. Hope sparked in her heart. If Gwilym managed to get himself and the king to the sewers, he might have a chance at escaping. She pocketed the rope and kicked the bloody brick into a corner. After a moment of internal debate, she returned to Antonio and lifted his slight frame from the floor. Disgust and shame washed over her, but she shoved the feelings aside. She was buying Gwilym time. The gods would forgive her.

After laying Antonio on the grubby floor of the cell, she shut the door behind her. A touch of magic set the lock. Next, she kicked dirt and straw over the pool of blood left by Antonio's head wound. When confident it wouldn't be noticed right away, she hurried to the small storage room.

It was empty, as she knew it would be, and desperation filled her heart. She'd wasted too much time with Antonio. Gwilym was close, and yet still far away.

She pushed aside the pile of crates in front of the wooden door and almost laughed with relief at the hole in one of the planks. Clever Gwilym. She closed the door and used a tiny amount of magic to lock this door as well. Then she slipped through the small door in the wall and reached through the hole to pull the crates against the wooden slats. Again, she used magic to keep the door closed and hidden from prying eyes either from inside Antonio's cellars, or someone in the sewers.

The little fragments of magic she'd used were adding up, and she couldn't risk using any more. Thus far, she hoped she hadn't alerted anyone to her presence. Despite Heshen's Purge and his outlawing magic, she'd seen enough evidence in the past two days to convince her others in Eidyn practiced magic to varying degrees. Whether friend or foe, she couldn't be sure, and she'd need to be hypervigilant.

The torch lit her way through a tall tunnel and into the sewers proper. She glanced at the other tunnels leading off from the main sewage line. They each led to a district in the city. Which would Gwilym choose?

A thin strand of shimmering light stretched from one tunnel to another. Her magic. Flox it, she'd forgotten about the little spy on Dante's boat. Of the two tunnels, only one led to the dock. It was most likely where the urchin had come from, and then he went through the other tunnel. It connected to several spin-off channels that could lead to anywhere on the west side of the city.

The magic trail could wait. Her priority was finding Gwilym. She searched the ground for clues and found several drops of blood, and scuff marks. Either of which could be from Gwilym...

or any number of people. The blood went in one direction and the scuff marks the other. She chose to follow the blood first.

After twenty paces, the drops ended abruptly. She bent low with the torch and studied the grimy bricks, then checked the nearby wall. But there wasn't a passage or any sign what happened to whomever had been bleeding.

Sounds came from one of the tunnels behind her, and she rushed to find cover. The magic thread twinkled in her torchlight, and she sprinted to that passageway just as looming shadows came into view. Men shouted at her to stop, and she bolted deeper into the tunnel, her heart beating as quickly as her feet raced through the muck. Sounds of footsteps pounded behind her and she sped up.

The bastards couldn't leave it alone. They had to pursue her. Barnacleballs. She wove in and out of spin-off paths, some no more than crawl spaces. The shouts ebbed and flowed, but she kept running. The men's voices echoed against the ancient bricks and she recognized several of them—one of which was Gerzer.

Fuck. If he saw her, and then discovered Antonio's body, he'd for sure think she killed him. But he didn't know she was in the city. Unless Antonio shared his suspicions with him after she left the manor.

Her chest heaved with her labored breaths, and she slowed to a jog. It had been ages since she'd had to run for her life and seven years of guaranteed meals hadn't kept her as fit as she'd once been. Fortunately, the men weren't spry things either. They cursed the shadows and threatened torture when she was found.

Amaleigh plastered herself against a brick wall and put a hand over her chest. The torch sputtered and cast shadows down the tunnel, giving the sewage waters an unnatural glow. She needed the light it provided, but it was a beacon to her whereabouts. This far underground, she might be safe using magic to light her way, but she was already in enough danger. She didn't need to add more. If she stayed in the main tunnels, light from the streetlamps casting through grates would give her enough to see.

She extinguished the torch in the putrid water and crept forward until she could see other passageways. The gentle gurgle of running water was the only sound she heard. She kept close to the wall as she made her way through the tunnels toward the palace. At the third turn, she saw her thread of sparkling magic leading down the only tunnel that connected to the palace.

The urchin had come this way. She checked her surroundings, still clutching the cold torch with trembling fingers. Drips echoed into small puddles. Carriage wheels squeaked several feet above her head. No voices. No footsteps. She let out the breath she'd been holding and crept closer to the palace.

She silently begged the thread to continue beyond the palace grounds, to not turn down a slim alley that led to the stables of the palace. It did no good. The thread glistened a path toward the small grate that opened into the stables. Whoever sent the boy to spy was in the palace. It could've been anyone, but her heart told her it was either Cassia or the fake prince. There was only one way to find out.

CHAPTER

TWENTY-EIGHT

Amaleigh entered the palace through a side door after having to convince the guard she was, in fact, a guest of Prince Gwilym and Princess Cassia. Her disheveled hair and sodden clothing didn't help, but eventually she persuaded them to let her pass. It might've had something to do with her mentioning that she was happy to wait while they tracked down the prince to verify her story. And hinting that the prince was in a rather foul mood, but it was their call whether they wished to risk the prince's ire any further.

She'd guessed correctly that the prince was indeed in a fit that day and they had no desire to tempt fate. As she half-ran to her rooms, she noticed several servants with their heads bowed, their hands clasped tightly at their waist. She'd seen the same reaction when she and Gwilym used to hide from his father's rage. Whatever the reason for the fake prince's anger, she needed to be extra cautious.

The door to her room stood ajar, and Amaleigh entered, prepared for an ambush. She wasn't half-wrong. Cassia and her ladies rose when she entered, their faces identical expressions of concern and alarm. As one, they took in her appearance from head to toe.

"What are you doing in my rooms?" She brushed past Isla on her way to the bathing room. "Haven't you heard of privacy?"

Cassia laughed a jolly little peal. "Oh, darling. There's no privacy in a palace." She followed Amaleigh into the small space and turned the taps to run her a bath. "We were worried. When I came for breakfast and found you gone, I assumed you'd return before lunch, but you didn't. And now it's almost dinner time and, well, look at you!" Cassia pointed to Amaleigh with an exasperated huff. "What happened to you?"

"It's a long story. Too long to tell it all. And right now, I need to bathe. Alone."

Cassia scrunched her nose. "You stink."

"Yeah, thanks for that. That's why I need a bath." She made shooing movements with her hands. "Go. I'll find you when I'm presentable."

"Would you like Meri to assist in your bathing?" Cassia beckoned the beauty.

"No. Definitely not. I'm fine. I promise, as soon as I'm dressed, I'll find you."

"We'll be in the queen's sitting room until it's time to dine. Do please hurry. There's so much we need to discuss."

Cassia stared at Amaleigh with meaning, but she didn't understand the intention behind the words.

The temptation to as what they needed to discuss was strong, but her stench stronger.

She'd find out later. First, she really did need a bath.

The princess left with her ladies, and Amaleigh locked the door after them. She took the key with her to the bathing room and set it on a marble shelf. Her clothes she left in a heap on the floor. The hot water soothed her aching muscles, but this wasn't a luxury bath. She made quick work of scrubbing the sewer from her skin and untangling her braids. Cassia's ladies would be mortified at the mess she'd made of their lovely braids.

Her hair fanned out beneath the water like wings. For a moment, she felt her dragon stirring and her heartbeat spiked. She was there, just under the surface of Amaleigh's magic. If she concentrated...but it was no good. The dragon receded into the shadows, and Amaleigh was left feeling hollow and alone.

She toweled herself dry and dressed quickly in a simple gown of rust velvet. Her hair she fingerbrushed and wrapped into a loose bun. Merigold might have something to say about it, but she didn't have the time or the patience to placate the Fianna Bel'en. A quick check in the mirror confirmed she was mildly presentable. It would have to do. Cassia waited and, in truth, Amaleigh was curious what the princess had meant with her meaningful glare and ominous words. "There's so much we need to discuss." It could mean anything.

Cassia and her four ladies-in-waiting stood in a tight group when Amaleigh entered the queen's sitting room. Her gaze went to the large mural, but the tapestries had been pulled closed to conceal the painting. A jab of disappointment stung her heart.

"You're here." Cassia approached with her arms outstretched as if to embrace Amaleigh, and she hesitated.

Did princesses hug everyone they met? It seemed strange, but then, nothing about the girl wasn't odd. Cassia's arms encircled her, and she returned the hug with a slight squeeze.

They sat on the sofa, and the princess tutted at Amaleigh's hair.

"I didn't have time to style it." She patted the sloppy bun, a lopsided grin on her face.

"You're here now. That's all that matters."

A tray with tea, biscuits, and scones sat on the low table. "May I?" Amaleigh indicated the tray, and Cassia nodded.

They were dining soon, but she was ravenous after her romp through the sewers. As she spread jam on a scone, she debated how much to tell Cassia about her day. If the urchin spy had been sent by the princess, then she already knew what had transpired that morning. But Antonio and the rest? She wasn't sure.

Merigold hovered on the periphery of her vision. When she turned to face her, the beauty wrung her hands and rolled her bottom lip between her teeth.

"Oh, all right then. Go on." Amaleigh shook her head when the ladies scrambled for combs and pins. "But not as many braids, and I could do without the magical enhancements."

The women glanced at Cassia.

The princess chuckled good-heartedly and shrugged. "I guess that answers one question." She motioned for the ladies to continue. "It relaxes them."

Cassia's tresses flowed down her back, with several braids intertwined with one another to make a complicated pattern over her crown.

"I suppose being a lady-in-waiting is, as the name implies, a bit boring. I mean, you're always waiting, right?" Amaleigh snorted at her joke and got a grimace from Cassia for her trouble.

The ladies brushed and tugged her hair, being as gentle as they could with the snarls she'd left in her haste.

"What did you wish to discuss?" She sipped her tea with nonchalance, but alert all the same.

Cassia went to the mural and pulled aside one of the tapestries to reveal the queen, but not Amaleigh's mother.

"Did you know dragon mages are susceptible to raging

fevers? If not treated quickly and in the correct manner, they'll perish." The princess ran a finger along the dragon's scales.

"I didn't know that." It was true; she'd never heard of dragon fevers.

"The queen had such a fever, which caused her death and that of her second child. But it wasn't just the fever that killed her." Cassia's voice lowered, and she gazed up at the queen's smiling image. "She was betrayed. By her own brother."

"Betrayed? How?" Amaleigh rose, ignoring the gripes of the ladies doing her hair. She joined Cassia at the mural. "I've never heard this part of the story."

"No one has, I would suspect. I doubt even the king knows the full extent of what happened." Cassia cocked her head and met Amaleigh's questioning squint. "Before you ask how I know, she talks to me." She stroked the mural. "The queen's spirit is restless. The time has come to right the wrongs of the past."

"Her own brother killed her?"

Cassia shook her head. "Not directly. He'd been stealing her power for years. At first, it was in small amounts, but as his power and prestige at court grew, so did his lust for her magic. She didn't realize it, as those who are powerful rarely do. He had no magic of his own, you see. But by robbing her of power, he made himself appear to be a great mage."

"Surely, killing her meant he lost his supplier." Amaleigh placed her hand over the queen's painted thigh.

A subtle vibration ran along her skin, and she closed her eyes. A darkened room came to her mind. The queen lay on her bed, tossing with sickness. Amaleigh's mother knelt at her side, comforting her queen. In the shadows, a figure stood waiting. Ghostly threads connected him and the queen. Her power. He sucked the strength she needed to fight the raging fever. It was true, he didn't kill her outright, but his greed made her too weak to survive the illness and subsequent premature birth of her child.

"There is a prophecy which says, 'Dragon fire will light the heart of the kingdom.' The queen's brother corrupted the true meaning of the prophecy and used the queen's fever to convince the king that dragons would tear the crown asunder." Tears streaked down Cassia's cheeks. "The queen's own brother, a man who should've loved and protected her, incited the king to commit his atrocities during the Purge."

"If the queen knew her brother was vile, why did she allow him to stay in the palace?"

Cassia ran a finger over the dragon's scales. "I suppose for the same reason anyone stays with an abuser. They believe if they love them enough, they'll change. They believe there's still good in the person. But the queen was wrong about her brother, and she paid with her life."

Amaleigh put a hand on Cassia's forearm. Power twisted beneath her touch, and she gasped at not only the amount of magic the princess possessed, but her control over that power.

"I'm so sorry, Your Highness. More than you'll ever know."

"I believe you." She pulled the tapestry closed and returned to the sofa.

As soon as Amaleigh's ass touched the cushions, the ladies resumed their brushing. It was soothing, in a way. The tug and stroke of their hands. Almost lulling. She could've curled into the sofa and napped, except something about the way Cassia spoke of the queen's fever nagged at her mind.

"Are dragons sentient creatures?"

Cassia's lips thinned, and her eyes narrowed. "I wouldn't know personally, but I've read that dragons are quite intelligent. They are especially keen negotiators."

Just so. They were still playing the game that she was a simple princess from Aenglebreck.

A page entered to tell them it was time for dinner. Lousy timing, as far as Amaleigh was concerned. They had so much more to discuss, not least of which was Cassia's continued pretense.

Before they left the queen's sitting room, Amaleigh stopped the princess. "Do you know anyone by the name of Taryn or Rhoane?"

"I don't believe so. Who are they?"

"Just a couple I met today. They said the strangest thing to me. Do you know what *dearth lach nothrin de las vendrigas, der darathi vorsi* means?"

A gasp came from one of the ladies, and Cassia's face paled. Her eyes widened and nostrils flared. "What a curious language that is. Do you know it?"

The warble in her voice betrayed her lies.

"I don't." Amaleigh shrugged. "I suppose it'll remain a mystery. Shall we?" She swept from the room, unsure whether Cassia's reaction was what she'd been expecting. Certainly she thought the princess might be curious about the foreign phrase, but not altogether alarmed. It made her desire to learn the meaning all the more imperative.

It might've been a threat. Or it could've been a curse of some sort. Neither seemed likely considering the couple hadn't given her any indication they were violent. Although, they traveled with the white beast and both carried swords.

As they walked the short distance to the prince's private dining hall, Amaleigh replayed the conversation with the pair. Nothing alarming struck her. An image ghosted through her thoughts of the woman's sword. Two dragons intertwined, one silver and one moss green. And the woman had told the man when they walked away that Amaleigh had a dragon soul. It was a spectacularly accurate guess, unless the woman knew somehow. Maybe Aerlghots could recognize their kind. Which would suggest the couple had dragon souls as well.

Amaleigh didn't know who the couple were, but their words definitely upset the princess. The palace was awash in mysteries, and as much as she wished it weren't so, she was being dragged deeper into them.

TWENTY-NINE

Dinner that evening was a raucous affair. Several of the prince's friends dined with them, along with their lady companions. They drank to excess and shouted toasts to their host at regular intervals. The theatrics of this evening sought to top the bizarre pantomime of the previous night. Instead of a showy display of affection from the prince to Cassia, tonight Gwilym sulked at the head of the table.

He sat with his hands steepled, his wine glass full, but he didn't drink. Every time she glanced his way, his gaze was firmly set on her. She shuddered with each glimpse of those cold eyes. The princess and her ladies raised their glasses with each toast, but like the fake prince, they did not drink.

Amaleigh watched it all and counted the seconds until she could escape.

The prince barely spoke but when he did, it was to say something crude or cutting. His remarks were meant to belittle her, she was certain of it.

After pudding was served, she thanked her host and excused herself from the revelries. Several shouts arose from the drunken lords and ladies, none of them complimentary, and

Amaleigh dug her nails into her palms to keep from snapping at the useless lapdogs.

They postulated and primped for a pretender prince. What a bunch of idiots. That they couldn't see he wasn't the true Gwilym infuriated her.

Unless they did know.

Her rage simmered beneath her calm façade, and she curtseyed to the lords and prince. She hadn't considered that some at the palace knew the king and his son had been taken. Or who might be in on the plot. It made her dealings with these simpering nobles all the more dangerous.

The fake prince didn't deign to stand when she left and for that, she was genuinely grateful. She'd worried he might try to escort her to her rooms.

Cassia and her ladies caught up to Amaleigh in one of the large halls.

"Dear Erma, won't you join me for a nightcap?" Cassia did the intense look again, and Amaleigh cocked her head.

"Is there a reason you keep stalking me?"

Cassia took her arm and directed her toward the queen's sitting room. Along the way, the princess chatted about the paintings and furnishings, commenting on their value as well as their provenance. Anxious to get some answers, Amaleigh half-listened. When finally they were alone in the sitting room, Cassia turned to Amaleigh.

"Does the prince know you're an Aerlghot?"

Stunned, Amaleigh took a step backward and bumped into Isla's chest. The Fianna Bel'en didn't move.

"Why would you ask me that?" Denials sprang to her lips, but no further.

"Those words you spoke. They're from an archaic elven language. *Darathi vorsi* are what the elves call air dragons." Cassia spoke quickly and paced a long path and back. "Loosely translated, they mean, 'When you know yourself' or perhaps 'When you know love of self' or just 'know love; your dragon will know you in return.' Who said this to you?"

"I told you. A couple I met on the street." The food Amaleigh ate soured in her stomach, and her nerves tightened. "I've never seen them before. I don't think they're from here. Perhaps they're from Aerithilyn."

"It's possible." Cassia turned to confront Amaleigh. "Who are you really?" She waggled a finger in Amaleigh's face. "Your disguise is good. A little too good. I'll admit, I didn't notice anything amiss, but Merigold did. In the bath."

"When you tried to seduce answers from me." She kept her tone more sulky than threatening.

"For all the good that did me. You've got great power, Erma, but you hide it. Why?"

Amaleigh snorted. "I wish I had great stores of magic, but I don't. I can barely do the most basic of spells." Cassia already knew she had magic, so there was no sense denying it any longer.

The princess peered straight through her, as if she were reading her soul. "Interesting."

The tea tray had been removed, and in its place a variety of cordials with dainty glasses sat on a silver platter. Beside it, a selection of cheeses spread across a decorative board. Her stomach gave a vicious pinch. The royals ate more in one day than she'd had in an entire month growing up.

She poured herself a glass of something dark and offered one to the princess and her ladies. The alcohol burned the back of her throat in a satisfying way, and she swallowed a burp. Cassia poured her another glass and they raised their drinks to each other. The second time wasn't nearly as hot as the first, but it still left a warm trail to her belly.

A sweet wooziness came over her. Yes, delirious oblivion,

that's what she sought. One night of solid sleep to escape everything happening around her. She toyed with the cheese knife, her mind spinning.

Cassia knew she had magic. What harm would there be in showing the princess her true identity? She'd know once and for all whether Cassia was a friend or foe.

"I could ask the same of you. Who are you really?" Amaleigh turned to face the princess and met a wall of five women. None of them looked too pleased with her words.

"What makes you think I'm anyone other than who I say?"

In a trice, Amaleigh flicked her wrist and released the knife toward Cassia's heart. Equally as quickly, Merigold snatched the blade before it reached the princess.

"What the flox is wrong with you?" Cassia fumed, her face flushed. "You could've killed me."

"It's just a cheese knife. It might've scratched you, nothing more. Besides, you have your *ladies* to protect you."

Merigold gripped the hilt of the little knife hard enough, her knuckles turned white. "I will disembowel you for your impertinence."

"You'd probably enjoy it, too." The alcohol emboldened her words, and Amaleigh approached the beauty. "But not yet. Something's going on here and you're part of it." Her gaze slid to Cassia. "All of you. I'm tired, so if you'll excuse me, I'm going to bed."

Cassia grabbed her hand. "Don't. I mean, stay with me tonight."

Amaleigh grinned and swayed where she stood. Flox the stupid drinks. They made her giddy and vulnerable. "Like I said, thanks for the offer, but I'm just not capable of giving you what you so obviously desire. I wish I could."

A snort came from behind her, and she swiveled her head to face Jada. Or was it Oona?

"I'm not asking you to stay with me to fuck." Cassia said and Amaleigh turned to face her, regretting the movement instantly. "I don't trust the prince and think perhaps your life might be in danger." A nervous glance went to Merigold. "I had a nightmare last night. A shadow stalks you and wishes you harm."

Amaleigh shuddered with the memory of the fake Gwilym in her room. She didn't desire a repeat of his visit, but neither did she wish to stay with the dubious princess.

"I promise you will not be harmed in my care. On my honor as a princess."

"Is that really a thing? Like, do you princesses get together once a year and decide what honor to uphold? Is there a secret handshake? Maybe a special wave you all give so you know who's in the club?"

"Isla, escort her to my bedchamber. Make sure there's a chamber pot next to the bed, just in case." To Amaleigh, she said, "Perhaps it would be best if you didn't drink any more tonight. I don't think graslip agrees with you."

"Graslip? Never tried it."

"Obviously." Cassia lifted her chin, and Isla took Amaleigh by the elbow.

They left through one of the doors tucked into a corner. It led to the queen's private quarters. It didn't go unnoticed that Cassia had been given these rooms, and Amaleigh wondered what the relationship was between the real Gwilym and the mysterious princess.

"Do you think she loves the prince?"

Isla grunted and steered her toward a huge bed. "That's none of your concern. But no, she does not love him."

"Because she has you, her Fianna Bel'en, right?" Amaleigh grinned sloppily at the pretty woman. Not a stunning beauty like Merigold, but prettier than any of the ladies at Eidyn's court. Although, the glare she gave Amaleigh did a fair job of detracting from her beauty.

"Never say those words again, do you hear me? If you do, I will finish what Meri promised."

Amaleigh slid a hand around her midsection. Disembowelment didn't sound like fun.

Under her breath, Isla muttered, "Foolish human."

A second before she started to say, "Aha!" Amaleigh bit her cheek. The fool graslip loosened her tongue. She'd do well not to say anything else until morning.

Isla seemed to agree. She stripped Amaleigh of her gown and thrust a chemise in her direction. After she pulled it over her head, Isla sat her in a chair and brushed out her hair. Within minutes, she added several more braids and tied them off with a golden thread.

"Under the covers, now." The Fianna Bel'en nudged Amaleigh toward the huge bed, and she happily obliged. Once she was burrowed deep, Isla stroked her forehead. "The princess worries for you, which means we all worry for you. Please don't do anything stupid."

"I'll take that under advisement. Good night, Isla."

"Blessed dreams."

Isla blew out the candles until only one flickered in the corner. Amaleigh listened to her moving around the room and finally settle on a chair not far from the bed. She'd assumed the woman would stay to make sure she didn't get up to any mischief. She needn't have worried. The only plan Amaleigh had for the evening was to sleep as deep and as long as possible. She closed her eyes and darkness enveloped her with a sinister embrace.

A shadow chased her. She knew she was dreaming, but couldn't wake up to stop the masked man from coming after her. Sluggishness weighed her thoughts, and she shifted in the large bed. A physical heaviness pressed upon her body.

"Cassia, I said no." She pushed against the princess, and made contact with a hard chest.

A hand went over her mouth, and she cried out at the same time she kicked against the duvet.

"Quiet." A blade pressed against her throat, and she stilled. "Better."

It was too dark to see her attacker, but she knew who it was—the man pretending to be Gwilym. She slid a glance to her side and saw Cassia's blonde hair against the white pillows. She couldn't tell whether the girl was alive or not, and her bowels turned to liquid.

"Don't fight me."

His acrid breath burned against her cheek, and she struggled against the hand over her mouth. If she could find purchase, she'd bite him. The blade cut into her skin.

"I will kill you if you don't do exactly as I say." He wore a mask over his face, a swathe of black fabric that covered everything but his eyes. They were hard and dark and filled with unspeakable cruelty.

His weight lifted off her body, and she felt the duvet being pulled away. Cool air rushed over her bare legs. The fake prince stroked down her body and held the knife beneath her left breast. Warmth covered her nipple, and she tensed. He was going to rape her there, in the bed beside Cassia. Where were the princess's ladies?

Her mind spun with how to get out of the predicament, but her body wouldn't cooperate. She could feel everything he did to her, but her arms flopped at her side, useless. When she tried to kick her legs, they felt leaden and refused to obey. Only her head moved when commanded. What utter bullshit. He'd made sure she saw and heard everything but couldn't fight back. That more than the actual assault raised her ire. What a floxy fucking coward.

The man moaned and stroked down her abdomen to between her legs. He bit her nipple at the same time he ground the hilt of his knife into her soft pubis. She turned her head, but he pressed his hand harder against her mouth. Her teeth cut into her lips, but she wouldn't whimper. Wouldn't give him the satisfaction of hearing her pain. She slid her gaze to her right and saw the slumped form of Isla in the chair.

She hoped with all her heart he hadn't killed Cassia and her ladies.

The knife blade traced along her leg while his mouth suckled her breast, and she swallowed the vomit that rose up her throat. A stinging crossed her thigh from one side to the other where he cut into her skin. Warm blood oozed down her leg but all she could do was lay perfectly still.

He ran a finger across the wound, then brought it to his lips. She stared in horror as he opened his mouth and sucked her blood from his fingertip. He was insane. This madman who pretended to be her friend was going to kill her.

Like hell he would. She mustered her magic and breathed deep as it swirled through her veins. The fake prince moaned as if in ecstasy and lifted his face toward the ceiling. His weight returned to her body. Still clothed, he rubbed his erection against her bare skin, grunting and jerking.

Her magic slithered from her like a snake shedding its skin. She reached for it, but it wasn't there. Just an empty void where moments before she'd felt power. The more she fought to grab it, the more exhausted and weakened it made her.

The blade returned to her throat, and his cruel eyes bore into hers. With a final thrust against her pelvis, he grimaced and shivered.

She gagged and swallowed her own sickness. He raised the

knife, and she saw the blade flash in the scant moonlight. Harnessing the last of her energy, she thrust into the depths where her magic resided and tried to grasp her power. It vaporized into a haze that left her depleted.

The last thing she felt was the knife hilt smashing into her temple.

CHAPTER
THIRTY

Light filtered through wooden slats on the window, and Amaleigh blinked into the brightness. Her head pounded and her throat was dry. She raised a hand to her temple and recoiled at the rope binding her wrists together.

The events of the previous night flooded her mind, and she curled into a ball against the onslaught of horrid images. The fake prince had assaulted her in Cassia's bed. He'd somehow immobilized her body to hold her down and—she raised her fingertips to a small cut on her throat. Another gash throbbed on her thigh. Oh, gods. Every tiny detail cascaded, one over the other, until she was almost sick.

She curled tighter and sobbed silently while rocking against the rough stone wall. It didn't matter he hadn't internally violated her—his dry humping and mindfuck was just as awful. The expression on his face as he climaxed was scalded into her memory. A shudder hit so hard she rattled the little bed. He hadn't raped her completely, yet. The ropes at her wrist were a promise that he would soon finish what he'd started. The fact he hadn't gagged her meant she was somewhere he felt secure in the knowledge no one would find her.

He'd moved her from Cassia's room, but she wasn't sure where. Amaleigh shuttled the harrowing memories of the previous night aside and looked around the sparsely furnished room. There would be time later to unpack all that the fake prince had done, or sought to do, but right then, her only concern was survival. The walls she'd perfected building around her heart served her well now as she buried her disgust and revulsion to focus on escaping. First, she had to know where she was escaping from.

The small mattress she lay on looked clean. A serviceable stand with bowl and pitcher sat beside the door, with a single chair in the corner. A servant's room, perhaps. She shuffled to stand, hampered by the rope that held her ankles together. After a wobble or two, she managed to peer out the window. Gardens stretched into the distance.

She was still at the palace. Which meant, if she was in the servants' quarters, she knew how to get out without being seen. The only problem was—well, two problems actually—she was dressed in nothing but a chemise, and her ankles and wrists were bound.

Amaleigh reminded herself she'd survived worse and closed her eyes. Anxiety pooled in her gut, but she steadfastly ignored it. She didn't have time to fret. The fake prince could return at any moment.

She hopped to the door and listened, but it was quiet. The servants would all be downstairs, working. When she tried the doorknob, it was locked, as she'd suspected it would be. Her magic had deserted her the night before, but that was under duress. She sat on the mattress and rested her hands in her lap.

Instead of concentrating on her magic, she reached for her dragon. Warmth infused her veins, and she imagined flames surrounding her. She focused the flames on the ropes binding her limbs. Heat singed her skin, and she breathed deep.

She was one with the flames. She was a child of fire.

A spark flared on the rope around her wrist, and she fed her power into it. Her magic started and stuttered, but it didn't desert her. The little flare grew until the twines curled and burned of their own volition. In a matter of seconds, she'd burned through the rope.

Just as quickly, she undid the knots tying her ankles together. The lock proved no problem as she'd been manipulating them since she was four. Even without magic.

Dust motes drifted through the filtered light in the quiet corridor, and Amaleigh quickly shut the door behind her, locking it with a flick of her wrist. Having her magic swirl through her veins again made her feel whole, empowered. It was there, but tempered. She had enough to light the rope on fire and lock a door, but doubted she'd have the energy to make a portal.

She slipped into a secret passageway behind the main walls and hurried to a set of stairs used exclusively by the servants. If any of them saw her, they might tell the prince, but it was the only way she knew for certain she wouldn't run into him.

Twice, her mad escape was interrupted by servants, but she was able to duck into a darkened corner each time. At the hallway leading to her room, she hesitated. The fake prince might be waiting for her. She needed clothing and her belongings. She couldn't risk it.

Pivoting on her bare feet, she headed for Cassia's rooms. Flox and barnacleballs. The princess—was she alive? Cassia had been in the bed when the fake prince assaulted her. He must've drugged all of them, but she couldn't be certain his vileness went so far as to kill Cassia and her ladies. No. Amaleigh shook her head. He wouldn't be that foolish. Even disguised, Cassia was a princess of high standing, and if she or her ladies were harmed at Heshen's court, the king of Aenglebreck would declare war.

She touched a finger to her temple, where dried blood caked her skin. The only way he could've drugged them all and not the other lords and ladies was to drug the graslip. That's why it had affected her so quickly. Bloody fucking hell. As soon as she found suitable clothing, she'd kill him. Slowly, painfully, and completely.

At the doorway to the queen's sitting room, Amaleigh heard Cassia's worried voice and breathed a huge sigh of relief. She couldn't make out their words, just tone and inflection. One of the Fianna Bel'en was angry, and rightly so. If not for her own rage, she would be curled into a ball, crying, at that very moment. Anger kept her moving, kept her thinking, kept her from totally, completely, losing her shit. The fake prince would be dealt with, of that she was certain.

She hurried to the princess's dressing room and rummaged through her clothes until she found a pair of loose-fitting trousers and a brocade tunic. As for shoes, all Cassia had were court slippers and a pair of riding boots. She shoved the flowy pant legs into the boots, not caring if she looked a fool.

Next, she went to Cassia's writing table and found a stick of wax that made a suitable writing utensil. Cassia wouldn't know what happened to her, and she wanted to let the princess know she wasn't dead. She needed to be clever and write something that only the princess would understand and yet wouldn't alarm the fake prince should he see it first.

She scrawled "fly *darathi vorsi*" on a sheet of paper and prayed the princess would know who it was from. She placed a hairbrush atop the folded paper and left Cassia's rooms.

At the kitchens, Amaleigh double-checked her magical mask before striding through the bustling rooms as if she had every right to be there. She'd learned on her adventures with Gwilym that confidence was rarely questioned. Don't make eye contact. Don't look around as if you're lost, and especially, don't appear nervous. Even though her legs trembled, she kept walking at a leisurely pace. A lady wouldn't run through the palace.

A hunk of bread tempted her, and Amaleigh picked it up as if she had every right to do so. No one stopped her. Gwilym had taught her all those years ago that all she had to do was dress nice, and thieving would be much simpler. But she never stole from him or the palace. That would've been a betrayal of their friendship. Her heart skipped a beat—until she stole the dagger. She'd told herself she was stealing from the king, and for a good reason, but it didn't absolve her of the fact that she'd broken her promise to her best friend.

"Kin I help ye?" A skinny woman with flour up to her elbows lifted her chin in Amaleigh's direction.

Her chest tightened, and she squared her shoulders. The door leading to the gardens was but twenty paces away. So close, yet so far.

"The princess wishes to relax in the orchard. I'm checking the perimeter for her."

"The perry what? Ah, never you mind. Go on, then." The cook waved her away, but Amaleigh's stomach growled its empty state.

"She'll require sustenance. May I take a few things?"

"Be quick about it. If'n the steward catches ye here, there'll be a demon to pay." She slapped a ball of dough and turned her attention back to kneading.

Amaleigh didn't linger. She grabbed a block of cheese and jug of milk. A quick scan didn't produce a bag to carry her items, which was a shame because the amount of food laying around would've fed her for an many happy days. Another roar from her stomach, this time followed by a pinch, quickened her steps.

At the door leading to the special gardens reserved only for the kitchen staff, she chanced a quick glance behind her, but no one cared what she was doing. They had their own lives to worry about.

Once outside, she jogged through the orchards, snagging several apples on her way to the far side of the palace grounds. She barely breathed the entire way. Only when she passed the high hedge that terminated the palace grounds did she stop to drink the milk and take a bite of the cheese. The rest she'd eat along the way. If only she knew where, exactly she was going.

She had no plan. Nowhere to run. Except the sewers. Or possibly Dante's ship. Remembering the little spy from the day before, she removed that from her list. Her attic, perhaps—the room she'd lived in before leaving Eidyn. By now someone else had surely found it and made it theirs. She didn't fancy another trip through the muck, but it was the last place the fake prince would look for her.

She strode through the side streets in the elite district until she reached a narrow alleyway she knew led to the sewers. She squeezed between the bricks, wondering when they'd gotten pushed together. Of course, it wasn't the bricks that had changed, but her. She grimaced as the expensive fabric of her tunic scraped along the rough stone.

Once through, she peered into the darkened path. Urchins called places like this home. She'd lived someplace similar for most of her life until she found the abandoned attic in the merchant district. She crept forward, wary. All of Antonio's thieves knew how to defend themselves—with a weapon and without.

A grubby little face emerged from the shadows and Amaleigh tensed. He held a long blade in his little hands. All urchins learned early on to protect their belongings. It was the second rule of the streets. The first rule was to protect yourself.

A cough came from behind him, followed by wheezing. The look of panic that crossed his features should've alarmed her, but instead it made her soften toward him. She'd been that filthy little blighter a lifetime ago. Had lived in a squalid alley much like this one. She knew the life he led and the fear that came with being too young to know anything except hunger and terror.

Amaleigh knelt in front of him. "I won't hurt you." She lowered the blade, but he brought it back to eye level. "What's your name?"

He glanced behind him again and shook his head.

"Is that a friend back there? Are they sick? I can help them." She held out the cheese and bread. "Take this. Don't eat it all at once or you'll hurt your tummy."

He couldn't have been more than five. About the age she'd been when she found Gwilym's study rooms at the palace.

The blade disappeared in a flash, and the boy snatched the food from her hand. Guilt flickered across his face, and he stepped aside so she could enter his hovel.

"Who's there?"

The voice that rasped from the shadows broke her heart. She knew that voice. Had been hearing it in her mind for several days.

She looked the boy full in the eye. "Did you help the prince?"

His cheeks bulged with food and he nodded, eyes full of apprehension.

"You did good. He's my friend. I'll help him now." She leaned back on her heels and peered into the dimness. They couldn't stay there. She'd have to find a place to hide. Her gaze returned to the boy. "I need you to get a message to someone for me. He'll give you food, and if you promise not to lie or steal from him, maybe even a job. Will you help me?"

His eyes grew larger and a smile broke over his little teeth.

"Go to the harbor and find Captain Danteneux on the *Sundancer*. Tell him Erma Kielder sent you and that she found her missing friend. Tell him I'm safe for now, but that I'd like him to take care of you. Can you do that?"

He swallowed and nodded. "I promise, miss."

Thank the gods, he could speak. She was beginning to worry that he hadn't learned to talk yet. "Good lad. Now, repeat what I said."

He said her words verbatim, and she pulled him into an embrace. His skeletal body hung limp in her arms.

"Go now. Tell no one about me or the people you helped. Promise."

"Promise." He spit on his palm and held it out to her.

She'd always hated this custom, but spit on her own hand and gripped his.

His dirty little head bounced down the alley and disappeared through the slim opening. Shuffling came from the dimness, and she rose on unsteady legs. Seeing the urchin brought back unwelcome memories.

A figure loomed from the shadows, and she turned to see a ravaged face.

"Gwilym?" Tears bit the backs of her eyes, and she sucked in air.

Until that moment she hadn't allowed herself to think about what would happen when she found Gwilym and now she shook with suppressed elation that he stood before her, alive.

He held a large stick in his hand. "Don't come any closer."

"Gwilym, it's me." She took a risk and let her mask dissolve so that her friend might recognize her.

"Amaleigh? How did you find us?" He stepped forward and blinked into the bright sunlight.

Wracking coughs came from behind him, and her nerves went taut. The king.

Warring emotions tormented her fragile heart. She'd been totally focused on finding Gwilym and hadn't let herself entertain the possibility the king would be with him. Yet, at the same time, she knew he must be and didn't want to consider the moment when she'd be face-to-face with him, as she was now, his life in her hands.

She could let the king die. Or she could kill him herself and finally have revenge for his savage murder of her family.

Gwilym stumbled closer, his breathing labored.

She winced at the battered face that was once handsome. Sadness, elation, joy, horror—her emotions spun out of control. He was alive. Her Gwilym. She wasn't too late. On impulse, she flung her arms around him and choked on a sob.

"I was so frightened," she whispered into his grimy tunic.

His arms wrapped around her like a dragon protecting its young.

A movement at his side drew his attention, and he released her from his arms. She ducked beneath the haphazard shelter and stifled a gasp. The king lay on soiled rags, his legs splayed as if broken in several places. The skin on his face hung in tatters and his arm bent at a wrong angle. It was a miracle he was still alive.

Something shifted in her heart. If she sought revenge, it would have to be later, when the king was healed and hearty. Killing him now would be a mercy.

The king lifted his head and peered at her, as if trying to place her face. A moment later, he flopped back onto the makeshift bedding.

"He needs a physic." Gwilym's fingers brushed hers. "I don't know who I can trust in the city."

Nor did she. "You can't go back to the palace. Is there a safe place, somewhere no one knows about?"

"All of the king's properties are known to the guardsmen. For his own safety." He made a disgusted snort. "For all the good that did him. How did you find us?" A note of suspicion edged his words, and sorrow filled her heart.

"I heard you." She tapped her temple. "In my head."

Relief crowded the worry in his eyes. "I had hoped, but as the days dragged on, I feared the worst." He took one of her braids between his fingertips. "You changed your hair."

"Not by choice." Warm flutters tickled her belly.

"You're hurt." His fingers brushed the wound at her temple.

"I'll live, but we need to get your father somewhere where he can be healed." Which meant, not in Eidyn.

Thank the gods she'd found them. Neither Gwilym nor his father looked as though they had much life left in them.

They didn't have time to consider their options. By now, the fake prince had discovered she was missing and would be searching for her. There was only one place she knew where they'd be safe. She'd need magic, though, and hers was elusive.

Gwilym slipped his hand in hers. "I trust you, Amaleigh."

His touch warmed her from the inside and stoked her magic. It sparked and sputtered, but it was there in all its potency. Something in his touch brought forth a memory, but it was just out of reach, like her dragon. Once the men were safe, she could figure out what it meant, but right then, she was grateful to have her friend's hand in hers, his heartbeat thrumming through their touch. He strengthened her, emboldened her, gave her purpose.

They held the king between them, and Amaleigh opened a

portal to the one place she knew for certain the fake prince wouldn't find them.

CHAPTER

THIRTY-ONE

The cottage spun, and she grabbed a chair to steady herself. She'd never used a portal with two others and the amount of energy it consumed surprised her. Even with her magic restored, she was drained. Gwilym staggered beneath the weight of his father, and she helped them to the sofa. She needed a moment to catch her breath, but there wasn't time.

She scanned the room for Cornelius, but he wasn't there. Probably out tending to the twins. Which meant she'd have to care for the king and Gwilym on her own until he returned.

They gently laid the king on the soft cushions. His moans whistled through clenched teeth. What he needed was a surgeon. A doctor skilled in medicine and anatomy. The village would be no help—they considered Amaleigh the best healer in the region.

Warring emotions railed in her heart. This was the man who murdered her family. He was the cause of a slaughter that killed hundreds of mages and dragons. Why were the gods so cruel as to put his life in her hands?

Gwilym sank into a chair, and his hands flopped to the side.

For him. For Gwilym, she'd set aside her hatred of the man, if only for a day. She rose and smoothed her hands over her braids. The immensity of her rash decision hit her full force. She'd brought her enemy to her home. The thought pummeled her skull that she couldn't pretend to forgive the king. Not for one minute, let alone a day. He deserved to die. If she let him, this far from Eidyn, no one would know.

She'd know. And Gwilym would know. She swiped at a tear and turned her attention to what needed to be done. She could unpack her complicated emotions later. Right now, she had to focus.

They'd need tea and potions and salves. All things she could make. But first she had to see what injuries she was working with. She shivered in the cold room and glanced at the empty hearth. It wasn't like Cornelius to let the flames die—they kept a low fire burning at all times to give the dragon's egg heat. She'd deal with Cornelius later. With an irritated flick of her wrist, she lit the fire. A whoosh of air and lick of flame shot toward them. Gwilym flinched where he sat, and Amaleigh swore beneath her breath. Emotions fueled magic—sometimes for good, most times not. She tempered her ire and returned her attention to the broken man lying on her couch.

The king resisted her touch when she tried to remove his arm from his abdomen. A spark of fury stung her heart, and she had to take a breath to keep from calling him a fucking murderous ass.

"Your Majesty, if you've any hope of living past today, I need to evaluate the extent of your injuries. I'm going to use magic to do so. It's the only way to save your life."

"You look familiar." The words squeaked from between his lips, and she had to untangle the syllables to understand.

His watery eyes drifted to her face, and she trembled, knowing he would now have a face to put to his death warrant.

No longer some anonymous girl who stole his dagger, she was a name and whole person.

"I'm the daughter of Helena and Selmar, your loyal servants whom you butchered." She wouldn't hide any longer. Let him see her face. Let him know who saved his life.

King Heshen nodded and removed his arm. A sliver of something crossed his eyes. Regret, perhaps, or annoyance, she couldn't be sure, but his features softened and a low sigh escaped his lips. Acceptance, if she had to guess. Of course he'd hate having his life saved by a mage. Well, flox him for being who he was and she who she was. Fate threw them together and it was up to her to decide whether she'd run from her past or face it.

She was done running.

Her examination took longer than she would've liked, but the king's injuries were numerous. She placed her hands on his chest and sent her magic beneath his skin to his blood cells and muscles. She stretched her healing to his broken bones and torn ligaments. His recovery would be difficult and long. She didn't envy him the days ahead, but at least he'd have breath to draw.

With her magic sustaining the king, she next checked Gwilym's damage. Not as horrific as the king's, he suffered several broken bones, including most of those in his face. The king's attackers had been brutal, but something about Gwilym's injuries led her to believe it was personal. Whoever beat him hated Gwilym.

She repeated the steps she'd taken with the king and sent her magic into Gwilym's body. Her fingers shook as they rested on his chest. His inconsistent heartbeat thrummed and skipped beneath her touch. If only she'd found him sooner. Tears flowed to drip from her chin, and she wiped them with her shoulder. She'd not lose him. Not again.

He cupped her cheek with his hand. "That bad, huh?"

"Not as bad as your father, actually." She leaned into his touch. She wanted to tell him she was sorry for abandoning him that night and for not finding them sooner, but the words stuck in her throat.

"Don't worry about me. Save the king."

She shook her head. "How can you love him after everything he's done?"

A crooked grin shifted the cuts on his face. "He's my father. The only family I have. I can't abandon him if there's a chance to right his wrongs."

"You can't change the past."

"No. But I can make a better future." His thumb brushed softly against her skin. "For everyone."

"I need to make preparations."

Gwilym clasped her hand in his. "Thank you." His gaze swept to his father and back. With a sigh, he closed his eyes.

To sleep, hopefully. He needed all the rest he could get.

"Don't thank me yet. You both have a lot that needs fixing." She rose and kissed his forehead, lingering to inhale his scent of sweat and blood and death. There would be time later to avenge him. Antonio already paid with his life, but she still had the real culprits to deal with.

The cottage door opened, and Cornelius strode inside. He stopped short when he saw Amaleigh and Gwilym. Then his gaze went to the king, and fury crossed his features.

"What are they doing here?" He waggled a finger at her. "Are you mad?"

Amaleigh stood to face him, her shoulders set. "It was the only safe place I could think of. They would've died, Cornelius. Was I supposed to just leave them?"

"Yes! Let them rot for all I care. Bloody hell, Amaleigh, I never would've taken you for brainless, but this is suicide." His rage came through in the harsh words. Then he took a long breath and looked at the ceiling. "I'm sorry. Of course you couldn't let them die, but why bring them here? This is our safe haven away from them, remember? What have the past seven years been about if you're just going to throw away what we've built by bringing them to our home?"

She understood his anger, truly she did, but there was a time for compassion and he wasn't in the right place to find his.

"I'm tired, Cornelius. Either stay and help or find something to keep you occupied outside. What's done is done." She brushed past him to the kitchen.

"The twins missed you. When you get a chance, see to them, will you?" His voice softened, and he joined her by the little cooktop they used to make tinctures.

"I will. Thank you." She put her hand on his sleeve and smiled up at him. "I know it's hard but put aside your anger for the moment. When they're healthy, then we can deal with our past."

He nodded and pulled her into an uneasy embrace. She kept her hands at her side, too upset with him to return the hug. When he released her, she glanced at Gwilym, who watched them with keen interest. A sliver of guilt cut through her heart. She tucked the feeling aside and focused on her work. They needed strong potions for both Gwilym and the king. Something that would speed their healing while they slept.

"Where's your locket?"

Amaleigh's hand went to her throat, and she frowned. "I left it at the palace. Cassia was asking questions, and I couldn't risk her seeing the portraits inside."

His jaw tensed and a cloud passed over his features. She waited for a scolding, but it didn't come. Instead, Cornelius turned away and began to gather ingredients. An apology hung on her lips, but she had nothing to apologize for. The locket held proof of her true identity. Surely, he understood why she had to leave it. Once more, she chastised herself for not hiding it with the dagger.

Struggling against a sense of shame, Amaleigh lit a fire under the burners. Their well-used pots hung above their heads, and she reached for the largest at the same time as Cornelius. It was something they'd done dozens of times, usually laughing at their synchronicity, but Amaleigh didn't feel like laughing. His presence was necessary, but a thin layer of tension hung over them. She tried to ignore it and focus on her work, but his passive-aggressive grunts and little jerks of annoyance kept interfering.

"Stop it," she hissed between her teeth.

"What?"

"This stupid game you're playing. Bumping into me, fretting about this or that. Make the potions and get on with it. I know you're upset. You don't have to behave as if I should be punished. I'm not a child, you know."

Cornelius tossed the pan he'd been swirling onto the cooktop and stormed out of the cottage, his fingers twitching at his side.

THIRTY-TWO

Amaleigh stared at Cornelius's retreating back, surprised by his anger. The door swung closed with a thud, and she winced against the sound. Tears threatened, but she refused to let him see her hurt. She righted the pan he'd carelessly toppled and filled a kettle for tea. While it brewed, she resumed her work, doing her best to forget Cornelius's tantrum.

Gwilym shuffled to where she stood and hovered close, but didn't touch her. "Can I help?"

With a grim smile, she nodded. Two hands were better than none. She poured three mugs of strong tea and added a healthy dose of honey to each, followed by a dollop of fresh milk. After taking one to the king and placing it where he could reach it easily, she returned to the cooktop and showed Gwilym how to swirl the liquid in Cornelius's discarded pan until it became a light amber. Gwilym used the back of a chair to support himself and did as she instructed. They worked in silence for several minutes before she gave him another task.

Her mind fought to remain calm and focused, but Cornelius's behavior perplexed her more than she cared to admit. She wasn't thrilled to have the king in her home either, but she'd determined to put aside her bitter anger long enough to treat the murderer. Maybe Cornelius couldn't. He'd been in his late twenties when the king slaughtered all the mages and dragons in Eidyn, and Amaleigh only three. She didn't remember much of that time, nor did she know anyone who was murdered besides her parents and brother. Cornelius had known them all—was friends or colleagues with all of them. How stupid of her to think he could set that pain aside.

As soon as she finished the potions, she'd find him to apologize.

"You have twins?"

Gwilym's voice brought her back to the moment, and she chuckled.

"It's complicated."

"Are you and Cornelius..." His voice trailed off, and Amaleigh glanced up to see sorrow lurking in his bruised eyes. "Are you together?"

"You mean are we lovers?" A wince of something dark flashed across his face, and she regretted her blunt words. "We're companions and friends, nothing more." She sighed as she stirred a thick liquid in her pan. "Apparently, I'm incapable of loving someone that way." She tapped her chest. "Cold, dark heart, I'm afraid."

Gwilym nudged her shoulder with his own. "I don't believe that for a minute. You would've left us to die if you didn't care. Or at the very least you would've left my father." His voice cracked. "I can't say that I'd blame you. He doesn't deserve your kindness, Amaleigh. I know it, and so does he. He's changed in the last few years—mellowed about so much. But that doesn't take away from what he did. He was a tyrant and murderer. I think he's trying to atone for his atrocities."

"Does he still celebrate the Purge's anniversary?"

A low sigh came from deep in his chest. "Yes, but it brings him no joy. He's afraid of disappointing the citizens of Eidyn if he cancelled them."

"They don't give a flox what the celebrations are for. They just want an excuse to party." Multiple days and nights of fireworks, feasting, and street parties where orgies happened in every villa and manor across the city. The citizens didn't honor the Purge during the celebrations as much as they saw it as an excuse for excess.

Antonio had adored the celebrations. It was his most lucrative time of the entire year. Drunken citizens with fat purses were easy pickings for thieves like Amaleigh. She'd done her fair share of separating a wealthy elite from their coins. Men or women...she hadn't cared. It was a long time ago for her, but having the king in her home brought the memories too close.

"I went to the palace looking for you. I met a rather gorgeous princess named Cassia. Do you know her?" Amaleigh's hands shook, and she set the pan clanging onto the cooktop.

Gwilym took her hands between his own and held her tight. "What is it? Are we in danger?"

She shook her head, unsure how to tell him about the pretender at the palace. He might not even know someone was masquerading as the prince. Damn it, she'd known something was off. Cornelius always told her to trust her instinct, and he was right.

"I'm fine. Really. It's been a long day and using magic depletes your energy. Let's get these finished and then we'll talk." She resumed her work, stalling the conversation she knew they'd have to have. It wouldn't be easy on either of them. She told herself she meant about the pretender and those who abducted them, but she couldn't deny that she also meant about Cassia. It shouldn't bother her if they were together, but the truth was, it did.

Quiet enveloped them, the only sounds coming from King Heshen's soft snores and the occasional scrape of pan against metal.

"What you did—risking everything by going to the palace —even though you knew to do so might've meant your death... how can I ever repay you?" Gwilym's soft words broke the silence.

She shrugged and looked into his battered face. "Don't die."

His eyes bore into hers with an intensity that brought a flush to her cheeks, and she licked her lips.

"I don't plan on it. Besides, I have the best healer in—where are we, exactly?"

A flutter of nerves upset her gut. Taking them to the cottage was one thing; telling him the name of the world was a whole other level of trust. She was already in too deep. And this was Gwilym. Her Gwilym.

"We're on a world called Cilachaem. You won't find it on any of your fancy maps. It's a simple place, but there are good people living here."

He put a hand on hers, and she exhaled slowly. "I understand. He doesn't need to know names or places." Gwilym inclined his head toward the sleeping king.

"When I heard you cry out, the anguish in your voice—it hurt as if I were being tortured, too. I don't understand why."

"I should never have involved you. I just didn't know where to turn or who to trust."

She squeezed his hand. The way he looked at her stole her breath and her words. She'd been his last and only hope.

He raised her hand to kiss her palm. Her heart did little flips and blips, and a strange tickling came from low in her abdomen. Warmth spread through her veins. The way he made her body react to a simple touch confused her. She was a cold, heartless witch. Or thought she was. Apparently not around Gwilym. Her mind cast back to the kiss they shared that night seven years ago.

She'd always had an attraction to him that she suppressed with the rest of her emotions. It was too much to hope he wanted her as much as she wanted him. By the look on his face, he did. Great, now she was deluding herself thinking it was anything more than a kiss.

He never really answered her question about Cassia. Maybe he did know her and they were just friends, or maybe it was something more. Even if there was a relationship, he was a prince and Cassia a princess. Flippin 'eck. Talk about lousy timing. The gods were having a laugh at her expense.

"We'll let these cool while you bathe. You stink."

A half grin quirked his lips, and he snorted. "Never one to mince words. I see some things never change."

They left the pans on the cooktop, and she led Gwilym to the little room they used for bathing. A good-sized tub dominated the room, but even it didn't fully fit Gwilym's height. Amaleigh turned on the faucets to full and set the temperature.

"Indoor plumbing, impressive."

She swatted his arm playfully. "We may not have all the luxuries offered in your palace, but you'll find the service incomparable."

"What about a change of clothes?" He plucked at his grimy shirt.

Cornelius was too short for his clothes to fit, nor did she think he'd be pleased to find the prince wearing his garments. The king would need freshening as well.

"I'll see what I can do."

He struggled to unfasten his court jacket, and she moved his hands out of her way. Once the buttons were undone, she gently slid it off his arms. Next, she lifted the cotton tunic he wore over his head. Gwilym gritted his teeth and shifted to accommodate her movements. She mumbled apologies with each grimace he made. At his trousers, she paused.

"Shall I continue?"

"Please." A devilish smile twisted his lips.

She unfastened his trousers quickly. "I'll let you slip them off." She took a step back and gasped at the angry red welts and bruises covering his skin. Not an inch wasn't marred or broken. "How the bloody hell are you still standing?"

"No idea. The more I'm with you, the stronger I feel."

"Yeah, right." She snorted.

"It's true. I can feel you," he tapped his chest and his temple, "in here. Although, I've always sensed you, but now it's like you're with me, healing. Not your magic—you."

He moved closer until their faces were mere inches apart.

"Gwilym—"

"Yes?" He closed the gap between them.

"I just—we shouldn't—what about the princess?" She hadn't meant to blurt the words, but she had to know.

"We're friends, nothing more. If she's interested in anything else, I'm certainly not. At least, not with her."

"Oh."

He bent until their faces nearly touched. "Yes, oh." Then his lips claimed hers.

She stilled, ready for the kick of disappointment, but it didn't come. Instead, her belly quivered with a flittering of nerves. Heat seared from his kiss, diving straight to her core. She hesitated, all too aware of his injuries and not wanting to cause more.

Gwilym didn't seem at all concerned for his welfare and nudged her lips open with his tongue.

He tasted of tea and milk and honey.

A dull throbbing started below her solar plexus and grew in intensity the longer the kiss went on. Her hands snaked up his back to curl in his hair, and he held her firmly against him. One hand tightened around her hip while the other cradled her head. For the first time she could remember, she felt safe. Protected. Even in the maelstrom of what her life had become, this was the center of the storm where all was calm.

Gwilym loosened his grip and drew back, a shy smile on his lips, rapture in his eyes. "Much better than that timid kiss I gave you the night you left. I was a fool and should've done that dozens of times before. The gods knew I wanted to."

"But we both know why you didn't. You're a prince, Gwilym. And I—well, I was a thief and now I'm a mage. Your father has a death warrant on me."

She could scarcely believe what he was telling her. He'd wanted to kiss her before. And often. Knowing why he hadn't didn't lessen the sting of remorse for what might have been. Maybe this was how it was supposed to happen. Now, here, this moment. She had to believe everything happened for a reason and trust in the timing.

"All of that will be forgiven. You saved his life. He owes you, Amaleigh. As do I."

Saving the king's life was one hell of a bargaining chip. She stroked his cheek, skimming her thumb across a nasty cut that was raw and ugly. Suddenly, she felt the cut as if it were her own. It was the one he received the night before when she'd had the vision of him at dinner. The horror of that moment replayed in her mind, and she shook her head against it.

"What is it?" Gwilym stroked her shoulders, terror dancing in his features.

"That sensation you described of feeling me inside of you...I have it too. Only, I relive your torture when I touch your wounds."

He gently removed her hand from his face and kissed her palm. "Then we should make new memories to erase the old."

"Am I interrupting anything?" Cornelius's tart words came from the doorway, and Amaleigh turned with an apology on her lips.

"Gwilym needed help undressing." Her cheeks flamed, and she balled her fists with a silent command to just shut up. She wasn't helping the situation.

"I brought clothes." Cornelius held out a bundle of plain brown fabric.

"Thank you." Amaleigh took them from him and set them on a stool in the corner. "If you don't need anything else?" she asked Gwilym. She'd expected to find him grinning, but there was no mirth in his eyes.

"I can manage." His gaze flicked from Amaleigh to Cornelius and back.

"Right, well, I'll be tending to your father if you change your mind." She scooted out of the room and ducked beneath Cornelius's outstretched arm.

Men were a complication she didn't need at the moment. She touched her lips and suppressed a grin at the memory of Gwilym's lips on hers.

A foreign throbbing started down low. Insistent, needy. She'd never believed herself capable of what she felt at that moment—desire. A shift happened internally, and she knew, in that moment, nothing would ever be the same.

CHAPTER
THIRTY-THREE

For two days, Amaleigh stayed at the cottage, caring for Gwilym and his father. The prince regained his strength quickly, but the king lingered between consciousness and deep sleep due to the strong draughts she gave him to help ease his pain and speed healing. Even with her constant care, she wasn't sure the king would live.

Cornelius stayed nearby, mostly to interfere in any privacy Gwilym and Amaleigh might share. Whether he knew he was intruding or not, she couldn't quite tell. His random disappearances always coincided with Gwilym's rest periods. Despite her best efforts, she struggled with her emotions. What had the kiss meant? To her? To Gwilym? He hadn't tried to kiss her again, but then, Cornelius hadn't given them a moment's peace.

Whenever he was around, Gwilym turned cold and distant. She didn't know why or whether it had to do with her or Cornelius. They knew each other from before the Purge, but she didn't know the extent of their relationship. It was one of the many questions she longed to ask him once they were alone.

On the third day, Amaleigh decided Gwilym was strong enough to show him the twins. Her heart stuttered at the same pace as her breathing as she led him out to the barn. He knew she was a mage, but not that she was also an Aerlghot. Albeit a struggling one. Still, in Eidyn before the Purge, dragon mages were revered. For centuries, they advised the king and had an amicable relationship with other kingdoms. After the Purge, all of that changed.

Amaleigh wasn't sure how Gwilym felt about Aerlghots, or even mages. They never talked about them growing up, and now she feared what he might say.

She waited until Cornelius left on one of his mysterious errands and woke Gwilym from his nap with a finger to her lips. He'd risen without question and followed her outside, where she stood on shaky legs.

"What you're about to see would get me arrested in Eidyn. I'm already in over my head by showing your father my face and mage abilities." She implored Gwilym with her eyes, begging him to either tell her to stop, or to continue.

"Whatever it is, my father doesn't have to know."

The bruising on his face had faded to a yellowish-olive hue, and his handsomeness was beginning to re-emerge. A rush of desire swept over her; she looked away, frightened of her newfound passion. If mooning over someone was love, then she was better off before when she didn't twitter at every touch or wait for Gwilym to speak just so she could hear his voice. She was being ridiculous with her constant need to be near him.

She held Gwilym's hand and called for the twins from the gate. Slight tremors vibrated against her skin, and she gave him a squeeze.

"Don't be frightened. They're just babies right now and can't do much harm."

The twins romped out from the barn, all wings and tails and horns. They were at the adorably clumsy stage when they tripped over their own feet and sneezed fireballs. About the size of a large dog, they looked far more ferocious than they were.

"Cor biscuits!" Gwilym took a step back, but she held firm to his hand.

"The ochre one is Mali, and the darker red is Shen. We found their eggs in a cave with the corpse of their mother. They won't hurt you. Go on."

Gwilym stepped forward to stroke Mali's snout. "Can we go inside with them?"

"Of course. I wasn't sure how close you'd want to get." She unlatched the gate and let him inside before closing it behind her. Thus far, the fence had kept the twins contained, but as soon as they learned to fly properly, they'd be off on their own, creating havoc around the countryside.

Shen nudged Gwilym with his horns and head-butted him several times. "Ouch! Easy now." Gwilym put out a hand and flinched when Shen tossed his head. "Don't eat me. I don't taste so good right now. Your mum's been poisoning me with all kinds of potions and elixirs."

"That's not true and you know it." Amaleigh grabbed a handful of hay from the loft and held it out for Mali. The dragonling nibbled at it before shaking her head and knocking Amaleigh's hand. "She's upset with me for leaving her." Amaleigh stroked Mali's scales. "I'm sorry, my pretty girl. It was important and I had to go."

Amaleigh closed her eyes and held Mali's head between her hands. She spoke the language of dragons in her mind, explaining as well as she could about Gwilym's capture and escape. Shen lifted his snout and made a strange little cry before rubbing his head against Gwilym's leg. She stared at him, shocked that he'd heard what she said without physical contact. She had to tell Cornelius. Her heart leapt, then sunk.

Cornelius wasn't there. She was so accustomed to his presence, it was odd not to have him underfoot.

"Did he just speak to me?" Gwilym stroked Shen's scales and patted his thick neck.

"What?"

"This one, Shen, right? I could've sworn he said something." He shook his head and knocked a fist on his temple. "Those beatings must've scrambled my brain."

Amaleigh considered him for a long moment, her lips pursed. "Or loosened something else. Come on, I have something to show you."

They walked side by side to the edge of the cliff. Wind swept up from the ocean far below, and she lifted her face to feel the force of nature. Salt air stung her skin while her loose curls twisted at all angles.

"So beautiful."

She turned to find Gwilym not looking at the horizon, but at her. "Shut up."

He nudged her shoulder with his own and did that stupid grin that made her belly flip. "It's true. Even when you were little and covered in grime, you glowed. Positively shined with some inner power that I never understood. But I knew even then, when I was too young to comprehend the throne and all being a prince encompassed, I knew you were special. And now look at you. A mage."

She cocked her head, a genuinely happy smile relaxing her features. "Thank you. It wasn't easy, my life growing up, but I always knew I had you to look forward to. No matter how brutal my punishments or how tired I was from training, you were waiting for me. The time I spent in the palace with you are the happiest memories from my entire life."

"Oh, come now. Surely you've had better days since then? I

mean, you have old man Cornelius to pal around with. What could be terrible about that?"

She knew he was joking, and it was mostly true, but still. He didn't understand how Cornelius had offered an escape from Eidyn or that it was Cornelius who had found her the night her parents were murdered by Gwilym's father. If not for him, Amaleigh wouldn't be alive.

"He's not that bad. Just...protective, and rightly so." The question was there, on her lips, but she couldn't speak the words to ask Gwilym shy he disliked Cornelius so much.

"Because of my father, I know. At least Cornelius took you away from Eidyn and gave you a decent life. It was more than I did." Gwilym turned to face the ocean and closed his eyes. "He's in love with you, and I don't mean in any sort of platonic way."

Amaleigh slipped her hand into Gwilym's and squeezed. "I know. He's made his feelings for me well known, and I've also explained to him that I don't return those affections. I love him like a brother, or an adopted father even, but not with any kind of passion." She let go of his hand and crossed her arms over her midsection, gripping her elbows. "Until recently, I feared I was incapable of loving anyone not platonically, as you say." She'd said too much. Given too much away.

"Until recently? How recently?"

She rubbed her arms and shivered. "I first felt it when you kissed me in Eidyn, but convinced myself it was a fluke and built walls to keep those emotions locked up tight. Then you had to go and kiss me again here, and well, I can't deny it any longer. You've quite literally stripped all my walls and defenses away. I spend my days mooning over that stupid kiss and wishing for more."

Now she'd really said too much. She clamped her lips shut and watched his reactions for signs of rejection.

He scraped his hair off his face and blew out his cheeks with a quick shake of his head. "I had thought I, too, was incapable of love. I loved you the moment I first saw you in the palace when you were a grubby little bean, but I hid those feelings out of some sort of loyalty to you. Or maybe because I didn't want to have my heart broken. Then, after you left, I too built walls to protect myself. The moment I saw you in the alley, those walls crumbled. I knew it was you. Had always been you. Would only ever be you."

"But I'm not a princess. Isn't there a law about you marrying only a princess or something?"

He laughed and turned to face her. "There's no law. Besides, there's only one princess in residence at the palace, and she's not interested in me in that way. At all."

A zippy little flare of excitement ran through her veins. "How long has she been there?"

He tilted his head side to side. "Six months, maybe? She came as an exchange and the first my father ever allowed. I think he started fearing I'd never marry and produce an heir. It's customary for nobles to send their offspring to foster with other high-ranking families. Builds alliances and often ends in marriage between two kingdoms. I'm sure Aenglebreck would love to have their princess as queen of Eidyn one day, but they and my father will be disappointed. I don't think Cassia would be too upset, however. She spends more time with her ladies-in-waiting than with me."

Amaleigh grinned at that. Fianna Bel'en were as dangerous on the battlefield as they were in the bedroom. "Her ladies are gorgeous. That Merigold? Oof."

Gwilym's expression turned from sympathetic to surprise. "Did she try to seduce you, too?"

"In the bathtub. I told you, I'm incapable of lust. Her efforts were wasted on me."

"And now? Are my efforts wasted as well?" His eyes narrowed and lips quirked.

The throbbing down low returned, and her vision tunneled to just him. She opened her mouth slightly, willing him to kiss her. It was dangerous, this feeling she had. His father murdered her parents. He was heir to the throne. None of that had mattered growing up because she didn't know Heshen's role in her life, and the throne was something far off in the future. She didn't have the luxury of thinking a day in advance back then, but she did now.

"What happens when you're healed and go back to Eidyn? Do you honestly believe your father will welcome me with open arms? Once he's healed, he'll forget any kindness I might've showed him. Tell me I'm wrong. Tell me you believe your father has changed and would accept a dragon mage for a daughter-in-law. You have a kingdom to consider. Surely that's more important than me."

"One of the things I always admired about you was that you never, not once, referred to me as a prince. You never curtseyed or pretended loyalty. You alone never called me Your Highness. I was always Gwilym to you. Your friend. You never judged me, Amaleigh, so don't start now."

"I'm not judging you. I'm being realistic."

He turned his attention back to the ocean and sighed. "'Tis a beautiful sight. I'm glad you shared it with me, Amaleigh." A cold distance entered his voice, and she shivered.

The wall around her heart she'd allowed to crack rose higher, stronger. What a fool she'd been to allow herself to believe she was capable of love.

THIRTY-FOUR

They returned to the cottage in silence, and Amaleigh busied herself with making tea. Gwilym needed rest, and she had some hard decisions to make. There were things he wasn't aware of and she was the one to tell him. Plus, she had a score to settle with the fake prince for attacking her, something she probably shouldn't share with the real Gwilym. If she said anything, he'd demand to return to Eidyn and fight the fake prince.

She still didn't know who was pretending to be the prince or why. Before the real Gwilym and the king returned, she wanted to make certain they wouldn't be put at risk. She hadn't worked this hard just to have some upstart undo all her healing. Even so, he deserved to know the truth.

"Gwilym." She set down his teacup and sat opposite him at the little table. She hated seeing him upset, especially knowing she was about to destroy him further. "There's something you need to know."

He wrapped his fingers around the cup but did not drink. "This sounds serious."

"It is." She glanced toward the king, who slept fitfully on the makeshift bed they'd erected near the fire. "I'm returning to Eidyn today, but you need to stay here and care for the king." He opened his mouth to speak, but she held up her hand. "Before you say it, no, you can't come with me. There are extenuating circumstances you aren't fully aware of. The reason no one searched for you is because those in the palace believe the king is hunting and you, well, you're there."

His face scrunched with a perplexed look. "But I'm here."

"And you're there. Someone is impersonating you. I believe whoever is pretending to be you is the one responsible for your kidnapping. I sensed something was off with the fake Gwilym, but I must admit, he's good. Whoever they are, they're skilled with magic. I couldn't see through their mask, and I'm certain neither could Cassia."

Gwilym leaned forward, his hands spread over the table. "An imposter? But how?"

"It's easy enough to do for a talented mage. This is how I disguised myself at the palace." She fixed the mask in place that she wore to the palace, and Gwilym whistled.

"No wonder I didn't recognize you." He peered closer and inspected her from every angle. "It's remarkable."

"The pretender didn't recognize me either, even with clues as to who I was."

"Clues?"

"I called myself Erma Kielder."

"Like my dog!" Gwilym's face lit up, and he grinned at the mention of his favorite pet. "What a scamp he was. Do you remember how we used to pretend he was a winged horse and we gods?"

"I do. That's why I used that name. I had hoped you'd recognize it, as you just did, but the fake Gwilym didn't react at all. That's when I suspected something wasn't right. Then his appalling behavior at dinner with the princess. Blargh."

"What do you mean? Did he harm her?"

The concern in Gwilym's tone showed he cared for the princess more than he was willing to admit. Amaleigh swallowed a bitter lump of jealousy.

"He made a show of affection that turned my stomach. I don't think Cassia appreciated it much. She tolerated his gross display, but only just."

"Good for her. She's far stronger than she appears, you know."

Amaleigh narrowed her gaze and bit her lower lip to keep from speaking everything she knew about the princess. The question nagged at her—if Gwilym didn't know she was really an elven princess and not from Aenglebreck, she didn't want to be the one to surprise him. That was Cassia's secret to tell.

"I've seen her strength. That's why you must stay here and I return alone. I believe Cassia is an ally we can trust. I'll have her there, if necessary."

"I don't like it, but if there's an imposter at the palace, bringing my father back there before he's recovered might be the worst possible thing."

It was exactly what she'd hoped he'd say.

She made extensive notes of what he needed to give his father and at what intervals. Next, she checked their stores to make certain he had enough food to last a few days. Satisfied he'd be reasonably well kept without her there, she led him to her room and opened a secret door in the little table she used as a vanity.

"If I need to send word, I'll write a note and have it delivered here. Do you remember the language we made up as children?"

"Our secret pirate's code? Of course."

That he remembered they used to pretend to be pirates was trivial in the larger scheme of things, but that small fact wedged a hunk of affection in her throat. Tears threatened, but she blinked them away.

"Good. If you need to get word to me, write your note and place it here. Before you ask, I can store things in time and space. It's complicated and not easy to explain, so just trust me."

He looked at her as if she'd sprouted six arms and a bushy tail. "When this is all over, I want to know everything about you. Even then, I think you'll continually surprise me."

A bubble of giddiness lifted her cheeks with a sloppy grin. "You should be careful what you wish for. I have some secrets that might shock you." Like that she was an Aerlghot, for one.

If her dragon would ever surface.

"No worries of that happening." The chill in his voice from the cliff was a distant memory. Warmth infused his words. "We used to tell each other everything, Amaleigh. Remember? There's nothing you can say that changes how I feel about you."

The emotion in his quiet statement was like a blow to her solar plexus. He stood close and smelled so good. That damned wall around her heart cracked, and she steadied herself against the vanity.

"Notes in here, written in code. Got it?" She couldn't look at him. Didn't want to see the need in his eyes. Instead, she placed her hands on her hips and looked around the small room. Her bed and a few chests were the only furniture. An old rug covered the stone floor. It was a far cry from his palace, but for her, it was enough.

"Amaleigh." He held her hands in his own and met her eyes. Concern danced in the dark depths. "Be careful."

There was more he wanted to say, she felt it in his stare, but he only uttered those two words.

"I will."

He bent and covered her lips with his own. His scent of salt air and vanilla mingled with a woody oakmoss. Gwilym. She took him into her mouth and gripped the nape of his neck, not wanting to let go. His tongue entangled with hers, and she moaned softly. The wall shattered and the rapid beat of her heart pulsed through her chest hard enough she was certain he could feel it.

Need built in that place she'd thought was cold and barren. She squeezed her thighs together, hoping to halt the throbbing, but it only made it worse. Gwilym shifted and his hip brushed her ribs. His erection pressed against her midsection. A flutter of insecurity gave her pause. Cornelius might return any moment.

As if hearing her unspoken thought, Gwilym reached a leg and shut the thick door. He gazed at her with lust pooling in his gorgeous blue eyes. There was a question in them, too, as if he waited for her permission.

She wanted this. Needed this. In answer, she tugged his tunic and stepped backward to the bed. Before she reached it, Gwilym stripped off his shirt and stood in front of her, bare chested. She sucked in a breath at the sight of his broad muscles. A smattering of dark hair teased her to scrape her fingers through the soft curls.

Her gaze swept over his abused skin, noting that most of the bruising had faded, with a few of the cuts still healing. "I don't want to hurt you." She tentatively touched one of the more vicious wounds.

His chuckle rumbled to her core, and she trembled with a passion she'd suppressed for far too long.

"There's no need to worry about that. You could never hurt me."

Not true. He was a prince and she a commoner. But for the moment, she wouldn't allow anything to prevent her from loving him as much as she was able. Emotionally, physically, wholly.

With slightly trembling fingers, he unfastened her stays and lifted her gown over her head. She fidgeted with the sleeves of her chemise, unsure where to put her hands. Next, he untied the ribbon holding the garment in place and gently slid it down her shoulders until it puddled at her feet. She stood naked before him, exposed. Vulnerable.

No words were spoken as he gazed at her from head to toe, but his eyes told her how much he desired her. She shifted under the scrutiny, unsure what was expected of her. Her heart beat strong and steady, if a little too fast, and her face flushed with his continued appraisal. It was thrilling and terrifying to be standing there, the sole object of his attention. Those lovely blue eyes of his gazed at her, and all worry that she wasn't enough faded. A small smile lifted his lips, and she bit her own to keep from weeping with unbridled joy.

In that moment, she was his. Truly, completely. And he was hers.

His head lowered to take a nipple in his hot mouth, and she gasped at the sensations coursing through her body. This was nothing like the fake prince's assault, where she'd lain frozen and terrified. This was her Gwilym. His touch made her skin first chill as if from a winter's breeze, and then burn from a flame lit deep within. Each caress brought fireworks and breathlessness all at once. Her vaginal muscles spasmed and clenched with want. It was too much and yet not enough. She craved more.

Her hands fumbled in his hair, and she by turns pulled and smoothed his curls. When his mouth left her breast, she whimpered until he suckled the other and the sensations began anew. She rocked with anticipation, scratching down his back and caressing his shoulders. Everywhere her fingers glided over his skin, the injuries healed until his flesh was unmarked.

His tongue swirled around her nipple, driving her to distraction. He nipped her lightly with his teeth and she cried out, but not in pain.

When he stood, that silly half grin teased her, and he made a lazy lap with his tongue around his lips. Emboldened by his cockiness, she gripped the fasteners on his trousers and tugged them open. He helped her slide the pants over his hips and down his legs before stepping out of them completely.

Her gaze traveled instinctively to his protruding cock, and she gasped. It wasn't the first she'd seen, but never had she been this close, nor had they been as eagerly elongated. She wrapped her hand around the shaft, delighting in the silkiness of his skin. A drop of liquid formed at the tip, and she bent low to lick it off. He arched and moaned a deep sort of animal growl that made her throb down low. She took the tip into her mouth and razed her tongue over the soft surface like he'd done to her nipple. He rocked with her movements, his hands tangled in her hair. More salty liquid dripped from the tip, and she greedily lapped it up.

His breathing deepened and his moans turned to groans as he guided her head and pumped harder into her eager mouth. His entire body stiffened and a moment later, he filled her with his semen, and she swallowed it all. When she licked his shaft clean, he trembled and shuddered at her touch. Knowing how much enjoyment she'd given him empowered her in a fascinating way. Though she knelt before him, it was she who was his goddess in that moment.

Gwilym lifted her gently and laid her on the cotton mattress. Her skin tingled with anticipation as he hovered over her, his lidded eyes locked to hers. She could lose herself in those eyes. They narrowed slightly as he cocked his head, with yet another wicked grin.

What was the cheeky bugger planning? Whatever it was, she welcomed the torment.

As if hearing her thoughts, he winked and lowered himself, leaving featherlight kisses down her abdomen. A delicious thrill went through her as she watched his head disappear between her legs. A moment later, she jerked at the touch of his tongue on her most private parts. Hot and wet and ooohhhh, yes, please just there. A low moan came from deep within, and she relaxed her bent legs, allowing him better access.

What he did to her was pure bliss and decadent torture. His tongue lashed her clitoris while his fingers delved into her pussy. It was ecstasy and agony that she wished would never end, but also craved the euphoric release of her climax. His fingers teased and lips sucked until she arched and groaned with her building need. He slid his tongue up her labia in a long swipe, and then lifted himself over her body. The loss of his hot mouth on her was subdued when his cock nudged at her opening, and she lifted her hips in silent invitation. Her body quivered with impatience; the need to feel him, for him to fill her, was all-consuming.

His lips sought hers in a kiss that was more of a claim than a question. He tasted of her juices, and she reveled in the sensation. Perspiration dotted his forehead as he slid his cock fully into her. A sharp thrill twitched from her clit, and she bucked to take him deeper. Slowly, he began rocking into her, with her hips matching his rhythm. As the pace increased, her breathing shortened to quick gasps as her desire grew and she cried out. Her pussy clenched against his cock, and she spiraled into a climax that was burning sparks and chips of ice. Magic swirled through her, around her, enveloping him in her embrace, tightening the sensations of her release, bringing him closer until he felt as if he were part of her. They were one.

Her mind exploded with an expansive sensation of love that overrode everything.

He arched and grunted with his own release and his hot seed filled her womb. She lay gasping and staring into his face with a sense of wonder. He returned her gaze with a sloppy, satisfied grin before he drooped his head and breathed heavily against her shoulder.

They lay together for some time without speaking, instead letting their hands explore their bodies. She didn't want the moment to end. If she could, she'd stretch their time to infinity and never let the outside world intrude. But that wasn't possible. Their lives were still at risk, and that meant she needed to leave Gwilym to find out who was behind it all.

Something monumental had happened with their lovemaking, but she couldn't put a name to it. Instinctively, intuitively, she felt the shift and knew nothing would ever be the same. The enormity of responsibility she felt overwhelmed and humbled her. In the distance, she heard the rustling of wings as if her dragon were waking from a deep sleep—only this time, it wasn't just her dragon she sensed.

CHAPTER

THIRTY-FIVE

He was infuriating. Handsome, certainly, but maddening as hell. Amaleigh turned toward her bed and frowned. If he felt the shift, she couldn't tell by his behavior—his rather lewd behavior that insisted they make love one more time before she left. Which they had, and now, she really did need to leave, but he wasn't making it easy.

"The least you could do is put on some clothes." She hid the little thrill it gave her to see him naked.

Gwilym reclined against the wall, an arm behind his head. His muscled, gorgeous body stretched the length of her bed. His semi-hard cock twitched between his legs. "Why? Then you might forget what you're leaving and not come back."

"I'll come back. I promise." She leaned forward and kissed him on the forehead. He grabbed her around the waist and spun her onto the bed. She yelped and struggled to right herself. "I have to go."

"Surely there's time for one more? You've been away from the palace several days already. What's a few hours more? Besides, this is helping me heal and that means I can return all the sooner."

Amaleigh traced a finger along his jaw. He was right. Whether she returned in a minute or a day wouldn't make a difference. But staying with him longer changed everything. With each passing second, she was more lost to his touch, his taste, his very being. Her magic expanded to fill her veins with power she'd only dreamed of having. And with each caress, his bruises lessened, his wounds healed. They made their own kind of magic that she didn't understand, but accepted without question. An unreasonable fear nagged at her that if she delved too deeply into the mysterious connection, it would snap, and she'd be left alone and unloved. Or, she might discover what the shift meant and deepen their connection even further. Fear was a liar. And fear wasn't nearly as sexy as the prince laying naked on her bed.

What the hell. She stripped the chemise over her head and tossed it to the floor. Eidyn could wait. Gwilym was her priority, and she would spend as many hours as possible giving him whatever healing she could. He lifted her until she straddled his legs and gently lowered her onto his impatient cock, and she swooned. Never in her wildest imaginings had she thought lovemaking would be this good. But then, it might have something to do with her partner.

For the rest of the afternoon, Gwilym showed her just how good it could be. They explored each other's bodies by taste and feel. They tried positions Amaleigh didn't think humanly possible, yet found gave an even stronger release. By the time she was dressed and ready to leave the little cottage, she was sore in places she didn't know existed. It was worth it. Every kiss, every touch, every sigh had been locked in her heart, as if she might never experience a day like this again.

It also meant she had more to lose if she failed.

Gwilym filled the doorway of the little cottage and waved as she stepped into the swirling air of her portal. She raised a hand in farewell, urging the pit in her stomach to go away. Her conflicted emotions made the portal unstable, and she turned away from him to focus on where she was going. It would do no good to think of what she was leaving. Ahead of her lay the unknown. She had to overcome that before she could think about the future.

As much as she'd wish otherwise, Gwilym's place was in Eidyn. He was the rightful heir and, if she were totally honest with herself, the people of Eidyn needed him as much, if not more than she did. She was done running. She wanted to go home.

The air shimmered around her, and she set in her mind the little area behind a privacy screen in her room at the palace. She'd been gone several days. For all she knew, someone else was staying there now. It wouldn't do to barge in on some unsuspecting guest.

She stepped out of the portal and waited until it blinked out of existence before she peered around the screen. The room was empty and silent. She hurried to the armoire where she'd left her bag, and cool relief swept over her that it was still there. Her belongings were folded neatly in a pile beside the bag, indicating someone had gone through her things. She searched the pocket for the locket, but it was gone. Silent fury warmed her veins, and she breathed through flared nostrils. It was irresponsible of her to leave it in the bag. Floxy fool that she was, she'd let sentiment get the best of her and now she'd lost the bloody thing.

She sat back on her heels and forced her heart to calm, her mind to stop spinning. Someone in the palace had the locket. That didn't mean they knew her real identity. She touched her face where magic hid her features. If anyone confronted her with the locket, she'd play innocent, or tell them the king gave it to her. If they pursued the matter, she'd come up with a new excuse. And another, until the questions stopped. Gods' truth, she really hated palace intrigues.

"So, you've returned. The princess said you would, but I wasn't as certain. It looks like you've ruined my braids in the process."

Amaleigh turned toward Meri's voice and chuckled. "Guilty. I suppose your princess would like an audience with me?"

"How did you know?"

"Lucky guess."

Amaleigh stood and walked to the door, only to be stopped when Merigold grabbed her by the wrist. She lifted Amaleigh's arm and sniffed from her hand to her shoulder blade.

"Gross." Amaleigh twisted her arm out of Meri's grip. "Haven't you heard of personal space? What the hell is wrong with you?"

"You've been with a man." Merigold squinted at Amaleigh, and she did her best to hide any sort of reaction. "Recently."

"Again, gross. It's no concern of yours who I bed."

"On the contrary. It matters a great deal to me. My princess was most vexed by your disappearance, especially after receiving your note. You'll have to explain what happened."

Amaleigh softened her features. "Is she well, Princess Cassia? Did the prince harm her?"

Meri's body shook with a snort. "I would love for him to try, but no. He's been strangely quiet the past few days. Come, we must see the princess."

Amaleigh followed Merigold to the same sitting room where the painting of the two women on dragons hid behind a tapestry. Her heart thrilled a little knowing her mother's image was close by.

"This one returned," Merigold announced, then added, "Like you predicted."

If Fianna Bel'en rolled their eyes, Amaleigh was certain Meri would've at that moment. But she doubted expressing childish behavior was tolerated by the warriors.

Amaleigh dropped a curtsey before facing the princess. Cassia sat on the sofa and patted the cushion beside her. Amaleigh took the chair opposite with a demure smile.

The princess tapped her lips and nodded. A grin peeked from beneath her fingertip. "I was worried about you when you didn't return the other day. We all were. Isn't that right, ladies?"

The four women murmured their agreement.

"Did you get my note?"

"I did. I'll admit, at first I wasn't sure what it meant. What happened that night?" Some of her smugness wore away. "We woke the next morning with dreadful headaches and you were gone. The bed linens were stained with blood, though. Oona thought it your monthly cycle, but I'm not convinced."

Amaleigh sat with her hands on her knees, her back straight. How much should she tell them? Just because the fake prince had drugged them didn't mean Cassia was an ally.

When Amaleigh said nothing, Cassia leaned forward. "Truly, I worried for you. The prince has been inconsolable. Have you seen him yet?" She glanced at Merigold, who shook her head.

"Merigold is the only person I've encountered since returning."

"Of which, you did not do by the front door of the palace. I'm curious then, how did you get into your bedchamber? More specifically, how do you manage to get into and out of the palace without being caught?"

Amaleigh rubbed her sweat-slicked palms down her gown. "You're being kept here, aren't you? The prince won't let you leave and you're afraid to use your magic."

A collective gasp popped through the air.

Cassia scrunched her face in mock confusion. "I'm just a

human girl from Aenglebreck. We have no magic in our kingdom."

"You and I both know that's not true. Listen, Your Highness, we can sit here and play cat-and-mouse all evening, or we can both start being honest. You go first, and I'll tell you how I can get into and out of the palace."

"She's been with a man." Merigold paced behind the princess, a bored expression on her face. "Recently, too." She leaned down to stage-whisper in Cassia's ear, "His scent is changed, but I would wager it's the prince."

Amaleigh, not being constrained by any warrior code of ethics, rolled her eyes hard enough to give herself a spasm. She played innocent while inside her nerves tightened. Merigold's obsession with her sexual encounters was disturbing. "Oh, please. How can you tell who I've been with? It could've been any man."

"Who was it?" Cassia glared at Amaleigh.

A shiver snaked its way down her back. If Cassia wasn't being honest with her and the princess was attracted to the fake prince, admitting she'd been with the real Gwilym would put both their lives at risk. Then again, their lives already were.

It was time to test her theory of being honest with each other. At best, she'd gain an ally; at worst, she'd be strung up by her entrails. If she was lucky.

CHAPTER
THIRTY-SIX

Amaleigh stalled in answering Cassia's probing question, trying and failing to find a way out of her predicament. Yes, she thought they should be honest with each other, but her relationship with Gwilym had always been her secret. Something shared between the two of them and no one else. If felt like a betrayal to tell Cassia that they'd made love.

She cricked her neck and glanced upward as if seeking answers. Gorgeous murals she'd not noticed previously caught her eye. Colorful paintings of centaurs and other beasts romping across the countryside with winged horses flying above their heads covered the entirety of the domed ceiling. In the distance, dragons circled a castle. It was there, for anyone to see. No tapestries hid it. No one had tried to paint over the beautiful figures. She could've wept for seeing the artwork. The vibrant colors made the figures seem alive. Gold highlights gave the mural an ethereal shimmering effect.

When she lowered her gaze, Cassia watched her intently.

Amaleigh swallowed her worry and spoke the truth. "I was with Prince Gwilym, but not the same man who's here, in the palace. He and his father are safe, but please don't ask me where."

"He and his father? But the king is hunting."

"Your Highness, how long have you been at the palace?"

Cassia chewed a cuticle but Merigold tutted, and she stopped. "Six months, one week, and four days. Why?"

"Oddly specific. And how long have you been prevented from leaving the palace grounds?" Amaleigh had a hunch it coincided with the fake prince's appearance.

"I'm not sure. A week? Two at most. Before then, I didn't really try, though."

"What changed?"

The cuticle returned to Cassia's teeth and this time another of her ladies tutted. She glared at the women and sat on her hand. Something had changed in the time Amaleigh was away, taking care of Gwilym and his father. The princess was nervous now, unlike the giddy woman she'd been when they first met.

"The prince changed. Before, he was charming and caring, but not solicitous. You might not believe this, but I had no intentions of a romantic dalliance with him. Quite the opposite, actually."

"None? Really? But you're a princess and he's a handsome prince. Surely there was, at some point, a conversation about uniting your two kingdoms?" Cassia's story coincided with Gwilym's, but she had to be certain there was nothing romantic between them, at least from the princess's perspective.

"Oh, there's always speculation and innuendo when two royals are in the same room. But I assure you, I am not besotted with the prince, nor he with me. That is, until recently. Now, I can't get him to leave me alone for more than a minute."

"Did his behavior change around the time the king went hunting?"

Cassia looked to her ladies. They murmured and nodded in unison.

"So, less than a fortnight ago, the prince suddenly changed and became overly interested in you?" The puzzle pieces were slotting into place, but Amaleigh was still missing a few details.

Cassia grunted and crossed her arms over her chest as if to protect herself from the fake prince. "Why do you think I spend so much time in here? It's the one room he won't barge into."

Amaleigh took a closer look at the room, peering into the corners and hidden spaces. There might be a ward around the rooms to deflect male visitors, but she couldn't be certain. If so, then it had been placed there more than two decades before. Back when mages were the king's advisers and magic wasn't forbidden. Before the Purge.

"Did you ward these rooms? Please don't tell me you don't have magic. We're beyond those lies."

Cassia sighed and glanced at Jada. "I didn't, but Jada did. Her ward is to prevent others from overhearing our conversations, that's all."

Amaleigh saw no reason the fake prince would avoid the room. Unless he objected to the beautiful murals. She was missing something important and it irritated her that she didn't have all the answers.

"If this counterfeit prince is a mage, or someone close to him is, they're probably the reason I can't leave the palace. It still raises the question of why you can, though."

"Maybe because I arrived unannounced and he doesn't know me? I have no real answer. I promise I'll show you how I do it later, but we need to focus on the fake prince. Who is he, and what's his end game?"

"You mean, besides the throne and all the king's treasures?" Isla snapped.

Amaleigh had to admit, those were compelling reasons to

assume someone else's identity. "Perhaps, but what if it's something else? We need to find out what. Who benefits most if the king and his son are dead?"

Cassia scooted to the edge of the sofa. "I do so love a good intrigue."

"This isn't court shenanigans, Your Highness. The stakes are very real. I found the real Prince Gwilym and his father near death from being tortured. Whoever is doing this, they aren't to be underestimated."

Cassia's face lost some of its color. "Tortured?"

Amaleigh smoothed her hair away from her face and breathed deeply. "Let me start at the beginning."

Her mind raced with all that had happened over the last few days, starting with the cry for help from Gwilym. But really, it began with her parents' deaths. She rose and went to the tapestry that covered the dragon mural and pulled it back enough to reveal the women's faces.

She let her mask dissolve, and she faced the princess. "My name is Amaleigh, and this woman was my mother Helena, an Aerlghot like me." She pointed to the smiling face of Helena. Tears threatened, and she didn't try to hide them. "She was the queen's protector and fierce dragon warrior. My father was the Lord High Mayor of Eidyn. They, along with my brother, were slaughtered during the Purge when I was too young to remember. King Heshen himself carried out their murders. I would've been killed that night as well, but in all the chaos, I can only guess that the king thought he had killed me. The only reason I'm still alive is because I hid in the fireplace behind the flames." Telling her truth was freeing, and terrifying. There was no place to hide, no secrets to protect.

"A child of fire," Cassia whispered. She and the other four ladies bent to one knee and placed a fist over their hearts. "A rare gem."

A buzz started in Amaleigh's gut and her vision swished, as if she were drunk on a boat during a raging storm. She reached a hand to steady herself and touched the painting. Scenes played out in her mind of her mother and the queen laughing and flying together. They were best friends and confidants, but they were more—both were Aerlghots.

She pulled her hand away and shuddered against the intrusion into her mind. The memories of her mother she craved, but it was the darkness behind the women that slid over her like pitch, burning across her skin.

"A child of fire is what my mother used to call me." She put a hand to her head and willed her vision to stop spinning, her gut to settle. "A rare gem. I remember." And she did. She remembered sitting at her mother's feet, listening to tales of dragons—lore handed down from one Aerlghot to another so that their history would never be lost.

Her dragon shifted beneath her skin, and she felt its ghostly wings unfurl behind her. When she looked, there was nothing there.

Cassia stood, and the pretense of her own mask fell away.

Amaleigh gazed into the face of the elven princess, a little bewildered by her beauty. The princess's true face was even more stunning than she'd glimpsed in the mirror. Deep golden-brown skin with high, angular cheekbones. Her frost-touched feathered eyebrows rose above the clearest pale-blue eyes Amaleigh had ever seen. Cassia's ladies dropped their masks and were equally dazzling. All five had ears that swooped upward with a sharp tip.

"I'm sorry to have lied to you, Lady Amaleigh, but it was for good reason. I am Cassia, First Daughter of Queen Ingrid and her consort, King Ezra." She indicated her ladies. "These are my shieldmaidens, sworn to protect the throne."

The warriors bowed their head.

Thrilled that she'd been correct about Cassia, Amaleigh allowed herself a rare moment of pride.

It was Amaleigh's turn to kneel and pay her respects. An elven princess, and the heir to the throne, was considered higher in rank than even King Heshen.

There was only one reason a high-ranking elven princess would be in Eidyn under false pretenses and disguised. As Amaleigh straightened and faced the princess, one word repeated itself in her mind: *Revenge*.

THIRTY-SEVEN

Instead of accusing the princess outright, Amaleigh thought it best to let Cassia admit her reasons unprovoked. If she was wrong, and Cassia was in Eidyn for another purpose, it wouldn't do to have her only ally turn against her. Besides Dante, Amaleigh had no one in the city she could trust. For now, her only option was to confide everything to Cassia and hope the princess returned her trust.

She resumed her seat on the chair and waited for the others to sit before explaining about her upbringing with Antonio and subsequent friendship with the real Prince Gwilym. Cassia listened intently as Amaleigh spoke, her eyes narrowing with any mention of Danteneux. Several times Oona would look at her princess, but none of the ladies interrupted Amaleigh's story.

When she came to the part about hearing Gwilym cry out, only then did Cassia speak up.

"You say you were not on Nasus? You were elsewhere?" She leaned back on the sofa and bit a nail. One of the maidens, Jada or Isla, tutted, but Cassia ignored them.

"That's correct. Yet I heard him as if he were sitting beside me. At dinner that first night of my arrival when I dropped the goblet, I felt the lash he suffered." She put a hand to her cheek. "I was surprised to find I didn't bleed, it was so real."

"This connection is rare, but not unusual for one of your kind. Your spirits call to each other through time and distance. You cannot be separated, even in death." Merigold's somber voice filled the room. "And," she grinned at Amaleigh, "Aerlghots mate for life."

Amaleigh glanced up, eyes wide, mouth agape. "Uh, what?"

Cassia giggled, and the air seemed to shimmer. "It's true. Oh, you might kiss or cuddle another, but when it comes to copulation, it won't happen except with your life mate. You can try, but something will always prevent you from achieving complete fornication."

"Can you please not use words like copulate and fornication? You make it sound so seedy."

She and Gwilym didn't fornicate. They— Her eyes grew even larger, and a wash of ice flowed from her head to her fingertips. They made love. It had been so easy with him, as if it were meant to be.

"Fuck." What had she done?

"Well, that's certainly a word for it, but far crasser than mine."

Amaleigh rested her elbows on her knees and ran her hands through her hair. "What happens if the other person doesn't know there's this unspoken life mate thing? What if they only wanted a quick release? Are they locked into something they don't want?" The last thing she needed was for Gwilym to feel trapped. She had to find a way to undue the bond if that was the case.

"It doesn't work that way. Once spirits are joined—and it can happen even when you're too young to realize—they cannot be un-joined. If you and the prince made love, it's because you are meant for each other." A softness covered Cassia's features, and she reached a hand to Amaleigh.

"Would this bond prevent someone else from, I don't know, forcing themselves on you?"

"Do you mean, can you be raped?" Cassia asked bluntly and Amaleigh grimaced against the word and the reality of what almost happened. "In a word, no." Her eyes narrowed and lips thinned. "Did something happen?"

Amaleigh waved her hands and shook her head. "Gods, no. I'm just curious how far the bond goes."

Cassia gripped her hand, her features smoothing. "They are absolute and can never be broken. And you have nothing to worry about with the prince. I suspected Gwilym was meant for another. As a test, I sent Meri to seduce him, but he wasn't interested. Hell, you've witnessed her seductive prowess. Yet you both denied her."

"It wasn't easy, I'll tell you that." Amaleigh snorted, unsure what to do with this new information. Knowing that she wasn't broken with a dead heart didn't help matters. They still had to deal with the fake prince. "Has Merigold tried seducing this new prince?"

The beauty snorted and crossed her arms. "Him, I wouldn't have to try that hard. He'll bed anything that looks at him sideways. It's trying to keep him off the princess that's the real challenge. He's determined to bed her and get her with child."

Amaleigh shuddered with the memory of him on top of her, his hand crushing her mouth, his pelvis grinding into hers. Bile inched up her throat, and she coughed against it. If she told the shieldmaidens what he'd done, she half suspected they'd string him up by his balls, which would be a pleasure to see, but they needed answers from him.

"We have to assume he's behind the abduction of the king and his son. He kidnaps them, has them tortured, then tries to impregnate the princess. To what end? To rule Eidyn?" Amaleigh went through possible motivations, spinning back around to nothing that made sense except taking over the kingdom. "Do you think he knows who you truly are, Princess?"

"Call me Cassia, please. And no, I don't believe he does. Why?"

"It's just a hunch, but if he knew you were the elven heir, marrying you or even getting you with child would secure both thrones." Her gaze drifted to the mural. The dragons' scales glittered in the candlelight, and she could almost envision them flying in the clear sky. "If he was a mage, then maybe it's revenge for what Heshen did during the Purge. Or, what if this is about the dragons? Could the pretender be someone from your kingdom?"

Cassia shook her head. "I'd see through their disguise. Our power is different from mage magic. That's why I couldn't see through your mask."

Yet Amaleigh was able to see through Cassia's in the mirror. Her heart stuttered beneath her ribs, and a chill swept up her back. "We need to confront the imposter and question him—by force if need be."

"Without the legitimate prince and the king, we have no proof. First, you must bring them back to the palace."

Cassia was right. Without Heshen and Gwilym, it was their word against the pretender's.

"Or," Amaleigh suggested, "we could do it clandestinely. Bait the fake prince and take him somewhere else to be questioned. Somewhere far from the palace."

"Then who would be here? A palace left ungoverned is ripe for chaos."

Damn and double damn, she had a point.

"The king is gravely ill but should be able to withstand the journey. You said you wanted to get out of the palace—now's your chance. I could use your help."

Cassia's face lit up and a wide smile stretched her cheeks. "Oh, yes, please. Let me change first. These court gowns are terribly inappropriate for intrigues."

They refitted their individual disguises and arranged to meet in Amaleigh's rooms. The princess rushed off with her shieldmaidens in one direction while Amaleigh went in the other. At the corner of her hallway and the path leading to the library, she paused. Gallivanting around without a weapon and hesitant to use too much magic wasn't the brightest idea, especially when she didn't know what kind of foe they might encounter.

Decision made, she spun on her heel and hurried to the library where King Heshen kept the decorative weapons he stole from those he murdered. It did her heart harm to think of the poor souls who owned the weapons, but time was short and she was too far from the armory to find anything else.

At the entrance, she breathed deeply and inhaled the scent of her childhood. A quick scan of the room came up empty. If others had been there, she would've aborted her plan. The cabinet stood as solemn as ever, and she hesitated before reaching for the door. If it resisted her now that she'd opened her magic, she'd pivot and find something else, possibly a steak knife. With shaking fingers, she touched the handle. It clicked open at her touch, and she breathed a sigh of relief. She snatched a dirk that would easily hide up her sleeve.

"Do you make it a habit to steal from those who offer you welcome in their home?"

The lilt in the fake prince's voice was almost enough to convince her he was the real Gwilym. This pretender was good. Too good. He'd avoided detection when she scanned the room, which made him dangerous as well.

Amaleigh set the dirk on a table and closed the cabinet door before turning to face him. She should gut him for what he did to her. Wanted to, so badly. Did they really need answers from him? Or just for him to be out of the palace? Her fingers itched to grab the dirk and shove it up his gullet.

"I admit I find it compelling. When I saw the weapons earlier, I knew I had to see them up close. If you consider that stealing, then I apologize for my supposed crime."

The fake prince approached, laughter in his dark eyes. "If it calls to you, then you shall have it. A gift from me to you." He trailed his fingertips along her forehead and tucked a strand of hair behind her ear.

Her legs trembled at his touch and her stomach twisted.

"I find you compelling, and as such, you could say my actions the other night were not stealing."

Her skin crawled where his touch lingered, and she bit back the cruel words that sprang to her lips. "I thought you were interested in the princess. The pair of you make a handsome couple."

"We do indeed. But she is meek and you are...not. I feared you'd left us for good when you didn't return after our dalliance." His head bent and lowered as if to kiss her.

Amaleigh pushed his chest, but he didn't budge. A force kept him solidly in her path and connected to him like a tether. She pushed again, and his moan made her stomach pinch. The bastard got off on her fighting him. She resisted the urge to flame him with her magic. He no longer had Gwilym and the king; it didn't matter whether he lived. Yet, she couldn't bring herself to murder him. All these years later, and she still wasn't a killer.

His lips touched hers, and she gagged against the intrusion of his tongue into her mouth. One hand held her head in place while his other hand caressed down her back to rest just above her ass. His fingers splayed out, strong and controlling in their grip.

She shoved him will all her strength and broke the connection between their lips. "Stop it."

The invisible force tightened, and he pressed his hardened cock against her hip. "Isn't this what you want? What you've always wanted?"

His sneer twisted his face into an ugly caricature of the man she'd known since childhood. He grabbed her between the legs and ground his fingers against her. She cried out against the pain and twisted to break free of his grasp. He lifted his fingers to his nose and inhaled. Shock crossed his features and the sneer lengthened into absolute hatred.

"You filthy whore." His hand whipped out and connected to her cheek with terrifying strength.

White heat seared where he'd slapped her, and she stumbled backward, into the table. Her fingers scrambled to grab the dirk, and she brought it up to the level of his nose. His fingers twitched at his side and sickness roiled in her gut. The finger twitch. The way he held her when they kissed. Her mind scrambled to deny it was possible, but her heart knew it was true. Cornelius. The imposter was her mentor, the man she thought protected her.

"You fucked him. Didn't you?" Cornelius shook where he stood, mania shining from his wild eyes. "You filthy fucking cunt. I'll kill you. I'll kill you both."

The dirk shook in her trembling hands as she stared down her one-time mentor. "Don't you dare touch him." Her magic flared, and she felt him sucking in her power. Immediately, she shut off her magic and his connection to it.

Cornelius's brutal laughter came from Gwilym's lips. "Are you going to stop me? You pathetic excuse for a mage."

Cornelius spun around and a portal opened in front of him. He stepped inside, his laughter trailing into the darkness.

She leapt for the opening but slammed into something hard and invisible. Bastard. Bloody floxing bastard.

Amaleigh sprinted for the door and jerked it open. She ran full out to her room, scanning the hallways for the princess. She might be able to defeat Cornelius alone, but having the princess and her elven powers would be better. Cassia barreled into her path, and Amaleigh slammed into her. They hit the wall with a shared grunt.

"Thank the gods." Amaleigh grabbed her hand and jerked the princess toward her room.

"Amaleigh, stop. You're positively quaking. What's wrong?"

"There's no time to explain. The imposter is Cornelius, my mentor. He's gone back for Gwilym. We must hurry." Amaleigh dragged her into the room and closed the door. "Hold my hand and don't let go."

She opened a portal to Cassia's astonished gasp and together, they stepped into the void between worlds. She just hoped it wasn't too late.

CHAPTER
THIRTY-EIGHT

The cottage was in shambles. Broken furniture, upturned chairs—there wasn't a space free of chaos in the entire place. Amaleigh took in the scene, her heart pounding in her chest and blood rushing through her ears. Fury ignited deep within, and she breathed in with measured counts.

The hows and the whys of what Cornelius had done would come later. Right then, she wanted to tear him from limb to limb. All those years believing he could be trusted, that he loved her...it was all a lie. Her gaze went to the little room where she slept, and through the open door she saw the shredded bed linens.

"This is where you live?" Cassia surveyed the damage.

"We lived all over. We've been on the run since I escaped Eidyn seven years ago. This was just the latest place we called home." Nothing in the cottage was irreplaceable, except the two people she didn't see.

She glanced at the smoldering embers, and her heart wrenched. No, dear gods, no. She rushed to the fireplace and jammed her hands beneath the still-hot ash, but it was gone. The dragon egg was gone. Next, she ran to her bedroom and checked the little drawer where she told Gwilym to hide notes to her. A small slip of paper rested within. She grabbed it and read the coded message. Her heart pinched with every word.

It wasn't a clue as to where they were, but four simple little words that nearly broke her.

You are my world.

She held the paper to her lips and fought the tears that threatened.

"Amaleigh, there's more." Cassia inclined her head toward the front door.

The twins. No.

She raced outside and flinched at the sight of flames coming from the barn. Cries came from inside, and she ran flat out to the gate. It wouldn't open so she burst through with her magic. Same with the barn doors. Flames rushed outward, toward her, and she held up an arm to shield her eyes.

Cassia stood to the side, swirling her hands in the air, and Amaleigh glanced up to see rain clouds forming over the barn. The twins called out, their little voices full of terror.

"I'm coming!" She called to them in the language of dragons, but doubt they heard over their own fearful wailing.

A spark landed on her hand, and she brushed it off. It didn't burn or even leave a mark. A memory of hiding behind the flames in the fireplace pushed through her worried fears, and she heard her mother's voice telling her she was a rare gem. A child of fire. The lullabies she'd remembered through dreams came to her lips, and she spoke the words that would allow her to walk through flames.

"Amaleigh, no!" Cassia called out.

But she couldn't stop. The twins would die if she didn't get to them quickly.

Their cries came from the far end of the barn, where they liked to hide beneath piles of hay. Hot flames licked up the sides of the barn, and a wall of fire stood between her and the dragonlings. Her hair sparked and sizzled, but she kept going. Heat blew against her, pushing her backward. She scrambled for footing, gaining only inches.

Despair roiled over her as she struggled to move forward, but she wasn't strong enough to fight through the blaze on her own. One of the twins screamed, and Amaleigh called out to them, begging them to believe in her. She would save them. Had to, or all was lost.

Her mother's words echoed in her mind. She was a child of fire. Fire fueled her. She could not burn. There was no better time than now to prove her mother right. Amaleigh sucked in a long drag of fire. Scorching heat filled her veins, warmed her heart, tightened her resolve. She did not burn, there was no pain, only a quickening of energy. Her thoughts settled, and she focused on the elusive dragon she knew existed inside her. The change came quickly and without hesitation. Whatever had been keeping her dragon locked inside her burned away in the flames and turned to ash.

Gorgeous ruby wings stretched wide, breaking through the boards of the barn. Not the bluish-green of abalone, her scales were now glittering gems that caught the firelight with each movement she made. What it meant, she wasn't sure, but it felt right. It was meant to be, as if she'd come into her own and was finally set free. Strength infused her as her talons scratched at the dirt, anxious to tear the barn asunder. The dragonlings needed her. Her vision sharpened, and she saw the twins huddled together in the far corner, their scales reflecting the flames that surrounded them.

She trampled through the barn and reached out her front legs to grasp one each between her long talons. The barn creaked and shuddered against Cassia's deluge of rain. Amaleigh snorted flames toward the ceiling and leapt up, beating her wings hard and fast to break through the fire-ravaged roof.

She soared high into the air, straight into the storm clouds. Rain pelted her snout, and she blew another stream of fire into the air. The twins struggled in her grasp, and she realized they didn't know her as a dragon. They didn't connect the ghost dragon she casted with the woman who cared for them.

"It's me, you sillies. It's Amaleigh. You're safe now." Her words were deeper, sharper, but still sounded like her human self.

The twins calmed and hung obediently from her talons. The poor dears were traumatized by their ordeal. Fire was a dragon's friend, but she'd failed in her duty to teach them how to use it for fuel. She'd been so worried they'd fly off and leave her, she'd done the very thing she promised them she wouldn't do—make them vulnerable. It was her job to nurture and protect them, and she'd gotten it so very wrong.

"I'm sorry, younglings." She swooped to the ground and set them down gently. Their little faces stared at her with awe and a little bit of fear. When she shifted back into her human form, they pranced and head-butted her with what she supposed was gratitude-filled love.

Cassia approached with a look of wonder on her face. "Look at you beauties." She spoke the language of dragons, and the twins turned from her to Amaleigh, confused.

"She's a friend," Amaleigh told them, and they wiggled their way to Cassia's outstretched hands.

"Do you have more?" Cassia scanned the barnyard and countryside.

"No, unfortunately. Cornelius and I have been searching for lost dragons, but so far, these are the only pair we've been able to rescue. I had an egg, but he's taken it."

"We can't leave them here. Is there someplace safe to take them?"

"There's only one person in Eidyn I trust, and he'll be none too pleased to see us with dragons. But he'll have to do. You hold Mali, and I'll hold onto Shen." She told the dragons what was happening and opened a portal wide enough for them all to fit through.

This was a very bad idea. Unfortunately, it was the best she had.

When she and Cassia stepped through the portal in Dante's cabin, he nearly fell over in his chair. When the dragonlings romped into the small space, his face lost all color and he spit curses that she'd never heard before.

"The clunge you doing, Amaleigh?" He pinned himself against the wall, his head bent against a rafter.

"Dante, you know I wouldn't come here if this wasn't important. I need you to keep these two hidden for me. Put them in the hold with some hay and they'll be fine. They're sweet babies, really."

The look he gave her suggested he thought differently. "First you send a half-starved wretch with some outlandish promise that I'll give him work and food, and now this? No. No, no, no. I can't have dragons on my ship. In case you weren't aware, dragons breathe fire and my ship's made out of wood. Bad combination. Baaaad."

"If they destroy your ship, I'll buy you a new one," Cassia said, and Dante's gaze swung to her.

His eyes widened and a slow grin spread across his face. "Well met on this day. And whose coin would I have the pleasure of taking?"

"Call me Cassia."

Amaleigh watched as Dante's mouth dropped. "As in, the princess? That Cassia?"

"Yes. That Cassia. Now, do we have your word these dragons won't be harmed?"

"On my honor, Your Highness."

Amaleigh snorted, and Dante waved her off. "You knew I'd say yes. Don't get your knickers in a twist."

"You're repulsive."

"You love me anyway." Dante patted Amaleigh's head as though she were a child. "When will you collect them?"

"I'm not sure." She told him a condensed version of events since she'd last seen him. With each new revelation, his expression morphed from mild interest to incredulity to horror.

"I don't give a sheep's teat who sits on the throne, but what you've described is bad for everyone in Eidyn. If you need swords, I have men at the ready." He shook his head and scratched his stubble. "Any idea where the king and prince are now?"

"None. I thought I'd check Antonio's again, but I doubt Cornelius is that stupid."

"Or he's hoping you don't think he's stupid. In which case, that makes an excellent place to stash them."

"We need to go," Cassia urged.

While Amaleigh bent to tell the twins what was happening, Dante whispered something to Cassia that made the princess chortle like a giddy child. She rolled her eyes and told the twins to behave themselves for Dante. She stroked their little faces and ran a thumb over their scales.

How could Cornelius have been so cruel? They were all deceived by him. Her, most of all, but now everyone else would pay the price.

CHAPTER
THIRTY-NINE

They hurried through the city using main thoroughfares and streets instead of skulking through back alleys. Cornelius knew they were looking for him. If he wanted a confrontation, Amaleigh would prefer it be in a more public setting.

At the corner to Antonio's manor, she slowed their pace to a casual stroll. Cassia kept glancing at the buildings, getting her first real glimpse of the city since arriving. Every so often, she'd grunt or snort with a quick shake of her head. It was all Amaleigh could do to not ask what she found so distasteful about Eidyn. As far as Amaleigh was concerned, Eidyn was one of the most beautiful cities she'd ever seen.

"It's just there." Amaleigh pointed to the quiet house. "The last time I was here, I spelled the door to allow reentry, but that means we're walking across open ground. We could be seen by anyone inside."

"Cast into the house and find out what we're up against."

"Cast? My dragon form? You're joking, right?"

"Not your dragon...you." Cassia screwed up her face as if she couldn't believe Amaleigh was that dense.

"I've never—I mean, I don't know how."

"It's dead simple. Same idea as casting your dragon, but instead, you focus on yourself. Here, I'll show you." Cassia closed her eyes, and a second Cassia appeared beside her.

Amaleigh gasped and took an involuntary step back.

"She doesn't bite. Feel her, er, me. This is rather confusing, isn't it?"

Amaleigh touched the duplicate Cassia's arm. Warmth emanated from the skin. "How is this possible?"

"Maybe it's not as simple as I said, but once you get it down, you could send copies of yourself all over. The only thing you can't do as a casted form is use your magic. Or, in my case, ShantiMari. Otherwise, no one's the wiser. I used to send my copies to my lessons until my father brought a mage to the castle and he snitched on me."

"It's remarkable, really. I wouldn't be able to tell the casted Cassia from the real you." Amaleigh touched the double's wrist, impressed with the solidness. "Can you cast yourself over large distances?" To say, other worlds? A terrible buzzing started in her gut.

"Of course. It takes more concentration, but the distance isn't important."

Cornelius could've been casting duplicates of himself even while he was at the cottage. Which raised the question of how long he'd been returning to Eidyn.

Cassia's double trotted across the street and jumped the front gate with ease. As the shadows grew around her, she disappeared completely.

"Where'd she go?"

"Oh, did I fail to mention? As a casted form, you control their opaqueness. She's jogging up the stairs as we speak." Cassia scrunched her nose and frowned. "It's worse than a pigsty in there. Oh! I see two people—a man and a woman.

They're arguing in," she counted the windows on the front of the house, "that room there."

"Antonio's rooms. Can you hear what they're saying?"

"Of course. The woman is angry with the man, Geezer something. Keeps saying he deserved whatever punishment the Master threw at him for getting Antonio killed and letting the prisoners escape."

"The Master? It could be the alias Cornelius used to convince Gerzer to abduct the king and Gwilym. Can you tell if they're in the house?"

Cassia shook her head. "There are others in the rooms upstairs. I'll take a look."

Amaleigh waited several tense minutes while Cassia's casted form searched the house. Several times the princess murmured or whimpered, but didn't share the reason why.

"I don't see them. That's one nasty lot in there, though. Several children are chained to their beds and there's a room in the cellars that will give me nightmares for years."

"That's probably where they were tortured. We'll come back for the children later. If Cornelius didn't bring them here, then where?" Amaleigh cycled through all the places she'd hide someone if she were Cornelius. The sewers perhaps, or a warehouse by the docks. It had to be someplace convenient. She smacked her forehead and swore several of the words she'd learned from Dante and Eaman. Cornelius would hide the king where Amaleigh was least likely to suspect—the palace. "I know where they are."

"Where?" Cassia arched as her casted form returned to her and cracked her neck. "If you show me how to make a portal in thin air, I'll teach you to cast yourself."

"You can't make portals? What do you use?"

"Doorways. We need something solid to walk through and a destination."

Amaleigh recalled the elf and silver-haired woman at the Shoogly Dragon.

"Let's get back to the palace. If Cornelius is going to do anything rash, we need to be there to stop him."

Two of Cassia's shieldmaidens, Isla and Oona, jogged toward them. They were dressed as Fianna Bel'en, with two slender swords strapped to their backs. Their braided hair trailed over their shoulders, and Amaleigh sucked in a breath. Gone was the pretty lady-in-waiting façade. The warriors showed their true faces.

"What are you doing here? And why aren't you disguised?"

"The pretender is in the palace and has the king with him. The prince has not been located." Isla's gaze went to Amaleigh. "I'm sorry, my lady."

"I'm not a lady. Just call me Amaleigh."

"But you are a lady. Your father was a lord and your mother a lady. Therefore, you are of noble blood," Cassia argued.

Amaleigh snorted and held her side. "It didn't feel very noble growing up in the alleys and sewers of Eidyn. Where's Cornelius now?"

"He's barricaded the palace doors and ordered his troops to stand guard outside the palace. They've been ordered to kill you on sight."

"What about the king? Do you know what he's planning to do with Heshen?"

Oona shook her head. "We think a public execution, but can't be certain."

"Why so dramatic? What's his end game?" Amaleigh held her temples and cleared her mind. "If he's ordered me killed on sight, then he has the palace warded against me coming in through a portal. But I never told him that I know of a dozen ways to get inside the palace where we won't be noticed."

She cocked her head in the opposite direction of the palace and jogged away from Antonio's manor.

"Shouldn't we be going this way, my Lady Amaleigh?" Isla asked.

"Not yet. We need to get to the right entrance first." The sewer she needed was behind the baths. They cut through a market square and down a flight of broad stairs before they came to the narrow alley she remembered from a decade earlier. She breathed a sigh of relief at seeing the plain wooden door. "Through here."

Amaleigh used magic to unlatch the door and shepherded the women inside. She scanned the alley to be sure they weren't followed and re-latched the door behind her, sealing it shut with a spell.

What might've taken five minutes through the streets took at least ten in the sewers. Each passing minute was like an ice pick to her heart. If they didn't arrive in time, she'd never forgive herself.

The women didn't speak as they sloshed through the city's sewage, but by their faces they weren't enjoying the adventure. Twice, they came upon urchins but didn't pause in their quest. The unarmed children were most likely in Gerzer's employ and would soon enough let their boss know they saw four well-dressed women running through the muck. She hoped to be long gone from the sewers by then.

"How much farther?" Cassia's voice came out labored and breathy.

"Not much. We're within the palace grounds now. I just need to find the right offshoot." They slowed, and Amaleigh searched the walls for the small gate that led to the palace cellars. "There." She pointed up ahead about ten feet.

"You!" A group of men ran at them, carrying torches and wooden clubs.

"Fuck." So close. They should've at least knocked the urchins out, but she couldn't bring herself to hurt children. Even those who sought to bring her harm.

Isla and Oona removed their blades from the scabbards on their backs and planted themselves into the shallow water. The men slowed their approach and appraised the situation. They were outnumbered, but she'd never known a man to believe a woman could best him.

The men fanned out and stalked the group. They were short and brutish, just the kind Gerzer would hire. Mercenaries, most likely. Bald, with thick beards, the torches glowed off their tattooed skin.

"Get it done quick, lads. The boss says we're needed up top."

Amaleigh shared a look with Cassia. They still had time. Whatever Cornelius was planning hadn't happened yet. If they wanted quick, they'd get it. She nodded to Cassia and the pair of them opened a thread of power. Amaleigh's magic glowed crimson in the flickering torchlight and Cassia's silver.

"Ain't nobody said nothing about no fecking mages."

"Don't matter nothin' to me. A skull's a skull." The brute in the middle lunged toward them, and Isla slashed forward with her blade.

The man's head bobbled a moment before tumbling from his shoulders to splash in the grime. The other two turned and ran full out toward the end of the tunnel.

"Really, Isla? You didn't let us play with them first. I'm terribly disappointed in you," Cassia complained with more than a hint of mirth in her tone.

"I'm sorry, Your Highness. I just figured with our time constraints it was for the best."

"Yes, you're right. What was I thinking?" She grinned at her shieldmaiden.

Amaleigh unlocked the gate with her magic and ducked beneath the brick archway. The three elves crouched low and shuffled into the tight tunnel while Amaleigh locked the gate and set another spell against anyone wishing to follow.

"I remember it being much larger. But then again, I was smaller way back then." She waddled her way through the mud up to the cellar door. Using her magic once more, she opened it for the women and secured it behind her. Thank the gods the kitchens needed drainage for the offal and whatnot they tossed out. It smelled rank, but that was a small price to pay for stealth.

They jogged up the stairs leading to the palace kitchens, and Amaleigh peered through a small gap. No soldiers could be seen, but that didn't mean they weren't nearby. She eased the door open and put a finger to her lips. The scullery maids cast their gaze downward or to the cook, but no one spoke. When the cook saw Cassia and her shieldmaidens, she placed a thumb first to her forehead, then to her heart before kissing it. Cassia acknowledged the gesture with a slow nod and they moved through the kitchens unobstructed.

"She's of fae blood," Cassia said once they were beyond the cook's hearing.

"As in, faerie? I didn't know Aerithilyn had fae folk."

"They're an ancient race, almost as old as the Eleri. Most of them have moved on, but some stay loyal to our throne."

"Eleri?"

"It's the archaic term for elves."

Either Isla or Oona grunted, and Amaleigh silenced her questions. She'd need several months at the elven castle to learn half of their history. Someday, perhaps. When they weren't under threat of death.

They stalked through the palace on silent feet and kept to

the lesser-used hallways. A commotion came from the state-rooms facing the grand square and they turned toward it. On the other side of the large passageway, Jada and Merigold hid behind life-sized suits of armor. Meri pointed to the balcony where Cornelius stood with the king at his side.

Shouts came from the square. A large crowd had amassed to see what the spectacle was at the palace. Eidynites loved their celebrations, no matter how revolting.

King Heshen's body drooped and Cornelius smacked his face, with an order to remain standing. The crowd roared. Whether cheering or yelling, she couldn't be certain. She hoped the latter.

Cassia moved forward, but Amaleigh put out a hand to stop her.

"We can't rush in without knowing what we're up against." Amaleigh scanned the balcony but didn't see Gwilym. She prayed to the gods that he still lived.

Amaleigh. His hoarse whisper touched her mind.

Where are you?

Somewhere dark, where else? His chuckle wasn't the least bit soothing, but she was grateful he still had a sense of humor. *It's Cornelius. He's the imposter.* Gwilym's tone lost all its mirth.

I know. I went back to the cottage as soon as I realized, but you were gone. Amaleigh watched Cornelius like a falcon its dinner.

Where's my father?

On the palace balcony, with Cornelius.

He's going to kill him. He never forgave him.

For what?

Everything. Gwilym's voice brushed her mind with a sigh. *Save him, please.*

She inched forward into the room until she had a clear view of her mentor. He still wore the mask of Gwilym's features. He meant to make it appear that the prince murdered his own father. Patricide in front of a crowd. It was ironic, really. Heshen had murdered hundreds of mages while the citizens did nothing. Now Cornelius would murder the king as entertainment for Eidynites.

Not if she could help it.

FORTY

Amaleigh signaled to Cassia before she opened her magic and rushed forward. So much for not running in without a plan. Her vision narrowed to the man with Gwilym's face, but who was not her best friend. This man, Cornelius, she didn't know anymore. He'd been more than a friend once. Mentor, big brother, family. Now, he was her enemy.

"It's over, Cornelius." She sent a thread of her magic toward him and ripped the mask off his face.

He screamed against the agony, and she flinched at the sound. The gathered crowd gasped and a cacophony of voices rose to the balcony. Merigold and Oona grabbed the king as he slumped to the stone floor. Amaleigh spied them carrying him to safety from the corner of her eye. Cassia stayed behind, a soft silver glow emanating from her hands.

"They stole everything from me. Everything!" Spit flew from Cornelius's lips as he spoke and his hands shook with anger. "He blamed me for my sister's death. I tried to save her! Then he blamed me after the Purge when I warned him. I warned him dragons would destroy the kingdom." He jabbed a finger at her.

"It's your kind that destroyed Eidyn. You disgusting mutations! I lost everything because of your kind."

The raw rage in his words took her aback. He'd always been supportive of her recovering her dragon. But that was all part of his lie, his deception. She'd wanted to believe him, to think he cared about her.

"You're talking madness, Cornelius. You're a mage, just like those Heshen murdered."

"Like your disgusting parents? No, I'm nothing like them."

"I thought you were friends with them. You said you loved them." She softened her voice and tried a different approach. "I loved my parents."

"You barely knew them! You speak of love, but you know nothing about what it truly is," he raged at her, and she flinched from the heat of his words. "You had your parents for what... three years? Pffft. You didn't even remember them. But him!" Cornelius pointed to inside the palace. "Him, you couldn't forget. Not even when I took you worlds away. Not even when I loved you more than anyone ever had. I promised him I'd keep you safe and I did. But you just couldn't love me in return."

"That's not true. I do love you, like a brother."

"I'm not your brother! I was her brother and she died."

"Who, Cornelius?" She had a suspicion and hoped she was wrong.

"Maire. My beautiful queen."

Holy hell, he meant Gwilym's mother. "She died of a fever. That's not your fault. What you're doing now, though...this is wrong."

He moved in front of her with preternatural speed, too fast for her to react. His hand whipped across her cheek, and she stumbled backward. It was the second time that day he'd struck her and she'd be damned if he did it again. She shoved a wall of flame at him, and he cowered against the heat of her attack. A moment later, her flames sizzled and popped as if water washed them away. She glared at Cassia, but the princess shook her head and showed her hands.

Cornelius chuckled, and her stomach dropped. He was stealing her magic. Crimson flames danced upon his upturned palms.

"You betrayed me far worse than they ever did." His voice dropped low as he advanced. "You healed the man who murdered your parents and brought him to our home. You deserve to die, just like them." His face reddened with each word and his fists shook.

He was well and truly past coherent discussion. But she had to try. Anything was better than him destroying the city or harming its citizens.

"I'm so sorry that you're hurt and angry, but this isn't the cure. Killing them won't bring your sister back. You've had your revenge on the king and Gwilym. It's time to forgive, Cornelius. To forgive and heal."

He flicked his wrist and a sword flew from one of the suits of armor toward her. She deflected it with a thread of her own magic.

"I'll never forgive them, and I'll never forgive you." He spun and made a portal, but Amaleigh was ready.

She leapt after him through the swirling opening, taking control of their destination as she did.

They landed on the charred ground beside the ruined barn, and Cornelius blinked at her in surprise. Wherever he'd planned to take them, she overrode those plans. A sneer lifted his lips and he looked ugly in that moment. The man she'd known—handsome, kind, caring—he was gone. She saw it in his eyes. This man would kill her without a hint of remorse.

"I'll keep fighting you. Either until you're dead or I am, but I won't let up." She set her shoulders and flicked hair off her face. "You know how stubborn I can be."

He started to laugh, and she noticed something was off with the way his mouth worked and the sound came out. As if he were distracted and not altogether there. A disquieting worry churned in her gut. She stepped backward and flung a fireball at him. He deflected it but didn't counter with magic of his own.

Bloody fool. He casted a copy of himself, knowing she'd follow him through the portal.

"Good luck getting back," his image mocked her. "I've surrounded the city with a wall of magic too powerful for you to break through. All those poor souls who were warded during the Purge, they're ripe for the picking." The ghost mage sucked in a delirious breath. "So much magic, all mine to steal. Now who's the better thief?" Sinister snickers came from the stupid thing.

He was stealing magic from poor souls like Eaman. Fuck. She made a portal and stepped into it, but was bounced back on her ass. She tried a second time, this one to open near the docks, but again, she was bounced out.

His casted form howled with laughter. "So pathetic."

She paced a small circle, her finger tapping her lip. Think, Amaleigh, think!

Cornelius must've put a ward over the entire city. One too powerful for her to break through. At least, too powerful for her human form. She tossed a spell at his copied self and froze him in place. A look of surprise twisted his face. She turned and ran full out toward the cliff and leapt off the edge into the air. A harrowing second later she made a portal and shifted into her dragon form.

Stars, it felt good to be her dragon. Her vision sharpened, and her heart thumped with strong, steady beats. Wind rushed past her snout, over her body, and across her wings, refreshing her spirit with its caress. To think this gorgeous feeling had been denied her by the conniving man made her blood boil. Her thoughts narrowed to retribution for all the harm he'd caused.

An angry howl followed her as she dove into the portal and cut off mid-screech. She crashed through his protective wards and skidded to a stop just below the balcony. The crowd parted with loud gasps. A few brave souls cheered her entrance, but not Cornelius. He glared at her, and her heart ached for the man she'd once respected. All those years of living with hatred. She knew the torment of rage all too well. It could isolate and destroy your soul.

With a dramatic flair, he reached down to grab something and lifted Gwilym by his hair. At first, she thought he held only the head and crushing sorrow ripped through her dragon veins. Then the rest of Gwilym appeared, and she shuddered with relief.

Fresh streaks of blood covered her beloved's face where he'd been beaten. This time, no doubt by Cornelius himself. To think, all those years he honed his jealousy when he could've been living his best life. All those years she'd run from Eidyn and her past. Wasted. But not completely. She shook out her wings and snorted flames at the balcony.

Cornelius countered by placing a blade at Gwilym's neck.

Gwilym elbowed Cornelius in the ribs and wrenched out of his hold. A moment later, he leapt over the banister and landed on her back with a grunt. He slid to the ground and stood at her side, breathing heavy.

"I could sure use a sword about now." He glanced over his shoulder at the approaching mob, led by Gerzer.

"Your Highness!" Merigold flung a sword down to Gwilym, and he caught it with one hand.

He tipped his fingers across his forehead in a salute.

Cornelius screamed at them, and she felt the force of his

anger as he stole her magic. It whooshed from her so quickly, it left her weakened. Without even trying, she shifted into her human form. All the lovely feelings from her dragon were gone in a breath. Energy spent, she went down on her knees. She had to find a way to block him from stealing her magic. Stealing any magic. He knew her weakness, and now she knew his.

Gwilym lifted her by her shoulders until she faced him. "Let me rescue you this time."

"Rescue me? How?" A madman was siphoning not just her magic, but her physical strength while spewing curses at her from the palace balcony, a mob was roaring toward them. It was the two of them against far too many. Even if she could reach her magic or her dragon, it wouldn't be enough.

"Trust me." Gwilym cupped her face between his strong hands. "You're not alone, Amaleigh. I've got you."

His lips pressed against hers with fierce protectiveness. He wrapped his arms around her in a tight embrace. Heat surged through her, loosening tendrils of magic that had shrunk with Cornelius's thievery. The longer they kissed, the more her magic grew stronger until she felt the full force of her power thrumming through her veins. Her depleted energy refueled with such force she could scarcely breathe. All from his kiss. He poured his love into her and she blossomed like a wilted flower.

Gerzer shrieked her name, and she reluctantly broke from the kiss to see him and his men advancing. They carried axes and swords. Some had double-ended pikes. All of them wore murderous looks.

"We'll do it together." Amaleigh brushed her lips against Gwilym's with one last kiss before turning to face the approaching mob. Crimson flames danced upon her open palms and she steadied herself.

She and Gwilym stood their ground while Gerzer and his men continued to advance. The crowd parted to make way for the mercenaries, and she swallowed her disgust at the cowardice of the people. A sliver of guilt went through her. They were scared. Nearly two decades of living in the shadow of the Purge had made them meek, exactly what men like Heshen and Antonio wanted. Some glared at her as she openly used magic, others looked on with curiosity, but it was those in the crowd that shrank from her that hurt Amaleigh's heart the most.

Magic was not to be feared. Fuck Heshen for making the people believe all magic was bad. If she attacked Gerzer and his men now with magic, she was only proving their point. And yet, she had no other means of protecting them. She couldn't win against Gerzer's mob, not as a woman. But as a mage, she would decimate their numbers. There had to be a way to protect the citizens without becoming the villain Heshen had led them to believe mages were.

Gwilym settled his shoulders, resolute. The sword glowed in his hands, and magic created a hazy aura around him.

A protective barrier. His magic, not hers.

"How? You're a mage?" She stared at the whirling threads of magic, entranced.

"I don't know and not in the least, but I learn quickly." His cheeky grin and half shrug made her chuckle. They'd needed a miracle, and Gwilym didn't disappoint. "I think that kiss helped me as much as it helped you." His brow rose and her belly tightened in all the best ways.

Not yet completely healed, he was willing to stand at her side and fight. It was foolish and yet, she felt immense gratitude. And pride. He'd accepted his magic without complaint or contempt. For the son of a king who murdered anyone with magical abilities, it was bold of him to publicly display power. But then, Gwilym had always defied his father for what he believed was true and just.

"Keep your focus and you'll do fine." They had each other.

"Yes my lady." He winked at her as if they were about to embark on one of their crazy adventures. "Don't die."

She laughed out loud and reveled in the simple joy those two words brought. If she had anything to do with it, neither of them would die. Not this night.

Gerzer strode closer, and she saw an unnatural light emanating from him. The glow of a fanatic. Magic infused. A mage controlled the man and now she knew who. Behind her on the balcony, Cornelius manipulated Gerzer like a puppet. It wouldn't take much to turn the man into a zealot—he'd always hated Amaleigh. She kept her gaze on Gerzer, trembling slightly at the vicious grin that widened the closer they came. He wasn't there to help Cornelius—his purpose was far more personal. He intended to kill her.

Gwilym tightened his grip on the hilt of his sword and rolled his shoulders. "If anything happens to me—"

"You'll tell me yourself after the fighting. Be ready."

Cassia and her shieldmaidens joined them, the princess dressed similar to her Fianna Bel'en. Six against five dozen. Not good odds.

Dante, now would be a good time to join the fun. She cast the thought toward the harbor.

Gwilym and the others rushed forward to meet the mob with their swords and magic blazing. The clash of metal rang out on all sides and she swallowed her fear. The first group of berserkers she came across were easily enough to handle. A flick of her fingers sent webs of magic to tangle their feet. Even faced with catastrophic odds, she couldn't bring herself to kill. A shrill voice called out her name and she saw Gerzer hacking his way toward her.

She wasn't a warrior like Cassia's Fianna Bel'en. Hell, even the princess was swinging her sword as if she knew what she was doing. Amaleigh was so far out of her element, she feared she would be more of a hindrance to the fight than a help. But there was something she could do to keep her friends.

Amaleigh stepped away from them and spread her arms out wide to embrace her dragon. Wings elongated where her fingertips had been. Ruby scales rippled across her muscular body. A new sensation of strength flooded her, and she blew a river of fire from her snout aimed at the stars. It would've been nothing to turn the advancing mercenaries to ash, but somehow that didn't feel right. She wasn't a murderer.

On the balcony, Cornelius wailed and shouted, "No!"

Gerzer skidded to a stop in the middle of the crowd, his face a mash of horror. A moment later, he turned and ran—away from her, away from the fighting. What a bloody floxy coward!

She swung her head toward the balcony where Cornelius continued to rail, his hands flailing. He paced from one side to the other, giving commands to men who weren't listening. A losing man was a desperate man. Curiously, though, he didn't use any magic. Nor did he try to steal hers. Whatever the change, she hoped it meant she was fully in control of her power and his time of siphoning from her was over. Just to be sure, she imagined a wall between her magic and her mentor. She sniffed the air and blew a ring of flame around him, effectively imprisoning him on the balcony. There were others she had to deal with first.

She dipped her snout toward the berserkers. Some had fled when she shifted, but many more stayed to fight. The crowd that had come to see what their prince had to announce were now either crouched behind statues or fighting. She scanned the square until she found Gerzer hiding behind a wall. In one leap, she was on him. With a single talon, she swept him into a building. His head cracked against the stone, and he slumped to the ground.

A cry caught her attention, and she whirled to see Cassia

struggling in the grasp of another dragon's great claws. Green scales so dark they almost looked black shimmered beneath the torchlight. Somewhere, in the back of her mind, she knew this dragon, had seen it before in her nightmares. This was the dragon that came the night of the Purge, after the killing, to take her away. Her heart knew what her mind refused to believe. Amaleigh accepted the truth like a child swallowing a bitter pill.

Flippin' barnacleballs, Cornelius was a dragon.

FORTY-ONE

Not once in all the years they spent together did he ever hint at being an Aerlghot; in fact, he denied her recollection of the night her parents were killed and swore he rescued her as a man. He'd hid it for some reason. Not only that, but he made a speech about revering her kind, banging on about how he wished he had that freedom, almost as if he'd been jealous. It didn't make sense. Unless he wasn't an Aerlghot and stole the power from someone who was. Amaleigh's gaze went to Cassia. Stealing magic, that she could understand. But stealing a dragon? She shuddered to think what that would do to a person.

Cornelius was a man desperate for power, and that made him dangerous.

"Put her down, Cornelius." Amaleigh advanced on him, her talons raking across the courtyard with screeching speed.

"It didn't have to be this way. You could've been my queen. We would've ruled Eidyn, Amaleigh. You and me."

"Eidyn isn't yours to rule, Cornelius. Nor is Cassia yours to harm."

"She's our enemy."

"How?" Amaleigh hadn't seen any evidence that the princess had harmed dragons.

"She came here for revenge. To kill the prince."

"She thought she was protecting her people. Same as you think you're protecting me." Amaleigh skidded to a stop in front of him. "Let her go. Please."

Cassia's Fianna Bel'en surrounded Cornelius, their vicious swords held aloft. Made from dragon scales, their swords would cut through his armor like a butter knife through cream. He blew a wall of flame, and they stepped away from the maniac. Their swords were powerful, but flesh burned all too quickly in a dragon's fire.

His words jumbled through her brain and she tried to make sense of it all. Cassia had come for revenge, but Cornelius hated the king and his son. Blamed them for his sister's death. Clarity gonged in her brain like a bell ringing out across the countryside.

All the pieces of the puzzle fitted into place, and she saw the scope of his plan, from the king's abduction to Gwilym's death and his taking the throne in his place. She saw him place a crown upon her head. It wasn't her face she saw, but that of the dead queen's. This wasn't about Amaleigh but had always been about Queen Maire. And she saw the truth of what he truly was. Human. Mortal. Magicless.

"You're not a mage, are you? You steal magic because you have none of your own. Why now? Why after all this time did you come back?" She had to hear the truth from him to fully believe it.

"You were getting too strong. My wards weren't enough to contain you."

He'd been warding her this whole time. His was the name Antonio had been reluctant to say. Her belly dipped with this new, disturbing piece of the puzzle.

"You didn't give me to Antonio, did you? You were going to keep me so you could use my magic, but he stole me from you and hid me among his urchins." Amaleigh watched the anger cross Cornelius's face and knew she had found the truth. "I was a child!"

"You were so much more than that. A child of fire! Your power would've sustained me for the rest of my life, but that drug-addled cretin figured out what I'd done and took you from me. I was too weak to fight him, so I bided my time until you stole your father's dagger."

A sea of voices rose around the square, and Amaleigh saw Dante rushing toward her, an axe held high. One hundred or so others jogged alongside him with weapons of all sorts and sundries waving to the sky. She blew a snort of flame high into the air. When they saw her, they slowed, eyes wild. She and Cornelius were the first dragons Eidyn had seen in more than two decades.

"You have nothing to fear from me, but this one was responsible for the Purge." She tilted her snout toward Cornelius.

"Amaleigh?" Dante stared at her, then at the greenish-black dragon. He inclined his head to her and turned toward Cornelius.

More men and women joined the fray. Citizens tired of being repressed or mages who'd been warded, she couldn't be certain, but was grateful for their numbers...and their enthusiasm.

Cornelius lifted into the air, and she followed. His talons gripped Cassia, pinning her arms to her side. She'd stopped struggling against his tight hold, but Amaleigh saw the grim determination on her face. The princess was planning something. Amaleigh rose into the air, ready to fight. No more worrying, no more fear, Cornelius must be stopped, and she was the only one who could end his reign of terror.

A flash of lightning lit the dark sky, and Amaleigh flinched from its electric brightness.

"Drink its power!" Cassia yelled above the rush of wind and sounds of fighting from below. "It won't hurt you."

Another flash cracked the air, and Amaleigh flew into the jagged afterglow. Her scales vibrated with the current left from the lightning, and she inhaled all she could take. Her nerves sizzled and popped with expanded power.

Cornelius flew above her, his mouth open, ready to suck in power. He screamed and shuddered as his body whipped away from the charged air.

Cassia's laughter floated to her, then cut short when Cornelius squeezed his talons. She'd tricked him into thinking the charged light would help him as well.

Clever princess.

The distraction gave her the opportunity to attack Cornelius. She blew a powerful burst of fire at his face, emboldened by the electrified air that filled her lungs and danced along her wings. He shrieked and released the princess as he raised his talons in defense.

Cassia plummeted toward the ground and Amaleigh dove quickly, catching her too close to the ground for comfort. She lowered the princess to the balcony and returned to the sky. Cornelius knew she'd save the princess and took advantage of her kindness to escape. His dark body blended into the night sky, but she saw between the stars and moonlight to where he circled the palace high above. The pretender couldn't go far—he needed Cassia's power to fuel his dragon.

Wind rushed across her snout the faster she flew, and she exalted in the freedom flying gave her. No wonder he'd blocked her from her dragon. If she'd known this kind of elation existed, she would've fought to keep it. Just like she would now. She built up the walls she'd once used to keep her heart protected, but this time she buttressed them against her magic. He wouldn't steal from her ever again.

Cornelius snarled and swooped toward her, less graceful than before, and with far less speed. Even so, she trembled at the hatred buried in his eyes. His dark-olive scales glistened in the bright moonlight as they rippled across his back.

"Please," Amaleigh whispered. "There doesn't need to be any more bloodshed."

Fire blazed forth from his snout, and she kept from flinching. It pummeled her scales, and she gulped in the heat, filling her lungs with his stolen power. Turnabout was fair play, after all. His roar would've delighted her, if she was the gloating kind.

Instead, she dove forward and snapped at Cornelius's long neck. He dodged her attack and banked to the right. She followed, sending a blaze at his back. Too quickly for her to counter, he swung around and clawed at her wing, nicking the delicate membrane. A shiver of pain raced across her back, but she couldn't stop. Wouldn't stop until Cornelius was either dead, or ran out of magic.

The sound of fighting continued on the ground as she and Cornelius battled in the sky. Again and again, they scraped long talons down scales and sought purchase with their sharp teeth. Their wings beat furiously as they rammed heads into torsos, swung tails against breasts. She didn't understand this kind of fighting, nor was she certain how best to use her dragon body. Her only saving grace was that it didn't appear Cornelius did, either.

He flew at her with surprising speed, and she ducked to avoid a collision. The movement opened her to attack, and Cornelius took every bit of advantage that he could. His sharp teeth pierced her scales, ripping into her right shoulder, and she cried out against the burning pain. Fury surged in her veins, and she whirled on him, slamming her tail against his snout. The force sent him tumbling backward, and she seized her opportunity to end this, once and for all.

Amaleigh reached into the void of the cosmos, between worlds and stars to where she hid the dagger. Her claw gripped the hilt, and she flew hard and fast toward Cornelius. Rage overrode all emotion as she pinpointed the dragon's heart. She could almost hear the rapid beating as she neared.

Her dragon was too large, her talons too clumsy to handle the dagger properly. It was foolhardy and dangerous, but she had no choice other than to shift into her human form if she wanted to hit her mark. Moments before impact, she released her dragon and gripped the dagger with both hands. She slammed into his chest and impaled the dagger between his scales. Flesh ripped against her blade, and she shoved it deeper, into his heart.

An all-too human scream rent the air, causing a rift in the sky. A great chasm opened and sucked her toward the darkness.

Amaleigh fought the pull even as she plunged the blade farther into his chest.

From the corner of her eye, she saw another dragon barrel toward them. Too late, she tried to pull free from Cornelius. The impact knocked the three of them toward the palace, tumbling wildly through the air. Cornelius landed hard on the stone pavers, with Amaleigh still clinging to the blade. Stars lit behind her eyes, and she rolled off the dragon onto wobbly legs. He shifted into his human form and lay wheezing. Blood spilled from the gaping wound her blade had left.

Honestly, she was surprised he was still alive. Hatred and spite were all he had to keep him tethered to life. Her own anger burned away as she watched him gasping his final breaths. This wasn't how it was supposed to end, not by her hand, and yet, she understood that it was the only way it could end. Tears filled her eyes, and she mourned the man she'd known as her mentor, her companion, and her friend. She knelt beside him and took his hand in her own.

Cornelius blinked up at her, his eyes dark. "I just wanted you to be happy. I wanted you to love me the way I love you. If only you'd loved me, none of this would've happened." He reached a bloody hand to her face and tucked a strand of hair behind her ear. "You failed me."

The compassion she'd felt evaporated, and ire burned through her blood. He dared to blame her for what he'd done. Her magic flared, but she held it in check.

"No, Cornelius, you failed yourself. You couldn't accept what I could give. And this?" She motioned to the carnage surrounding them. "This isn't love. This is madness."

"Forgive me, Amaleigh." He clasped her hand and shook violently with his coming death. "Please."

Her tears spilled forth, and she shook her head. He didn't deserve forgiveness, not for all the death and destruction he'd caused. He was the reason Heshen slaughtered her family. He stole her magic for years, only to use it against her. It was an easy thing to promise, but not if it wasn't true. She couldn't forgive him. Wouldn't.

A crowd had gathered and ringed them at a respectable distance. Jada approached, with several others at her side. They carried a litter, with the king sitting awkwardly against the cushions. His gaze went from Cornelius to her. Sorrow, deep and abiding, etched his features.

"The peace you seek, child, is here." King Heshen tapped his chest. "To forgive isn't to absolve one of their crime, but it is to release you from your own prison."

Heshen struggled to get out of the chair, and his servants helped him to kneel beside the dying man. Amaleigh's dagger stuck out of Cornelius's chest and the king jerked it free. He wiped it on his shirt sleeve, and then handed it to her. She took it with trembling fingers. The two men who had caused so much heartache not just in her life, but throughout the kingdom, were within her reach. She could turn them both to ash with but a single breath.

And oh, how she wanted to. But that was a prison she knew she'd never escape. Heshen was right. Forgiving Cornelius wasn't saying she accepted what he'd done, but it would free her from the shackles of guilt that burned against her soul. She'd never understand why he and the king did what they'd done, nor could she bring back the mages and dragons Heshen had slaughtered. But she could live. Live her life to the fullest, without fear or regret.

"I forgive you." Fresh tears streamed over her cheeks to drip on his brocade coat. She said the words to Cornelius as well as the king. "For my mother, my father, and my brother, I forgive you. For all those souls you murdered, I forgive you." But she would never forget. Their memories needed to be kept alive so nothing as heinous as the Purge could ever happen again.

Cornelius's breath rattled one last time before his body went limp. Amaleigh closed his eyes and bowed her head. His hand flopped to the side, and her locket spilled from his palm. She let out a sorrow-filled sob and wiped her cheeks with her sleeve.

The king picked up the pendant and clicked it open. His eyes shimmered with tears as he rubbed a thumb over the portraits. "I'm so sorry, my friends."

She reached for the locket, and he handed it to her with a deep sigh.

"They're my parents."

He blinked, as if not comprehending. Then he nodded and dabbed his cheeks with a silk cloth. "You're Amaleigh?"

"I am."

He took her hand in his, and she felt his anguish in the trembling of his fingers as they gripped hers.

"She healed you, Father."

She glanced up and saw Gwilym shake off his scales, eyes wild, hair standing at all angles. He stood beside her, his leg grazing her shoulder as if in support. He was there for her, just as he'd always been. If only she'd realized it sooner. But then, neither of them were ready or in a position to accept their fates. Perhaps it had to end this way for her and Gwilym to be together, fully and completely. She couldn't turn back time, couldn't take back the Purge or what Cornelius had done, but she and Gwilym could forge a new future for Eidyn.

"I didn't know I could do that. Was I really and truly a dragon?" Gwilym held out a hand to help Amaleigh stand.

She took it gratefully and sank against his body. "You're one of us." The realization spread through her, igniting a fire she'd thought dead. "You're an Aerlghot."

"I suppose I am." His voice was full of wonder. "But what does that mean?"

"Oh, my son." The king rose on unsteady legs with the help of several servants. "I am truly sorry. I didn't know."

Gwilym raised Amaleigh's hand to his lips. "Nor did I."

Cassia stepped from her group of swordmaidens, looking beautiful and fierce in her regalia. Gone was the mask, and her skin shimmered with a pearly iridescence. "I'm sorry to have deceived you, Your Majesty. What the traitor Cornelius said was true—I came here seeking revenge for the destruction you caused, and for the deaths of our lovely dragons." She knelt on one knee, a fist over her chest. "I do no seek your forgiveness, only that you understand our sorrow at the loss."

King Heshen placed a hand on her head. "It is I who hopes one day Aerithilyn will forgive us for our past misdeeds. Rise,

Your Highness, and may you never feel the need to hide your true self from us ever again."

Cassia stood tall and faced the man who she'd come to Eidyn to murder. "While I cannot speak for my parents, please know that I will personally tell them of what transpired here. If your words are true, then one day, you will get your wish." She turned to Gwilym with sadness in her eyes. "I'm glad to have known you before the traitor impersonated you. In truth, I didn't discover his treachery on my own. Amaleigh saw through his clever disguise, and for my idiocy, I am sorry. Though I must confess there were several times I wished to stab the pretender in the heart, and wish I had. It would have saved us all a fair bit of sorrow."

Gwilym rubbed his chest with a grimace. "I thank you for not murdering me." His gaze took in Cassia's shieldmaidens. "You or one of your ladies."

Merigold snorted and Isla grinned, her fingertips running along the blade of her sword. Amaleigh stood silent, watching the scene as if she were a patron at the theater. Her mind followed the play, with one question nagging at her.

"If Gwilym was unaware of his power, then who warded him?"

Cassia glanced at the king, who looked baffled, and then back to Gwilym. "When you were naught but a babe, your mother suspected her brother of misdeeds and placed powerful wards on you to protect you from his trickery." She inclined her head toward the king. "The late queen speaks to me from beyond the grave. It was important she tell me her truths so that I might pass them on to you."

"He told me the prophecy, 'Dragons will tear the crown asunder.'" Heshen's lips moved as if reciting more of the long-ago conversation with a man who sought to betray not just the king, but the entire kingdom.

"He lied. The actual prophecy speaks of peace and says that dragon fire will light the heart of the kingdom. We have a copy in the library at Aerithilyn."

Heshen peered at Cassia for a long moment before he spoke. Disbelief, then grief, then resignation crossed his battered features. "You can show the new king this document. He will be a wise and just ruler."

Murmurings and gasps went through the crowd.

At her side, Gwilym straightened.

The king waved a hand at those gathered. "My time of ruling has come to an end. It's a new beginning, and my son will lead his people to peace. There will be a formal proclamation forthcoming." Heshen glanced at Gwilym. "It's the least I can do after all the suffering I've caused."

Amaleigh saw the shake of Heshen's legs and used her magic to keep him upright. His wan smile was full of meaning she didn't quite understand.

"And his queen will restore the power of the dragon mages in Eidyn."

Gwilym squeezed her hand and the crowd cheered, but Amaleigh could only stare in horror at the man who continued to control events in her life.

Her, a queen? He was mad.

CHAPTER

FORTY-TWO

Two weeks after Cornelius's death, Gwilym found Amaleigh in the garden where she liked to sit and listen to birdsong. She turned toward him as he approached and smiled. All the wards placed on him when he was just a child had been removed—mostly by her, with a little help from his mother's spirit. The late queen shared every last sordid detail about her brother's mad quest to save Eidyn from itself. A quest that had cost her and her unborn child their lives. Once she'd helped Amaleigh release Gwilym from the bonds she'd placed on him, her spirit was finally able to rest and Amaleigh heard from her no more. It was a relief and also a bit of sorrow that she was gone. Amaleigh had hoped to ask Maire about her parents.

With her gone, that left only the king and she was reluctant to bring them up for fear it might cause him to relapse into the tyrant she'd always known him to be. Although he had a long way to go before he was completely healed, he'd been true to his word and publicly abdicated the throne in favor of his son. There were those in Eidyn who didn't want dragons to return, but they were few and would either adapt to the change, or leave. Gwilym had made several edicts outlining his feelings on the matter. Being an Aerlghot gave him an authority no other king before him had. From what they could tell in the records, Gwilym was the first Aerlghot king to ever rule Eidyn, but they both hoped not the last.

The official coronation wouldn't be for another month, which gave them time to escort Cassia to her kingdom. Amaleigh had counted the days until they could leave for Aerithilyn and now the time had come.

Shortly after the battle at the palace, Amaleigh and the others raided Antonio's manor and freed all the children being held there. When they'd cleared the house, she and Gwilym shifted into their dragon forms and razed the place with flames hot enough to melt iron and purify the ground. Amaleigh had plans for the land—they were going to build an orphanage on top of the ash of Antonio's manor. The subjugation of orphans was at an end.

They would also build a new university, where mages could study and learn. People like Eaman who'd been warded and shielded for all their lives could unleash their magic and use it for good, as mages had done for centuries. It would take time, but eventually Eidyn would once more be a respected city where mages were not feared and dragons soared through the skies.

She and Gwilym had spent many hours together working to understand their powers and learning all there was about being an Aerlghot. The only thing she had yet to confess to Gwilym was the life bond they shared.

Every time she thought to bring up the subject, she lost her nerve. If Gwilym rejected her or bristled at the idea that he was bound to her and none other, she couldn't bear it. Even though his father had said she'd be Gwilym's queen, he had yet to ask and she wasn't one to assume anything.

"Dante's here to see the twins." Gwilym sat beside her and slid her hand into his. "I think he's going to miss them."

Amaleigh blinked back tears. "I know I will. But Cassia's right. They need to be with other dragons."

They'd agreed the elven princess would take the twins with her to Aerithilyn. In her heart, Amaleigh knew it was the right decision, but she'd had the twins since they'd hatched. A jag of sadness cut through her. They still hadn't recovered the egg she'd found in the ruins of her family home. Cornelius had hidden it somewhere out of her reach. It was lost.

Dante entered the garden and whistled at the surroundings. "Not a bad upgrade, Erma."

Amaleigh laughed, a full-bellied chortle that shook out the doldrums that threatened at the thought of losing the twins.

Gwilym looked from Amaleigh to Dante and chuckled. "A thief and a pirate openly guests at the palace. Will wonders never cease?"

Together, they went in search of the twins, who were being housed in a separate stable from the horses. Not just the horses, but all the barn animals had never seen dragons and went wild when Shen and Mali arrived. For the safety of everyone, the twins were kept away from any livestock. Amaleigh seriously doubted the twins would ever eat a chicken, but they were dragons and chickens are delicious.

As they passed a corridor, Dante gave a long look in the distance before turning toward the archway. "I'll meet you there. I have something to do first."

Gwilym and Amaleigh glanced down the corridor, where Merigold leaned against a pillar, flipping a dagger between her fingertips.

"Do you think they're...?"

"Oh, I have no doubt they are. Probably all five of them."

"Together? As in, all at once?"

"Definitely."

Gwilym looked intrigued, and Amaleigh's heart sank.

"Is monogamy all that bad?"

He turned to her with a wide smile. "Not if it's with you." He pressed his lips against her forehead and breathed deeply. "Are you packed?"

She was. Had been since a week previously. No one from Eidyn had been to the elven kingdom in over twenty years. It was an honor to be invited as Cassia's friend. Since Cornelius's death, they'd spent hours together in the queen's sitting room, chatting about everything from dragon mages to healing properties of herbs. They'd also explored every district of Eidyn, always with Gwilym and the shieldmaidens in tow. Not for protection, but out of a genuine curiosity about the city.

Of the small group, Amaleigh alone knew the streets and hidden passages, but on their walks, she revealed all Eidyn's secrets. On each excursion from the palace, Cassia had marveled at the sheer size of Eidyn while simultaneously tsking at the architecture. "Too stumpy", she would say with a grimace. It made Amaleigh even more curious about the palace of Aerithilyn.

A giddy little hiccup tickled her belly. She was going to the elven kingdom. Her! An orphaned urchin who once called the sewers home. She nearly pinched herself to make sure it was real. But it was. All of it was real. The good, the bad, the deadly.

They retrieved the twins from the stables and herded them through the palace to the meeting place. Several courtiers scurried out of their way, and a few brave souls bent to stroke the dragonlings as they scampered across the carpeted floor.

"Are you ready to meet the elf queen and king?" As much as she wanted to see Aerithilyn, she was nervous what the elven rulers would think of her. A fine gown didn't make her past disappear. Nor did gems at her throat and wrists make her anxieties vanish. She could wear all the baubles in the world and still feel exposed as the poor thief she'd been.

"They'll love you." Gwilym directed her to the small room hidden behind the great hall where Cassia and the others waited.

Dante saluted her on his way out, a cocky grin showing his teeth.

Such a manwhore. She smiled and waved as he passed. Leave it to him to get in a quick shag before they had to leave.

He stopped to give the twins a cuddle, then left the room.

It was time.

Cassia stepped beside Amaleigh, her eyes narrowing at the locket she wore. Amaleigh raised a protective hand as if to protect the images of her parents inside. But there was no need to hide any longer. Everyone knew who she was, who her parents had been.

"When we first met, I sensed a spell on your locket." Cassia stroked a finger along the silver. "Whether to track you or spy on you, I can't be certain, but it is no longer there." She took Amaleigh's hand in her own. "I am happy that you and I became friends."

Amaleigh hugged the princess hard. "So am I." It didn't surprise her to learn Cornelius had spelled the locket. She should've guessed he would do something so deceitful. She shoved the spark of anger away and focused on the present. She gave Cassia a meaningful look. "Are you ready?"

Cassia nodded and watched Amaleigh closely as she opened a portal large enough to fit the entire group. With Cornelius's wards removed, her magic never exhausted her and was always present. No more failed attempts to grasp an elusive thread.

The princess held out her hand, circling it like Amaleigh was doing. The portal stretched and yawned into darkness. They shared an excited grin. With practice, Cassia would perfect her portal-making abilities. Just as Amaleigh had perfected her casting skills.

Jada and Isla took a dragonling each, and the group stepped into the void. Amaleigh's ears rang and her heart quickened. This was unlike her usual portals. It might've been Cassia's power affecting her magic; she wasn't sure. She took Gwilym's hand and kept alert to any danger.

A few moments later, light shone from the blackness and they stepped into—what, exactly, she wasn't sure. Ashen walls stretched to the sky, where branches arched to make beams. Their leaves provided shelter from the elements.

"Amazing." Gwilym tightened his grip on her hand, and she followed his gaze around the room.

They were in a tree, but not a tree. Lacy cornices framed windows and delicate furnishings sat atop fur rugs that dotted the polished wood floor.

"Welcome to Aerithilyn." Cassia cocked her head to the side. "This way."

They traversed through several walkways, all tiled with marble, but surrounded by the same ashen walls. Every so often, a tree trunk grew through the wall and disappeared into the ceiling. Amaleigh's mouth gaped, as did Gwilym's. Even the dragonlings were subdued in this mysterious, ethereal place. Amaleigh understood Cassia's tutting. Eidyn, though beautiful, was nothing like this place.

When they entered a great space, those gathered glanced up at the intrusion.

"Cassia! Darling." A lithe woman with ebony braids that reached her buttocks hurried forward and embraced the princess.

"Mother, Father, this is King Gwilym of Eidyn and his betrothed, Lady Amaleigh."

Amaleigh and Gwilym lowered in their respective curtsey

and bow. A refined-looking gentleman approached and held out his hand to grasp Gwilym by the forearm.

"Welcome to our home. We heard the news of what transpired and although we are grateful the sorrows have ended, we are sorry for your loss."

Gwilym placed his fist over his heart. "I hope our two kingdoms can once again enjoy the friendship we once shared."

Amaleigh's gaze traveled past the king and queen to a couple standing with a group of courtiers. The golden eyes of their beast met hers, and she gasped.

"What are you doing here?" She left Gwilym's side and stepped toward the threesome.

The silver-haired woman touched her partner's sleeve and indicated Amaleigh. He squinted in her direction, then a wide smile broke across his face.

Cassia and the others quieted while Amaleigh approached the ones called Taryn and Rhoane. She bent to one knee and bowed her head. The beast sniffed her several times, then licked her face from chin to forehead.

"Kaida senses your dragon," Taryn told her. "As do we."

Amaleigh rose and faced them. "Did you return the faerie to his home?"

Sadness flickered across her features, and she nodded. "He is with his queen."

"How is it you're here?" Amaleigh waved to indicate the room, but she meant Eidyn as well. Their meeting outside the Shoogly Dragon had felt like a chance encounter, but now, she sensed it had deeper meaning.

"Rhoane, look." Taryn pointed to something behind Amaleigh, and she turned to see the twins hiding behind Gwilym's legs.

Rhoane sucked in his breath. "So it is true." His gaze went first to Taryn, then to Amaleigh, and finally to the king and queen. "You were right, *mi carae*. We have at last found a home for the lost *darathi vorsi*."

The king clapped for silence and indicated the queen had something to say. The group quieted in respectful anticipation.

"Everyone, on this happy occasion of our daughter Cassia's return, we are also graced with Their Highnesses Taryn and Rhoane. Our mysterious visitors are from a world far from ours, one where dragons long ago were used against the citizens and then exiled by a malicious witch. Considering recent events, I'm sure you can all appreciate our horror at their circumstances. It appears they are searching for somewhere safe where their dragons can live in harmony with their caretakers." Queen Ingrid reached for her husband's hand. Amaleigh saw the slight shake in the queen's grip.

It broke her heart to hear of Taryn and Rhoane's troubles. Dragons, it seemed, were used as weapons not just on Nasus, but other worlds as well. She peered closer at the pair, a tickle in the back of her mind teasing her.

"With your blessing, Your Majesties, we would like to bring our *darathi* to live here, with you." Rhoane kissed his thumb and placed it at his forehead, then heart.

The elven king grasped Rhoane's hand. "We would be honored, *Surtentse*. They will be cared for and loved by all Eleri now, and in the future." He looked to Gwilym and Amaleigh. "Now that peace has returned to Nasus, the dragons will once more flourish."

From his lips to the gods' ears, be it so. Gwilym stepped to her side and slipped her hand in his. The twins approached with caution, their mischievous eyes darting to the white beast.

Taryn knelt and held out a hand. "Come here, my beauties. Kaida won't hurt you." She inched forward until Mali's little snout touched her fingertips. "That's a good girl."

Shen sniffed the air and sneezed a little fireball in Kaida's direction. She shook her head and pawed the ground. Amaleigh started to reach for Shen to pull him away, but Rhoane's words stopped her.

"You are home, little one." Rhoane bent down and stroked Shen's scales. Tears glistened in his magnificent moss-colored eyes. "*Dearth lach nothrin de las vendrigas, der darathi vorsi.* You are home."

He spoke to the dragonlings in their language, and the words struck Amaleigh's heart. No more hiding. No more running. No more jumping between worlds, looking for something intangible that she'd never had. What she longed for most was always there, in Eidyn, with Gwilym. He'd been her best friend, her family, and her true love. She'd just been too distracted by survival to see it. She gave his hand a squeeze and gazed into the face of the man she loved.

"What?"

His cheeky grin melted her insides. If only she could tell him what she truly desired. To be away from the others, naked.

As if reading her mind, he cocked an eyebrow with a slight shake of his head.

Duty first. Then fun.

Damn protocol.

CHAPTER

FORTY-THREE

Amaleigh arched into their movements, her breasts glistening in the moonlight. After the excitement of seeing the dragonlings had died down, and discussions were had about Taryn and Rhoane's dragons joining those at Aerithilyn, they had joined the queen and king for a sumptuous meal in the great hall. She still couldn't quite wrap her head around the fact that they were in a giant tree. Even so, Aerithilyn was one of the most beautiful palaces she'd ever been in. Not that her list was exhaustive. Fairytale came to mind when she thought of the soaring cathedral-like ceilings made from branches and leaves.

She glanced at the leafy canopy of their bed and sighed. Yes, a fairytale. Would that be how her and Gwilym's romance was remembered? Would their reign be one remarked upon in centuries to come?

Gwilym pinched her nipple, and she yelped.

"Where were you?" His hips thrust upward, and she giggled at his audacity.

"This palace is incredible. It oozes magic, and yet, I don't feel unsafe here. Just the opposite, in fact." She bent forward and simultaneously ground her pelvis against him and took his lips between her teeth. His low growl sent spirals of desire through her body.

She surrendered his lips and arched again, rocking harder with her coming release. His hands snaked up her abdomen to fondle her breasts, and her breath came in short gasps. Watching his face as he came undone was one of her favorite things in the world, and tonight was no exception. She clenched against his cock, her gaze locked to his. His hand slipped down her sides to her hips and gripped tightly, but not enough to hurt. She delighted in the pressure he applied and met his quickening thrusts with her own.

"Stars, you make me wild." The words were husky and full of want.

That wicked half-smile played upon his lips. "I like you wild."

Another thrust, and she grunted as she shifted forward just enough to hit her tender bud. A surprised yelp escaped her lips as her climax hit hard and fast. She gripped his shoulders, crying out as the delicious shivers ravaged her body. A moment later, he added his cry to hers, his face red with the effort, his veins straining with his release.

He pressed deeper, holding her hips still until the last of his seed filled her womb. She dug her fingers into the soft curls on his chest and laughed at how hard she was heaving.

"You'd think I just ran all the length of Eidyn, chased by a gang of urchins. Too much rich food." Another chuckle came between her gasps.

"I like the change." His hands smoothed over her hips. "You have curves now."

Truth be told, she didn't mind the curves or the rich food.

She kissed his nose and slipped from the bed to put on a

velvet robe he'd had made for her. It was the color of emeralds and set off her crimson hair brilliantly.

"You're gorgeous." Gwilym followed her and shrugged into a pair of loose-fitting pants. "I wish we could stay abed all day and night."

She giggled and poked his belly. "Is that all you think about? Making love?"

He wrapped his arms around her and guided her to the balcony that overlooked the glittering treetops of the elven city. He held her close and stroked her hair. "I think about what will happen after we make love."

She stilled, her mind circling to the lost egg. Her heart grieved its loss more than she'd grieved anything in her life.

Gwilym pulled away slightly, and she tugged his arms tightly around her.

"I can see how much you love it here. I'd understand if you wanted to remain with the elves. Eidyn hasn't exactly been kind to you. You could make a new home here, if you wanted." There was a tremor in his voice that spoke to his nervousness.

"Is that what you want?" She turned to face him, afraid of what she might find.

He held her face between his hands and looked deeply into her eyes. "I want you by my side, always."

"I've been running from one thing or another all my life. What I long for now is somewhere safe, where I never have to hide who I am or pretend. I want to belong. I want a home."

"My home is with you. Wherever that may take us." Gwilym's lips brushed hers. "I love you, Amaleigh. I always have but was too stupid not to tell you." His tongue flicked against her open lips, teasing. "It would be an honor if you would consent to being my best friend, my partner, and my queen for the rest of our days. Will you marry me, my love?"

She could scarcely breathe. She'd hoped the question was

coming, but now having heard it, the responsibility of his words slammed against her chest. It meant she would rule at his side as queen of Eidyn. What did she know of ruling? She couldn't even get raising dragons right. And hell, she hadn't known Cornelius was a complete fraud. What if she let her people down? Worse, what if she let Gwilym down?

As he gazed adoringly at her, she knew none of that mattered. They would figure it out together.

"Yes," she whispered. "I will be all of that and more."

He blew out a breath and grinned. "I had assumed since we're mated for life, it was a given, but it's nice to know you wanted me as well."

She pulled away with a frown. "You knew we're mated?"

He nodded, and a huge burden lifted from her shoulders.

"I want you, Gwilym. For a minute, a month, or a lifetime. As long as the gods see fit to keep you by my side, I want you. I've always loved you. I was just too afraid to see it or allow myself to hope you could love me in return. I was a fool."

"You're my fool and will make a wonderful queen."

She worried her bottom lip, unsure how to say what might undo all that they'd just said.

"The dragon egg is gone, Gwilym. Cornelius probably destroyed it out of revenge." She cupped his cheek in her hand, tears swimming in her eyes. "I'm sorry, Gwilym."

He shook his head, his own eyes shimmering. For Aerlghots, they couldn't have children without a dragon egg of their own.

"There's no need to be sorry. Whether we have children or not, I still love you and want you to be my wife."

Warmth embraced her—all consuming, powerful, intimate.

Amaleigh gasped and looked at Gwilym. His eyes were wide, full of wonder.

"Do you feel that?" He stroked her hair, and she nodded.

It was the same magic she'd felt coming from the couple—

Taryn and Rhoane, what Cassia called ShantiMari. It enveloped them with a soothing heat.

The egg you lost was never yours to claim. It belonged to your parents, but do not despair. You will have your own egg in time. Trust. Believe. Love. I promise you will have the family you so desire.

"That man, the one called Rhoane," Gwilym touched his forehead, "I can sense him in here, as if he's speaking to me, but it's not our language. *Dearth darathi firthglen fortuni.* The future of dragons resides within us."

Amaleigh nodded. "I heard him, too. I always thought it was the language of dragons, but Cassia says it's an ancient form of elven called Eleri."

Gwilym frowned, and then grinned. "She told me Taryn and Rhoane are gods. I thought she jested, but now? Do you suppose they are?"

She sighed and turned to face the forest, her back snuggled against his bare skin. "If they are, then perhaps we are blessed by them."

He wrapped his arms around her, and she rested her head against his chest. It wouldn't surprise her in the least if the strange couple turned out to be the very gods who created Nasus. Nothing surprised her anymore. Not after everything that had happened in Eidyn.

They'd cleared Antonio's mansion and made way for an orphanage and university, all good beginnings for a new Eidyn, but there was so much more to be done. As she stood with her love, she knew they couldn't fuck this up. Too much was at stake if they did.

Gwilym had said his home was with her. And her home was with him, wherever that might be. Together, they could accomplish anything. Their magic was raw and in its infancy—same with their dragons. To build a stronger Eidyn, they'd have to master both their magic and dragon souls, but that was a worry for tomorrow.

For tonight, she would love her king with all her heart. She sighed and curled against his strong body. No more running. No more hiding. She'd found her home.

The steady beat of his heart was the rhythm of her life. He was her world.

About the Author

Tameri Etherton is a USA Today Bestselling and award-winning author of dangerous fantasy and paranormal romance with magical ever afters. She grew up inventing fictional worlds where the impossible was possible.

It's been said she leaves a trail of glitter in her wake as she creates new adventures for her kickass heroines, and the rogues who steal their hearts.

She lives an enchanted life traveling the world with her very own prince charming. When at home, she enjoys many cups of tea and cuddles from their two massive Maine Coons, Pora and Ember.

Read More from Tameri Etherton and explore the Aetherverse at
www.TameriEtherton.com

AUTHOR NOTES

Amaleigh and Gwilym's story began in the short story *Child of Fire*, but I loved the characters so much, I knew I needed to give them a full-length story, and *Dragon Mage* was born.

I still wasn't completely satisfied, and so I combined *Child of Fire* and *Dragon Mage* into one book to give Amaleigh and Gwilym the story they BOTH deserve! I've added extended scenes, new chapters, and more sexy times in this updated edition. And, their romance will continue through two more books, Dragon Throne and Dragon Queen! At last, Eidyn will have the king and queen it deserves, but with some twists and turns along the way.

Anna Spies at Atra Luna Cover & Logo Art did an amazing job with the cover and interior artwork. Many dragon kisses and faerie hugs to her!

As always, Faith Williams did a fab job with the edits. If there are any typos or mistakes, they are all mine! I can't help but tinker after I get final edits back.

Last, but never least, a huge thank you to my very own Prince Charming, David. He is my world.

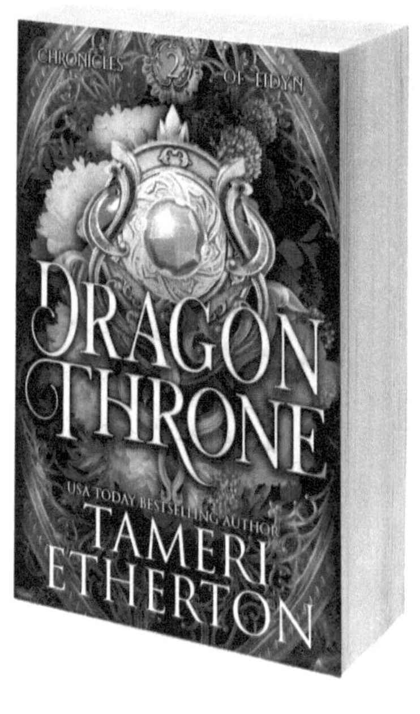

Continue the adventure with Amaleigh and Gwilym as they fight for their throne!

Coming in 2026...

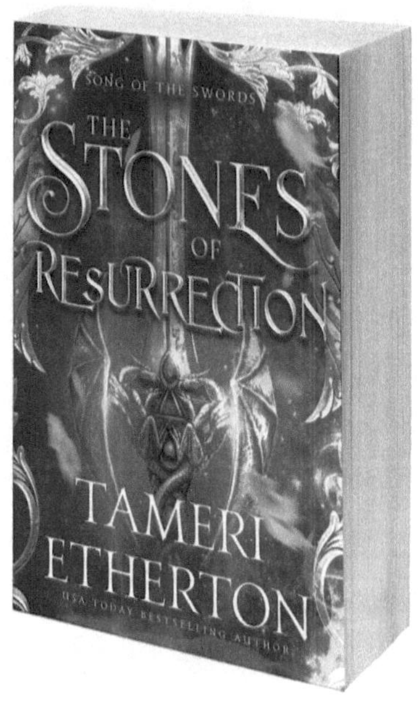

Otherworldly portals. Mysterious powers. Evil hungrily awaits her return.

Taryn's simple life is all she's ever known. Living above a busy London pub with her grandfather, they're ripped from their reality and plunged into a strange world to jumpstart an ancient prophecy. And when he's killed defending her from a vicious intruder's magic, Taryn's left nearly alone... and forced to trust a rugged savior.

Rhoane has one job. Sworn to protect the young woman who has returned to fulfill her destiny, the assassin dare not let his feelings get in the way of her training. But he knows the time will come when she accepts her power and recognizes he's her fated mate.

As Taryn learns her life on Earth was a lie, she must unlock her hidden talents to save an entire world from destruction. And though Rhoane will show no mercy to anyone who stands in her way, he fears her biggest threat comes from the family she has never known.

Will the destined pair rise to stop the annihilation of a vast kingdom?

The Stones of Resurrection is the enthralling first book in the Song of the Swords fantasy series. If you like ensemble casts, intense action, and dark family sagas, then you'll love Tameri Etherton's epic tale.

She's been hijacked by fate. He's running out of time. Can these magically mismatched outsiders find their forever-after before their realms perish?

Rori MacNair has learned to close off her heart. Molded into a spy to follow her legendary family's legacy, the faerie assassin is stunned to wake up in a strange forest and start reliving past traumas. Suspecting mind control, she shatters the spell trapping her only to stumble upon a handsome thief.

Therron Mistwalker is avoiding a cursed crown. Tracking a dark magic-wielder to end her vile acts, the elf-prince-in-disguise is unprepared to meet a captivating fae determined to slay the same villain. And realizing the prophecy he dreads has finally caught up to him, he teams up with his prickly new ally while worrying about the clock now ticking down to his doom.

Pursuing the evildoer through forbidden portals, Rori worries she's warming up to her mysterious pointy-eared companion far too easily. And a guilt-ridden Therron struggles to set aside his ever-growing attraction as their prolonged witch hunt leaves behind a trail of dead bodies.

Can Rori and Therron bring their foul target to her knees and rescue their worlds?

Fatal Illusion is the exciting first book in the Fatal Fae series of romantic fantasy adventures. If you like slow-brewing chemistry, imaginative worldbuilding, and the healing power of hope, then you'll love USA Today Bestselling and award-winning author Tameri Etherton's powerful page-turner.

Essence of elegance by day. Rampant with desire by night. Can she keep her deadly secret while she wins a prince's heart?

Lady Rainne Dequette hates her ugly magical curse. Transforming from dignified elf to reckless ogress every evening, she's resigned to dispatching bandits after sundown instead of dancing at magnificent castle balls. But when her epic skills with a blade save a handsome royal from ravenous wolves, revealing her shameful form could get her killed.

Prince Theo Mistwalker would rather be in his grand library than combing the forests for his wayward brother. But after he's attacked, he's smitten by the swashbuckling rescuer who plants an alluring kiss on his lips before vanishing into the trees. Though his loyalty weakens while he heals in a local duchess's home and develops feelings for her beautiful elven daughter.

After Rainne confesses her burden to the noble man she's fallen for, she has no choice but to deal with her self-hatred or risk losing her one shot at happily-ever-after. And to be with the woman of his dreams, Theo must embark on a dangerous quest to break the spell.

Can they find a way to end Rainne's torment and surrender to their destined passions?

Indulge in a mesmerizing tale of passion and danger, where an enchanted apple holds the key to forbidden desires.

Lady Eira Cannaid, blessed with unparalleled beauty, conceals the scars of her abusive past. Longing for escape, she is enticed to the grand palace, where a glittering ball promises a respite from the uncertainty of her days. But beneath the dazzling facade lies a treacherous plot woven by her scheming stepmother, who seeks to elevate her own status by sacrificing Eira's innocence to the king.

Lurking in the shadows is the king's heir, a prince willing to court the ire of his father to claim what he believes is rightfully his—and he'll do anything to ruin Eira before his father has the chance.

To evade the prince's threats, the shackles of an unwanted marriage, and her stepmother's malicious machinations, Eira must place her trust in a mysterious stranger. A captivating huntsman, whose intentions remain as enigmatic as his alluring presence. He could be her savior, or the instrument of her downfall.

Eira's journey towards a blissful ending is fraught with treachery, deceit, and betrayal at every turn. She will risk everything to claim her freedom, embarking on a perilous path that starts with an enchanted apple destined to seal her fate.

Enchant plunges readers into a spellbinding series of courtly intrigue, concealed royalty, and an intoxicating enemies-to-lovers romance. Immerse yourself in this enchanting tale, perfect for fans of fairytale retellings, where passion and peril intertwine in an irresistible dance. But beware, within these pages, mature content awaits, exploring profound and sensual encounters that will leave you breathless.